SIZE MATTERS

The Wizard Zulkeh was poking at the pile of bones with his staff. "These—*trifles*—are no cause for alarm. Merely the typical residue of that loathsome creature known to the unwashed masses as the Great Ogre of Grotum—"

"When will it come back?" interrupted Greyboar.

Zulkeh frowned. "Do you trifle with me, sirrah? 'Tis well known that the Great Ogre of Grotum never leaves its lair for any reason." He thrust out his staff, pointing to a dark corner of the room. "Indeed, the miserable monster lurks yonder."

Everyone gasped. Gwendolyn and Hrundig held up the lanterns. A voice came from the dark corner. A horrible, dry, croaking kind of voice. "Don't hurt me," it whined.

"Show yourself!" commanded the mage.

A moment later, the Great Ogre of Grotum scuttled into the light. I gaped. So did everyone. The damn thing wasn't more than two feet tall! Oh, sure, it was horrid looking, what with those bat ears and the bat fangs and the talons and the knobby limbs. But still—

"Ah, excellent," spoke the mage. "Not often does one encounter such a perfect specimen—"

Greyboar cut him short. "Why's the thing got the reputation it does? It can't be more than two feet tall."

Zulkeh spread his arms wide, exuding satisfaction. "Did I not say it was a perfect specimen? It demonstrates that absolute mastery of disguise—"

Greyboar frowned. "What disguise?"

"Its size, naturally. Marvelous. I was familiar with—"

"How big is it?" cried Jenny.

"I estimate—" The mage pondered. "Eight feet tall. Possibly nine."

"Nine and a half," said the ogre smugly. A moment later, the disguise vanished and the great slavering monster sprang.

The Philosophical Strangler

ERIC FLINT

THE PHILOSOPHICAL STRANGLER

A shorter version of "The Prologue" was published © 1993 as "Entropy and the Strangler" in *L. Ron Hubbard Presents Writers of the Future, Volume IX*.

A Baen Books Original

Baen Publishing Enterprises
P.O. Box 1403
Riverdale, NY 10471
www.baen.com

ISBN: 0-7434-3541-9

Cover art by Stephen Hickman
Map by Richard Roach

First paperback printing, March 2002

Library of Congress Cataloging-in-Publication Number 00-066733

Distributed by Simon & Schuster
1230 Avenue of the Americas
New York, NY 10020

Typeset by Brilliant Press
Printed in the United States of America

To David and Fred and Richard;
To Joanie, who fed us beer and spaghetti;
To Steve, on his couch;
And to the memory of Jerry O'Connell

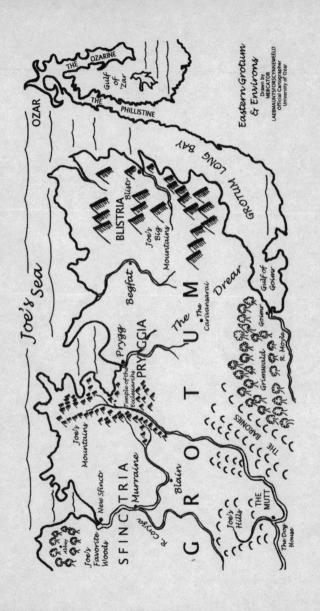

THE OZARINE

THE PHILLISTINE

OZAR

Gulf of 'Zar

GROTUM LONG BAY

Joe's Sea

BLISTRIA

Blistr

Joe's Big Mountain

Drear

Gulf of Goimr

Joe's Mountains

Begfat

Prygg

PRYGGIA

Temple of the Ecclesiarchs

The Caravansarai

Goimr

R. Moyle

Grimwald

THE BARONIES

G R O T U M

New Sfincr

SFINCTRIA

Murraine

Blain

R. Caijor

Joe's Hills

THE MUTT

The Dog House

Joe's Favorite Woods

Abbey

Eastern Grotum
& Environs
Drawn by
MERCATOR
LAEBMAUNTSFORSCYNNEWEELD
Official Cartographer
University of Ozar

Prologue.
Entropy, and the Strangler

"To the contrary," demurred Greyboar, toying with his mug, "the secret lies entirely in the fingerwork."

But the bravo wouldn't have it. " 'Tis rather in the main force!" he bellowed, and fell upon the strangler. The table splintered, the mugs went flying in a cloud of ale froth.

Needless to say, I scrambled aside. Like being a chipmunk caught between two bull moose, don't you know? Besides, there's no profit in this sort of thing.

Safe at a distance, I stuck my head between two cheering onlookers and saw that my client was in his assailant's grasp. The lout's great biceps, triceps, deltoids, pectoids and whatnot bulged and rippled as he worked at Greyboar's throat. Couldn't find it, of course.

They're a low lot, these tavern rowdies, not given to temperate debate.

Stupid, to boot. What I mean is, the outcome was never in doubt. "Professional fingerwork," as Greyboar calls it, is simply beyond the ken of hurlyburlies who lounge about the alehouses, until they encounter it firsthand.

For this particular clown, personal experience had now arrived. Casually, Greyboar sank his hands into his opponent's belly, kneading and squeezing. It must be like eating ten cucumbers at once. An astonished grimace came over the goon's face.

"Fouled our breeches, have we?" chuckled the chokester. A good lad, Greyboar, but his humor runs in a low vein.

His jest made, the strangler proceeded to more serious business. A quick flip of the thumbs popped the bullyboy's kneecaps. His victim now at eye level, Greyboar leaned back in his chair and shrugged off the hands which were still groping in the vicinity of where his neck would be if he had one.

"As I said," he concluded, "it's all in the fingerwork."

Then, just as I thought we'd gotten out of the silly affair with no harm, wouldn't you know it but that the barkeep had to go pour oil on the flames.

"And who's going to pay for all this broken furniture?" he demanded. The barkeep's voice was shrill, in keeping with his sour face. He looked down at the bullyboy, now writhing on the floor.

"Not Lothar, that's for sure," he whined. "Not much money to be made by a loan enforcer on crutches."

That's done it! I thought.

"Him?" exclaimed Greyboar. "A shark's tooth?" His good humor vanished like the dew.

"And here it is," I grumbled, "there'll be lawsuits, damages, weeping widow and wailing tots, and the Old Geister knows what else." I squirmed my way through the crowd.

"Greyboar, let's be off!" There's nothing worse than a usurer's lawyers.

"Not quite yet," growled the strangler, reaching for the doomee's neck. But luck was with us. At that very moment the porkers arrived, a whole squad of them.

"What's the disturbance here?" demanded the sergeant in charge, flattening the nearest patron with his bullystick. "You're all under arrest!"

If we'd been in our usual haunts, quaffing our ale at The Sign of the Trough in the Flankn, the porkers wouldn't have dared come in—not with less than a battalion, at any rate. Of course, if we'd been in the Flankn, where Greyboar's well known, no bullyboy would have picked a fight with him in the first place. But I'll give the patrons in that grimy little alehouse this much, they didn't hesitate but a second before the benches were flying and the fracas was afoot.

I seized the propitious moment. "Out!" I hissed, grabbing the strangler's elbow. "There's no money to be made here."

"Money, money, that's all you think about," grumbled Greyboar. "What then of ethics, and the meaning of life?"

"Save it for later." I pulled him toward the rear exit. Fortunately, the strangler was willing to leave. He's not the sort one drags from a tavern against his will, don't you know. On our way out, a beefy porker blocked the route, leering and twirling his club, but Greyboar removed his face and that was that. Fingerwork, he calls it.

Once in the back alley, Greyboar returned to the matter, like a dog chewing a bone.

"Yet there must be a logic to it all," he complained. "Surely there's more to life than this aimless collision of bodies in space." His thick brows knotted over his eyes.

"Wine, women and song!" I retorted. "There's sufficient purpose for a strangler and his agent. And it all takes money, my man, which you can't get rousting bravos in alehouses."

That last was a bit unfair. It had been my idea to go into the alehouse, to celebrate the completion of a nice little job with a pot or two. Bad idea, of course. The job had taken us to a grimy little suburb of the city, where we'd never been before. And there's something about Greyboar—his size, maybe, or just an aura of implacable certainty—that inevitably seems to arouse the local strong man to belligerence. As the wise man says: "Big frogs in little ponds are prone to suicide."

But it was just so exasperating!

"Still and all," continued Greyboar, like a glacier on its course, "I'm convinced there's more to it. 'Wine, women and song,' you say, and that's fine for you. You're a sybarite of the epicurean persuasion. But I, it is clear to me, incline rather to the stoic, perhaps even the ascetic."

"You're driving me mad with this philosophical foolishness!" I exclaimed. "And will you *please* curl up your hands?"

"Sorry." He has long arms, Greyboar, it's an asset in his line of work. But the sound of fingernails clittery-clattering along the cobblestones gets on my nerves.

By now we had reached the end of the alley and were onto a main street. I looked around and spotted a hansom not far away. I whistled, and it was but a minute later that we clambered aboard. It was an extravagance, to be sure, but we were flush with cash and I'd no desire to walk all the way back into the city.

"Take us to The Sign of the Trough," I told the driver. "It's in the Flankn, right off—"

"I know where it is," grumbled the cabbie. "It'll cost you extra, you know?"

I sighed, but didn't argue the point. Cabbies always charged extra for going into the Thieves' Quarter. Can't say as I blamed them. It was one of the disadvantages of living in the Flankn. But the advantages made it worth the while—hardly any porkers to bother you, hidey-holes galore, a friendly neighborhood (certainly no pestersome bullyboys!), a vast network of information, customers always knew where to find you, etc.

As the hansom made its way back into New Sfinctr, Greyboar continued to drone on about philosophy's central place in human existence. I struggled manfully to control my temper, but at one point I couldn't resist taking a dig.

"You're only doing this philosophy nonsense because of Gwendolyn," I grumbled.

Of course, that made him furious. This is not, by the way, a stunt I recommend for the amateur—infuriating Greyboar, that is. But I'm the world's expert on the subject, and I know exactly when I can get away with it.

His jaws clamped shut, his face turned red, he bestowed a ferocious glare on me.

"What's my sister got to do with it?" he demanded.

I glared right back at him.

"It's obvious! You never gave a second thought—you never gave a first thought!—to this philosophy crap until Gwendolyn said you had the philosophy of a weasel."

He looked away from me, his face like a stone. I felt bad, then. He was such a formidable monster, that I forgot sometimes he had feelings just like other people. And before their fight, he and his sister had been very close.

Still, it shut him up. The rest of the ride into the Flankn took place in a cold silence. Uncomfortable, yes, but it was a damned sight better than having to listen to him prattling on about epistemology and ontology and whatnot.

The cabbie dropped us off in front of our lodgings. We had some small rooms on the top floor of a typical Flankn flophouse. I paid the cabbie and we headed for the door.

Just as we started up the steps to the landing, a voice sounded behind us.

"Hold there, sirrahs!"

We turned and beheld a bizarre sight, even for the Flankn. A small man stood before us, clad in the most ridiculous costume: billowing green cloak, baggy yellow pants tied up at the ankles, tasseled slippers curling up at the toes, his head bound in a bright red strip of cloth. A "turban," it's called.

"Who're you?" I demanded.

The fellow glanced about. "Please, lower your voice! My business is confidential."

"Confidential, is it?" boomed Greyboar. "Well, out with it!"

The man hissed his agitation. "Quietly, please! It is not to be discussed on the public thoroughfares!" He cupped his ear.

Greyboar snorted. "It's as good a place as any. There's none to listen but the urchins of the street, who're loyal to their own." The strangler gazed benignly over the refuse, debris and tottering tenements that encompassed a typical street of the Flankn. His eyes fell upon a ne'er-do-well lounging against a wall some steps beyond. "And the occasional idler, of course." Greyboar cracked his knuckles; it sounded like a coal mine caving in. The layabout found urgent business elsewhere.

"Nevertheless," continued the turbaned one, "I must insist on privacy. I represent a most important individual, who demands the utmost discretion."

Left to his own, Greyboar would have quitted the fellow with no further ado. But that's why he needed an agent.

"Important individual, you say? No doubt he's prepared to pay handsomely for our services?" I spoke softly, since there was no reason to aggravate a potential client. Strangler's customers were always a twitchy lot.

"He can be quite generous. But come, let us arrange a meeting elsewhere."

"Done!" I said, cutting Greyboar off. "In three hours, in the back room of the Lucky Lady. Know where it is?"

"I shall find it. Until then."

"It'll be twenty quid for the meeting—whether or not we take the job." For a moment, I thought he would protest. But he thought better of it, and scurried around the corner.

And that's how the whole thing started. It was bad enough when Greyboar was wasting his time (and my patience) searching for a philosophy of life. But now that he's *found* one, he's impossible. If I'd known in advance what was going to happen, I wouldn't have touched the job for all the gold in Ozar. But there it is—I was an agent, not a fortune-teller. And even though we were flush at the moment, I always had an eye out for a lucrative job. "Folly ever comes cloaked in opportunity," as the wise man says.

Three hours later we were in the back room of the Lucky Lady. The tavern was in the Flankn, in that section where the upper crust went slumming. Greyboar didn't like the place, claimed it was too snooty for his taste. I wasn't too fond of it myself, actually. Much rather have been swilling my suds at The Trough, surrounded by proper lowlifes. But there was no place like the Lucky Lady for a quiet business transaction. Especially since almost all our clients were your hoity-toity types, who'd die of shock in The Trough.

Mind you, my discretion was all in vain. The man was there, all right, accompanied by a fat, frog-faced lad barely old enough to shave. And both of them were clad in the same manner, except that the youth's costume was even more extravagant. *Customers.* As the wise man says: "Wherefore profit it a man to be learned, if he remains stupid in his mind?"

"You could have worn something less conspicuous," I grumbled, after we took our seats across the table from them.

The stripling took offense. "I am the Prince of the Sundjhab! The Prince of the Sundjhab does not scurry about in barbarian rags!" Typical. Sixteen years old, at the most, and he was already speaking in ukases.

Greyboar's interest was aroused. "The Sundjhab? It's said the Sundjhab is a land of ancient learning and lore. Sages and mystics by the gross, you stumble over 'em just walking down the street."

"Let's to business!" I said, rather forcefully. Once let Greyboar get started on this track, we'd never get anything accomplished.

The Prince's companion nodded his head. "You may call me Rashkuta. My master's name"—a nod to the Prince—"is of no import. His involvement in this affair must remain completely hidden." He cleared his throat. "Our business is simple. My master's birthright is barred by another, his uncle, whom we wish removed that my master may inherit his kingdom."

"What about his uncle's children?" demanded Greyboar. "D'you want I should burke the whole brood?" Sarcasm, this—Greyboar drew the line at throttling sprouts, save the occasional bratling.

The gibe went unnoticed. "It will not be necessary. In the Sundjhab, the line of descent passes from uncle to nephew. There are no others between my master and his due."

"Odd sort of system," mused Greyboar. "In Grotum, a man's own children are his heirs."

"Yours is a preposterous method!" decreed the Prince. "That a king's children be his own is speculation, pure solipsism. But that a king's sister's children be of his own royal blood is certain."

"A point," allowed Greyboar. The royal nose lifted even higher.

"Let's keep it to business," I interjected. "There is a problem with your proposal. The Sundjhab is known to us here in New Sfinctr, but mostly as a land of legend and fable. Three obstacles are thus presented. First, it is far away. Second, should we arrive there, we are unfamiliar with the terrain. Finally, how will we make sure to collect our fee once the job is done?"

"Your concerns are moot," replied Rashkuta. "My master's uncle is touring the continent of Grotum. For the next week, he will be residing in New Sfinctr. The work can be done here. Indeed, it *must* be done here. Fearsome as are the guardians who accompany him on his travels, they are nothing compared to what surrounds him in his palace in the Sundjhab."

His words jogged my memory. I had heard vague talk in the marketplace about some foreign muckymuck on a visit. Couldn't for the life of me understand why. What I mean is, if I'd been the King of the Sundjhab, I'd never have left the harem except to stagger to the treasure room. And I'd certainly not have come to New Sfinctr! The place is a pesthole. Probably some scheming and plotting going on. A dirty business, politics. Of course, it was great for the trade.

But a chokester's agent can't afford to let his mind wander. "Who are the King's guardians?"

"They consist of the following," replied Rashkuta. "First, the King has his elite soldiery, a body of twelve men, the cream of the Sundjhabi army—"

"Not to be compared to the buffoons in Sfinctrian uniform," sneered the Prince.

"—secondly, he is accompanied by his Grand Sorcerer, one Dhaoji, a puissant thaumaturge—"

"Not to be compared to the fumbling potion-mixers called wizards in these heathen lands," sneered the Prince.

"—and thirdly, should you penetrate these barriers, you will confront the Royal Bodyguard, Iyesu by name, who is a master of the ancient martial arts of the South."

"Not to be compared to the grunting perspirers called fighters in your barbarous tongue," sneered the Prince.

I looked at Greyboar. He nodded.

"We'll take the job. Now, as to our fee. We will require ten thousand quid, payable half in advance and half upon completion. In addition, of course, to the twenty quid you owe us for this meeting."

Our clients gaped. "But we were informed that you only charged one thousand quid for, uh, for your work!" protested Rashkuta.

"And we *are* only charging you a thousand quid for strangling the young master's uncle," I agreed cheerfully. "In addition, however, it is necessary to charge two thousand for the elite soldiers, three thousand for the unexcelled sorcerer, and a clean four thousand for the incomparable master of the martial arts. As a rule, such trifles come with the job. But—I am only respecting the Prince's fiat—his uncle's protectors are not to be compared to the riffraff we normally encounter in our work." A nice touch, this. To be sure, I was demanding an outrageous fee. But I'd be a poor agent if I didn't milk the Golden Cow when I could. "Greater greed is the greedy man's gratuity," as the wise man says.

"We can find another to do the job!" countered Rashkuta. But it was weak, very weak.

"Greyboar's the best." No boast, it was a simple fact. And by the look on their faces, our clients had already learned as much in their investigations.

Rashkuta tried to bargain, but His Adolescence cut him short.

"Pay them. We are not peasants, to squabble in the bazaar."

You could always count on royalty. Why the world was such a madhouse. Buggers'd rather slaughter each other's plebes than compromise their noble dignity. Parasites, the lot of them. I'd always agreed with Greyboar's sister on that point, even if I thought Gwendolyn's ideals were a lot of utopian nonsense.

"Going to be a bit of trouble collecting the back half of our fee," I said to myself. It was clear from his glare that Tadpole the Terrible was not pleased with us. But I wasn't worried about it. Greyboar was the dreamy type, true, but he was always quick enough to squeeze what was owed to us out of recalcitrant clients. That is not a metaphor. He fed them the money first. Crude, I admit, but the word got around.

Rashkuta counted out the money and slid it across the table. Naturally, he made a big production out of it, hunching his shoulders, eyes flitting hither and yon. As if a Flankn cutpurse this side of an asylum would intervene between Greyboar and his commission.

Naturally, too, he had to add: "How can we be certain that you will do the job, now that you possess such a princely sum?"

"Matter of professional ethics," growled the strangler. Rashkuta made to press the point, but Greyboar transmuted a chunk of the oak table into sawdust, and that was that. An easy-going and tolerant sort, Greyboar, but he'd always been testy about his professional ethics.

"Where can we find the Prince's uncle?" I asked.

"He retains a suite at the Hospice of Stupefying Opulence. You are familiar with the establishment?"

"Of course." Wasn't quite a lie. I'd seen the outside of the place. I was even familiar with the servants' quarters in the back, due to a brief but torrid affair with one of the maids in my earlier years. But I'd never been in the guests' portion of the Hospice. They catered to a rather different clientele.

"However," I continued, "it will prove a wee bit difficult for us to saunter through the main entrance, don't you know. Exclusive, it is. They'd as soon let in a measly baronet as a leper. Doormen standing on porters on top of bellhops. Professional busybodies, the lot of them, they send 'em to the Royal Academy of Officiousness. Desk clerks get three years' postgraduate training. What I mean is, we can't very well march in and announce we've come to throttle the King of the Sundjhab. We'll need help getting in. Are you staying there too?"

Hem, haw, squirm, squirm. Customers. Eventually, they confessed to a small room tucked away in an obscure corner of the Hospice, practically a broom closet in the maids' quarters, to listen to them.

"Fine. There's a rear entrance, leads off the kitchen. At midnight, tonight, one of you will be there to let us in."

Of course, they squawked and quibbled, but they finally gave in. Greyboar and I arose. "Our business is then concluded, for the moment," I said. "We'll meet you here the night after tomorrow, same time, for the balance of the fee."

"It's the wizard what bothers me," said Greyboar some time later, as we discussed the job over pots of ale at The Trough. "The soldiers are meaningless, and the martial artist will be interesting. But sorcerers are tricky, and besides, I hate to extinguish any bit of knowledge that brightens this dark and murky world."

"Oh, give me a break! That so-called wizard is nothing but another pretentious trickster. 'Secret lore,' 'hidden mysteries,' 'opaque purports of the unknown'—it's all rot for the weak-minded. Reality's what is, and the truth is there for all to see it. A pox on all philosophy!"

Greyboar would have continued the argument, but I cut him off. "I'll deal with the sorcerer. I've got just the thing—a small potion Magrit made up for me the last time we were in Prygg."

"Really?" Greyboar's curiosity was aroused; best way to distract him. "What is it?"

"How should I know? Since when does Magrit divulge trade secrets?"

"True," mused the strangler. "A proper witch, she is."

"Best in the business. None of your epistemology for old Magrit! Cuts right to the quick, she does. As for the potion, all I know is that when she gave it to me she said it was tailor-made to take out any obnoxious wizard that got in the way."

"But how will you get him to drink it?"

I snorted. "Intravenous injection, that's the thing."

In the blink of an eye, I whipped out the little blowpipe from its pouch in my cloak. A second later, a dart was quivering in the bull's-eye of the dart board against the far wall. The crowd playing darts looked over, frowning fiercely, but when they saw who the culprit was they relaxed. Fergus even brought the dart over and handed it back. I was popular with the lads at The Trough.

"If that big gorilla wasn't here, I'd bust your head," grumbled Fergus.

"Don't let me stop you," said Greyboar instantly. I cast him an aggrieved look. Fergus smiled, then shrugged.

"Ah, what the hell? The shrimp's good for comic relief. And if we ever get bored with darts, we can always use him to play toss-the-midget."

A round of laughter swept The Trough. I was not amused. After a while, my glare finally quieted Greyboar's bass braying.

"Oh, stop glaring," he chuckled. "It serves you right, showing off like that. All this fancy stuff you do with darts and knives—it's just overcompensation 'cause you're such a little guy. Now, if you'd apply yourself to a study of philosophy—"

And there he was, off again. Injury added to insult.

At midnight, Greyboar and I slipped through the back door of the Hospice. Rashkuta was there to let us in, as promised. It was obvious, from his twitchy face and trembling limbs, that his nerves were not of the best. A bloodthirsty lot, your strangler's customers, when it comes to the theory of the thing. But when the deed's to be done, their knees turn to water. Else why hire a chokester? It's a simple enough matter, all things considered, to shorten a man's life.

Quickly, Rashkuta guided us through the Hospice's maze of stairways and corridors. We encountered no one, which was fortunate, as Greyboar and I were rather stunned by the place. Not our normal haunts, don't you know? Eventually, we arrived at an immense double door carved out of a solid slab of some exotic hardwood. There was enough gilt on the handles alone to drown a whale.

"The door is locked," whispered Rashkuta, "with an intricate and powerful lock constructed by the King's master locksmith, brought especially from the Sundjhab for the occasion."

"No problem," grunted Greyboar. He looked at me. "Are you ready, Ignace?" I shrugged.

"A moment, please!" hissed Rashkuta, and scurried down the corridor. Customers, like I said.

Greyboar seized the handles and tore the doors off their hinges. Entering, we beheld an antechamber, empty except for four guards. These lads were bare from the waist up, clad in baggy blue trousers tied up at their ankles. Curl-toed red slippers completed their uniforms. Funny-looking, sure, but each one held a huge scimitar, and there was no denying they were splendid soldiers. Though caught by surprise, they were on top of us in a heartbeat.

Upon Greyboar, to be precise, for I naturally took myself to one side. Not for me, this sort of melee.

The foremost soldier, muscles writhing like boas, swung a blow of his scimitar that would've felled a cedar. But Greyboar seized his wrist in midstroke and tore the arm out of its socket and clubbed the other three senseless and that was that.

"Aside from the professional fingerwork," Greyboar liked to say, "I think of my methods as a classic application of Occam's Razor."

To the left stood an open door, leading to the guards' quarters. Beyond, a group of soldiers were scrambling from a table where some exotic game was in progress. The most enterprising of the lot was even now at the door, scimitar waving about.

"Bowls!" cried Greyboar, slamming the door in the soldier's face. You could hear them falling like tenpins beyond. The door now closed, Greyboar sealed it by the simple expedient of wrenching the frame out of shape. He had a way with doors, Greyboar did. On those occasions when we found ourselves guests of the porkers in the Durance Pile, they kept us in a special dungeon equipped with sliding stone slabs instead of the usual gate and grill. "At great expense to the State," Judge Rancor Jeffreys sourly noted.

The preliminaries accomplished, Greyboar and I burst through the right-hand door. This new room was obviously a sleeping chamber. But the bed and all other items of furniture had been shoved against the walls, leaving the center of the room empty. Even the carpet that would normally have covered this portion of the floor was rolled up and standing on end in a corner. The purpose of this unusual arrangement was clear. For there, in the center of the room, squatting in a pentacle drawn on the bare floor, was a man who could be none other than the sorcerer Dhaoji.

I won't attempt to describe him. Wizards are usually bizarre in their appearance, and this was a wizard among wizards. Even at that very moment, the fellow was bringing some fearful-sounding incantation to a close, which I had no doubt would have transmogrified us right proper. Mind you, I've no use for their extravagant theories, mages, but there's no denying the better ones can wreak havoc on a man's morphology.

"My job, this," said I. A moment later, two of my darts were sprouting from his neck. Dhaoji cried out and clapped his neck. He broke off his incantation and tried to remove the darts. But the potion was already at work.

Nor did Magrit fail us. A dire potion, indeed.

"Horrible!" gasped Greyboar. For even now was Dhaoji locked into his doom.

"Yet 'tis clear as day," we heard him whimper, quivering, hunched like a hamster, eyes gazing into The Terror, "that an arrow can only travel its course by traveling half the distance first. But then, to cover the second half, it must cover half of that half first. And in order to cover half of that half, 'tis necessary that it first cover half that distance again. How, then, can it ever complete its course? Yet it does!" A hideous moan ensued.

Xenophobia hastening our steps, we entered the room beyond. At last, the royal chamber, no doubt about it. Luxuries like sand on the beach. And our prey stood before us.

Or rather, lounged before us. Astonishing sight! Here we had a mighty king, his death at hand, all his protectors destroyed (save one—a moment, please), and all he could do was laze about on a divan, chewing a fig. I was rather offended, actually.

But we'll get back to him. First, there was the matter of the final bodyguard. Even as foretold, this wight was there: a smallish man, though very well-knit in his proportions.

"You'll be Iyesu, master of the martial arts," said Greyboar. The man bowed courteously.

"Well, be on your way. There's no point in a useless fracas. It's your boss we've business with."

Iyesu smiled, like an icon.

"I fear not," he replied. "Rather do I suggest that you depart at once, lest I be forced to demonstrate my incomparable skills upon your hapless body. For know, barbarian, that I am the supreme master of all the ancient arts of the South—I speak of the blows, the strikes, the kicks, the holds, the throws, the leaps, the bounds, the springs, eschewing not, of course, the subtle secrets of the vulnerable portions of the musculature and nerves. Observe, and tremble."

And so saying, Iyesu leapt and capered about, engaging in bizarre and flamboyant exercises. Many boards and bricks set up on stands to one side of the room were shattered and pulverized with sundry blows of well-nigh every part of his body.

"As you can see," he concluded, "your crude skills cannot begin to compare with mine."

"No doubt," replied Greyboar, "for I possess no such skills, other than professional fingerwork. Of the martial arts, as you call them, I am as ignorant as a newborn babe. A simple workingman, I, who worked as a lad plucking chickens, as a stripling rending lambs, as a youth dismembering steers. A meatpacker, employed now in a related but much more lucrative trade."

Iyesu gibbered his disgust. "The insult to my person!" he cried, and sprang into action. And a pretty sight it was, too, to see him bounding and scampering about, landing many shrewd and cunning blows of the open hand, the fist, the knee, the elbow and the foot upon those diverse portions of Greyboar's anatomy which he imagined to be vulnerable.

So great was his interest that Greyboar stood immobile for no little time.

"Most proficient!" marveled the strangler. Then, recalling his duty, Greyboar seized Iyesu in mid-leap and pulverized his spine and that was that.

"Master, I am undone!"

Iyesu's shriek stirred the King to a flurry of activity. He raised his head from its pillow.

"Can you do nothing?"

"The probability is small, Your Highness. Indeed, were it not for my incomparable training in the mystic arts of bodily control, I would already be dead. The spine is rather central to all human endeavor. But I shall make the attempt."

And so saying, the master of the martial arts slithered his way to Greyboar's side and tried a few blows.

" 'Tis as I feared, the leverage is no longer available. On the other hand," he mused, "there are possibilities for the future. Perhaps even a new school!"

"Too late, I suppose, to prevent my assassination?"

"Indeed so, master. Even the great Ashokai required four years to found his school. I fear it shall take me longer. There are, it must be admitted, certain obstacles to overcome." Here he seized Greyboar's ankle and attempted a throw. "Just as I predicted," he complained, flipping and flopping about, "it's the leverage."

"So be it," yawned the King. Greyboar advanced and seized his neck. "Yet do I regret the truncation of my philosophic endeavor."

Greyboar's fingers halted in mid-squeeze. A great fear seized my heart.

"What philosophic endeavor?" demanded the strangler.

"Greyboar!" I shouted. "Burke the bugger and let's be off!"

"One moment. What philosophic endeavor?"

The King stared up at the strangler. "Surely you are not interested in such matters?" he wheezed. His round face was very flushed, which was not surprising, given that Greyboar's hands were buried in the rolls of fat adorning the royal neck.

"To the contrary," replied Greyboar, "philosophy is my life's passion."

"Indeed!" gasped the King. "It seems . . . an odd . . . avo . . . cation . . . for an as . . . sassin."

"Why? It seems to me quite appropriate. After all, my trade brings me in close proximity to the basic metaphysical questions—pain, suffering, torment, death, and the like. A most fertile field for ethical ponderations."

"I had . . . not . . . con . . . sidered . . ." The King's face was now bright purple. "But . . . I . . . ex . . . pire."

"Oh. Excuse me." Greyboar released the royal gullet. "Professional reflexes, I'm afraid."

"Quite so," agreed the King. His Royal Rotundness managed to sit up, coughing and gagging and massaging his throat.

Well, you can imagine my state of mind! By now I was hopping about in a rage. "Greyboar! Will you cease this madness and get on with the job?"

The next moment I was peering up Greyboar's

massive hook of a nose, his beady black eyes visible
at a distance. So does the mouse examine the eagle's
beak just before lunch.

"You will annoy me," he predicted.

"Never," I disclaimed.

"That is not true. You have annoyed me before, on
several occasions."

Prudence be damned, I'm not the patient type. I
was hopping about again. I fear my voice was shrill.

"Yes, and it's always the same thing! Will you *please*
stick to business? Save the philosophy for later!"

"I cannot discuss metaphysics with a dead man." He
turned to the King. "Is this not so?"

"Indeed," concurred His Majesty. "Although the
transcendentalists would have it otherwise."

Greyboar's fingers twitched.

"Not my school," added the King hastily.

I saw my chance, while they were distracted. I drew
my dagger from my boot and sprang for the royal throat.

I know, I know, it was stupid. But the aggravation
of it all! Of course, Greyboar snatched me in midair.

"As I foretold, you have annoyed me." Moments
later, my arms and legs were tied up in knots. Square
knots, to boot. I *hate* square knots—they're not natural
to the human anatomy.

"Last time you tied me in a granny," I complained.

"Last time you got loose."

He turned back to the King. "And now, Your Highness, be plain and to the point. What is this philosophic
endeavor of which you spoke?"

"I have discovered the true philosophy, the correct
metaphysical basis upon which to construct the principles of human conduct. Even when you entered, was
I perfecting my discipline."

"Liar!" I shouted. "You were lazing about, eating a
fig!"

Greyboar glared at me and I shut up. Tongue knots are the worst.

The King gazed at me reproachfully. "You misinterpret these trifles," he said, waving a vague hand at his surroundings.

Trifles! His silk robe alone was worth enough to feed all the paupers of New Sfinctr for a year. And New Sfinctr has a lot of paupers.

The King got that long-suffering look in his face. You know, the one rich people get when they talk about the triviality of wealth in the scheme of things.

"These small luxuries are but the material aids to my philosophy," he said, "necessary, I regret to say, solely because I have not yet sufficiently advanced in my discipline to dispense with them. I am only, as yet, an accomplished Languid. I am on the verge, however—I am convinced of it!—of achieving Torpor, whereupon I will naturally dispose of these intrinsically worthless comforts."

"What is this Torpor you seek?" asked Greyboar.

"To a question, I respond with a question. What is the fundamental law of the universe?"

"He's stalling for time, Greyboar!" Sure enough, I was tongue-tied. A half hitch.

Greyboar turned back to the King. "Conservation of matter and energy."

His Highness began to sneer, thought better of it.

"To be sure, but the conservation of matter and energy is at bottom a mere statement of equivalence. From the ethical standpoint, a miserable tautology."

The strangler scratched his chin. "I admit that it does not appear to bear upon one's moral principles."

"Course not!" snorted the King. "Subject's fit only for tinkerers. No, sir, the whole secret lies with the *second* law of thermodynamics."

Greyboar's frown has to be seen to be believed.

"Surely it's obvious!" exclaimed the King. "Philosophy—ethics, that is, the rest is trivia—concerns itself with the *conduct* of men, with the *direction of their actions*, not the substance of their deeds. To place our ethics upon a sound metaphysical basis, therefore, we must ask the question: To what end do all things in the Universe, without exception, conduct themselves?"

Greyboar was still frowning. The King's jowls quivered with agitation.

"Come, come, my good man! To what destination does Time's Arrow point?"

"Maximum entropy," responded the strangler.

"Precisely!"

"But life works against entropy, human life most of all. At least, in the short run."

"Yes! Yes! *And there's the folly of it all!*"

I hadn't the faintest idea what they were babbling about, but all of a sudden Greyboar's eyes bugged out. Never seen it happen before. What I mean is, he wasn't what you'd call the excitable type.

"I've got a bad feeling about this," I mumbled to myself.

"Of course!" bellowed the chokester. He swept the King into his embrace. "Master! Guru!"

"I've got a *very* bad feeling about this," I mumbled to myself.

Then everything fell apart at once. A loud crash indicated the escape of the King's soldiers from their makeshift prison. As if that weren't bad enough, I could hear the squeals which announced the arrival of the porkers. Bound to happen, of course, a strangler's got no business dawdling on the job.

Fortunately, Greyboar hadn't lost his ears along with his senses.

"Time presses, master." He set the King back on the divan. "Quickly, what is the Way?"

The King frowned. "Why, 'tis simple enough, in its bare outline. The achievement of ethical entropy lies along the ascending stages of Languor, Torpor, and Stupor. In turn, achievement of these steps requires following the eightfold Path of Chaos through application of the Foursome Random Axioms. But where is the haste? I shall intercede on your behalf with the authorities. You can be sure of it! Long have I sought a true disciple. We shall discuss our philosophy at length."

"Languor, torpor, stupor, eightfold path, foursome axioms, languor, torpor, stupor . . ." muttered Greyboar, like a schoolboy reciting his tables. He seized the King by the throat. "I fear not, my guru."

The King's face swelled like a blowfish. "But . . . but . . ."

Greyboar shook his head sadly. "Matter of professional ethics."

The whirlwind was upon us! Alarum! Alarum! Hack and hew! The King's guards filled the room, the porkers close behind. Bobbing, weaving, ducking, dodging—he can be nimble when he has to be—Greyboar scooped me up and headed for the door. He was handicapped at first, what with me in one hand and the King in the other. But once the choke was finished—I'd like to stress that point, there've been allegations in certain quarters; I'll admit he was eccentric, but his craftsmanship was impeccable—he had one hand free and that was that. Guards and porkers went flying and we were out of the King's chamber.

But by then, of course, we'd been recognized.

"It's Greyboar and his shill!" squealed the porkers.

"I resent that!" I cried, finally tongue-loose. (I'm good at half hitches.) "I'm a bona fide agent!" But it's hard to pull off dignified reproof when you're being carried like a cabbage. I got an upside-down view of the sorcerer as we made our way through the madding crowd. He was still rooted to the spot, paralyzed by the Void.

"—for if what is were many it must be infinitely small, because the units of which it is composed must be indivisible and therefore without magnitude; yet, it must also be infinitely great, because each of its parts must have another before it from which it is separated and this must be likewise—"

Magrit, there's a proper witch. Mind you, if I'd known what the potion was, I'd never have used it. I'm not what you'd call soft-hearted, but that doesn't make me a bloody *sadist*.

Once we got into the corridor, it was easy going. Porkers all over the place, of course, and the Hospice's staff and filthy-rich clientele ogling and staring, all agog and atwitter, but give Greyboar some finger room and it took a small army to pull him down.

Truth to tell, it wasn't long before we were out on the street, and from there into the sanctuary of the Flankn, with its maze of alleys, byways, tenements, cellars, attics, and all the other accouterments of the Thieves' Quarter. On our way, I gave Greyboar a good talking to, you can be sure of it, but I doubt he heard a word I said. His mind, plain to see, was elsewhere.

Eventually, I ran out of breath, and besides, we'd arrived at one of our hideouts. "All right," I concluded sourly, "untie me and let's split up. Hide yourself somewhere and don't move around—you're too conspicuous. I'll make the rendezvous with Rashkuta and collect the rest of our fee. Meet me in the attic over old Fyqulf's place the day after tomorrow. At night, mind you, if you move around during the daylight, you'll get spotted for sure."

Two days later, I was sprawled on the attic floor counting our money. Things were coming up roses. I'd expected some haggling over the balance owed, but nary a peep. I suspect, after viewing the carnage in the Hospice, that His Acneship gave up any thought of stiffing us.

It was by far the biggest fee we'd ever collected, and I was feeling quite pleased with the world. "Lucre," I gloated, "abundance, riches, affluence, pelf, the fleshpots! the cornucopia! the full measure!—and then some! O wallow, wallow, wallow, wallow, wallow, wallow—" I'm afraid I got quite carried away. I didn't even notice Greyboar come in until he tapped me on the shoulder.

"Snap out of it," he grumbled. "It's only money." Imagine my indignation. But it was no use. Greyboar slouched against the wall, gazing at his hands.

"Without my guru to lead the way, the road will be long and hard."

"Ha! With what we've got here you can slobber around in all the extravagance you need to achieve— what'd the old geezer call it?—sloth, wasn't it?" I giggled; Greyboar glared. "No, no, that's not quite right! Languor—of course, that's the word!"

"I fear not," said Greyboar. "The hunt's up all over the city. The whole army's been turned out. The Flankn's crawling with informers and stool pigeons. We'll need every copper we've got just to bribe the porkers and get out of Sfinctria. Starvation rations, we'll be on, until you scrounge up some work. Even that'll be hard, being in a different city and all."

I laughed, gay abandon. "Is that what's troubling you? Fie on it! D'you think I hadn't figured this all out before I took on the job? Sure, for the moment there's a little heat. Looks bad, prominent tourist getting throttled. But what does the Queen of Sfinctria care, when all is said and done? Unless there's pressure from the Sundjhab—zilch, that's what Belladonna cares! And the Prince—remember him, he's our client?—he's the new King of the Sundjhab now. He'll cool things down right quick."

"I fear not." He scowled. "It's not the loss of the money that bothers me, it's the dislocation—the interruption of my habits, the distractions. It'll make it difficult to concentrate on my Languor."

"You're mad! The main thing the little—pardon, His Puissant Pupness—wants is for the hubbub to die down. After all, if we're caught, how's he to know we wouldn't sing like birds? No, no, Greyboar, take my word for it—the one thing you can be sure His Pimple will be doing is to move heaven and earth to get the hunt called off."

"Under other circumstances, no doubt he would." Greyboar rubbed his nose thoughtfully. "I think our best bet's to make for Prygg. I know the captain of the guard at the southeast gate; we can bribe him. And once we get to Prygg, Magrit'll put us up till the heat's off. Have to do a job for her, of course. No freebies from Magrit. Proper witch, she is."

"What're you running on—" A queasy feeling came to my stomach. "Wait a minute. What d'you mean, 'under other circumstances'?"

Greyboar looked at me, surprised. "Those circumstances under which the Prince would call off the hunt."

"But why wouldn't he—" A *very* queasy feeling. "You've seen him!"

"Last night."

"Why? Rashkuta had the money—I collected it."

"Money." He waved the subject away. "To refute his disrespect for philosophy. Imagine—hiring me to strangle my own guru!"

"To refute his disrespect for philosophy?"

"Well, naturally, what did you expect? I found it

necessary to acquaint him with the second law of thermodynamics."

"You—*what*? What did you say to him?"

"Say to him? Nothing."

I was on my feet. "*What did you do to the Prince?*"

"I aligned him with Time's Arrow."

I was hopping up and down in a fury. "*What does all that gibberish mean?*"

Greyboar grinned, a cavern in the abyss.

"The Prince has achieved maximum entropy."

PART I: *THESIS*

Chapter 1.
The Sign of the Trough

But that was all in the past. Ancient history. Forgotten unpleasantness.

Things were looking up!

First of all, we were back in New Sfinctr.

Not many people, I'll admit, would share my delight at returning to New Sfinctr. Home town or not, the simple truth is that the place is a pesthole, even by the standards of Grotum. "Armpit of the continent," they call it, when they're not calling it something obscene. But it was a great city for a strangler and his agent. Business opportunities everywhere, you tripped over them.

As soon as we arrived back in town, of course, I headed straight off to The Sign of the Trough. Best ale in the world they've got at The Trough. Although I'll admit The Swill As You Will in Prygg comes in a very close second. And the Free Lunch in the Mutt is always entitled to honorable mention.

But before we go any further in our story, I should take the time here to describe the setting. Much of the action—and most of the thinking—will transpire in this sacred place.

The lowlife's temple. The world's finest alehouse. The Sign of the Trough.

It's in the Flankn. New Sfinctr's Thieves' Quarter, as I believe I mentioned. Right in the very center of it, in fact. The heart and soul of the Flankn, The Trough's often been called.

From the outside, The Trough looks like a huge building—bunch of buildings, maybe, all crunched into each other; it's hard to tell—some three or four stories tall, depending on which angle you look at it and how drunk you are. (Rumor has it that some of the towers are five stories tall. Could be.) The thing covers an entire block, and—I'm talking frivolous architecture, here, not serious drinking—makes absolutely no rhyme or reason.

Just think of an edifice put together by some kind of architect's crazed patron saint in a drunken stupor. Insane, and huge.

But it's way, way bigger than it looks.

On the *inside*, that is. Don't ask me how it works, but every real Trough-man knows that The Trough is bigger inside than out. The famous mathematician Riemann Laebmauntsforscynneweëld once visited The Trough. Rumor has it that's where non-Euclidean geometry got started.

So we'll skip over the rest of the exterior description. Who cares, anyway? The ale's inside.

Though I might point out, as we head for the door, the huge feeding trough hanging over the entrance. It's The Trough's only sign. Stolen, they say, from some minor farm god's hogpen. Wouldn't know, myself. I didn't consort with deities. Even the lesser ones were bad news, even though the Church said they didn't exist.

And I might also suggest, as we reach the entrance—my civic duty, this—that we give the door itself a moment's scrutiny. The thing's big, and heavy, but it swings open well enough on account of it's kept well-greased. The door's made out of oak, mainly, but there's plenty of wrought iron to give it some extra strength. Which it needs, as the many deep gouges and gashes demonstrate. Been many the desperate deed been done at the entrance to The Trough. And, yes, those dark stains covering the door are blood. Along with some other stuff. Delicacy forbids precise description.

Inside! Into the holy chambers!

As soon as you step into The Trough, you find yourself in the taproom. The "main" taproom, I suppose I should say, since there's any number of smaller ones scattered through the place. But, by hallowed tradition, it's just called *the* taproom. (I don't have much truck with the smaller ones, anyway. Those are for sissies.) You cast your eyes about, examining its cavernous interior. Immediately, you notice—

You can't see a blessed thing. You're blind as a bat.

Yes, the lighting is dim. *Dim.* That's the way your proper Trough-men like it. Keeps the snoopy eyes of officialdom under a handicap, of course. But, what's more important—your porkers don't venture into The Trough too often, and when they do they come in such hordelike numbers that there's always plenty of warning, anyway—it allows the Trough-man planted on his favorite stool that blessed moment wherein he can discern the figure of the new arrival before the new arrival's eyes have had time to adjust to the gloom.

Important, that. A lifesaver, it's been, often enough. Many's the Trough-man who's alive today, with sane spirit and functioning kneecaps, on account of how he had time to slip into the maze back of the taproom before the newly-arrived grudge holder, enforcer, bill collector, feudist, outraged (and-now-armed) victim, disgruntled husband, insensate father, insensate mother, insensate wife, insensate you-name-it, serial killer, homicidal maniac, gibbering lunatic or evangelist had time to spot him in the throng and nail him.

Soon enough, your eyes adjust, and now you can make out the full splendor of the vista.

The taproom's huge, huge. A single room, basically, though the thick wooden pillars give the illusion of walls. The ceiling's a bit on the low side, which allows the smoke to gather properly. On a busy day or night— and which aren't?—the pipe and cigar smoke is so thick that you can't really see the further corners of the room. Through a glass, darkly, your poets might say. If you squint, you can spot the multitude of little nooks, crannies, alcoves and corners which adorn the various sides of the room. (How many sides? I'm not sure. Sober, I'd say the taproom's more or less hexagonal. Other times—more sides. Lots more.)

But fie on all that! Never bother with the nooks and alcoves, myself. I'm for the main floor, I am, along with all your other proper Trough-men stalwarts. There's tables scattered all over the place, and plenty of chairs. Crowded, true—always is—but there's usually a chair to be found somewhere.

Be a little careful walking, if you would. The floor's so clean it would actually glisten, if there were any light worth talking about, and it can be slippery to walk on. Novices to The Trough are always surprised at how well scrubbed the floor is. If they survive the first month, they understand the reason for it. If they don't, they're the latest occasion for the mop.

First, though, it's time for genuflection. Turn to your right, and worship—

The Bar Itself.

O, Eighth Wonder of the World!

The Bar Itself runs the entire length of one side of the taproom. You can't usually see the end of it, on account of the smoke and the gloom. It just kind of fades away, like all your first-class religious mysteries. It's wood, of course—none of your foppish hoity-toity stuff. Oak, mostly, although you can find almost any other kind of wood used to patch up the many busted sections.

Contemplating the Bar Itself is the closest I ever get to philosophy. Willingly, I mean.

I'm serious. All the fancy problems that philosophers waste their time fretting over can be solved just by studying the Bar Itself.

The distinction between Essence and Appearance, for instance, shows up in the way the Bar Itself actually dissolves into its many components. Each portion of the Bar Itself has its own distinct identity.

First and foremost, there's the Old Bar. That's the first twenty or so feet of it, right by the door. The Old Bar is actually an upturned watering trough which, legend has it, served as the original bar when the place first opened in the dim mists of ancient history. (Yeah, I know—that conflicts with the legend of the minor farm god. So? Legends conflict, it's the nature of the beasts.)

In modern times, this original section of the bar—also known as The Trough Proper, by the way—is reserved by right and custom for the most aged of The Trough's customers. These heroes—sure, they're a lot of doddering oldsters, but you have to be a genuine hero to survive the number of years it takes to be elevated to the Old Bar—sit there for hours on end quaffing ale through toothless gums and squabbling over their reminiscences of days gone by. They also,

I might mention, serve The Trough as its Court of Final
Appeal.

Next to the Old Bar, as we move away from the
door— Oh. Yeah, I should mention that there's an
elaborate nomenclature by which directions in The
Trough are specified. I won't get into it—way too
technical for laymen, don't you know?—but, for the
record, moving down the Bar Itself away from the door
is called "nethering," or, by your real hard-core Trough-
men, "nether-reaching."

Anyway, *nethering* from the Old Bar we come to
Anselm's Cursed Yard-and-a-Half, as the next stretch
is called. But we won't linger on Anselm's Cursed Yard-
and-a-Half. Nobody ever sits there, not since Anselm
cursed it some two hundred years ago. (And if you
don't know who Anselm was, or why he cursed it, or
why anyone worries about an old curse, that's tough.
I'm a proper Trough-man, I am, and there's some
things you just don't talk about.)

The next stretch, comprising some thirty-five feet
in length, are called the Blessed Planks. The oak slabs
which make up most of the Bar Itself are absent here.
Sometime back in the dawn of history—after the
Suspected Soap Bead Uprising, according to legend—
they were replaced by planks of cheap pine. Miracu-
lously, as century succeeded century, the pine lasted.
Unscarred, ungouged, uncarved, pristine and perfect.
This, given the nature of The Trough, is an obvious
miracle. Most Trough-men believe that a pot of ale
served up on the Blessed Planks is better than any
served elsewhere.

Superstitious sots. I've got no truck with that nonsense, myself. Ale's ale, and there's an end to it. The
ale at The Trough is the best in the world, and that's
that. Doesn't matter where it's served or where you drink
it, just as long as it makes its way down your throat.

Our hearts lighten, now, as we come to the next portion of the Bar Itself. This is where I hang out, whenever I'm not sitting at a table like I usually am on account of how Greyboar and I are too couth to belly up to a bar like your average lowlifes.

Eddie Black's, it's usually called. If you want to get formal about it, it's The Stretch Where Eddie Black Was Probably Conceived. And if you really want to go black-tie over the matter, it's The Stretch Where Eddie Black Was Probably Conceived If You Believe His Slut of a Mother and If You Ignore The Bloodstains Which Is What's Left of Smooth-Talking Ferdinand After Eddie Black's Father John-the-Ill-Tempered Carved Him Up On Account of How Eddie Black's Pop Was Convinced That Eddie Was Actually Conceived Over There In What's Now Called Ferdie's Folly.

My spot, this. Always has been, since I was old enough to prop my chin on the Bar Itself.

And that's the end of the tour. I'm thirsty, and enough's enough.

"Welcome back, Ignace," said Leuwen, shoving a mug across the bar. I contemplated the sacred object for a moment, before its contents disappeared into my gullet. Leuwen was obviously bursting with curiosity, but he's the best barkeep in New Sfinctr—hands down—and so he waited for me to quaff two more full mugs before he started questioning me.

"So, how's Prygg?" he asked. This, of course, was a meaningless question, nothing more than dancing around before he got into the juicy stuff. Leuwen's interest in Prygg ranked somewhere below his interest in the taxonomy of flatworms.

I could dance too.

"Still there," I replied.

"Glad to hear it," he intoned cheerfully. "How's Magrit? Still the same old proper witch?"

We were now bordering on a real question. Normally, I would have responded with a polite and reasonably informative answer, but the truth was that Magrit happened to be on my shit list at the moment—very high up on the list, in point of fact—and so I satisfied myself with a noncommittal grunt.

Leuwen wouldn't let it go. "Hear she had to take it on the lam."

Another grunt.

I didn't think it would work. And it didn't.

"Word is," Leuwen plowed on, "she was mixed up in that business that brought in the Ozarine troops."

Now we were treading on dangerous ground. I decided a grunt would be worse than an answer, so I tried to head Leuwen off.

"Yeah, that's what I hear," I said casually. "Wouldn't know myself, Greyboar and me only bumped into her the once or—"

"Word is," interrupted Leuwen, "she had some help in that little business. Real serious help. *Serious* muscle-type help, in fact."

I sighed. It's just as the wise man says: "Wisdom drops dead. Stupid shit'll haunt you forever."

There was no point dancing around it. Leuwen looked like a walrus, but nobody had ever accused him of having anything between his big ears but brains.

"All right," I growled. "What've you heard?"

Leuwen grinned and started wiping his hands on the rag he always kept tucked into his belt. I watched the project carefully. The experienced Trough-man could gauge Leuwen's exact mood and manner by the precise way in which he wiped his hands on that rag. Don't ask me to explain the subtleties. Can't be done. You either knew how to read them or you didn't.

The hand-wiping looked ominous. I could read avid interest combined with rabid curiosity combined with— this was bad—shrewd deductions combined with—this was worse—experienced surmises combined with—oh, woe!—detailed half-knowledge of way, way, way too many facts.

"Well, let's see," he mused. "First off, I heard the proper witch managed to get into the Ozarine embassy and wreck the gala affair being held there to celebrate the recent wedding between Prygg's very own Princess Snuffy and the Honorable Anthwerp Freckenrizzle III, scion of Ozar's third richest multi-zillionaire. Trashed the social event of the season, she did. Or so people say."

I frowned. Bad, but I could live with it.

"But," continued Leuwen, as I feared he would, "the word is that Magrit's little comet strike on high society wasn't nothing but a cover. A diversion, people say, so that *other* parties could sneak into the top-secret super-security part of the Ozarine embassy and steal one of Ozar's three Rap Sheets."

I tried to control the wince, but I couldn't. Leuwen didn't miss it, of course, and the hand-wiping went into high gear.

"Yeah, no kidding, that's what people say. Can you imagine that? Stole a Rap Sheet! One of the real Joe relics!" He pursed his lips, frowned, pretended to be thinking idle thoughts. "What are there—five Rap Sheets, total, in the whole world? Maybe six?" He shook his head mournfully. Wipe, wipe. "But that's what people say." Wipe, wipe, wipe. "Among other things."

"What else?" I grumbled.

Leuwen wasn't even trying to keep his grin under control anymore.

"Well, people're saying that whoever snuck into the embassy and took the Rap Sheet must've had some real bruiser along with 'em. On account of what happened to all those elite-type embassy guards. Broken necks, snapped spines, crushed windpipes—even say one of 'em had his spine tore out and that same spine used to garrote another. Can you imagine that?"

I was glaring into my mug.

Wipewipewipewipewipewipe.

"Now, who could *do* such terrible things?"

By rights, the ale should have started boiling by now, just from my glare alone. It was one of the many problems with having the world's greatest professional strangler as my client. He couldn't stop showing off.

One glance at Leuwen's wicked smile told me there was no point in trying to act dumb. Leuwen knew what it said on Greyboar's business card as well as I did:

GREYBOAR—*Strangleure Extraordinaire*
"Have Thumbs, Will Travel"
Customized Asphyxiations
No Gullet Too Big, No Weasand Too Small
My Motto: Satisfaction Garrooted, or
The Choke's on Me!

Leuwen was now in full steam:

"Yeah, that's what people say. Whoever stole the Rap Sheet—and thereby pissed off the world's most powerful empire so bad they up and *invaded* not only Prygg but three other sovereign nations of Grotum—also managed to get away with it—and thereby also pissed off the Church and sent the whole Inquisition into a frenzy—and even seem to have dropped out of sight entirely and are wandering around loose with one of the real Joe relics—thereby plunking themselves right smack in the middle of all that Joe business, which is the worst business anybody can possibly get mixed up

in, on account of sooner or later God Himself is bound
to come down on them like a ton of bricks."

Wipewipewipewipewipe. Wipewipe. Wipe, wipe.
Wipe.

"Who knows?" I asked glumly.

Leuwen shrugged. "Nobody actually *knows*, Ignace.
Cheer up. It's not all that bad, really. The authorities
are too stupid to figure it out, and the lowlifes what
aren't too stupid to figure it out won't really believe
it on account of"—here his face grew solemn and
serious—"no lowlife in his right mind is going to believe
for one minute that Greyboar would have been stupid enough to get himself mixed up in such a mess.
Much less you."

I relaxed, slightly. Only slightly, however, because I
could see the next—yeah.

"So why *did* you get mixed up in it?" he asked
quietly. "More of Greyboar's philosophy? Wasn't it
enough he got you chased out of New Sfinctr with that
foolishness?"

"Wasn't philosophy," I grumbled. "Worse. Gwendolyn."

"Ah." Wipewipewipe. "Ah."

I scowled at the bar top. "What was I supposed to
say? No—we wouldn't do it?"

Scowl, scowl, scowl. "You know with a Rap Sheet
in Grotum, Gwendolyn's as good as dead. Every porker
in the land's been looking for her for years. The
damned thing's a Joe relic. Most powerful magic there
is. They'd find her in a heartbeat. Then—chop, chop,
chop."

The bar top was suddenly subjected to a vigorous
cleansing. "Ah."

"Can't you say anything else?" I demanded crossly.

He shrugged his fat shoulders. "What's to say,
Ignace? Gwendolyn's family. Only family Greyboar's got
left, now. For that matter, she's the only family you've

got left. After your parents all died when you were youngsters—their mom and your pop—the three of you brought each other up. Like your own little miniature clan."

He chuckled. Leuwen's chuckles were kind of a signature piece. Large, rolling, heavy—and somehow very dry at the same time.

"And just as fierce in your feuding as any clan of Groutch legend, too! God, the three of you were ferocious, if anybody messed with any of you. Even you, tiny as you were. I still laugh, now and then, thinking about that time old Stinky Gerrin started pawing at Gwendolyn when she got off work at the packinghouse after her first day on the job. What was she then? Twelve? Maybe thirteen?"

"Twelve," I muttered. "We'd just celebrated her birthday two days earlier. Greyboar'd caught a juicy rat—one of those fat ones that hang around the slops—and I'd, uh, obtained an apple pie that some baker must have misplaced." I smiled for a moment, remembering. "We even spent the money to buy a candle for the pie. Couldn't afford but the one, so we invented a new arithmetic where one equaled twelve. Laughed, we did, telling ourselves we'd revolutionized mathematics."

Leuwen's ensuing chuckle rolled over in a laugh. "Good old Stinky! Never could resist a girl just coming of age." Another chuckle rolled over. "Wish I'd seen it! They say you were on his shoulders biting his ear off before Gwendolyn even started breaking his fingers."

I couldn't help chuckling myself. "Stinky was right! Yuch! Nastiest-tasting ear I ever bit into. Spit the damn thing out as fast as I could. And I can't tell you how happy I was that I didn't have to take off the other one. By then, of course, Gwendolyn was breaking his wrists and it was pretty much all over."

A companionable silence followed, for a few seconds. Then Leuwen mused: "Yeah, good old Stinky. He disappeared the next day. When they dredged his body out of the river a few weeks later, the corpse was in such wretched shape they almost couldn't identify him. But the cause of death was obvious enough. They say his neck hadn't been broken so much as pulverized."

Leuwen gave me a speculative glance. "Even at the time everybody figured that was Greyboar. His first choke."

I kept my mouth shut. Actually, it'd been Greyboar's second choke. Stinky hadn't been the first lecher to think a dirt-poor orphan girl would make easy pickings. But the first one had been a vagrant, so nobody had noticed. In his own way, Stinky had been a well-known fixture in the Flankn. After he, ah, "came to a bad end," nobody bothered Gwendolyn much anymore.

Leuwen accepted my silence readily enough, and didn't try to pry anything loose. Even a man with his curiosity can accept a stone wall when he sees one. He went back to wiping the bar, chatting idly.

"Yeah, I can still remember the first time the three of you came in here. Three kids—even if two of them were already huge—swaggering into The Trough bound and determined to order their first real, by God, ale pot. *Trying* to swagger, I should say."

He emitted another chuckle. "You couldn't afford but the one pot to share. I remember the three of you counting out the pennies, almost sweating blood you wouldn't have enough."

"We *didn't* have enough," I growled. "Short one lousy penny, we were. We tried to wheedle you into giving us credit. Chintzy bastard! You wouldn't budge an inch."

He smiled, shrugging. "You know how it is, Ignace.

But look at the bright side—I *did* agree to give you a pot not quite full. Bent the hell out of professional ethics, if I say so myself."

He gave the bar an idle swipe, before pointing with the rag to a stool several feet down. "That's where the three of you sat. Gwendolyn had to hoist you onto the stool. You couldn't get up that high on your own." He laughed outright, now. "The thing that impressed me the most was how all three of you split the pot. I thought for sure you'd get shorted, what with those two giants. But—no. You got your fair share, just like they did."

I could feel the old ache coming, and shoved it under. Ancient history, dammit! Let it stay buried with the rest of the ruins. Then, sighing, I drained the mug and pulled the handful of coins out of my pocket.

I stared at them glumly. To my surprise, Leuwen filled the mug up.

"On the house," he said.

That was a lie, actually. Under the circumstances, "on the house" meant: as long as you keep my interest up, you can keep drinking. Bullshit me and you die of thirst.

Terrible thing, death from thirst. It took me all of two seconds to decide to spill the beans. The fact is, there wasn't much harm in it anyway. He obviously knew too much already, and, being as he was the best barkeep in the world, Leuwen practically wrote the book on Barkeep Professional Ethics.

Barkeep Moral Imperative #1: Confidential information transmitted over a pot of fresh-poured ale is *confidential*.

It was only midafternoon, so the crowd at The Trough was relatively light. Leuwen had no trouble keeping the customers supplied with the necessities of life while I regaled him with the whole story.

Experienced raconteur that I am, I started with a proper topic sentence:

"Prygg was a fucking disaster. A pure, unmitigated, unadulterated, fucking disaster. A *disaster*, I tell you."

I fell silent, staring with anguish at my empty mug.

"Good topic sentence," pronounced Leuwen, quickly replenishing the staff of life.

After drawing off half the mug in a single draught, I immediately launched into the background to the disaster.

"To begin with, we lost all our money bribing the guards to get out of New Sfinctr. Then, once we got out of the city, we had to make our way across Joe's Mountains in order to get to Prygg. Would have been easier, of course, to take the southern route, skirting the mountains altogether. But that meant going through Blain."

Leuwen winced. "Blain's dicey."

"Tell me about it! On the way back—never mind. Yeah, Blain's a bad luck city, pure and simple. And with the manhunt on, we knew there was bound to be at least a full company of the Queen's Own Cuirassiers stationed there, looking for us."

Leuwen shook his head. "Nasty lot, the Cuirassiers."

I nodded, took another draught. "*Nasty*. We found out later they speared every pig the farmers tried to bring through the town, on the off chance Greyboar and I were hiding in their bellies. The farmers themselves got force-fed emetics, so the Cuirassiers could inspect the barf.

"So we decided to take the mountain route. But that posed its own set of problems. The main road through Joe's Mountains goes right past the Great Temple of the Ecclesiarchs. The very seat of God's Temporal Power on Earth."

An aggrieved looked crossed my face. "Not that we'd

done anything to call ourselves to the attention of the
Inquisition, mind you. Fact is, to my way of thinking,
the Church stood in our debt. Hadn't we throttled one
of the world's most powerful heathens? The King of
the Sundjhab himself!"

Leuwen shook his head. "The Ecclesiarchs have
always been schizophrenic on the subject." Wipewipe.
"If you go out and slaughter a *poor* heathen, of course,
you're a hero in the eyes of the Lord. But if you croak
a rich and powerful one, well, that's a different matter altogether." Wipewipewipe. "That smacks of bloody-
handed red revolution, which ranks a whole lot higher
in the scale of sins than simple heathenry."

I nodded sagely. "Yeah, that's the way we figured
it. So we decided it would be best, all things considered, to just avoid the Temple. But *that* meant we had
no choice but to take one of the less-traveled routes
through the mountains. 'Less-traveled route,' you'll
understand, is what they call a euphemism. 'Goat path'
better captures the reality.

"And *that* meant—I still shudder at the memory—
that we had no way to replenish our funds through our
customary, dignified, professional skills. Instead, we had
to hook up with one of the flea-bitten, mangy little
caravans which avoid the Temple and— Well. You
know. *Work.*"

Leuwen grimaced with sympathy. He even wiped his
rag once or twice to show his proletarian solidarity.

I continued: "A nightmarish period followed. The
labor was bad enough. What was worse was listening
to Greyboar be philosophical about it! But, eventually,
we toiled our way through the mountains and onto the
plain of Pryggia. Now back in civilized lands, I
scrounged up a little job in one of the larger towns
along the way. Had to accept an outrageously low fee,
of course—*country rubes*—but the job was quick and

easy. The good thing about country rubes—the *only* good thing—is that even the local lord of the manor doesn't expect to receive the attentions of a world-class professional strangler. So, a quick and simple choke, and we had enough cash to pay our way into Prygg with no more of that toiling nonsense."

I then proceeded to regale Leuwen with the tale of our adventures in Prygg itself. Of that tale, however, I will say nothing here. Secrets which I'll spill to Leuwen, bound as he is by the barkeep-sot privilege, I'm not going to blather about openly. My lips are sealed. I vow eternal silence. I still have hopes—getting fainter all the time, I admit—that our part in the madness which ensued will remain hidden from the public eye.

Just as I was finishing up my tale of our misadventures in Prygg, a sudden hush came over The Trough. You couldn't help notice it—by that time, late afternoon it was now, the place was getting packed.

I turned in my seat to see what had caused the unusual dip in the usual cacophony. A woman had entered The Trough, and was making her slow progress toward the bar.

The Cat.

"I'll be damned," I whispered. "I never thought she'd show up."

The Cat was half blind to begin with, and, as dark as the room was, she had to fumble her route. Halfway to the bar she passed the Belly-Ups, groping and feeling her way.

Good lads, the Belly-Ups. Always sat at the same table, always friendly, and they were the bedrock of The Trough's business. So they were very polite about the whole thing, even though their eyes were suddenly a lot less bleary than they had been.

She could produce that effect, the Cat. Strangest

woman you'd ever meet, but there was no denying she
was beautiful, in her own way. Tall, great figure, gorgeous yellow hair, bright blue eyes, a striking face—
if you didn't mind the long nose and the spectacles like
beer bottles. Oh, yeah, and the three-foot sword belted
to her waist. Put some guys off, that razor. Can't imagine why.

Anyhow, she eventually found her way to the bar.
I said hello and she nodded at me, vaguely. I'm not
sure she really even saw me, her eyesight's so bad.
Then she ordered a vodka martini.

I'll give him credit, Leuwen didn't even blink an eye.
Not your normal order in The Trough, a vodka martini, but Leuwen had one in front of her in seconds.
She paid him, tried it, looked impressed. Hell, I was
impressed—it was the first expression other than indifference I'd ever seen on her face. Except when she
got onto the subject of Schrödinger, of course.

"That's a good vodka martini," she announced.
Leuwen nodded placidly.

"Haven't made one in a while," he commented.
"Nice change from pouring ale. You're new here. What's
your name?"

"Schrödinger's Cat."

I kept a straight face. I'd have given thousand-to-
one odds on Leuwen's next sentence.

Yep, I'd have won again. He did a double take, then
blurted out: "Who's Schrödinger?"

"I wish I knew," she replied. "I'm looking for him."
She took a sip. "When I find the bastard, he's dog food.
Haven't seen him, have you?"

Leuwen said he'd never even heard of him. That was
probably true, but even if Schrödinger was sitting next
to her, Leuwen would've said the same thing. Neutral,
he is, like any barkeep in the Flankn. Professional
ethics, you know.

So then the Cat groped her way over to an empty table and sat there, slowly sipping her martini. Waiting for Greyboar, I guessed, though with her you never knew what was on her mind.

"You know her?" asked Leuwen.

I shrugged. "As much as anybody does, I imagine. That is one strange woman. Leave it to Greyboar to get the hots on the world's weirdest female."

Leuwen's eyes widened. "She's *Greyboar's* girlfriend?"

I laughed. "In his dreams! We met her in Blain on the way back from Prygg. There was—"

I choked on the sentence, fell silent. It occurred to me that Leuwen hadn't given any indication that he knew the slightest thing concerning the unfortunate affair in Blain, and I saw no reason to enlighten him.

Greyboar and I had run into her at Blain, on our way back from Prygg. "Run into her," I admit, is a delicate way of putting it. But—it's all part of that accursed business in Prygg, which was caused by Magrit taking up with the philosopher Zulkeh.

You want to know the main reason to avoid philosophy? It's because where there's philosophy, there's always a philosopher. The real thing, too, not an amateur like Greyboar. As the wizard Zulkeh would put it, "the personal reification of the abstract essence."

In this case, himself. Zulkeh of Goimr, physician. The most dangerous characters in the world, philosophers. None more so than the sorcerer Zulkeh, as I found out to my eternal chagrin when we got mixed up with the guy in Prygg. (That was Magrit's fault, and accounts for the extreme altitude of her position on my personal shit list.)

It's in the very nature of things, you see, that philosophers insist on mucking around in philosophy. And if you muck around in philosophy you'll find yourself,

soon enough, mucking around with such risky stuff as
the nature of God. And if you go mucking around with
that you'll sure as hellfire find yourself right up against
the Joe business. And then—well. The rest follows as
night from day. Inquisition. *Auto-da-fé*. The Godferrets
hot on your heels. Ruin and damnation.

Sure enough. On our way back—just when I thought
we'd made a clean getaway—that idiot Zulkeh dragged
us into the trial of the heretic Alf at Blain and that's
where Greyboar saw the Cat when she barged in looking for Schrödinger and started hacking up guards and
scientists when they took offense at her interrupting
the proceedings. In the event, once the dust settled
down (the ashes, I should say—the Cat caused the
whole courthouse to collapse in a fiery conflagration),
Greyboar and I found that we had been separated from
the wizard and his apprentice and there was nothing
for it but to wend our separate way to New Sfinctr.

No loss, that, so far as I was concerned. Zulkeh and
Shelyid were heading south to the Mutt, anyway, so
we would have been parting company in any case. And
I was purely delighted to shed the sorcerer from my
back. Let the Fangs of Piety chase after *him*. I wanted
no part of that Joe business.

Then, not a few miles up the road, who should we
encounter but the Cat, ambling her way along as if she
hadn't a care in the world. As soon as Greyboar found
out she was heading to New Sfinctr, he invited her to
travel with us. She agreed, not seeming to care much
one way or another. Of course, the Cat didn't seem to
care much about anything except finding Schrödinger.
Greyboar had hopes, but he might as well have tried
wooing a wall. She didn't reject him, exactly. Does a wall
say "no"? She just ignored him. But any mildew on the
big guy's tongue was gone by the time we got to New
Sfinctr, the way it was hanging out the whole time.

Greyboar was always stubborn. I should know! Absolute pighead about this philosophy foolishness. So, even after we got here, he right off invited her to have a drink with him that evening at The Sign of the Trough.

She showed a mild interest. "Any chance Schrödinger might be there?" she asked. Greyboar ran a line about how everybody in the world shows up at The Sign of the Trough sooner or later. True enough, of course, but I doubted this guy Schrödinger would ever show up—especially if he heard the Cat was hanging around!

So they set up a time to meet later in the evening. And damned if she didn't show up. Early, in fact.

I was delighted, to tell you the truth. The Cat was a nut case, of course, but what did I care? I wasn't chasing after her, Greyboar was. The main thing, far as I was concerned, was that the big numbskull had something else on his mind beside his damned philosophy. Hadn't practiced his "ethical entropy" in days, he'd been so pre-occupied with figuring out how to make an impression on Schrödinger's Cat.

I saw that Leuwen was eyeing me suspiciously. Any moment and he'd be pressing me about Blain.

Fortunately, there was a timely interruption. There was all kind of ruckus going on at the table where the Belly-Ups were sitting. A real uproar. Howling laughter, fists pounding the table, heads back, elbows jamming into ribs, ale slopping right and left. I wandered over to see what the fuss was about.

Right at the center of the fun, like the eye of the storm, sat O'Neal.

"Pinched me, she did!" he insisted in a surly tone.

More howls. Angus saw me, said: "D'ye hear him, Ignace, d'ye hear him?" He mimicked O'Neal's voice: " 'Pinched me, she did!' " Howls.

O'Neal's face was an artist's dream. *Seated Man With Mug, Disgruntled*.

"Well, she did, dammit!" Stiff lip. Eyes front. *Still Life With Amour Propre, Injured*.

More howls. I was grinning myself. O'Neal loses when he *cheats* at solitaire. Like the wise man says: "Some're fast, some're slow, and some dummies can't even find the starting gate."

O'Neal finally blew his stack. *"Will somebody explains what's so all-fired funny?"*

Angus stopped laughing long enough to speak. "She wasn't pinching *you*, Wetdream, old boy! She was just finding her way through the room. Trying to figure out if you were a chair in the way, or just a big ugly dog. Look at her, dummy—she's blind as a bat!"

But O'Neal was dense, like always. He tried to make a living as a scalper once. Sold tickets for half the price they were asking at the box office. He couldn't figure out why he was broke when he had so many customers.

"I say she pinched me," he announced, trying for some dignity. "And by the Old Geister, that's an invitation in anybody's book!"

He glared around the table. "And what's she doing here anyway, if she's not looking for a handsome lad like me?" He stood up and sucked in his gut. At least three geometric axioms were refuted.

"She's here to meet Greyboar," I announced. "He should come—there he is now."

Sure enough, Greyboar was already halfway across the room, headed for the Cat's table. Good thing nobody was in his way, he'd have trampled them. Not on purpose, of course! Greyboar was normally as polite as you could ask. But does a bull moose in heat pay attention to the odd field mouse in his way?

O'Neal was like a statue, white as marble. Slowly,

slowly, that certain smile inched across his face. "Coprophagic," the scholars call it.

"Gee." A mouse squeaks louder. He cleared his throat.

"No need to mention this to Greyboar, is there, Ignace old buddy? I was just kidding anyway. Ha. Ha. Ha. Buy you a drink?"

"Oh, siddown," I said. "I didn't mean to scare ten years off your life. Why would I tell Greyboar? And even if I did, so what? He's the phlegmatic type, he is. Not the kind to get all worked up into a jealous rage, don't you know?"

"True, true," opined Angus. "Nice easygoing lad, Greyboar. Still and all, everybody's got their off days. Fat lot of good it'd do O'Neal here, his neck like a tapeworm, being the exception to the rule."

Anyway, that was the Cat. Weird, like I said, but did I care? Long as she was around, Greyboar wasn't wallowing in that damned philosophy.

Yessir. Things were looking up!

Chapter 2.
A Choking Dilemma

Or so I thought. Mind you, I'd always known life wasn't fair—first thing I ever learned. My pop used to whup me for no reason, just to drive the lesson home. But the way things were going! Unfair is one thing. Being singled out by Fate for merciless persecution is another.

The next day I landed a simple, straightforward job. Easy money, put us right back in the pink, no complications. Ha!

Naturally, Greyboar started grousing as soon as I explained the job to him.

"I hate these jealous-lover jobs," he growled. "First of all, they're boring—never any professional challenge to 'em. Second, they're stupid. I mean, what is it with people and jealousy, anyway? I figured it out when I was twelve: the only rational philosophy when it comes to this fidelity business is solipsism. If you didn't see it, it didn't happen. And don't go looking for it, if you don't want to see it, because then it won't have happened. Sensible, right? Logical, right? But no! And finally, it's always disgusting. I suppose this client of ours wants me to wave his ex-girlfriend's new lover's dead tongue in front of her face, like usual?"

I nodded.

"Never fails! Sadistic bunch, ex-lovers." He glared at me. "And then there's the fee! *Five hundred quid?* Our going rate's been a thousand for the last three years!"

My voice got shrill. Unreasonable lug! "That's because rumors are flying all over that we might have had something to do with that business in Prygg that brought in the Ozarine troops!"

Greyboar shrugged. "Which we did."

"I know it! I'm still mad about the whole thing. We wouldn't have even been in Prygg if it hadn't been for you and your damned philosophy!"

I bestowed on him my best glare. (And it's a hell of a glare, too, if I say so myself. Though I'll admit it was a bit like a minnow glaring at a shark.)

"Scares off customers, don't you know, us maybe being mixed up in politics? Not to mention heresy—Joe business, no less! Especially with things the way they are in New Sfinctr—you know Queen Belladonna's tight with the Ozarines. She always has been, and since this Prygg business—how many times do I have to tell you, you big gorilla?—politics! Sure, and it's good for the trade, but you've got to know how to finesse the thing! But no! Not the great philosopher Greyboar! No! He's got to—"

"All right, all right, I'll do the job!" He waved his hands. "Anything to shut you up! But I trust that you explained to this—what's his name? Baron de Butin?—that I won't choke the girl. It's one of my rules, you know that. I don't choke girls."

"Yeah, yeah, I know," I grumbled. "I told him. Cost us, too—as usual."

The Baron had offered to double the fee if Greyboar'd burke the girl along with the Baron's "rival," as he put it. But once I explained Greyboar's rules he finally agreed to settle for having my client wave "the rival's" pop-eyes and purple tongue in front of the girl's face. They're really a cruddy lot, your "jilted suitors," Greyboar was right about that. Still and all, fine for him to wax philosophical, I was the agent. I was the poor slob who had to go out there and get his hands dirty rounding up the business—while he lounged around worrying about philosophy, mind you! And the fact is there was a lot of business in your aristocracy's "alienated affections." Steady, steady, steady work. I think they must be inbred or something, all the trouble they seem to have.

Actually, this whole problem with choking girls wasn't so much Greyboar's philosophical obsession. It was really on account of his sister Gwendolyn. She was purely furious when he and I told her, years before, that we were quitting our jobs in the packing plant to move on to more lucrative work. Right nasty she got: "cold-blooded killer," "murdering bastard," "nothing but a cheap thug with a fancy label"—those were the terms she used that weren't just plain obscene. Anybody else'd said stuff like that they'd be pushing up daisies, but the truth is Greyboar was afraid of his sister.

Couldn't say I blamed him. Woman terrified me. She wasn't as strong as he was, but when she was in the mood she was the meanest person who ever lived. Anyway, Greyboar and she went back and forth about it for hours. I kept my mouth shut. I'm normally on the talkative side, but around Gwendolyn in the mood I kept my mouth shut, shut, shut, shut.

Finally, Gwendolyn gave up. But she made Greyboar swear two things: One, he'd never work for a boss as a strikebreaker. Two, he'd never choke a woman except in self-defense—and then the way she defined "self-defense" he'd have to have some harpy drive three stakes into his heart before he could lift a finger!

The strikebreaking stuff was no problem. Greyboar and I wouldn't have done it, anyway. I mean, it's not like both of us hadn't been good union men since we were kids.

The woman question, now—that was a little stickier. Lots of money in choking women. Truth to tell, it was the bread and butter of the trade. So Greyboar tried to make a compromise—he'd only choke purely evil women, she-devil types. But Gwendolyn wouldn't budge. Said that, first, she'd trust him to tell a good woman from a bad one about as far as she'd trust a wolf to pick between saint and sinner rabbits. Second—she'd always been unreasonable when it came to women!—she said: "Besides, I don't care if the woman's as foul as a demon. There's just something about men hiring other men to kill women that makes me cross. Really, really, really cross." Then she'd looked him straight in the eye and said if she ever heard he'd choked a woman, she'd track him down and kill him. Yeah, just like that. Cold as ice.

So the two of them stared at each other for about a minute. Ever been a squirrel trapped in a cage with two tigers about to square off? That's how I felt—but I kept my mouth shut, shut, shut, shut. And then suddenly they were hugging each other and crying like babies.

I felt pretty bad, actually. The career move was my idea in the first place—not that Greyboar wasn't willing! We were both sick of that slaughterhouse—work your life away for nothing and die in the poorhouse. But they were all the family each other had, and I guess I'd sort of put something between them. Between her and me, too, for that matter.

So then Greyboar swore, all choked up, that he'd never harm a woman no matter who else he squeezed. He stuck to the promise, too. Never even bent it a little.

Yeah, I thought it was going to be a simple, neat little job. Five hundred quid, easy as pie.

There was no point in dawdling, so we decided to do the job that very night. Following directions I'd gotten from "the jilted one," we found ourselves in a part of town we weren't very familiar with. Not surprising, of course. I know this city as well as anyone, but nobody really knows all that much about New Sfinctr, the place is such a mess. But we were surprised, because the area where "the rival" was to be found wasn't much better than a slum.

Odd, that. Your typical "alienated affectionee" usually wound up in a part of town that was at least as posh as the one she fled. Usually quite a bit more posh. Natural feature of the "alienation of affection process," don't you know? Upward social mobility, I mean.

"You should have seen the Baron's—what'd he call it?—oh, yeah, his 'modest townhouse,' " I commented to Greyboar. "His girl dumped him in that palace for this place? This 'rival' has got to be hung like a moose."

Greyboar made a sour face. After that I tried to keep the quips to a minimum. He really did hate jealousy jobs. I wasn't too fond of them myself, when it came down to it. Made the slaughterhouse seem like a spa, disgust-wise.

Eventually we found the address. It was a small two-story house, nestled in between a couple of classic tenements. Shabby, but poor-shabby rather than sloppy-shabby, if you know what I mean. Cleanest, best-kept place on the block.

"You sure?" asked Greyboar quietly.

"The address is right," I answered. "And, yeah, there's the flower box outside the window, just like the Baron said. This is it, all right."

Greyboar shrugged. I snuck up the front steps and checked the lock. What a joke! I'd been all geared up for the usual—armed guards in front of the mansion, mastiff watchdogs, locks like they were guarding the Crown Jewels of the Kushrau Kaysar, the works. Have a vastly overrated opinion of their real worth, your noble types. But this!

I picked the lock in six seconds flat. A moment later we were both inside the front room downstairs. I checked for a possible watchdog. But the only thing on watch was a mouse, who disappeared into its hole quick as lightning.

Everything downstairs was dark, but we could see the room well enough to size it up. Much like the outside—shabby, everything threadbare, but well kept. Little woman's touches here and there. Homey like, I mean to say. Definitely not your usual rich young bachelor's love nest.

"Must be her poor old mother's place," I whispered. "Probably she's trysting here with some guy who's so noble he can't soil his palace with the likes of some money-grubbing trollop. Gold runs through his veins, I bet." Greyboar motioned me to silence. He pointed up the stairs to the floor above. Listening closely, I could hear voices. Couldn't make out any words, though.

But by the time we got to the top of the stairs, moving like cats, I could make out the words all right. Such as they were, yes sirree. Mostly just meaningless noises, don't you know? Well, not exactly meaningless— it was impossible to miss the emotional content, so to speak. You know: passion, ecstasy, etc., etc.

We crept up to the bedroom door. The noises

beyond the door seemed to be reaching that stage which genteel society likes to call a "climax." Silly word, really, like you were struggling up a mountain, huffing and puffing and gasping for breath, instead of whooping like a kid while you slide down—well, let's keep it couth.

Greyboar reached for the doorframe, his huge shoulder muscles starting to move like a tidal bore. His normal approach to opening doors, don't you know? But before he got halfway into it he dropped his arms and stared down at the doorknob. I looked around him and saw what he was staring at. The door wasn't even closed, much less locked!

For a moment, Greyboar and I looked at each other, almost as if we were helpless. I mean, what a ridiculous situation! The greatest strangler in the world—he was, too, don't ever doubt it—and he'd been hired to do a job a ten-year-old could have handled, at least so far.

I made a face and a couple of gestures, which more or less expressed the idea: what the hell, maybe the guy inside is built like a bull. He must be, judging from the noise coming through the door.

Greyboar took a deep breath, shook his head, and charged through the door into the bedroom, his hands ahead of him ready to deal death and doom and destruction.

Well, the next few minutes were touch and go. I do believe the wings of the Angel of Death brushed me more than once. I do, I do, I do.

Never did a mouse staring up an eagle's beak talk faster than I did. Trying to convince the big bird to forego lunch.

Funny thing was, it was probably the girls who saved my weasand from undergoing the Really Big Squeeze.

I talked just fast enough and long enough that they stopped screaming and started listening to what I was saying and eventually they started talking too and what they said backed up my story. Not a moment too soon, either. First time I'd ever seen Greyboar's eyes red with rage, actually. Not a sight I recommend for tourists.

Eventually, the red started fading into a kind of pink-orange, and I knew I'd make it to another sunrise. Still had to keep talking, of course. It's nice to live, but not all that nice when you've managed to get yourself into Greyboar's Black Book, page one, line one. I grant you, it was a small black book, Greyboar's—he wasn't the type to nurse grudges, don't you know? But, oh, it was a very very very very black little book.

"He told me 'his rival,'" I said, for maybe the tenth time in the last few minutes. "I told him 'no girls' and he nodded," I said, for maybe the twentieth time in the last few minutes. "How was I supposed to know?" I said, for maybe the thirtieth time in the last few minutes. "It's not my fault!" I said, for maybe the hundredth time in the last few minutes.

The girls were still scared to death, clutching each other, trembling, pale as ghosts down to the soles of their feet. Oh yeah, you could see the soles of their feet, all right. Not surprising, they were both naked as the day they were born. Under other circumstances, it would have been distracting, as young and good-looking as they were. But at the moment, my thoughts were entirely focused on the survival of me rather than the species.

Plucky girls, though, I'll say it now. As terrified as they were, they managed to think quick and talk almost as quick as me.

Greyboar and I, as it turned out, had definitely accomplished the first part of the job—tracking down the Baron's ex-girlfriend and "the rival." Caught them, in fact, in the very act of "alienating his affections." Marooning his affections on the moon, more like. What the upper crust calls *in flagrante delicto*, don't you know? What we crude plebes call humping like rabbits. Having a grand good time of it, too, like teenagers usually do.

The ex-girlfriend's name was Angela. She was the one on the left. Cute as a button, which wasn't surprising given that she was all of seventeen years old. She was a short girl, with one of those lush figures that looks so striking on a small woman. Her complexion was dark. Not as dark as Greyboar or Gwendolyn, who look like desert nomads, but at least as dark as an Ozarine. "Olive-skinned," they call it. Her eyes were big, colored one of those rich dark brown hues. Almost the same color as her hair, which was on the short side but so curly that it framed her head like a halo.

The "rival" was the one on the right. Jenny, her name was. Eighteen years old—the predatory older woman of song and legend! Other than being almost as young, Jenny's appearance was very different from Angela's. She was taller and slimmer, with long blondish hair and green eyes. Where Angela was drop-dead gorgeous, Jenny was what you might call "country-girl pretty." But even in the tension of the moment, I was struck by her eyes. In their own way, they were just as lustrous and sparkling as Angela's.

The story was simple enough. The Baron had bought Angela from her father the year before. The Baron's "affections," as Angela described them, did not make him a candidate for the World's Greatest Lover. His most attractive characteristic was cold indifference. His other qualities went very rapidly downhill from there.

Jenny had been hired on some months back as Angela's seamstress. After the terrible epidemic in the Year of the Jackal, she'd been orphaned. She managed to stay out of prostitution because she'd learned to be a seamstress from her mother. Starvation wages, of course, but Jenny hadn't been able to accept the alternative. She was a stubborn girl, that much was obvious.

Over time, close proximity led to this and that, and eventually they'd planned and carried out Angela's escape. Since then they'd lived here, in the little house Jenny had inherited from her parents. Jenny was teaching Angela how to sew, and the two of them had plans to open a little shop in the room below.

"Of course he'd call me his 'rival,'" snapped Jenny. "Think the mighty Baron'd admit his girl got stole by a girl?" I swear, the two of them even giggled at that point. Plucky, like I said.

"But why'd he do it?" I demanded. Well, screeched. I fear my voice was shrill. "We'd have found out sooner or later, and I told him a dozen times if I told him once—I swear it!—'Greyboar won't choke girls.'"

Greyboar had calmed down by now. Actually, he was almost as pale as the girls were. In fact, not to put too fine a point on it, he was looking positively ragged. He looked around for a place to sit. Angela and Jenny moved over, still clutching each other, giving him room to sit on the bed. When he sat down, the bed creaked alarmingly. He must have weighed twice what the two of them did together.

"He knows my reputation," growled Greyboar. "That's what the rotten bastard's counting on. All professional chokesters have to keep their reputations clean as a whistle. Not a very trust-filled business, strangling. If you don't take your professional ethics seriously, you're soon out of business; it doesn't matter how good your fingerwork is. And my reputation is as good as gold. Never violated professional ethics.

Never. Not once." His nostrils flared, it's a sight to freeze a man's blood, believe me. "I even strangled my own guru!"

I cleared my throat. Couldn't believe what I was about to say—me, his agent, of all people! But, well, I'm a hard-boiled cuss, sure I am, but—well, the truth is, they—the girls—they—

Couldn't do it. Just couldn't.

"Maybe this once, big guy. I mean, what the hell, we'll tell the Baron if he complains we'll tell the world the truth about his rival. We'll shout it from the rooftops! He'll be the laughingstock of New Sfinctr! Of all Grotum!"

Greyboar shook his head. "Won't work. Two reasons." He held up two fingers like cucumbers and counted off.

"One. If the Baron's like most Groutch noblemen I've known, he values his reputation for ruthlessness a lot more than his reputation for lovemaking. Rich as he is, he can always buy another bedmate, and what does he care what she really thinks? But if he loses his reputation for being a snake—well, you know what these highborn scum are like. We both do, it's what puts the food on our table. Word gets out he's been made a patsy and he's not long for the world. Not in New Sfinctr!"

"He's right," said Angela, in a voice like a mouse. Jenny nodded her head about a hundred times. Her long blonde hair rippled like a curtain in the breeze.

Greyboar went on. "Two. It's all beside the point anyway. Professional ethics is professional ethics. Period. It's the way it's got to be. You don't understand that, Ignace. You never have and you never will. Nothing personal, it's just—sure, you arrange the job and you always go along, and I wouldn't even look at another agent—but." He took a breath. "But I'm still the one that does the squeeze." He looked down at his hands. "More times than I can remember, now."

He was silent for a moment, then continued.

"It's a stinking, rotten trade, Ignace. My sister was right about that, I always knew she was." I started to say something but he held up his hand.

"Don't say it! 'Pay's good. Work's steady. What else do you ever get in this world?' I've heard you say it once, I've heard you say it a million times. Don't disagree, either. Fine for Gwendolyn, she's got her fairytale dreams of revolution and justice and rights to keep her going. But me—" He stopped and took a deep breath, looked at his hands again. "Me, I've got my professional ethics."

As the wise man says, "It's all nuts, anyway." Sure and I crossed the line, then. I motioned to the girls. They slipped off the bed and came over to me. I waved them behind me. Cleared my throat.

"I'm afraid I'll have to take a slight exception here, big guy." I even managed a feeble grin. "Just can't do it. Just can't."

I could feel the girls huddled behind me, up close. Angela was about my height, and was clutching my right arm, pressed into me. Even in the peril of the moment, the feel of her nude form against my back was incredibly distracting. For that matter, having Jenny's blonde hair floating over my left shoulder and her arm wrapped around my belly was just as unsettling. She was shivering with fear even more than Angela, and while her figure was on the lean side there wasn't any doubt at all that it was purely female.

I almost burst into hysterical laughter. At least I'd undergo the Final Squeeze with a light head! It seemed like all the blood in my body had rushed somewhere else. Dizzy, I was.

Greyboar stared at me. I think that was the only

time, in all the years we'd known each other—since we were kids scraping in the gutter together—that I'd ever really impressed the damn monster.

He smiled a crooked smile. No comfort to me at all, that smile. Reminded me of a crocodile.

"Ignace! After all these years, don't tell me you've discovered philosophy?"

Well, you can imagine! That did it! I hit the roof! I was hopping around in a fury! I mean, the insufferable nerve of the guy!

"You and your damned philosophy!" I roared. Well, sort of what you might call a high octave roar. Your operatic baritone types don't actually lose a lot of sleep worrying about my competition for their jobs.

"The sleep I've lost because of your philosophy madness! The money! The peace of mind! Dragged me all over Grotum! Got me mixed up with high politics! Heresy! And now this!"

I shoved my face into his great granite block of a so-called visage.

"All right, big guy! Put up or shut up! You're the great philosopher! You're the student of heavy thoughts! I'm just the mental pip-squeak here, right? You're the one learned from the *guru*! You're the one spent the Old Geister knows how many hours on the way back here from Prygg discussing the whichness of what with the great wizard Zulkeh! Wish he was here! He's the world's biggest windbag, Zulkeh is, but he'd figure a way out of this in his sleep! That's why he's a great wizard and you're a great lump of gristle with delusions of grandeur! You're in a—what would you call it, you genius, you—you *philosopher*? A dilemma, that's it! The great philosopher Greyboar, what just happens also to throttle necks on the side—just to pay the rent and keep his pea-brain agent in ale, you understand?— why, he's faced with an ethical dilemma, he is!"

I actually started pounding the top of his head with my fist. Regretted it later, of course—like pounding a rock—no, a lump of solid iron.

"Well, philosophize your way out of this one! Sure, why not? I bet your *guru* could've philosophized a nice greasy little escape clause in a minute! And Zulkeh? He could conjugate dilemmas like a grammarian teaching schoolkids—find any conditional subjunctive ethical hatch he needed! So why don't you?"

I finally fell silent, panting for breath, glaring at him like a, well, to be honest, like a maniacal mouse. Then, slowly, Greyboar's eyes got that dreamy look I hated so much. He began stroking his chin.

"Well," he said, "let me think a minute." And so he did. For more than a minute.

There were times afterward—*hundreds* of them— when I thought I should have kept my mouth shut and gone down like an honorable mouse. Sure, I'd have been dead, and the girls with me. But it'd have been quick and clean—Greyboar could've snapped all three of our necks at once with two fingers, tops—and then? Oblivion, that's what—peaceful, restful, untroubled oblivion. Not so bad, really, when you think about it. I mean, it's not as if this world is such a great joy, is it?

Instead—an endless future of aggravation I created.

Because, naturally, Greyboar philosophized a way out. Was he proud of it? Does a peacock preen? Does a rooster strut? Did he talk about it afterward, a million times? Does a dog howl at the moon? Does a cock crow at dawn?

Did he tell me—oh, maybe twelve times a day from then on until forever—how essential philosophy is to daily life? To hourly life? To figuring out which fingernail to trim first? Did he? Did he? Does a—oh, never mind. It's too aggravating to talk about.

So we left. But before we got more than halfway down the stairs, with me leading the way, Greyboar stopped.

"Wait a minute, Ignace," he said. He thought for a moment, then: "It occurs to me that there's a little matter of professional ethics still to be taken care of." He turned and called back up the stairs.

"Jenny! Angela! Are you decent? Need to discuss one last little thing."

Their heads peeked around the door. "We're dressed now," they said.

Greyboar turned back to me. "Your job, this, Ignace. You're the agent."

It didn't take me any time to figure it out. I went back up into the bedroom, grinning from ear to ear.

Chapter 3.
Sans Tout But the Beast

The following night we presented ourselves at the Baron's "modest townhouse." Of course, we had to go through the usual routine. First the guards searched us for weapons. We didn't have any, naturally. Why would anybody in their right mind carry around weapons when Greyboar's got his thumbs?

Then the dogs sniffed us. They looked up at Greyboar. He gazed down at them. The great mastiffs whimpered and slunk into the corner.

Then the butler lifted his nose higher than the mountain peaks and announced we'd have to wait "for His Lordship's pleasure." Then we waited for His Lordship's pleasure.

Eventually, it pleased His Lordship to allow us into his august presence. We were ushered into his "study," as he called it. Quite a place, that "study." Maybe six books in the whole room. The rest of it—every wall and most of the floor space—was covered with pelts, mounted heads of more animals than I even knew existed, great stuffed bears and lions and tigers roaring their eternal fury at the bold big game hunter who'd bagged 'em—not without the assistance of maybe five hundred beaters and bearers and guides, I don't imagine.

And there he stood before us, the big game hunter himself, just as I remembered him. Nobility incarnate, from the top of his well-coiffured hair to the tips of his feet. His Lordship, the Baron de Butin. He stood by the mantel, dressed in a smoking jacket made of some kind of material would probably cause me brainstroke if I tried to guess at the price. A great fire roared in the fireplace.

"You may leave us, Jeffrey," he instructed the butler. "I have private business with these gentlemen."

His Lordship was in a man-of-the-people type mood. Right away, the Baron was chatting away like we were three gentlemen discussing the weather over brandy. Eventually, he came around to the point. When he heard what we had to tell him, the man-of-the-people mood went like last year's snow. Most displeased, he was, His Lordship.

After a while, his denunciations and recriminations wound themselves up and he closed his mouth. He bestowed upon us a look of contemptuous dismissal— head back, eyes sighting in down the long aquiline nose like a hunter drawing a bead.

"You may go," he announced.

Greyboar made a motion. I hauled out the leather sack containing the Baron's advance on the job. Broke my heart, this, but Greyboar had insisted and I wasn't going to press the point. Got testy about his professional ethics, Greyboar did.

"We're returning your advance, Your Lordship," explained Greyboar. "Only proper, given that we didn't finish the job."

The Baron's nose lifted higher. "If you think this'll set things straight, you're quite mistaken, my man," he declared. "The issue here is ethics, not money. You are a scoundrel, sirrah, and you may be sure I shall see to it that your despicable behavior in this entire affair is known to the world."

Then Butin's reserve cracked just slightly. "I simply don't understand!" he cried. "A chokester of your reputation!"

Greyboar spread his hands. "Well, Your Lordship, it's like this here. Sure and I was in a dilemma, torn between my professional ethics and my solemn vow never to choke girls. Fortunately, I am—as you may have heard—a student of philosophy. A fortunate man, I've been—I was trained by the King of the Sundjhab, you know?" Greyboar coughed. "A very brief apprenticeship, to be sure—but he was a great guru, the King! Incredible man, to have taught me so much in such a short time. And then! Postgraduate polish applied to me by the great sorcerer Zulkeh. A master dialectician!"

The Baron was staring at Greyboar like he was looking at a madman. I hate to admit it, but I actually had a moment of empathy for His Lordship, for just that one fleeting second.

Greyboar continued. "Of course, once I applied their teachings to my dilemma, the solution came to me almost at once. Hadn't the wizard Zulkeh taught me to seek the higher synthesis which arises from the contradiction of thesis and antithesis? Didn't my guru explain that entropy is the guiding principle of all ethics? So I realized that the dilemma could only be resolved by rising to a higher plane. And what plane could be higher than the increase of entropy, the pursuit of disorder from order?"

The Baron, his face now red as a beet, began to speak. He didn't get far.

"I have not finished," said Greyboar, in that tone of voice he occasionally used. Could silence the surf, that tone of voice.

"So I asked myself, what is really the ethical issue here? What course of action would flow with Time's Arrow, what course resist it with futile immorality? The answer was then obvious! Wonderful girls, Angela and Jenny! Really—natural-born ethical entropists! Not only did the little rascals humiliate a great Lord, but they went further and broke down these old and hoary rigidities concerning the proper sexual order—and with great thermodynamic energy, too! I know, I was there!"

Greyboar was now smiling broadly. "Yes, marvelous lasses! Instinctive *philosophes* of the second law of thermodynamics! Pioneers of entropy! Explorers of disorder! Of course they had to survive—they were an example for us all!"

Greyboar coughed modestly. "I myself, perhaps. Well! Ignace and I have been close for many years. Perhaps an even greater closeness, perhaps we too could contribute—" He eyed me speculatively. I was furious, you can imagine! Him and his little jokes! I didn't think it was a bit funny!

"Well, perhaps not," admitted Greyboar. "A good lad, Ignace, but he's really quite set in his ways. Not a philosophical bone in his body, I'm afraid. In any event, Your Lordship, I trust I've explained the thing to your satisfaction."

By now the Baron had quite lost his aristocratic reserve. "You are not only a scoundrel, sirrah," he stormed, "you are a pervert and a madman! Leave! At once!"

Again, Greyboar coughed apologetically. "Well, actually, Your Lordship, there remains one small matter which we need to resolve before we go." He held up a hand, forestalling the Baron's next—no doubt peremptory—sentence.

"Won't take but a moment, Your Lordship," said Greyboar soothingly. "I assure you—just a brief moment of your time. You see, oddly enough, I have acquired another client. Two of them, actually. An unusual situation all the way around. Cut my rates to the bone, for one thing."

He turned to me. "What am I being paid again, Ignace?"

I glared at him. As the wise man says: "Fun's fun, but money's money."

"One penny, as you damned well know," I snarled. "They scraped together a shilling and tuppence, but you made me give the rest back. Just needed the one penny, you said, to satisfy the requirements of professional ethics."

"Why, yes, so I did," rumbled the strangler. He turned back to the Baron. And then he grinned.

Even a man as stupid as the Baron finally figured it out at the end. An artist's dream, that momentary tableau. *The Great Hunter. Sans Beaters. Sans Bearers. Sans Guides. Sans Tout But the Beast.*

He tried to scream for help, but he couldn't get out a sound, even before The Thumbs closed around his throat. I'm not surprised, really. I'm sure it was Greyboar's grin moving toward him. Must have been like staring into his own open grave.

Well, much to my surprise, the whole thing turned out to have quite a few bright spots. "Every storm drowns a few rats," as the wise man says.

First of all, we got out of there without the slightest little ruckus. Always nice, a job that doesn't require a messy getaway. I hear it was five hours before the butler got up enough nerve to peek into the Baron's study, and by then we'd already knocked down eight pots of ale in The Sign of the Trough.

Then—lackeys babble, it's the nature of the breed— the word got all around town, especially among the upper crust where most of our business comes from. Greyboar had set a new world record! The Baron's neck was tied into a double sheepshank. Never been done before. Of course, I made sure the Records Committee got it into the books. But even before they made the official announcement, clients were pounding on our door. Displeasure of the Queen and the Ozarine be damned! Greyboar was back in fashion—big fashion. I even cranked our standard rate up to 1500 quid.

Then, what would you know but two weeks later I got a note from Jenny and Angela inviting me over for dinner. Quite a nice dinner, too, they must have scraped for a week to put it together. I offered to help pay for the food, but they wouldn't hear of it. Wound up staying there quite a while. Well, the whole night, actually. It turned out they weren't really all that rigid in their ways, so to speak, so maybe Greyboar was right about the moral advance of disorder (whatever that meant).

In fact, I found myself spending quite a bit of my time over there, in the days that followed. Well. Actually, to be honest, I found myself spending *most* of my time over there, when I wasn't attending to business. To my astonishment, whole days would go by— two or three in a row, sometimes—where I didn't even make a token appearance at The Trough. And when I did, more often that not, it was just to conduct a little bit of quick business. Then—off.

Of course, the proper Trough-men made a big deal over it. But I was impervious. Serene in my disregard. The sniggers were flat; the ridicule, limp; the derision, as hollow as an aching tooth.

Eat your hearts out, boys.

Yet, oddly, I didn't boast. I just maintained a dignified silence. No way to explain it, really, that wouldn't have gotten me into the soup with the Trough-men. Sure, and I was having fun. More fun than I'd ever had in my life, in fact. But—

The truth is, it was mainly the peace of mind. I found myself treasuring the moments when Jenny and Angela were asleep even more, in some ways, than the excitement when they were awake. Just listening to them breathe softly in the dark was a treasure I hoarded even more than I'd ever hoarded any coin. And me—a champion miser!

I think— I don't know. Hard to explain. I think it was maybe that being around them made me feel like I might have felt if I hadn't grown up to be me. Or something like that.

Of course, I didn't neglect my managerial responsibilities. Even when it meant grinding my teeth for hours and hours listening to Greyboar droning on about his progress with "Languor" and his hopes for eventual "Torpor" and his daydreams about final "Stupor."

Then—finally! Just when I was sure I'd never hear the end of Greyboar's bragging and boasting about his philosophy—the big loon got distracted. Really distracted.

The Cat had been gone for a week or so. Where? Who knows? Looking for Schrödinger, I expect. But, anyway, one night she showed up again at The Trough. Greyboar invited her over to our table right away, of course. Stubborn, like I said. She sat down, off in her own world. Eventually she got around to asking Greyboar what he'd been up to lately, with about the same interest you might ask a rock how it's feeling. Wouldn't you know it but Greyboar started off and told her the whole story, droning on and on about the philosophical intricacies and the dialectical subtleties and all the other goobledygook he learned from Zulkeh. I mean, not the sort of thing your normal wooer with half a brain would touch with a ten-foot pole, don't you know?

Strange, strange woman. About halfway through the story, the Cat took off her telescope-lens spectacles and gave them a good cleaning. She put them back on and stared at Greyboar until he finished the whole story. Never took her eyes off him once. After all this time, I think it was the first time she actually looked at the guy.

When Greyboar was finally finished, she continued staring at him for a while. Then she said, very abruptly: "Stand up." Greyboar stood. The Cat got up and slowly walked around him—for all the world like a lumberjack sizing up a tree.

She sat back down and stared at him a bit more. "You know," she said, with an actual tone in her voice, "you're kind of cute. For a gorilla."

Well, I'm a man of the world, so I quickly made a graceful exit. Figured I'd leave the two of them alone for a half hour or so—just long enough to let a little warmth get started, but not so long that Greyboar would ruin it with another philosophy lecture.

But when I went back to the table, they were gone. Didn't see either of them for two weeks. Furious, I was—you wouldn't believe the business I had to turn down!

Finally, Greyboar showed up, smiling like an imbecile, laughing at everything like a tot, practically had to have his chin wiped. Said he'd fallen in love, no less.

It figured. Leave it to a philosophical strangler to fall in love with the weirdest woman in the world. But I was still happier listening to him babble about the Cat than babble about ontology. Leastwise, I could understand some of what he was talking about. Quite a bit, actually.

Chapter 4.
Portrait of a Strangler

But all that came later. In the immediate aftermath, the Baron's choke resulted in a completely unexpected hitch. Greyboar's sister Gwendolyn came back to haunt us. In a strange sort of way.

Late in the afternoon of the very next day, while we were at The Trough having a friendly argument over *my* idea of "life's big questions"—*stout or lager*—a stranger showed up. The first we knew of him was when Leuwen came over and started muttering and mumbling something incoherent. He was wiping his hands on his rag, too, in that particular way he has whenever he's got something to say to Greyboar that he thinks the big guy won't like.

Silly habit. Greyboar's never been one to blame the messenger, and, even if he were, he certainly wouldn't take his peeve out on a professional Flankn barkeep. Just isn't done. Your imperial-level ambassadors don't hold a candle to Flankn barkeeps when it comes to real diplomatic immunity.

"Stop mumbling," growled Greyboar. "Just spit it out."

"Well, see, it's like this, Greyboar. There's this guy here—he's a stranger. An outlander, actually, damned if he isn't an Ozarine—but he's vouched for by The Roach himself, if you can fathom that. It's the truth! He came here once before, Oscar and the lads brung him, and spent a fair number of hours quaffing ale with The Roach in one of the small private rooms, although The Roach let it be known in the main room right here—in no uncertain terms—that Benny—that's his name, this stranger I'm talking about—was a friend of his and not to be meddled with. If you know what I mean."

(What it means, if you're not familiar with the personage involved, is that The Roach passed the word in The Trough—the Flankn's combined heart and central nervous system—that if any Flankn cutpurse or mugger so much as looked cross-eyed at this Benny fellow, well, they'd have The Roach to deal with. And The Boots. Among the lowlife of New Sfinctr, that's as good as gold. Quite a bit better, actually. Even gold wears out, eventually. The Boots and their effects are eternal.)

Leuwen was still droning on and around and about and up and down and sideways, so Greyboar cut him short: "Get to the point."

Again, the frantic wiping of the hands. Then: "Well, you see, actually, the point is—he wants to talk to you."

Greyboar lifted his eyebrows. "So? Send him over, then."

Some few moments later, Leuwen was wending his way back through the crowded taproom with a stranger in tow. The man was carrying a cloth sack filled with something or other in one hand, and an odd-looking object of some sort in the other. The thing was flat, almost like a board, and about four feet wide by three feet tall. Couldn't figure out what it was.

As he drew near, the man subjected us to a very close scrutiny. Well, subjected Greyboar, I should say. He didn't give me but a glance. In and of itself, that wasn't unusual. Strangers often stared at Greyboar when they first met him, even if they didn't know who he was. If they did, the stare became an ogle.

But there was something odd about this fellow's stare. There was no fear in it, not even apprehension. Instead, there seemed to be some kind of weird recognition. Almost as if he were seeing a ghost, or something.

But I didn't spend much time trying to figure out what the stranger was thinking. I was much too busy wallowing in an immediate, overwhelming, intense, detestation of him.

I hate that man, was the overriding thought in my mind. *May he contract leprosy. May he stumble and disfigure himself. May he suffer from an incurable deadly disease which strikes him down before he takes another step. May a meteorite plunge through the roof and turn him into a crater. May—*

And so on, and so forth.

No man in the world has any right to be that handsome.

It was so disgusting. Mind you, I'm not normally given to envy over such things. There's no need for it. Your normal "handsome man" is an object of ridicule. Most of them are pretty-boy types, which the girls may swoon over but which any solid male bellied up to a bar can instantly dismiss with a sneer. "Cream puff. Break him like a twig."

Alas. I doubted that any man in The Trough could have broken this fellow, other than Greyboar and maybe a couple of your finest muggers. He wasn't just

impossibly handsome, he was also—brace yourself for
another sample of life's fundamental unfairness—tall,
broad-shouldered, lean-hipped, flat-bellied, the whole
works. His stride had a light, pantherish quality to it,
which went quite oddly with the soulful sadness in his
gray eyes. And his hands! Oh, the injustice of it all!
Women would gaze on those finely-shaped, long-
fingered, well-manicured objects with fascinated curiosity, and decide he was undoubtedly a charming fellow.
Men would examine the size of the sinewy things, note
how well they undoubtedly wrapped themselves around
the hilt of the sword scabbarded to his waist, and
decide likewise.

The sword, naturally, was not only a finely-made
rapier with a truly splendid hilt and basket, it was also
obviously well used.

By the time Leuwen brought the wretch to our
table I had damned him to a thousand deaths. Silently,
of course. Alas, Greyboar didn't share a natural male
reaction to such things. And, fact is, should the big
guy have chosen not to back me up in a little *con-
tretemps*—he'd been known to desert me in my hour
of need—things might have gotten a little tricky if the
stranger took offense at my conduct.

True, the man was obviously an Ozarine. The dark
complexion and the typical Ozarine cast to his features
gave him away even before he opened his mouth and
exhibited that grotesque Ozarine accent. But I was not
one of those dolts who thought all Ozarines were
overcivilized fops. Overcivilized fops do not, as a rule,
conquer half the world.

Greyboar gazed up at the fellow and spoke.

"May I be of assistance, sirrah?" Yeah, just like that.
Polite as can be.

The stranger bowed—I hated that bow; courteous
as you could ask for, without a trace of foppery; there's

no justice—and replied: "Indeed, sirrah, such is my very hope." He gestured to an unoccupied chair at our table. "May I?"

I scowled, but Greyboar immediately nodded his permission. After the man sat down, he said: "Allow me to introduce myself, gentlemen. I am an artist. My name is Benvenuti Sfondrati-Piccolomini. If I am not mistaken, I believe I have the honor of addressing the famous professional strangler Greyboar and his agent"—here he nodded politely at me and shrugged apologetically—"whose name, alas, is not known to me."

Naturally, I started to deny everything, but Greyboar cut me off. "His name's Ignace. And I'm Greyboar."

Since there was now no hope of claiming to be misrecognized, I decided to brush the fellow off.

"What d'you want?" I demanded, in my best brush-off tone. "We're busy."

Alas, the fellow took no offense. Instead, to my surprise, he beamed cheerfully. No simpering foppish smile, either. One of those manly-type grins. Naturally, his teeth were blindingly white. Naturally, the debonair dark mustache set them off perfectly.

"Perhaps you can help me with a problem." He reached back and lifted the strange object he'd been carrying. He turned it toward us. Now, finally, I recognized the thing. Artist, he'd said. Sure enough, the object was a portrait. A very large portrait. Oil on canvas.

Unfortunately for my *amour propre*, I was in mid-quaff when he turned the portrait. Seeing it full on, I couldn't stop myself from spewing ale all over the table.

Greyboar, whether from some weird premonition or simply because he has the nervous reactions of iron ore, simply took a long, casual draught of his ale pot. Then, after a satisfied belch, announced:

"Quite a good portrait of the Baron." He wiped foam from his lips. "Excellent, actually—though I'm no connoisseur of the arts."

"Connoyser be damned!" I hissed. I was on my feet like a shot.

"Blackmail!" I pronounced. "Choke him, Greyboar! Burke him, I say! He's a filthy rotten blackmailer!"

Greyboar, alas, responded with nothing more dynamic than a glance in my direction. "Choke him?" he mused. "Blackmail? Whatever are you talking about, Ignace?"

He turned his gaze onto the stranger. "Surely this fine gentleman's no blackmailer," he rumbled. "And if he were, so what? What crime have we committed to fear blackmail?"

The stranger glanced at me and laughed. "Too many for Ignace to count, I venture to say." The quick laugh was followed by a pleasant grin and a casual wave of the hand.

"But you may rest easy, Ignace," he announced. "You may have, but I most surely did not, mistake the emphasis in Greyboar's words. Where you heard 'what crime have we committed,' I heard the important words: '*to fear blackmail*.'"

He transferred his cheerful grin to the strangler. "I dare say you're not troubled by blackmailers often. And certainly not for long."

Greyboar cracked his knuckles. Several of the patrons in The Trough flinched and stared up at the ceiling.

"No," he said. "Not often. And not for long."

"Then what d'you want?" I demanded.

Again, he was unfazed by my hostility. He simply responded with his suave smile and said:

"I am in a bit of a predicament, sirrahs, as a result of the recent demise of the Baron be Butin. Some time ago, the Baron commissioned me to do his portrait."

He glanced down at the canvas. "As you can see, I had almost finished the work when word came that the Baron had shuffled off this mortal coil."

Comprehension dawned. I sneered. "So you lost the commission? Never got your money?"

He nodded. Again, I shot to my feet like a rocket.

"Extortion!" I pronounced. "Choke him, Greyboar! Burke him, I say! He's a filthy rotten extortionist!"

This time, Greyboar simply chuckled. The stranger frowned.

"Whatever are you talking about, my good Ignace?"

"I'm not your good Ignace! I know what you're up to! You lost out on your commission because Grey— because some unknown desperado choked the Baron, and now you're trying to squeeze the fee out of us!"

The artist's frown deepened. As if he didn't understand what I was saying, which was ridiculous, because it was plain as day—

Greyboar interrupted. "I regret your loss, sirrah, but I'm afraid I don't see what I can do about it. Alas, it's in the nature of my trade that third parties often wind up taking a loss, through no fault of their own." He shrugged. "You just have to be philosophical about it. The way I look at it, for every third party unfairly injured there's another third party unfairly rewarded. Heirs and such, for instance."

For a moment, a steely glint came to the strangler's eyes. "But I'm afraid I can hardly be called upon to make good such losses to third parties. Put me right out of business, that would."

He waved his great hand airily. But the steely glint remained. "And I'm afraid, should such a third party insist, that I would have to—reluctantly, you understand—come to the conclusion which my friend and agent Ignace came to, as is his unfortunate habit, much too precipitously."

Very steely glint. What people call The Stare, in fact. "*Extortion.*"

I was astonished. This Benvenuti fellow was one of the very, very, very few men I'd ever met who didn't seem in the slightest bit intimidated by The Stare.

He actually laughed! A real, cheerful, happy-go-lucky type of laugh, too. Not the least little quaver or tremor in the thing.

"You misunderstand!" he exclaimed. "I am not seeking financial restitution for my loss. Oh no, not at all. The idea's grotesque! No respectable craftsman such as yourself could be held responsible for unforeseen losses to third parties which arise as the natural result of his enterprise."

The Stare faded, replaced by a puzzled frown.

"But you said—"

The stranger nodded vigorously. "I said that you could be of assistance to me in my predicament. But— my fault entirely—I failed to make clear that the quandary is of an artistic rather than pecuniary nature."

Seeing the puzzled frown still on Greyboar's great looming tor of a brow, the artist explained:

"The Baron's estate, you see, has already made clear that they will not pay me for the portrait under any circumstances. Indeed, they refuse even to compensate me for my expenses. The commission, they say, was undertaken by the Baron, who is now deceased. The estate therefore bears no responsibility for it."

A steely glint came into his own eyes. "At the same time—you seem to have some peculiar legal customs here, if you'll permit an Ozarine to say so—the estate claims that the portrait is part of the estate and must therefore be delivered up. The completed work, mind you. Else I shall be liable before the law for embezzlement and breach of contract."

Greyboar quaffed his ale thoughtfully. "It's true that

the laws of New Sfinctr tend to be weighted a bit in favor of the rich."

He eyed the portrait. "So you must legally finish the work, though you will not be paid for it, and—to make matters worse yet—the model himself is no longer available." He shrugged. "But I still don't see the problem. Surely an artist of your skill could—"

Benvenuti cut him off. "Finish it from memory? Oh, to be sure! But that would only satisfy the legal side of my obligation. The problem, I said, was artistic."

The glint in the artist's eye was now pure steel. I took another look at his sword. A *very* well-used sword, it looked like.

Then, Benvenuti explained what he wanted.

Again, I shot to my feet.

"Insanity!" I pronounced. "Choke him, Greyboar! Burke him, I say! He's a dangerous lunatic!"

Greyboar now began laughing, if the term "laughter" can be applied to a rumbling earthquake. I glowered at him, then at the artist.

"See what you've done?" I demanded.

Greyboar's great paw patted my shoulder. "Relax, Ignace. I'll tell you what. Let's put the question before the ancients."

Good idea. The ancients of The Trough would have no truck with this madness.

"O'Doul! Flannery!" I shouted. Then, I had to shout louder still. By that time of night, the sound of The Trough was like a heavy surf of conversation and camaraderie.

"O'Doul! Flannery! Come over here!" Then, the traditional, hallowed words: *"We need sage advice and wise counsel!"*

In an instant, the uproar in The Trough died away. A multitude of heads turned our way in sudden interest. Immediately, two of the ancients sitting on their prestigious stools at the Old Bar drained their mugs and upended them ceremoniously. A moment later, they were shuffling their way across the room.

Proper ancients, O'Doul and Flannery. Took the customs seriously.

Before they had even arrived at our table, Leuwen was already there bearing new pots of ale. I winced, but couldn't object. By right and tradition, ancients called upon to make an official Ruling of The Trough were entitled to free ale at the expense of those who called for the Ruling.

As soon as O'Doul and Flannery arrived and took their seats, I laid out the case before them. I was careful to present both sides of the dispute, fairly and dispassionately. Not my natural inclination, that sort of judiciousness, but I had no choice. The worst thing that can happen to you, in a Trough Ruling, is to be charged by the ancients with "special pleading" or, even worse, "lawyering." The penalty for special pleading is official Trough derision. The penalty for lawyering is outright ostracism. Extreme cases are even banned from The Trough for life.

By the time I was finished, a huge crowd had gathered around the table. Outside of a brawl, there's nothing proper Trough-men love more than a Ruling. The comments from the crowd were loud, drunken, and, often enough, obscene. As was hallowed tradition.

My presentation done, I glared at the artist and waved my hand majestically, inviting him to argue his side of the matter. I was hoping, of course, to trick him into special pleading. I figured he'd fall right into the trap, being an Ozarine. To my chagrin, however, he smiled good-naturedly, loudly admired the fairmindedness of my presentation, and simply added a few little details which, though they highlighted certain charms of his argument, could hardly be accused of legalism.

The ancients launched into the case. O'Doul began with the traditional appeal to precedent.

"Reminds me o' the time Hammerhand Hobbs throttled that gov'nor while he was engaged with one of the girls o'r to Madame Henley's House of the Purple Lamp. The lady o' the evening wanted Hammerhand should pay her on account as how he'd robbed her of rightful wages for an unaccomplished labor o' unspeakable debauchery, whilst Hammerhand claimed he owed not a farthing inasmuch as the girl hadn't actually had the chance to perform the act o' grave moral depravity, inasmuch as Hammerhand had burked the old guv'nor before he'd even got it up, though he allowed as how iffen he'd done the terminal deed *after* the guv'nor 'ad managed—doubtful though that latter event might be in any case, in light o' the guv'nor's advanced years and state of inebriation at the time—that he'd've per'aps owed her recompense—"

"Oh, stop blitherin' on," interrupted Flannery, "the situation's no way comparable at all! The gentleman 'ere's not claimin' Greyboar owes him no money on account o' no financial loss. Indeed, 'e's most graciously conceded right from the start that 'e 'as not the least claim on th'infamous strangler's purse on account o' th'desp'rate villain's recent act o' callous murther 'n' mayhem—"

I shot to my feet.

"*What* murder? *What* mayhem?" I demanded. "We haven't admitted to any part of such crime!"

Bad, bad mistake. I knew it as soon as I shut my mouth.

"D'y'ever hear sech foolishness?" demanded O'Doul.

"The two o' yers choked th'Baron," pronounced

Flannery. "I know it, 'e knows it, th'gentleman knows it, y'knows it yerself, th'dogs in th' alleys knows it, th'babes in th'woods knows it, th'man in th'moon knows it, th'tooth fairy knows it, th'owl an' the pussycat knows it, th'Queen knows it, th'constables knows it, ever'body knows it."

Alas, my mouth had a mind of its own.

"*Can't be proved!*" I cried. The next moment, I flinched with dismay.

The whole crowd around the table was hissing me down.

"*Prove* it?" demanded O'Doul. His face was pale with outrage. "*Prove* it?"

"What's *proof* got t'do with it?" demanded Flannery. "What d'ye think this is, y' mangy cur, some kind o' court o' law?" Flannery tottered to his feet, waving his alepot about. "This is not a court o' law, y'little guttersnipe! This 'ere is th'ancient an' venerable Bar o' Troughly Justice!"

"Verges on outright *lawyering*," muttered O'Doul, glaring at me balefully.

I tried to make myself invisible.

Flannery resumed his seat. By now, another half-dozen ancients had shuffled up and drawn chairs about the table. Within moments all of them were deep into the wrangle. Chapter and verse were hurled about—not from lawbooks, of course, but from the hallowed precedents established by true and proper Trough-men, as codified in the collective memory of the ancients of The Trough. Most of the wrangling, as always, involved the reliability or lack thereof of the respective memories of the various ancients. Mutual derision gave way to an interchange of condemnations which, in turn, soon ceded central stage to a cross-blowing blizzard of personal insults and defamations of character.

In short, it was shaping up as a classic Ruling.

It was going to be a long evening. But, at that point, I was just as glad. By the time the ancients reached a Ruling, they'd hopefully have forgotten my lapses from custom.

Then, to my surprise, Greyboar settled the question. "I'll do it," he announced.

Silence fell upon the table, and over the crowd surrounding us. Disapproving silence. *Very* disapproving silence.

"The ancients haven't rendered decision yet!" I protested.

"We most certainly 'aven't!" exclaimed these latter worthies, in one voice.

"I don't care," replied Greyboar. "I've decided I agree with Benvenuti and I'll do as he asks."

He rummaged in his pocket. "Of course, I mean no disrespect to the ancients, and I'll naturally make recompense for lost ale." He drew forth a fistful of coins, which, given the size of his fist, made a small treasure. I squawked, but the ancients were mollified. Moments later, the venerables were tottering back to the Old Bar, hollering for ale pots. Only the original three of us were left at the table.

Greyboar cleared his throat. "I do have one condition, Benvenuti."

"Name it."

"Well, it's—it's a bit personal. There's a lady, you see—"

I rolled my eyes. Greyboar stammered into silence.

"You'd like her portrait painted," stated the artist. Greyboar nodded. Shyly, if it can be believed.

"I should be delighted," exclaimed Benvenuti. I started to squawk again, but he silenced me with a gesture. "Fear not, doughty agent! I shall be glad to perform this service entirely free of charge."

Hearing that, I relaxed and took another draught of ale. Then, for the first time since we made his acquaintance, I grinned. He was still too damned handsome, but—you've got to make allowances for a man's faults, when he has that kind of *wicked* sense of humor. Not to mention that fine appreciation of vengeance.

Benvenuti drained his mug and coughed apologetically. "I'm afraid," he said, "haste is now necessary. The portrait must be turned over to the estate tomorrow."

Leuwen provided us with an alcove on the second floor of The Trough. The Colon Coign, it's called, so named following that famous episode in Trough lore and legend when, in the course of a friendly argument, Ethelbert the Murtherous accused Handsome Jack of being full of shit and Handsome Jack challenged him to prove it and Ethelbert the Murtherous did.

The lighting was terrible, of course, dark as a cellar. But it didn't seem to bother the artist in the least. And I'll say this—Benvenuti was an expert at his trade. It didn't take him but a couple of hours to finish the painting, which was quick work given that he had to redo the Baron's face as well as add the new material. Greyboar was so fascinated that he stayed to the very end, even after his own part as a model was finished. I stayed, too, as it happened.

Really, a *wicked* sense of humor.

When Benvenuti was finished, Greyboar and I examined the portrait intently.

"You're good," announced Greyboar.

By now, my initial hatred for the man had ebbed considerably, and I was positively awash with simple ill feeling. If there's one thing I admire in a man, it's a proper sense of retribution.

"Good?" I demanded. "He's bloody *great*! The portrait's perfect! Perfect, I tell you. I know—I was— uh, I have it on good authority."

Benvenuti began packing away his supplies. "Sirrah Greyboar, I thank you for your gracious assistance. I shall need tomorrow morning to render up the portrait to the estate. Beginning in the afternoon, however—or anytime thereafter at your convenience—I shall be available to do a portrait of your lady. I can do it here, if you wish. But, if I might make the suggestion, it would go better at my studio. The lighting is much superior."

Greyboar coughed and looked away. I grinned.

"Bit of a problem, that," I chuckled maliciously. "Fact of the matter is, Greyboar hasn't the faintest idea where the lady is, where she's gone to, nor when—if ever—she'll be back."

Benvenuti raised his hands. "You needn't say more, Ignace. Indeed, please don't. The lady's whereabouts are none of my business."

"They're none of Greyboar's business either," I cackled. "The fact of the matter is, she's not really his lady. Fact is she's—"

Greyboar stared at the wall stonily.

"—pure and simple crazy."

Again, the Ozarine artist was delicacy itself. "As I said, the matter's none of my affair. But I repeat, Sirrah Greyboar: I shall be delighted to paint the lady's portrait, whenever and wherever the occasion should come to pass."

"Don't hold your breath," I giggled.

Greyboar tried to lay The Stare on me. But I'm immune to it.

"Oh, come on, big guy!" I grinned from ear to ear. "You've just got to learn to be *philosophical* about these things."

In time to come, the portrait became famous. The Baron's estate had conniptions when they saw it, but the fact is that Benvenuti had stayed within the letter of the law. Eventually, the Baron's portrait was sold by the estate to some other mucky-muck—the Duke de Croûte, I think it was; one of the Baron's longtime enemies—who promptly put it up for public display at a grand soiree. Greyboar and I were tempted to go, but, under the circumstances, we decided that would be a bit imprudent. But I did get a chance to see it, eventually, after it was acquired by the New Sfinctr Museum. It's one of their most popular exhibits, in fact.

When I finally saw the portrait again, I was flattered to see that Benvenuti had even given it the title I'd suggested.

The Great Hunter. Sans Beaters. Sans Bearers. Sans Guides. Sans Tout But the Beast.

Beautiful portrait. Perfect likeness of the Baron in his last moments. Perfect, I tell you. The bulging eyeballs, the blowfish cheeks, the purple veins popping out on the forehead—most of all, the hopeless sense of doom gleaming from his eyes. Greyboar was in the portrait, too, of course. At least, his thumbs were.

Chapter 5.
A Delicate Affair

We didn't see Benvenuti again for a time. Winter was upon us, and that was always a busy season for the trade. Noblemen and financiers and men-about-town came down with cabin fever, got cranky, decided what's-his-name was the cause of all their misery, sent for Greyboar.

Then, alas, came spring. I hated spring. Everybody's mood turned gay, flowers, birds chirping, all that crap. Business went into the toilet except for the run on brides by jealous rivals, and that didn't do us any good on account of Greyboar wouldn't choke girls. Fortunately, we did pick up the occasional groom. (Hired by rivals, sometimes; but usually it was the in-laws who came knocking on our door.) Otherwise we'd have starved.

So, anyway, come late April Greyboar suddenly decided to visit Benvenuti in his studio. The Cat happened to be around that day, and she agreed readily enough to the proposal. And when Jenny and Angela heard about it, they were practically bouncing off the walls in their eagerness to come along.

I wasn't too happy about *that*, remembering how good-looking the damned artist was. But after I stalled for a few minutes, Greyboar—the treacherous dog—started making snide remarks about jealous shrimps. Then Jenny and Angela started making sarcastic predictions about midgets suddenly put on a regimen of total abstinence and I withdrew my objections. I did, however, insist on coming along.

"What's this, Ignace?" asked Greyboar slyly. "Have you developed a sudden interest in art?"

I maintained a dignified silence. Jenny and Angela did not, but I see no reason to repeat their childish remarks.

Benvenuti's studio was located in a part of town which Greyboar and I hadn't visited in quite a while. But we had no trouble finding the place. The driver of the carriage which Greyboar hired was familiar with the studio. Partly, he explained, that was because Benvenuti had become rather famous since he arrived in New Sfinctr a year or so earlier. An artistic rocket blazing into the heavens, to hear the cabbie tell it. And partly, he explained, it was because Benvenuti had become rather notorious since his arrival. A matter of several duels, it seemed, fought with jealous husbands and suitors. And finally, he explained, it was because Benvenuti was located in a most peculiar place for an artist's studio.

When the carriage dropped us off in front of the studio, his remarks became clear. Benvenuti's studio was located on the second floor of a grim-looking gray building. The first floor was occupied by a *salle d'armes*.

Hrundig's *salle d'armes*, in point of fact.

Awkward.

"I thought you said you didn't know the place," grumbled Greyboar.

"He moved," I snapped. "This isn't the joint I cased out. That was over—"

Greyboar waved his hand. "Never mind, never mind."

We stood there for a moment, staring at the door.

"He kept the same sign, though," I muttered.

Oh, there was no doubt about it. Not the sort of sign you forget, especially when its owner is someone you've been approached to give the big squeeze.

> Learn the brutal martial arts of Alsask!
> The Thrusts! The Chops! The Strokes!
> Study Impromptu Amputation!
> Develop Disemboweling Skills!
> Master of arms: Hrundig, Barbarian of Alsask,
> Veteran of the Ozarean Legions.

Greyboar shrugged. "What the hell?" He started lumbering toward the door. "We turned down the job, didn't we?"

I began to follow, with the Cat and Jenny and Angela in tow, when the door suddenly opened. Hrundig himself appeared in the doorway. He was wearing half-armor and carrying a sword. In his hand.

"Are you here on business?" he asked. Very mild, his voice was.

We stared at him for a moment. Hrundig's a rather remarkable-looking man. Rumor has it that he's human, but you have to wonder a bit. There are those odd discrepancies.

First off, his skin. Alsasks are pale, to be sure, but Hrundig's flesh was as white as an albino's. Yet his skin had none of that translucent, pinkish appearance which a true albino's does. No, *his* flesh looked like the wall of a glacier.

And that's not a bad image, actually, to convey the essence of the man. A walking, talking—glacier.

It wasn't his size, so much. True, Hrundig was a little bigger than the average man—the average Alsask, for that matter, who tend to run on the large size—but he was no giant like Greyboar. No, it wasn't his size. It wasn't even his musculature, impressive as it was. It was the sense he exuded of a man whose body was as hard as a glacier and whose soul was just as cold. And both of which—body and soul together—were inexorable.

Oh, yeah, and his eyes. Ice blue.

Greyboar shrugged. "We're simply here on a personal call, Hrundig. We're not looking for you, as it happens. We're looking for Benvenuti Sfondrati-Piccolomini."

No expression registered on Hrundig's face beyond a slight sense of calculation.

"I'm being quite honest," added Greyboar. "The truth is, we had no idea you even lived here."

Hrundig's smile was, as they say, chilly. "I'm trying to remember," he mused, "if lying directly to the chokee—protestations of innocent intentions, to be precise—is allowed under the Professional Stranglers' Official Code of Ethics. As a means of gaining access to the chokee's gullet."

Greyboar looked slightly embarrassed. "Well, actually, as a matter of fact, it is. Hallowed by tradition, actually. To be precise."

"That's what my memory was just telling me."

Greyboar shrugged again. "Why would I do it, Hrundig? We turned down that little job offer, you know."

The smile was now, as they say, wintry. "Not exactly.

As I heard the tale, you turned down the *price* offered for the job."

Greyboar grinned. "Turned it down flat. Can you believe that idiot Sk—well, no names; matter of professional ethics—offered us the usual rate?"

For just a fleeting instant, a faint look of curiosity came and went in Hrundig's deep-set eyes. "What was your counteroffer?"

Greyboar looked at me. I sighed.

"I offered triple rate. And no bargaining."

The memory was still a bit hot. "And would you *believe* that jackass Sk—" I choked down the words. "Well, no names. Matter of professional ethics, you understand."

Hrundig's smile widened, slightly. "It was Skerritt," he stated. "Irked, he was, that I was taking so much business from his own *salle d'armes.*"

Widened further. "Pity, what a sad end he came to. I hear they found him in an alley, a bit later, rather badly hacked up."

(Actually, they found Skerritt in several alleys. His limbs, that is. His guts they found hanging from a lamppost. And his—well, let's just say that Skerritt's demise gave vivid proof that the expression "head up his ass" was no mere metaphor.)

I'm not sure to this day whether Hrundig would have allowed us to come any nearer, if it hadn't been for Jenny and Angela. The two girls had held back a bit, almost hiding behind me. (So to speak. There's not actually that much of me to hide behind. Especially for Jenny, who outtops me by several inches.)

But if there was one characteristic both of those girls had in spades, it was curiosity, and so they couldn't help sticking their heads over my shoulders to get a peek.

"And who are you two?" asked Hrundig.

Jenny and Angela's heads ducked down. Then, a moment later, reappeared. Curiosity, like I said.

"I'm Jenny. And she's Angela."

Hrundig's cold blue eyes fixed on Angela.

"So you're the one," he stated. "Beautiful girl. I can see why the Baron was so distraught by your departure."

Angela scowled. "Damn the Baron!" she snapped.

For the first time, Hrundig's smile had an actual trace of warmth in it. "Oh, my, I've no doubt of that, lass. Imagine he's feeling quite toasty at the moment."

Then, suddenly—I swear I'm not lying—Hrundig's eyes actually *twinkled*. "You cost me one of my best customers, you know."

Angela pressed her lips together, but she stood her ground. She actually *glared* at Hrundig.

The Alsask chuckled. "Oh, I'm not peeved about it, girl. There's plenty more where he came from. Customers I'm not lacking, they stand in line. I don't like the most of them, but the Baron was a particular disfavorite of mine."

For a moment, Hrundig held his gaze on her, then transferred it back to Greyboar. Again, that faint look of calculation came to his face.

"I'm trying to remember," he mused, "if your famous prohibition on burking girls extends to throttling men in front of girls."

Greyboar shrugged. "Well, no, in point of fact. Although—"

The strangler stopped, exasperated. "There's no point to this, Hrundig," he rumbled. "If you don't want to let us get near you, fine. Just tell Benvenuti we were here and I'll make arrangements to meet him elsewhere."

Suddenly, Hrundig scabbarded his sword.

"Oh, I don't think that'll be necessary." He eyed

Jenny and Angela again. "Somehow, I don't think you'd do a job in front of *those* girls."

The blue eyes seemed to bore into Greyboar's soul. "Your reputation's rather interesting, actually, to a man like me. Contradictory, you might say. I like that in a man."

He stood to one side of the door, and politely waved us inside.

Greyboar strode through the door. I followed. With dignity, I dare say, although I thought my hair would stand on end when I passed by Hrundig. I'd seen what was left of Skerritt, as it happens, and I wasn't a bit happy knowing that sword was behind me, and but two feet away. Scabbarded, sure. So what? How long does it take a tiger to bare its teeth?

Within, we found ourselves in a very large room. The actual *salle*, as it were, of the *salle d'armes*—and now I knew why they called it that. The floor was a beautifully finished parquet, perfect for footwork. And the walls—it was grotesque! The walls were literally covered with every conceivable hand weapon known to man. I didn't even recognize most of them, and I haven't exactly led what you'd call a sheltered life.

The girls gaped. The Cat, who until that moment had seemed to be off on another planet, immediately headed over to one wall and stood there, fixedly studying something that looked like a homicidal maniac's nightmare version of a double-ended straight-bladed scythe.

"What's this called?" she asked.

"That's a *lajatang*," replied Hrundig. "It's from one of the southern provinces of the Sundjhab."

The armsmaster came over and stood by her side, examining the monstrosity with a look of warm regard. "Beautiful, isn't it? It's quite a rare weapon, you know.

Even in the Sundjhab, not many people are proficient in its use. It's a difficult weapon to master."

"How much?" demanded the Cat.

Hrundig's eyes turned ice cold. "It's not for sale. None of my weapons are."

The Cat snorted contemptuously. "Of course not! You damned idiot, how much is it to train me to use it?"

Hrundig actually started. Slightly.

"*Train* you? In the *lajatang*?"

The Cat turned her gaze full on him. Magnified through those incredible spectacles, her own blue eyes seemed even icier than Hrundig's.

"Are you hard of hearing?" she demanded. "Or just stupid?"

Blue glare met blue glare. Glaciers collided.

Greyboar looked worried. I looked for the door. Too far. But there was a big shield on the wall nearby. I thought maybe the girls and I could hide behind it.

Suddenly, Hrundig laughed. A real, genuine laugh, too. Full of mirth and good humor.

"No, lady," he said—still laughing—"I'm neither deaf nor stupid. Just caught by surprise."

He shook his head, eyeing the Cat admiringly. "A hundred quid," he announced.

The Cat immediately transferred her gaze to Greyboar. The strangler coughed, glanced at me—I could see it coming!—and caved in.

"Sure, sweetheart. I can swing it." To Hrundig, in a feeble attempt to recapture a smidgen of manly frugality: "That's a hundred a week, I imagine. But for how many sessions?"

Hrundig shook his head. "You misunderstand. One hundred's the total price."

Greyboar's jaw dropped, just a bit. Mine probably hit the floor. Hrundig wasn't precisely what you'd call upper crust—to put it mildly—but he was still the most exclusive armsmaster in New Sfinctr. He charged noblemen a hundred quid just to show them how to draw a dagger out of its sheath.

The Cat nodded. Not graciously, not thankfully— just, Cat-like. Hard to explain. As if the way things turned out were the way they naturally would, since nothing makes any sense to begin with.

I didn't even bother squalling. No point in it. I just dug into my purse and handed over the money. Although I did manage a marvelous scowl.

Greyboar had enough sense to avoid my glaring eye. He ambled toward a far door and disappeared into the stairwell beyond. A moment later, I followed, eager to depart the scene of the crime. (*A hundred quid!* So's a crazy woman could learn to handle a crazy weapon!)

On the floor above, in a large studio, I found Greyboar staring at something over the shoulder of a man seated on a stool, working on a canvas. As I approached, I recognized the fellow as Benvenuti. He seemed to be totally preoccupied with a portrait of some kind. Hearing my footsteps, he turned his head. Then, seeing the huge figure of Greyboar looming over him, he made a little gasp of startlement. It was obvious that he'd had no idea of the strangler's presence.

I couldn't help grinning. Huge as he is, and as much as his walk looks like a lumber, Greyboar can move with absolute silence.

"Soft-footed, isn't he?" I chuckled. "You wouldn't think such a huge lump could move like a cat, but he does. Quite an asset in our line of work, actually."

"I can imagine," said Benvenuti, frowning in bemusement. He gave Greyboar a very keen scrutiny, then. A *keen* scrutiny. You always hear about the "artist's eye," but for the first time in my life I got a real sense of the thing. And there was something different about the way Benvenuti was studying Greyboar now, compared to the way he had done so at The Trough. This time, I sensed, he was focusing not on the man, but the strangler.

Greyboar himself was oblivious. He was completely preoccupied with studying the portrait.

"Since when did you become an art connoyser?" I demanded.

The chokester shook his head. "You should see this, Ignace," he said. His tone combined admiration with—something else, I couldn't tell what. "I swear, it's the spitting image."

I moved closer. Recoiled. "Saints preserve us," I muttered.

Benvenuti tore his eyes from Greyboar and glanced at the portrait he was working on. A raffish grin came to his face.

"I should certainly hope so!" he exclaimed. "The portrait alone should do the trick. After all, he *is* a holy man."

Greyboar mumbled something. I didn't catch all of it, but the words "slimespawn" and "scumbag" came through clearly enough.

Benvenuti must have caught more of it, because he started shaking his head with mock chagrin. "Such language! To refer to a Cardinal."

"Luigi Carnale, Cardinal Fornacaese," growled Greyboar. "If ever pure corruption took human form, it's him."

Benvenuti gave the portrait a clinical study. "Dare say you're right," he mused. "I do know it's taken all of my skill—to keep the image accurate, on the one hand, while not portraying the foulness which oozes from the man's every pore."

"You've met him, then?" grunted Greyboar.

"Oh, yes. Spent several hours in his company, while he sat. Fortunately, I was able to keep him quiet. Told him I needed absolute stillness to catch his image properly."

A small commotion caused us to turn. Jenny and Angela had come into the room, with the Cat drifting in their wake. The girls were eagerly examining the various portraits hanging on the walls, oohing and ahing with admiration.

I got a bit tense, then, I'll admit. Bad enough the guy was so good-looking! Now the girls were goggling over his talent, too.

Artists. Ought to hang the whole lot. It's unfair competition for the working stiff.

I was relieved to see that Benvenuti gave them no more than a passing glance. A *keen* glance, mind—I didn't care for that at all—but a quick one. His attention was almost immediately riveted on the Cat.

With another man, I would have assumed a certain kind of interest. The woman's nuts, but she really does have a great figure. But with Benvenuti—

No. It was that "artist's eye" again.

I couldn't help laughing. "Yeah, that's her, Benny. Your model. Good luck! You're going to need it."

The artist was now studying her with ferocious intensity. "How does she move?" he muttered. His hands made vague wandering gestures. "So hard to follow. Seems she's going one way but she's not, and then—never gets there when you think she's going to."

Then: "Fascinating!"

He continued staring at her for some time. The Cat, of course, took no notice at all of the attention she was drawing. She was just—drifting—through the room, looking at everything and nothing in particular.

Again, I laughed. My laugh jerked Benvenuti out of his trance. The artist looked at Greyboar. The expression on the chokester's face was a combination of pride and bemusement.

"Yeah, she's the lady I told you about. Can you do her portrait? Her name's Schrödinger's Cat, by the way."

I held my breath. Then, when Benvenuti said nothing, exhaled with disgust.

I hate losing money. Really, really, really hate losing money. But I was already digging into my pocket before Greyboar spoke the inevitable words.

"You owe me a quid." His ugly oversize mitt was already extended. Sourly, I dropped the coin into it. Poor little coin looked like a lost sheep in that vast expanse.

"We had a bet," explained Greyboar. "Ignace was sure you'd ask who Schrödinger is, like everybody else does. But I knew you were too refined and gentlemanly, unlike the slobs Ignace hangs out with in The Trough."

"Of course he is!" exclaimed Jenny. "He's an artist—a real one!" She pointed to one of the portraits hanging on the wall. "Just look at this! It's beautiful."

She turned and bestowed a gleaming smile upon him. "I'm Jenny, by the way. And this is Angela. Ignace should have introduced us, but he's *not* refined and gentlemanly."

Jenny now turned toward the Cat, who was standing at the far wall, examining one of Benvenuti's paintings. "Hey, Cat!" she hollered. "Come over here and meet the fellow who's going to paint your portrait."

The Cat swiveled her head and fixed her gaze on Benvenuti. Through the thick lenses, her eyes seemed huge. And very blue. Ice blue.

"Not like this, I hope," she stated forcefully, jabbing her finger at the portrait before which she was standing.

Benvenuti laughed. "I should think not! The portraits you see hanging on the walls are the results of commissions which went unpaid. The Sfinctrian nobility, I am afraid, has a lackadaisical attitude toward paying their debts. I simply keep them here as advertisement."

For a moment, he fell back into his "artist's trance" way of staring at her, before turning to Greyboar and saying:

"It's your decision, of course. You're the customer. But I do not actually think that a formal portrait would do justice to—uh, Cat."

"*The* Cat," Greyboar corrected. He rubbed his chin. "Well—you're the professional." He glanced at the Cat, who was off again, wandering about. "I'll admit it would be difficult to get her to sit still for a formal pose."

Benvenuti shook his head. "And it wouldn't—how shall I say it? It wouldn't be her. It would be—" He waved at the various portraits on the walls.

Greyboar looked at them. "Yeah, I see what you mean. They all look like they're constipated or something." He shrugged. "All right. Do whatever you think's best."

For about the next hour or so, Benvenuti drew a whole series of charcoal sketches. Within minutes, he was oblivious to anything else. Greyboar stayed and watched for quite some time, but the rest of us started wandering around. (By "the rest of us" I mean me, Jenny and Angela. "Wandering around" doesn't really apply to the Cat. She wanders around when she's standing still, if you know what I mean.)

Jenny found them first. Wandering into a room where she shouldn't have been wandering, with me and Angela not far behind like we shouldn't have been, she suddenly started oohing and ahing again.

"You've got to see *these*!" she squeaked.

Angela scurried into the room. A moment later I heard her oohing and ahing too.

"Oh, they're *wonderful*."

Tiresome. Like I said, they ought to hang all artists just on general principle. Male ones, anyway.

I moseyed into the room, just to bring the presence of masculine sanity and nonchalance. A bedroom, it was. The artist's, apparently. But I didn't have much time to examine the furnishings, for my eyes were immediately drawn to the portraits which lined every single wall in the room.

I froze. Utter shock.

The portraits were all of a single woman. The same woman, over and again, in a variety of poses. Except they weren't really poses. I'm no artist, but even I could tell that these paintings had been done from memory. These weren't your typical studio portraits.

All kinds of portraits, there were. The most of them, mind you, were eminently proper. A woman—*the* woman—fully clothed, riding a horse. The same woman, sitting on a chair staring out a window. Same woman, singing.

But, then—there were the others.

The same woman—*the* woman—lying on a bed.

You know.

Artists call them "nudes." Us lowlifes call them nekkid wimmen.

There were a *lot* of those paintings. The same woman, in a variety of different poses and attitudes. None of them were actually what you'd call pornographic, mind you. Even in my state of shock, I could tell that these were the kind of paintings that aesthetes go berserk over but don't do all that much for your normal regular-guy-type lecher.

Still. I mean—*naked*.

Her.

That woman.

I finally found my voice.

"Get out of here!" I hissed to Jenny and Angela. "If

we close the door and act like nothing happened, maybe we can still keep—"

Jenny and Angela were glaring at me.

"And just what's your problem *now*, Ignace?" demanded Jenny.

"Yeah!" chimed in Angela, planting her hands on hips. "Still protecting your little cherubs? Boy, do you—"

I tried to shut them up with frantic hand motions. Too late. Greyboar was already standing in the doorway.

I sighed. "And here it is," I muttered. "Murther and massacree. So much for pleasant social outings."

Greyboar was motionless—all except his head, which was slowly scanning the room. His eyes—I swear it— were starting to bulge out of their sockets. And that's some feat, believe me, when you've got a brow like his.

"Aren't they wonderful, Greyboar?" piped up Jenny.

Greyboar made no reply, beyond a faint noise which sounded like a man strangling to death. I was seized by a sudden urge to giggle. I suppressed the urge manfully. (Well, more like a despot suppresses insurrection.)

The chokester scanned the portraits, wall to wall. His head swiveled back, scanning. When he was done, he turned and walked out of the room. There was a kind of slow but inexorable pace to his movement. Think of a glacier advancing on a rabbit hutch.

"What's wrong with him?" demanded Angela crossly.

I rolled my eyes. Pointed to the portraits.

"That's his *sister*," I hissed. "*Gwendolyn*."

Their eyes grew round. They stared at the portraits. Me, I just sighed and left the room.

In the studio, I found Greyboar standing in the center of the room. He was staring at the artist, who was still seated and working on his sketches.

I started to head toward the chokester. Not quite

sure why, really. I mean, it's not as if a guy my size is really going to restrain the world's greatest strangler when he's hell-bent on—

What would you call that, anyway? Throttling your sister's squeeze? Sororicopulicide?

But, to my surprise, Greyboar turned away. And then, to my utter astonishment, went and got a chair against the far wall, hauled it out, and planted himself upon it. And there he sat, his face like a stone, watching the artist finishing his sketches.

Out of the corner of my eye, I saw Hrundig enter the room. His eyes quickly flitted about, taking in the whole scene. Greyboar, seated, staring at Benvenuti. The door to Benvenuti's private room, open. Jenny and Angela, now standing in that door, staring pale-faced at Greyboar. Me, standing in the middle of room, looking like—whatever I looked like.

Yeah, Hrundig looks like your classic barbarian low-brow, but there's really nothing at all wrong with his brains. It didn't take him but the instant to size up the situation. His expression grew grimmer—some trick, that—and his hand moved to his sword.

For a moment, everything was frozen. Then, suddenly, Benvenuti sat up straight, blew out his cheeks, and exclaimed: "Finished!"

He held up the sketches and turned his head. For the first time, he became aware of his surroundings. His eyes flicked about, absorbing the odd poses and expressions on the people in the room. He cocked an eyebrow.

"Is something amiss?" he asked. He glanced down at the sketch pad. "You don't care for them? I think they're quite excellent—and I'm usually my own harshest critic."

"It's not that," I muttered. "It's those other—"

"You should perhaps have kept the door to your private room closed," said Hrundig.

Angela and Jenny started scurrying forward.

"We shouldn't have gone into that room in the first place!" squeaked Jenny.

"That's right!" chimed in Angela. "The gentleman has as much right to privacy as anybody!"

Greyboar spoke then, his voice sounding even more like an avalanche than usual. "There's an interesting set of portraits in the other room," he rumbled.

Benvenuti's face grew absolutely still. Not scared-shitless-still, though. Just—still. As stony as Greyboar's own.

I was impressed. *Really* impressed. Most people, when Greyboar gives them The Stare—men, for sure—turn pale, sweaty, sickly looking, etc., etc., etc., including, usually, serious bowel-control problems.

Not this guy. Artist he may have been, and an Ozarine to boot, but he had steel balls.

I made a last, desperate attempt to head off slaughter and mayhem. "Hey, big guy," I said, placing a restraining hand—so to speak—on Greyboar's shoulder, "I'm sure his intentions were quite honorable. It doesn't mean anything, you know. Women are always posing stark nak—uh, *nude*—for artists. It's not the same thing as—you know. Different rules."

"That's right!" squeaked Angela. Jenny nodded her head about a million times.

Benvenuti rose, dropped his sketch pad on the chair, and walked over to the door to his private room. He started to close it, when a thought apparently came to him.

"Cat," he said. The Cat turned away from a portrait and gave him that bottle-glass stare. Benvenuti's face was expressionless, still, and then he said—in a voice with nary a quaver (boy, was I impressed):

"I believe you are the only person here who has not yet examined the paintings in my private chambers. You might want to take a look at them. They're far better than the ones out here." He made a slight gesture with his hand, politely inviting her in.

The Cat drifted past him into the room. Benvenuti turned back to Greyboar.

"The woman in those paintings," he said harshly, "was not a model. Nor did she ever pose for me. She was my lover, once, and I did those paintings from memory."

I sighed, and covered my face with a hand. "Oh, boy," I muttered. "It's like the wise man says: 'why waste a good excuse on a dummy?' "

Through my fingers, I saw Hrundig stiffen. His hand was now gripping the sword tightly.

Angela—bless the girl—made her own desperate attempt.

"It must be someone else!" she piped. "Just a passing resemblance."

"It's Gwendolyn," rumbled Greyboar. "There isn't another woman in the world who looks like that. Besides, the paintings are perfect. Every detail. Even got—you remember, Ignace, that time you bit her when you were kids?—even got that little ragged scar on her left knee."

Suddenly, Jenny charged forward and planted herself before the strangler.

"You behave yourself, Greyboar!" she admonished. "We're having a pleasant afternoon and I won't stand for anything spoiling it!"

"That's right!" cried Angela. A moment later, she was standing next to Jenny, wagging her finger in Greyboar's face. "We won't stand for any of your roughneck ways!"

Benvenuti started laughing. Everyone stared at him.

"What's so funny?" demanded the girls.

"You are," he replied cheerfully. "You look like two mice lecturing a bear on table manners." He shook his head. The gesture expressed admiration combined with wonder.

Greyboar's face suddenly took on an actual expression. The Stare vanished, replaced by a peeved frown.

"I'd like to know why," he grumbled, "everybody seems convinced that I'm about to turn this place into a slaughterhouse."

"There's a bit of a body count in your past," said Hrundig.

"That's business," replied the strangler. A glance at Hrundig's hand, followed by an irritated shrug. "Oh, stop clutching that stupid sword, Hrundig. There's no need for it, and it probably wouldn't do you much good if there were."

"I imagine not," replied Hrundig. "Still—Benvenuti is my friend."

Greyboar looked up at Angela and Jenny—or, I should say, looked straight at them, for even seated his eyes were on a level with theirs. Suddenly, he grinned.

"Benvenuti's right. You do look like two mice lecturing on protocol."

The girls flushed. Greyboar took a deep breath and gazed up at the ceiling. "It was quite obvious that Gwendolyn never posed for those paintings, Ignace, so you could have saved us *that* ridiculous suggestion."

"Worth a try," I muttered.

Still staring at the ceiling, Greyboar sighed. "Ignace, not everyone in this world is as hot-tempered, choleric and pugnacious as you. Nor, Jenny and Angela, am I quite the homicidal maniac you seem to think I am. But, even if I were, I still wouldn't have done anything about those paintings."

His gaze dropped; he glanced toward Benvenuti's private room. "Only one person in the world scares me," he muttered, "and that's my sister. I imagine she'd take it badly, if I was to go out and do something like choke her former boyfriend on the grounds that he had sullied the family name." He grimaced. *"Real* badly."

He looked at Benvenuti, now, and for what seemed like endless seconds they stared at each other. I understood that stare. Two men, both of whom in their own way loved a woman, simply acknowledging that fact. I found myself swallowing. There were times—now and then—

When I found myself missing Gwendolyn. A lot.

The Cat came back into the room. She wasn't doing her usual drifting, though. She headed straight for Benvenuti. For an instant there, I could almost follow her progress.

"Is that it?" she demanded, pointing at the tablet on the chair.

Benvenuti nodded. The Cat picked up the sketches and studied them. Then she studied the artist.

"You're good," she pronounced. She looked back at the sketches. "Is that really what I look like?" Then, without waiting for an answer: "It's exactly what I feel like."

She transferred her stare to Greyboar. "You should see the portraits he has in the other room. They're wonderful. They really are. Not at all like the crap on the walls out here. The funny thing is, the woman in the paintings looks kind of like you, except she doesn't look like a gorilla."

"My sister, Gwendolyn," rumbled the strangler. Abruptly, he rose.

"Well, I believe our business here is done," he announced. "The Cat's happy, which is what matters."

Then—I almost laughed, here—Greyboar actually nodded very politely to the artist. Almost like one of your real upper-crust salon-type bows, that was.

"I thank you, Benvenuti." Greyboar hesitated, adding:

"Someday, if you'd like, come visit me at The Trough. I—would like to hear about Gwendolyn."

"I will do so, then," replied the artist.

Greyboar turned and left, after ushering the Cat through the door. I started shooing Jenny and Angela after them, eager to make an escape.

"One moment, please," came Benvenuti's voice. We stopped and turned around.

The artist was smiling at Jenny and Angela. "The moment I saw the two of you," he said, "I wanted to do your portrait. Now, after witnessing your gallantry in my defense, I must insist. At no cost to yourselves, of course."

Jenny beamed. "Oh, that'd be great!" exclaimed Angela.

Well! *I* didn't think it was great!

"I don't know about this," I growled, in my best man-of-the-world tone. "Two innocent young girls—an artist—who knows what might—"

"Oh, shut up!" snapped Jenny.

"Yeah, what's your problem?" added Angela.

I bore up stoically under their childish complaints. "Well, you know, he'd probably want you to pose, you know, with your clothes off."

"And so what if he does?" demanded Angela.

"*You* always like us to pose with our clothes off," added Jenny.

I tried to think of a riposte. Alas, I failed. The only thought in my mind was: *Ought to hang all artists. On general principle.*

Fortunately, I had enough sense not to say it.

Benvenuti grinned, enjoying, I darkly suspected, my predicament.

"Actually," he said, "I wasn't thinking of a nude portrait. In fact, I wasn't thinking of any sort of formal poses. I would just like to try and capture your spirit, if I could. The two of you are like liquid sunshine."

"Oh, how sweet!" exclaimed Jenny, blushing. With her peaches-and-cream complexion, a blush made her look especially angelic. Angela smiled, like a sultry cherub. Then, to me, in a loud whisper: "*You* never say things like that to us."

I tried to think of a riposte. Failed.

"Let's be off!" I said, and started hustling the girls out the door. Over my shoulder, I glared at Benvenuti.

He shrugged. "I assure you, sirrah, my intentions are quite honorable."

I was not mollified. "Intentions be damned," I muttered. "Anybody who'd seduce Gwendolyn is out of his mind in the first place, so who knows what he'd do?"

On our way back, Jenny and Angela chattered cheerfully. The Cat stared at her sketches. Greyboar was silent. Lost in thoughts of Gwendolyn, I imagine, but I didn't ask.

I was too busy thinking my own silent thoughts.

Dark thoughts. Dark.

Despite what you might think, only some of my gloom was brought on by the prospect—inevitable, I could tell, from their chatter—that my two girls would soon be cavorting about in the studio of a damned artist who was not only the handsomest man I'd ever seen but had all the other accouterments, to boot.

But, mostly, my gloom was brought on by more general considerations. Almost philosophical, you might say, much as I hate the term.

I could feel the net of Fate closing in. Destiny's doom. The Kismet Kiss of Death.

Or, to put it in my crude layman's terms:

Shit kept happening, no matter what I tried to do.

One damn thing after another. Philosophy! Leads to mad and reckless impulses. Leads to desperate flight. Desperate adventures. Hooking up with crazy women. Dragged back into the life of a crazy revolutionist sister. Mad artists.

Mad mad mad mad mad. All of it.

This is going to end badly. I just know it!

Those sorts of thoughts.

When we finally pulled up in front of Jenny and Angela's house, I tried to restore my usual good humor.

"Tomorrow—back to business!" I exclaimed cheerfully. "Enough of all that other stuff."

Greyboar shook his head. "Won't matter, Ignace. Entropy rules. There's no getting around it. It's just the second law of thermodynamics, that's all. The essence of the universe."

I grit my teeth.

"You'll see," he said stoically.

I ground my teeth.

Greyboar grinned. "You can refuse to recognize philosophy, Ignace, but philosophy recognizes you."

PART TWO: ANTITHESIS

Chapter 6.
Thermodynamic Fortune

You wouldn't think the strangler would be sentimental about a client, but he was.

"He's been our most regular customer for years," complained Greyboar.

"Big deal," I sneered. "The old bastard's a cheapskate. And he drives me nuts! Every time he hires us he insists on haggling for hours. I wind up giving him a discount just to stop listening to his voice. Fine for you to wax philosophical about fond memories—you just do the jobs. *You* aren't the one who has to listen to that quavering whine for hours. *You* aren't the one—"

"All right, all right!" Greyboar glared at me. "I'll do the job—just so's I won't have to listen to *you* whining for hours. But I'm not happy about it."

He held up his hands, forestalling my outburst. "I know, I know," he grumbled, "you're the agent. You're the wizard manager. You're the financial genius. I'm

just the muscle what does all the work and probably
ought to be happy with whatever crumbs you drop
from the table. But I still think it's stupid, at least in
the long run."

"What long run?" I demanded. "He's got to be a
hundred years old by now. How much longer do you
think he's got, anyway? No, no, trust me on this one—
better we take a big lump payment now instead of
hoping for a few pennies later."

He was still glaring at me, so I glared right back
and stuck in the knife. "Or have you got some cute
little philosophical angle on this I don't know about?"

Of course, that made him furious. But I wasn't
worried. Stick it to the strangler on his philosophy, and,
sure he'd get mad as a wet hen—but he wouldn't do
anything about it. Nothing physical, I mean. It was a
matter of pride with Greyboar. He considered it boorish
to refute a philosophical challenge with his thumbs.

So he glared at me for a full five minutes, frowning all the while in that inimitable fashion which would
cause a lifetime of nightmares to any poor child which
saw it. But he couldn't think up a logical riposte, and
he finally gave up trying. He nodded once, indicating
his official approval of the engagement. That was all
I needed. I was out of the room in a flash, down the
stairs, up the street, around this corner and that, and
back in The Trough. I was in a hurry because I wanted
to close the deal. Once we'd taken the money for the
job, Greyboar wouldn't back out even if he did think
up some idiotic philosophical objection. Professional
ethics, don't you know?

Our prospective client was still there, at the same
table in the corner. The silly jackass was all scrunched
up, trying to make himself as inconspicuous as possible.
His eyes were flitting hither and yon, flicking fearfully
over the other occupants of The Trough. Dozens of

lowlifes, there were at that hour, every one of whom—
not to mention all of them taken together—was a
source of fear and loathing for our client. Nothing
unusual about his reaction, of course. He wasn't the
first little rich kid who'd sat in that corner table,
huddled and shivering with terror, while I left him to
finalize the deal with Greyboar.

As soon as I sat down he started whining. "I could
have had my throat cut fifty times over while you've
been gone. You said you were only going to be a few
minutes. You were gone for hours! I was alone at the
mercy of these—"

"Oh, shut up," I snarled. (One of the things I always
liked about the strangling trade—you really didn't have
to fawn over your customers the way a greengrocer
does.) "You were safer here than anywhere in the
world. D'you think for a minute that any of the characters in this room would even think of scaring off one
of Greyboar's clients?"

I sneered. "There isn't a cutthroat anywhere in the
Flankn who'd try to come between Greyboar and a
commission. Certainly not in The Trough! There's
probably more pleasant ways to commit suicide, but
there's sure none quicker."

I let the sneer slide off after a few seconds. It's good
to put the piglets down, but you don't want to overdo
it. As the wise man says: "Pissing on 'em's fine, but
don't drown 'em."

"Besides," I added, "I wasn't gone all that long. Took
me longer than usual, because Greyboar's not happy
with the job. Your great-grandfather's been one of our
steadiest clients for years. The big guy hates to let him
go. In fact—"

Well, I won't bore you with the rest. Naturally, I
used Greyboar's reluctance as my excuse to jack the
fee up even higher. And, naturally, I succeeded. I

wondered, sometimes, what Greyboar would have done without me as his agent. Probably been strangling crocodiles in a circus sideshow for peanuts.

I'll give the little rat this much, he put up a good struggle. No matter how scared they are—of their surroundings and of the very idea of hiring a strangler in the first place—I never saw one of these greedy heirs apparent who'd cough up the fee without squabbling. But it didn't bother me. The kid wasn't a shadow of his great-grandfather when it came to haggling. And Greyboar could say what he wanted—personally, I was looking forward to getting rid of that ancient horse trader. Wouldn't ever have to listen to him again, the venerable Monsoor Etienne Avare.

Yep, the Merchant Prince himself—our newly contracted chokee-to-be. The richest man in New Sfinctr, some said. That wasn't actually true. There were several dukes and archbishops—not to mention the Queen—who had fortunes to make Avare's look like a child's piggy bank. But he was certainly the wealthiest member of the parvenu classes. And, in any event, after a while the whole point becomes moot. Even somebody as greedy and tight fisted as me thought hoards that big were ridiculous. I mean, what's the fun of having so much money that you can't even count it?

Quite a guy, actually, Monsieur Etienne Avare. He'd amassed a fortune as a young entrepreneur, and then kept it growing all through his later years. Even when his years got later and later and later. Over a hundred years old, he was. He'd outlived all his sons and daughters, all his grandsons and granddaughters, and was halfway through the next generation.

Not without some help, of course. Greyboar was right about that—Avare had been a steady customer over the years. Every few months we'd get invited to his mansion, have a nice gentlemanly chat over brandy, and then get a commission to burke whichever one of his descendants had succeeded in convincing Avare they were worthless bums not worthy of inheriting his money. Very high standards he had, the Merchant Prince. Two generations had failed to meet them already.

Greyboar always liked the work. It was not only steady, but it was completely free of petty nuisances. The porkers who examined the deceased would invariably report them as suicides or accidents. One of the benefits, you'll understand, of having a merchant prince as a client. But, of course, he'd never had to deal with Avare's haggling. As soon as the brandy was finished, and the deal agreed to, Greyboar would make his grand exit while I had to stay and do the dirty work. The brandy snifters would disappear in a flash, replaced by a tumbler of salted water. After the first such session, I never made the mistake of drinking from it again. Hard to negotiate when you're dying of thirst, don't you know?

But it was all in the past now! We had a new client, one of Avare's half-dozen surviving great-grandsons. Marcel Avare, his name was. He'd gotten tired of waiting for the old man to croak, and since he was one of the few Avare scions who'd managed to make some money on his own, he'd been able to save up enough to hire Greyboar to bring him his inheritance. Much dumber than the old man, of course—he'd even let slip how much of a nest egg he'd saved up. I cleaned him out of every penny of it. But, then again, his loss would only be momentary. He'd soon enough be the richest merchant in New Sfinctr himself.

The deal made, our client scurried out of The Trough like a rodent fleeing a lion's den. I would have liked to have stayed myself, celebrating. But Greyboar always liked to do a job quick, and I'd need a clear head to figure out a plan of action. The truth was, it was going to be a tricky job. The old miser's mansion was built like a fortress, and he had bodyguards and watchdogs like you wouldn't believe.

So I left and went back to our apartment. Well, it'd be more accurate to say our garret. Three small rooms we had, on the top floor of one of the Flankn's tenement buildings. We could have afforded a nicer place, easily, but I never saw any reason to waste money on inessentials. Greyboar'd make noises now and then about "the dump," but he really didn't care that much himself.

By the time I got back, Greyboar had reconciled himself to reality. Sort of.

"You know how hard it's going to be, just getting to Avare to put the thumbs on him?" he demanded.

"D'you mind if I sit down first, before you start grousing?"

Once seated, I said: "Yeah, I know it's going to be more difficult than our usual jobs. But look at the bright side—I was able to crank our fee way up, moaning and groaning to the little snot about the insuperable challenges ahead."

"How much are we getting, anyway?" he asked sulkily.

I played the trump card. "Five thousand quid."

The sulky look vanished. Greyboar whistled. "Not bad, Ignace, not bad at all."

"Not bad?" I demanded. "It's better than three times our normal fee! It's as much as the old miser would have paid us for five or six jobs. And I didn't have to spend hours listening to the old coot demanding a discount for volume trade."

"All right, already," grumbled Greyboar. "I don't want to hear it again. I'll admit, it's a very good commission. Still and all, I think this job's going to prove a bad move in the end. Entropy, you know? The natural tendency of the universe to run down. You think you can get around it, but—"

"*Will you shut up about your damned entropy?*"

Once again, we were glaring at each other. Greyboar gave it up first.

"All right. I'll shut up about the entropy if you'll stop crowing about the job. I still think—never mind. Let's get down to brass tacks. How are we going to get to Avare?"

Before I could answer, there was a knock on our door. I got up and opened it. Surprised, I was.

"Henry?" I'm afraid my jaw was probably hanging down. The last person I'd expected!

But it was him, no question about it. Henry—old man Avare's manservant and general gofer. We knew him well. He was always the one who came and told us that Avare "desired our company."

Sure enough. Henry nodded politely, and then announced: "Monsieur Avare would desire the company of you gentlemen. Tonight at eight o'clock, if you would."

Greyboar started to say something, but I silenced him with a gesture. "Certainly, Henry. Greyboar and I would be delighted to come. Eight o'clock—we shall be prompt."

As soon as Henry left and I'd closed the door, Greyboar started right in.

"What are you doing, you little squirt? You know we can't take another job from old Avare now!" He glowered fiercely. "There's a matter of professional ethics involved here!"

"Who said anything about doing a job for him?" I demanded. "Was there any mention of a job? Did Henry say anything about a job? Did we agree to do a job? Did any money change hands? Was the crude subject of money even mentioned? No! We were simply invited over to the old miser's mansion for brandy. What better way to get in to see him? Without having to fight our way through an army of guards and watchdogs? We just waltz into the mansion, and then, as soon as Henry's poured the brandy and left the room, like he always does, you do the choke. Then we leave. By the time anybody figures out something's wrong, we'll be long gone."

Greyboar was frowning ferociously. Before he could say anything, I continued:

"Sure, and it'll be obvious we did the choke, but so what? We'll have to hide out for a bit, while the porkers make a show of looking for us. But we won't even have to leave the Flankn. And you know the porkers won't try all that hard to find us. The truth is, Avare's made himself plenty of enemies in this town—especially among the upper crust, half of whom owe him a fortune. There'll be counts and barons and earls and who knows what greasing the porkers' palms to let the whole thing slide."

He sighed. "Yeah, yeah, I know it'll work. But I don't like it. Your scheme bends professional ethics into a pretzel."

"And so what?" I couldn't pass up the opening. "You're a philosopher, aren't you? What else is philosophy good for if not splitting the hair between bending and breaking?"

Here I did my imitation of the wizard Zulkeh:

" 'Tis a truth known to babes in swaddling clothes, the epistemological distinction 'twixt bending and breaking! Did not the great sophist Euthydemus Sfondrati-Piccolomini himself, in his ground-breaking *A Loop Is But A Hole*, argue that—"

Greyboar, the sourpuss, was not amused. But he gave up whining about professional ethics. Still and all, he made the rest of the afternoon miserable, muttering about "unforeseen entropic consequences" and such-like nonsense.

When the time came to leave, I was right glad of it. We hired a carriage. Bit too far to walk, and besides, wouldn't be proper showing up at Avare's mansion without suitably snooty transport. As much money as we were making for the job, I wasn't about to quibble over a few shillings. The more so since it was midwinter. New Sfinctr's winters are fairly mild—it's about the only saving grace the city has, business opportunities aside. But a mild winter's still not summer.

My misery wasn't over, though, because Greyboar started whining all over again after I explained the details of the plan. It was the part about the brandy that upset him.

"And why shouldn't we wait until after we've had the brandy?" I demanded. "Avare's brandy is the best in town, you know that."

"I don't care," grumbled the strangler. "You can twist professional ethics all you want, you miserable little lawyer, but I still think it's going too far to drink a man's brandy when you're planning to put the big choke on him."

"What's the difference? He's a chokee no matter how you look at it. And enough about professional ethics! He won't start talking business until after the brandy, you know it as well as I do. So we finish the brandy—the best in the world, that brandy is—and then, when he starts in about a job, we just politely decline. If you want to be an absolute stickler about it, you can explain to him that we have a prior engagement which prevents us from accepting his commission—professional ethics, don't you know? Then you give him the squeeze."

He hemmed and hawed, but he came around

eventually. I knew he would. He loved good brandy, Greyboar did, but he was too cheap to buy any for himself. Well, actually, it'd probably be more accurate to say that I was too cheap to let him.

At eight o'clock sharp, we presented ourselves at the front gate of the mansion. Henry himself came out to let us in. He ushered us through the grounds—waving off the dogs and their keepers—and into the mansion itself. He took off our overcoats and hung them in the vestibule. Then he led us up the main staircase onto the second floor, and from there it was but a short distance to the study.

I don't know what it is about rich people that they always have to have a "study." Not the scholarly types, as a rule, your robber barons. I'll give Avare this much, his study actually had a lot of books in it. Nary a stuffed animal in the room. And the books all looked well read, too.

Of course, his library was highly specialized. One whole wall was taken up by much-thumbed copies of *The Encyclopedia of Exploitation*—all 788 volumes, he had the entire set. Another wall was taken up by leather-bound first editions. Top-flight stuff. All the great classics on the subject ever written by either one of the world's great scholarly clans: Rockefeller Laebmauntsforscynneweëld's trilogy: *Plundering the Poor*, *Pillaging the Plebes* and *Peeling the Paupers*. J. P. Sfondrati-Piccolomini's *Beg and Be Damned*. On and on.

Secular writings, mostly, but he had a fair number of the Ecclesiarchy's "Tomes for Troubled Times," too—for instance, Paolo Pipa, Cardinal Bufo's *The Sin of Wages*.

His proudest literary possession was encased in glass and mounted on the wall above the fireplace. The first time I saw it, I couldn't believe it. But Avare assured us it was genuine. Only four authentic copies in the world, according to him. An ancient piece of vellum, bearing a fragment of the legendary *Primitive Accumulation of Capital*, by Genghis Laebmauntsforscynneweëld.

As usual, Avare greeted us from his easy chair by the fireplace. In all the hours I spent with the old guy, I never once saw him out of the chair. "At my age," he'd explained, "one must conserve one's energies. My legs have long since withered to sticks, but one doesn't need legs to ruin rivals."

The truth is, Avare looked like he was already a corpse. The twitching fingers and the moving eyeballs were the main signs of life. When he talked, even his voice sounded like it came from the grave. Hoarse, faint, dry as dust.

"Be seated, gentlemen," he rasped. "Henry, pour these good men some brandy."

As soon as our brandies were before us, Avare raised his own glass in a feeble semblance of a toast. Greyboar and I drank deeply. The one downside to the whole business, I thought at the moment, was that we'd not be tasting any more of that terrific brandy. A sad thought. I drowned my sorrows. So did Greyboar.

"Goodness," said Avare, "you are both certainly thirsty tonight. Henry, leave the bottle next to the gentlemen. I shall ring for you when I need further assistance." Here he gestured to the small bell which he always kept by his side. But I wasn't worried about the bell. As feeble as Avare was, he'd never get hold of it before Greyboar got hold of his weasand. Very quick-moving, the chokester, when his mind was on business and not philosophy.

Henry left the room, closing the door behind him. A nice thick door, I noticed, perfect for deadening sound. Yes, indeed, things were looking good.

Greyboar was uncomfortable, fidgeting. And, of

course, Avare noticed immediately. There was nothing decrepit about the old man's mind.

"You seem ill at ease, Sirrah Greyboar," he commented. "Not at all your normal self."

Greyboar muttered some silly stuff about indigestion. The old man wasn't fooled for a moment, I could tell. And the worst of it was that Avare decided to get right down to business instead of whiling away a pleasant half hour in well-brandied conversation. I decided then and there that I'd sneak the brandy bottle out with us when we left. Have to make sure Greyboar didn't notice, of course. The chokester would be bound to make a stink about it, yapping on and on about the fine points of professional ethics.

"I have requested your presence tonight," said Avare, "because I have concluded that yet another of my would-be heirs has demonstrated that he is unfit for the inheritance."

He frowned peevishly. "Really, I am so tired of the whole business. You'd think that one of my descendants would show some capability. I'm on to the fourth generation now. Such a sad and sorry lot they've proven to be! Most distressing! It's why I cling to life, you know? Personally, I'd as soon be done with it. At my age, the grave is a thing to long for rather than fear. But I have a grave responsibility to the family fortune. It's my plain and simple duty to ensure that it falls into competent hands."

Not to worry, old-timer, I thought to myself. *Your toil and trouble is almost over.* I made a little motion to Greyboar, signifying: okay, choke the geezer and let's get out of here.

But, naturally, that was too simple for the great philosopher! Oh no, he had to make a great ethical issue out of the whole thing! I couldn't believe it, I just couldn't! The huge numbskull started jabbering away as to how he couldn't accept the commission because, don't you see, he'd already taken on another client, don't you see, and given the nature of his commission, don't you see, there'd be an irremovable stain on his professional ethics, don't you see, if he accepted Avare's commission, don't you see, because—

Well, like I said, there was nothing wrong with Avare's brain, whatever condition his body was in. Greyboar hadn't stumbled his way through the first two clauses before the old man figured everything out. I could tell by the sudden gleam in the ancient eyes. There'd be no way now that Greyboar could get to the bell before Avare rang it. And besides, it was plain as day from his furrowed brow that Greyboar was completely pre-occupied with trying to elaborate the ethical whichness from the whatness. He wasn't even thinking about the bell!

But Avare didn't even look at the bell. He leaned forward and held up his hand. Surprised me no end, that—it was the most energetic action I'd ever seen the old man perform.

"Sirrah Greyboar!" he said. "Stop! There's no need to continue. I am in complete sympathy with your situation. But before you get on with the job, I must know—who employed you to strangle me?"

Greyboar—pardon the expression—choked.

"Uh, uh, I'm not sure, uh, wouldn't be proper—"

"Come, come, my good man!" snapped Avare. "What possible objection could you have to informing me of the identity of my murderer?"

Greyboar looked over to me. I shrugged.

"Well," said the strangler, "I was hired by your great-grandson, Marcel."

"Wonderful!" cried Avare. "I knew it! I knew it! I had all my hopes pegged on that boy!"

Then, before we could think to stop him, he started

ringing the bell furiously. The truth is, Greyboar and I were both a bit confused at the moment. And before we could think to take action, Henry was already in the room.

"Henry!" exclaimed Avare. "Bring more brandy! The sealed bottle!"

Henry gasped. "The sealed bottle! Is it—"

"Yes, yes!" replied Avare. "And tell me—which one do you think it was?"

Henry shrugged. "Well, Monsieur Avare, as you know, I have always been partial to Marcel."

"Yes, Henry, your instincts were correct. Marcel it is. The marvelous lad!"

Henry left the room hurriedly. Avare turned back to us.

"Gentlemen, if you could postpone your business for just a moment longer, I would appreciate your joining me in another glass or two of brandy. The world's greatest brandy, I might add. I've had a sealed bottle of Derosignolle waiting in the cellar for the past thirty years. Surely you won't pass up the opportunity. Only twelve bottles left in the world, you know."

Well, the long and the short of it was that Greyboar and I spent the next hour finishing the bottle of Derosignolle with Avare and Henry. The situation by then was so bizarre that it didn't seem odd to have the old man's manservant take off his coat, roll up his sleeves, and pull up a chair for himself.

"Been with me for years, Henry has," explained Avare. "Closer to me than any of my family, in truth. It's only fitting that he should be part of this grand celebration."

Seeing the look of befuddlement on our faces, Avare snorted. "Gentlemen! Why do you seem so out of sorts? Haven't I already explained that I've simply been clinging to life long enough to make sure that one of my descendants was worthy of the family fortune? And for it to be Marcel! I had hopes, of course, but I was getting a bit distressed that it seemed to be taking him so long to get about it."

"He's still quite young, Monsieur," said Henry.

"Not that young!" replied the old miser. "Why, by the time I was his age—well, let's have none of that. No one wants to hear an old man's ruminations on the past, not even the old man himself." He took a sip of brandy. "Won't even have to change the will. I'd already named Marcel the sole heir. Purely on speculation, of course, but then"—here he grinned evilly—"I've always been a great speculator."

When the brandy was finished—and, by the way, it *was* the greatest brandy I'd ever had, before or since— Avare became all business.

"I believe it would be best to have the choke administered right here. I haven't actually left this chair in years, except for—well, no need to be vulgar. Very fond of this chair, I am, I shall be most pleased to expire in it."

He turned to Henry. "I can trust you to make the usual arrangements with the police, Henry. We certainly don't want Marcel's inheritance to become complicated by busybody officials."

Henry nodded. Avare thought a moment longer, then frowned.

"There is one small point, Henry," he said. "I really should not like the cause of death listed as suicide. Wouldn't want any of my rivals, what few still survive"—here he cackled horridly—"to gain even the slightest comfort from my demise. Much rather have them think I died in a state of complete satisfaction with my life. Which, after all, is the plain and simple truth."

"I completely agree, Monsieur," replied Henry. "The

police coroner would never agree to suicide as the cause of death, in any event—no matter the size of the bribe. He'd be the laughingstock of New Sfinctr. His career would be ruined! Who would believe it? Does a shark commit suicide? Nonsense!"

Henry coughed apologetically. "If Monsieur will forgive me, I have given some thought in the past to the proper way of handling this joyous occasion. As it happens, the timing is perfect. The miserable incompetent, Emile Vantard, was thrown into debtor's prison just yesterday. I thought it would be suitable if I had the rumor spread that, in your glee at the ruination of a long-standing rival, you leapt from your chair and began capering about, howling like a wolf. Alas, your aged legs failed your spirit and you fell, breaking your neck."

"Perfect!" cried Avare. He cackled again. "Perfect, perfect." Then, after stroking his chin:

"One last little point. Now that Marcel has shown his mettle, I must insist that his inheritance remain undisturbed." He gave Greyboar the rheumy eye.

The strangler shrugged. "I'm bound to be approached by the other heirs after the will is read. The disgruntled heirs-that-aren't, I should say. Be a line of them outside my door, I expect."

I saw my chance and leapt at it. "Of course, we'd be forced to turn down the offers, if we were prevented from taking them by a prior commitment. Clear matter of professional ethics."

I leaned back in my chair, restraining a sigh of satisfaction. Then, smiling innocently at Avare, reached for my brandy.

Stopped. How the hell he'd done it without my noticing is a mystery, but Henry had already switched the snifter for a glass of salt water.

"To be sure," wheezed Avare. "Professional ethics—

of course! I shall have to provide you with an honorarium. Something substantial enough to offset any possible later counteroffer from Marcel's rivals."

My heart sank. I stared at the glass of salt water in my hand.

Wheeze, wheeze. "To be sure, to be sure. I foresee a lengthy negotiation." Avare's ancient vulture's eyes seemed to be glowing at the prospect.

Greyboar rose hastily from his chair. "Not my job, this." He patted me on the shoulder. "I leave the matter entirely in the hands of my trusted agent. I'll while away the time in the kitchen, with Henry."

Bitterly, I watched Greyboar hurriedly drain what was left in his own snifter. Then, heard alum poured over bile.

"Take the whole bottle with you, my good man!" urged Avare. His eyes were fixed on me like a carrion eater on a dying mouse. "Ignace, I'm sure, won't have any need for it. Professional ethics, you know. No reputable agent would befuddle his mind with strong drink whilst in the midst of *protracted* bargaining."

I think I let out a whine. Not sure.

But, finally, it was done. To my surprise, I even managed to squeeze a bundle out of the old buzzard after I raised the specter of Marcel's rivals forming a consortium. I think his heart wasn't entirely in it anymore, now that he was eagerly looking forward to his eternal rest.

And so was I, so was I.

"Make it quick," I hissed to Greyboar, as I opened the door. "Before the old bastard changes his mind."

The strangler snorted and lazed his way past me into the salon. As I began to close the door, I heard the Merchant Prince speak his—hallelujah!—last words.

"I believe the time has come. I can trust you to do the job properly, I am sure."

"You won't feel a thing," rumbled the strangler.

And he didn't, either. At the end, I couldn't resist peeking. I've got to give Avare his due. He went out of this world the same way he passed through it. The satanic grin never left the old pirate's face.

Chapter 7.
The Second Law At Work

Well, it's like everything in life—there's an upside, and then there's a downside.

The upside turned up almost at once. Only a day after Marcel came into the inheritance, Henry secretly told all the remaining now-disowned non-heirs the true manner of Avare's passing. It was an act of complete treachery, of course—not only to Marcel, but to his great-grandfather's last wishes.

"Least I could do to pay back the miserable old tyrant for years of semi-slavery," he told me later, sharing a friendly ale at The Trough. Personally, I suspected there was another motive as well, judging from the fancy clothes which Henry was wearing. I do believe Henry'd been skimming the old man's till for years, I do. Hard to explain the manservant's newfound riches otherwise. I figure he decided Marcel would want a complete audit done of the estate, first thing, and so best to get rid of him quick.

Anyway, before you knew it the strangler and assassin trade in New Sfinctr was booming. I had to turn down all the offers, of course—professional ethics—and leave the business to others. But I wasn't chagrined in the least.

Why? Simple. I really had gotten a *big* bundle from Avare. Enough to keep Greyboar and me in the pink for quite a while. Long enough, I was certain, for someone else to do away with Marcel. At which point, of course, our obligation to the old Merchant Prince would have been satisfied and we could pick up on all the *aftermarket* trade. We'd be rich!

Oh, I was such a shrewd fellow. Heh heh.

And, at first, everything seemed to be going according to plan. Even with the second-raters that the disgruntled heirs had to settle for, it didn't take much more than a week before the new Merchant Prince of New Sfinctr was a chokee. Throttled, apparently, by someone hired by Marcel's brother Antoine.

The next day, we were approached by Antoine's cousin Pierre. I rubbed my hands, foreseeing well-nigh-endless work. The Avare extended family was huge.

Heh heh. Shrewd!

Except—

I couldn't believe it! Greyboar went mad!

"I can't see it, Ignace," he insisted. "My interpretation of our obligation to old Avare is that we can't burke *any* of his heirs. No dice."

The moron! But, since he was clearly prepared to be stubborn, I raced down to the Ethics Committee and got an official ruling. The Ethics Committee, being made up of sane and sensible men, naturally ruled that our obligation extended to Marcel alone.

Didn't matter! Greyboar still refused to budge. He babbled some gobbledygook about the downhill nature of Time's Arrow and the intestines of entropy and God

knows what other silly nonsense—all of which led him
to the firm opinion that the Ethics Committee was
shaving the thing way too close and that since he wasn't
bound to actually take on the job by their ruling, he
wasn't going to do it.

Ethics, he said. And he wouldn't budge an inch.

It broke my heart. Antoine was gone in four days.
Pierre and his five brothers—one after the other, like
tenpins—lasted ten days, thanks to the commissions
someone got from his sister Amelie. *Big* commissions,
according to rumor.

I spent those two weeks sulking, brooding over ale
pots in The Trough. I didn't even pay much attention
when that artist Benvenuti showed up one night and
spent hours at another table with Greyboar, chatting
over this and that. The crazy sister/lover, I imagine.
Didn't care!

Which, of course, was sheer stupidity on my part.
Because Greyboar then disappeared for a few days and
I was too disgruntled to wonder about it.

Stupid.

Stupid! I should have known better than to let the
numbskull roam loose on his own. By the time I finally
thought to track him down, the damage had been done.
The *further* damage, I should say.

I found him at Benny's studio, posing for a portrait.
He must have been at it for days, because the portrait
was almost finished. When I saw it, I almost had a
heart attack.

Not the cost of the thing, so much—although that
was horrendous enough. (And can you believe the nerve
of that artist, claiming he was only charging us "family"
rates? What family? The nematodes?)

No, no. It was the portrait itself. Havoc on canvas!
Ruin in oil!

~ ~ ~

Even a lowlife like me could spot it. Benvenuti hadn't given it a title. Didn't need to. Take your pick:

The Brooding Strangler, Pondering the Futility of His Wicked Life.

Chokester, Gazing Into Eternity, Soulful.

The Gleam of Reason Within the Beast.

Ogre, in Repose, Regretting His Fangs and Talons.

Yeah, *that* kind of portrait. And I couldn't, no matter how hard I tried, get Greyboar to relinquish the monstrosity. At first, he tucked it away into a closet. But then, the first time the Cat drifted by for a visit, he hauled it out for her opinion.

"You aren't that cute," she promptly announced. "Be nice if you were, though."

Thereafter, Greyboar left it prominently displayed in his little cubbyhole of a room. Used to spend hours there, just staring at it. Practicing his "ethical entropy," he said.

Then, thankfully, my pain was eased because business hit what would have been a dry spell for us anyway, because Greyboar wouldn't have taken any of the six commissions offered to burke Amelie. Tough cookie, Amelie. She hired stranglers to strangle stranglers, and managed to stay unchoked for a fortnight. But then she died of poisoning.

The dry spell would have continued, however, because the courts ruled that the last sister on that side of the family—Arianne—was the heir. But Arianne only lasted a day. Committed suicide. Stabbed herself twelve times in the back.

Then the inheritance started running back through the masculine branches of the family. And, again, my heart was broken watching the lost commissions. I even started avoiding The Trough, so I wouldn't have to see the smug looks on the faces of all the hoi polloi stranglers lounging about the place in their newfound riches. By now the business was well into second and third cousins and every mangy ham-thumbed chokester in the trade was getting a piece of the action.

Then—finally!—there looked to be a break in the clouds. One of the remote cousins, like an idiot, decided to bring in some lawyers. Didn't take long before the estate started getting gobbled up by legal fees. At first, I was worried that the gold mine would dry up. But I needn't have feared. It seemed the smaller the estate got, the more hysterical the feeding frenzy became. Pretty soon we had lawyers hiring stranglers to choke other lawyers—and offering (can you believe it?) to let them bill by the hour.

Paradise! Not even Greyboar could claim any ethical problem with strangling lawyers!

Nor did he. "Glad to," he rumbled.

But—but—I couldn't believe it!

He insisted on doing the work *pro bono*!

"A professional is obligated to return *something* to the community, Ignace," he explained solemnly. "I just wouldn't feel right, charging for this sort of thing."

He even left off his damned Languor and charged into the thing with vigor and enthusiasm. And, of course, with him back on the job, the whole thing was settled within a couple of weeks.

There was one point where it got a little sticky. A pair of lawyers hired us to choke the other simultaneously. One of them went through me, following proper procedure. But the other one—on the very same day—accosted Greyboar himself on the street. He was so insistent that Greyboar took his money (one quid—just a token to satisfy protocol) without sending him to his agent. Naturally, having screwed the whole thing up,

Greyboar started moaning and groaning about his professional ethics. I finally had to get an official clarification from the Ethics Committee. They ruled that since both commissions had been accepted in good faith, that they were both valid. But the Ethics Committee also fined Greyboar half the fee for not going through his agent like he was supposed to. It was a moral victory for me, you understand. But, on the other hand, I hated to lose the money. True, it was only half a quid. But the way Greyboar was throwing around his *pro bono* labor, I figured we needed every pence we could get.

Like all good things in life, of course, the gold mine eventually played itself out. Within three months there weren't any heirs left and there wasn't any estate left and what few lawyers were still alive had already gorged themselves full. The way it finally ended up, the only thing left of the estate was a single bottle of brandy. The courts ruled that the bottle should go to Henry, since there were no heirs left and he was, after all, the faithful servant who had loyally served old man Etienne for umpteen years.

Ironic, it was.

Henry certainly thought so. He came by The Trough with the bottle and insisted that Greyboar and I drink it down with him. Leuwen the barkeep normally frowned on liquor being brought into The Trough instead of purchased on the premises, but when we explained the situation he gave his wholehearted approval. Even came over and had a glass himself.

"Here's to treacherous servants!" he toasted.

So, I can hear you asking, where was the downside? Where do you think? Philosophy, of course.

I started getting wind that something screwy was going on when I noticed that Greyboar was getting more and more cheerful as the *pro bono* commissions rolled in. Not at all like him, that. The truth is that Greyboar was lazy even before he discovered his "ethical entropy." After that he was impossible. Days on end he spent lounging around, grumbling about the smallest little job, whining and complaining that he had to practice his Languor. Usually, I had to crack the whip to get him to work. But here he was, charging around like a kid with a new toy, squeezing like mad, grinning all the while like an idiot.

Finally, I demanded an explanation.

"Isn't it obvious?" he boomed cheerfully. "You're seeing entropy at work! I told you this whole scheme of yours was goofy, in the long run. It makes me laugh just thinking about that old idiot! There he was, the great Etienne Avare, Merchant Prince of New Sfinctr, bumping off one relative after another so he'd be able to keep the fortune intact. A futile attempt to outsmart the second law of thermodynamics if I ever saw one! And what happened? Tell me! What happened?"

By now I had my hands over my ears. Damned if I was going to listen to this gibberish! Greyboar grabbed my hands and pulled them away. I resisted, of course, but it was like a mouse resisting an elephant.

"What happened?" he continued. "No sooner does Etienne get what he's been working for—for decades, no less!—than it all falls apart in months. It's perfect, perfect! Classic example of entropy in action! Total verification of my philosophy!"

"What a load of bullshit!" I fired back. "Sure and the Avare fortune are history—so what? We've made more money out of the deal than we've ever made in our lives! And I've saved up most of the old bastard's honorarium, too!"

I know, I know, I know, don't tell me—bad move, Ignace. As the wise man says: "A braggart and his brag are soon parted."

Sure enough, Greyboar grinned from ear to ear and stuck out his paw. His great, ugly paw.

"Fork over, Ignace," he said. "The Cat and I are going off on a spree. I figure, why try to save the money? It'll just go the way of all energy, anyway—scattered to the wind."

Insult, naturally, was now added to injury. "It's entropy, Ignace," he said solemnly, "you can't fight it."

So I had to cough it all up. Everything I'd hoarded! Blown in a week!

Chapter 8.
A Week in the Country

I would have stayed in our garret, sulking, but when Jenny and Angela heard about the spree they came and dragged me out. Made me go along. Greyboar had invited them, of course. "Natural-born entropists," he called them. "The perfect company for an outing devoted to the second law of thermodynamics!" He was not all that enthusiastic about me coming along. Called me a sourpuss, if you can believe it? But Jenny and Angela put their foot down, and that was that.

Then, Jenny and Angela got the crazy idea to invite Benvenuti along, too. Said he was such a charming man that he was bound to add something to the festivities.

I was utterly against the idea, but I had enough sense to keep my mouth shut. I knew the silly girls would accuse me of jealousy, as absurd as it was. And given that Greyboar was still being a bit grouchy with me, I realized that my opposition would be sure to swing it the other way.

Besides, I wasn't worried. I knew that Greyboar wouldn't really want someone around for a whole week who would remind him constantly of Gwendolyn. I knew it for a certainty, because *I* didn't want to be reminded of Gwendolyn. Not that much, anyway.

And, sure enough . . .

"Well, I don't know . . ." he muttered, scratching his head. Greyboar was sprawled on the couch in Jenny and Angela's living room. The Cat was curled up next to him, half asleep, her head nestled on his shoulder. Angela was perched on the armrest of my chair, looking like a cheerful little bird.

The strangler's black eyes glanced around the little room, like rats looking for a place to hide. I tried not to look smug.

"Well, I don't know . . ."

"Oh, come on!" chirped Angela. "Sure, and just having him around will probably makes you feel sad, reminding you of your estranged sister and everything. But you're always sad about that, anyway."

"So's Ignace," chirped Jenny. She was standing right behind me, her hands on my shoulders. I stiffened and started to utter a protest, but she clapped her hands over my mouth. "Is too!" she chirped. "Keep talking, Angela!"

"And besides," Angela chirped on, "it's your plain and simple philosophical duty." Greyboar's eyes almost bulged. "Didn't Ignace say anybody who'd fall in love with Gwendolyn is nuts? And an artist! He's *bound* to have an angle on entropy, whatever the silly thing is, that you never even thought of. Probably lots of them."

Greyboar's eyes got unfocused. *Oh, no!* I thought.

"Good point," he said. "Sure—why not?"

So Jenny and Angela and Greyboar and the Cat hired a carriage and charged off to see the artist. I stayed behind, sulking.

Then—*then!*—when they got back, it turned out they'd decided to invite Hrundig, too. That had been Angela's idea, seeing as how she'd been charmed by how nice Hrundig had been the first time they visited, even if he was a brutal barbarian mercenary.

"He's a brutal barbarian mercenary!" I protested.

Angela frowned at me. "And so what? You and Greyboar are brutal mercenaries, aren't you? And without even the excuse of being barbarians!" She patted me on the cheek. "But we don't hold it against you, now, do we? Not much, anyway."

I choked and spluttered, trying to come up with a counter. Greyboar just looked sheepish. "Well . . ." he muttered. "Well . . ."

"Are too!" chirped Jenny. "Depraved and horrible desperadoes, even if you're actually kind of sweet and Ignace isn't but he's real cute and Angela and I like the way he fusses over us even if he is a pain in the ass sometimes."

I choked and spluttered, trying to come up with a counter. Greyboar just gave me a sweet smile. Sickening, it was.

Then—*then!*—it turned out that Hrundig had a girlfriend and he asked if he could bring her along. By that point, Greyboar and I were completely at sea. "Sure, why not?" one of us muttered. Can't remember which one.

Then—*then!*—it turned out Hrundig's girlfriend was a widow with three daughters and she wanted to know if she could bring *them* along. I don't think either Greyboar or I even muttered, at that point.

The thing was turning into a damned migrating barbarian horde!

And the worst of it was—who was going to pay for all this? As if I didn't know.

Yup. "It's our treat, you little tightwad," growled

Greyboar. "*Try* to be a little gentlemanly about it, will you?"

About the only bright spot in the whole thing was that after we decided we had to rent one of those expensive pleasure barges, it turned out that Benvenuti was an experienced yachtsman—was there *anything* the damned man couldn't do?—and Hrundig, of course, was an experienced sailor in a different kind of way—*not that we're planning to plunder any monasteries, of course*—so we were able to save money on hiring a crew as well.

Which, of course, didn't really save us any money at all because as soon as they heard that, Jenny and Angela started oohing and ahing over the most expensive and luxurious barge at the piers instead of the perfectly good little commercial fishing craft that I had my eye on—*okay, so it smells a little, so what?*—and the Cat made some offhand remark about the pleasures of wallowing for a week in offal and that was that. One gold-plated barge coming up.

I admit it was a nice barge. Very nice, in fact. Everybody had staterooms and everything, and the "accouterments," as they say, were, as they say, "nonpareil." And once we pushed off from the wharf and I resigned myself to the inevitable, I found myself actually starting to look forward to the trip. Especially once we sailed up the river out of the city, heading south into the countryside.

Mind you, I'm really not that big a fan of "rural scenery." Plants are pretty much all green, when you get down it, and if you've seen one tree you've pretty much seen them all. Still—it *was* nice to get away from New Sfinctr. Much as I'm a city lad, I'm not about to claim the place isn't a pure and simple eyesore.

Not to mention nose-sore. True, New Sfinctr does

have what they call a "sewer system." Queen Bella-donna prided herself on what she called her "modern-ization program," also referred to as the "window to the east."

But it doesn't really do much good to build a sewer system when the work is contracted out to cronies and the powers-that-be are spending too much on their palaces to waste money on such frills as hiring actual sewer workers. Instead, the powers-that-be would periodically order the porkers to round up some "vagrant" dwarves and set them to work in the sew-ers. Which is the kind of idea that only Sfinctrian dimwit officials would come up with, since once you let a dwarf get underground you can pretty much kiss that dwarf good-bye.

New impromptu and unplanned sewer, coming up—and off he goes. The end result being not only that the sewers *still* aren't cleaned but you soon have a "sewer system" that's more system than sewer, if you know what I mean. You know that kind of cheese that's mostly holes instead of cheese? If so, you get the picture.

Ah, yes. Fresh air, sunshine, the lot. It really was pretty nice. Especially after we popped open the wine and the nice bread Jenny and Angela bought, and they dug into their baskets and brought out the meat pies and the kind of cheese that's mostly holes instead of cheese, which is fine by me because I don't like cheese.

Then it got even better because Madame Frissault—Hrundig's girlfriend—opened up the huge baskets she and her daughters had brought along and it turned out they'd spent a whole day baking practically anything that can be baked. And they were good bakers.

At that point, I became reconciled to the whole thing. I admit, my change of mood was helped along by the fact that Madame Frissault—Olga, as she insisted we call her—was a very jolly kind of lady and her daughters were pleasant enough. Very pretty, too, all three of them. Which, for me, was what they call an "academic question," but it was still nice to see.

Soon enough, it became clear that all three girls had a massive crush on Benny. Especially the oldest, Beatrice, who was maybe a little older than Jenny. Beatrice looked a lot like her mother. Dark-haired and dark-complexioned, almost as much as Angela. A little on the plump side, in an attractive buxom kind of way, with a face that wasn't exactly pretty but so pleasant that it was really *very* pretty, if that makes any sense at all. I thought the pince-nez spectacles perched on her nose were a little silly, but from the way the girl devoured books the whole trip, I suppose it wasn't really an affectation.

But while Benny obviously felt very affectionate toward the daughters, and was always flirting a little with Beatrice, there wasn't anything in it. If you know what I mean. A very handsome and sophisticated man in his mid-twenties handling a teenager's crush on him with ease and gentility and a heart of gold.

It was *so* tiresome. Especially having to listen to Jenny and Angela babble on in our stateroom about the artist's splendid personal qualities. Which, needless to say, they highlighted with the occasional contrast to another individual. So tiresome.

"Why d'you put up with me, then?" I snarled at one point. "And stop telling me I'm cute! Just because I'm a red-headed freckled shrimp doesn't make me a pet!"

I was sitting cross-legged at the head of the big bed in our stateroom. Jenny and Angela were sitting in the same position in the center of the bed. I crossed my arms over my chest and assumed a pose of great dignity.

"Pout—pout—pout!" squealed Angela gleefully, clapping her hands.

Jenny grinned. "I do believe his feelings are hurt," she cooed.

Angela squealed again. "Feelings! We're making progress!" A moment later both of them had me on my back and were tickling me mercilessly.

And I *hate* being tickled!

Well . . . usually.

In this case, it wasn't so bad, because one thing led to another and maybe an hour or so later I was feeling better. A lot better, actually. Especially after Angela fell asleep with her head nestled on my chest and Jenny kissed me and whispered, "Don't worry about it, Ignace. We're a little family now, sort of. Even if it's illegal by law and we're dead meat if the Church catches us. A real one, not like what Angela had and I lost."

I turned my head and looked at her, and saw that for once Jenny wasn't teasing me. There wasn't any smile at all on her lips, just in her eyes. Blue eyes as clear as the sky almost never gets in New Sfinctr.

I felt an ache coming up and pushed it under. I guess my lips must have tightened or something, because Jenny started shaking her head. "Sooner or later, Ignace, it's going to come out."

I guess I must have shaken my own head, because Jenny put her hands on my cheeks and made me look at her. "Yes, it will," she whispered, and then pulled my face into her neck. "Got to."

It was a tender moment, really was. Then, of course, Jenny had to go ruin it by laughing and saying: "Got to! You fuss too much over everything to leave anything alone! S'true!"

Needless to say, I started denying the ridiculous charge—and vigorously, too!—but that woke up Angela and once she got wind of the argument I was outnumbered again.

And I *hate* being tickled!

That night, we pulled into one of those spas that they have for rich people up the river and took rooms in what they called The Lodge. Silly name for a hotel, if you ask me. Like calling a restaurant The Eat. But I kept the sarcastic thought to myself, lest I be accused of uncouthness or something.

To be honest, I was a bit worried about the whole thing. While Greyboar and I were definitely "men about town," this was what you might call a whole different kind of town. I was half sure they'd take one look at us and pitch us out on our ear, even if Greyboar and I were wearing our best outfits.

But, again—life is *so* unfair—Benvenuti proved to be a master at the kind of suave assurance that gets all doors opened and the carpets rolled out. And Olga Frissault underwent a magical transformation from a cheerful mother on an outing to a grim, implacable matron of high society. Every desk clerk and bellhop in the place avoided her gaze like they would that of a basilisk.

So, even though Greyboar and I and Hrundig got a few skeptical glances, there was no trouble. In fact, Benny wrangled up an entire set of interconnected suites, complete with our own small little dining room.

"I think we should perhaps stay here for the rest of the week," Olga suggested tentatively, after the bellhops left and the door was closed. "There's really not much change in the scenery until you get to Murraine, and—"

Greyboar coughed. I think I started hacking.

"Not a good idea," I managed to get out. Hack, hack. "By all means—let's stay here!"

"By all means," rumbled Greyboar. "Splendid idea."

Olga seemed a little startled at our eager agreement. Hrundig gave us that humorless grin he does better than anybody I've ever seen except a shark I saw once in a nightmare.

"Job went sour, eh?" he chuckled.

I glared at him. For a moment—it was on the tip of my tongue!—I almost blurted out a hot retort. *Sour, my ass! We made a bundle!* But, under the circumstances, it would have perhaps been uncultured. Especially if I had to explain exactly why the Duke of Murraine might view our presence with disfavor. Not, mind you, that the gentleman had any reason to hold a grudge. Quite the contrary! But he might start wondering who *else* had paid for our services. And, dukes being dukes, might leap to the assumption that *his* heir apparent—

Well. No need to pursue that line of thought.

So, in the end, we wound up spending the whole week at that lodge. And, by the end of the stay, I understood why they called it a "lodge."

"Get moving, Ignace," hissed Jenny. "You can't live in luxury forever."

"Why not?" I whined. "I *like* this magnificent four-poster—"

Alas, Angela dislodged me from the royal bed in question. None too gently, either, I might add. And neither she nor Jenny were any gentler about the way they more or less frog-marched me out of our suite.

On our way through the door, I cast a despairing glance backward. Jenny chuckled and kissed me on the cheek. "Memories, Ignace. We'll always have them."

"Memories," I muttered. "Damn things are worse than ghosts."

Chapter 9.
Downhill

When we got back, I was in the best mood I'd been in years. But it didn't last for very long. Sooner than you could believe, things started going downhill. Greyboar called it entropy. I called it the innate tendency of life to get fucked up. He insisted we were talking about the same thing, which absolutely infuriated me.

My way of putting it was simple common sense, backed up by long experience. It had nothing to do with any damned *philosophy*.

Oh, and sure, we didn't fall into poverty. Somewhat to my surprise, even after that luxurious spree, we still had quite a bit of Avare's honorarium left. Enough to last us for quite a while, even after Greyboar got pressured by the Cat into moving us into swankier digs. Well. Less hovelish digs, it might be better to say. I was able to hold the line *somewhere*.

In addition to what was left of the honorarium, business kept picking up. Partly that was because the life and times of Sfinctria—all of Grotum, in fact—was sure and purely going to hell in a handbasket. After the fiasco in Prygg—I repeat: my lips are sealed; I vow eternal silence—the Ozarines got so furious they just invaded eastern Grotum outright. No more of that namby-pamby "covert action" stuff. (Weird phrase, that. What I mean is, the action's never covert to the covertee, who's presumably the guy that's supposed to be kept in the dark.)

Queen Belladonna, naturally, immediately hailed the invasion and signed about eight million treaties with Ozar. The upper classes sided with her to a man— cleaved to her bosom like newborn babes, more like— chattering about *realpolitik*. The middle classes more or less went along, muttering glumly about devils you know and devils you don't. The intelligentsia—the young ones, anyhow—screamed about collaboration and rioted in the streets. The great unwashed masses went on about eight million general strikes and built barricades every other Tuesday, bellowing rowdy slogans in which the terms "boot-licker" and "toady" vied in popularity with "puppet" and—always a crowd pleaser—"worthless cocksucker."

The Ecclesiarchy also gave their blessing to the enterprise. The Ozarine Empire was officially anointed with the title "Protector of the Faith," which the Twelve Popes even managed to say with a straight face. Nice trick, that, given that Ozarines are notorious free-thinkers and keep the Church on a very tight leash in Ozarae. A civilized folk, the Ozarines.

The "blessing of the Ecclesiarchy," needless to say, translated itself into an inquisitorial frenzy and priests sermonizing about the "dwarf menace." Before you knew it, there were pogroms practically every week.

Would-be pogroms, I should say. In the event, all those years of forcing "vagrant" dwarves into the sewers paid off for the dwarves, because they had a million hidey-holes to scurry into. Stinky hidey-holes, sure, but smelling like crap beats smelling like a roast.

For a while, the pogromist mobs were enraged by their slim pickings and started whipping themselves into a bigger frenzy. But then—we heard about it, we didn't see it—Gwendolyn and The Roach surfaced and organized a counterforce. One of the big mobs ran right into an ambush and by the time Gwendolyn and The Roach and maybe two dozen surly agitators and two hundred really surly proletarian types and two thousand *really* surly dwarves got finished, the pogromists had been pretty much pogromized to a pulp. I heard the sewers were clogged for a week in that part of the city.

When he got the news, Greyboar didn't say anything. He just went into his room and spent the next three days staring at that damned portrait. "Practicing my Languor," he said. "Practicing my Languor."

Ah, what the hell. I didn't feel too great myself. Even though all the reports we heard agreed that Gwendolyn had made a clean getaway when it was all over. Not that I was surprised. A completely unreasonable woman. But—

Heh. I'll admit I laughed, thinking about it. Gwendolyn had been a tough cookie even when she was a kid. I could just imagine what she was like now!

After a day or so, I bucked myself up. Life is what it is, and that's all there is to it. What else do you ever get?

Philosophy, my ass. Greyboar could call it entropy till he turned blue in the face, and practice his Languor, and pretend he was discerning the secrets of the eightfold whatchamacallit in the profound depths of the foursome whosit. Me, I stuck with the wise man's most profound saying: "Shit happens."

And, I reminded myself firmly, it was great for the trade! Business was absolutely booming, and nobody had to worry about the porkers anymore. Not stranglers and their customers, at any rate. Oh my, no. The porkers were running their tails off stamping out riot and revolution, ferreting out subversion, grappling the serpent of anarchy, etc., etc. Likewise, the army. Likewise, the Inquisition.

Greyboar, of course, refused to look at it rationally. He called it *fin de siècle* something or other—*angst*, I think. Me, I knew it was just that everybody— especially in the upper crust where most of our customers came from—was swept up in the sagacity of the wise man.

Shit was happening, indeed. At which time, as the wise man says: "Better to be the shitter than the shittee."

We were swamped with prospective clients. Greyboar's reputation was now sky-high. Nobody was in his league anymore. Nobody ever was, actually; but now even the cloddies knew it. Greyboar had always been famous in the scholarly journals, mind you. *The Journal of Contemporary Assassination*, *Asphyxiation Quarterly*, *Garrote Gazette*—one or the other always had a reference to him in a current article. And, year after year, like clockwork, *Jane's The World's Perps* listed him as, and I quote: "the state of the art in the trade" and "the standard by which professional thuggee must be measured."

But now there was a flurry of articles about him in the popular press, too. Most of which—brace yourself— were titled something like "World's Greatest Strangler A Recluse!" and "Greyboar Spurns Another Offer!"

I swear, it broke my heart. More business than you could shake a stick at—more *potential* business, I should say—and Greyboar turned down 99% of it.

He was—keep a straight face—"bored." He was—
don't laugh—"not challenged." He wanted—are you
ready for this?—"only jobs which are epistemologically
valid, ontologically rigorous, and adhere to ethical
entropic axioms."

I'm serious. The guy made a living crushing
windpipes—this is not, as a rule, considered intellec-
tually demanding labor—and he insisted on *philosophically correct* chokes.

Of course, I protested. I denounced. I sermonized
on sloth. I whined. I groused.

None of which did the slightest bit of good. Then,
seeing starvation looming, I scrounged up what jobs
I could which satisfied the great *philosophe's* dignity.

Weird, weird jobs. For instance: The Royal Astronomical Society hired us to strangle a vampire who was
bumping off its members in an observatory. I kid you
not. Actually, as it turned out, the whole thing was
really on account of the fact that the telescope in the
observatory in question was—

Never mind. Some other time. I just bring it up now
to illustrate the woeful life of a strangler's agent.

Then, naturally, it got worse, because I made the
mistake of complaining to Jenny and Angela about it.

"Pooh," sniffed Jenny. "Sniff," poohed Angela.

The next thing I knew, the two of them were hauling
me down to Benvenuti's studio, insisting that I get my
own portrait painted alongside their own. "In order to
improve my spirits," they said.

I protested at the cost, but that turned out to be
a bad move because Benvenuti was making a ton off
of his portraits of Jenny and Angela. Which astonished
me, since they weren't nudes. Turned out there was
a market for great portraits of youthful innocence, if
you can believe it. What a weird world. Oh, sure, he
gave them several free of charge, which would have

been worth a bundle—except Jenny and Angela refused
to let me sell them. Which, I'll admit, is not something
I pushed very hard. After a while, I got to like having the portraits around.

Then—then!—Benvenuti offered to do a portrait of
me. And—brace yourself for some vulgarity here—*free
of charge.* Artists, I decided, had the most disgrace-
ful set of professional ethics I'd ever heard of. A scan-
dal, what it was.

Well, I could hardly refuse under the circumstances.
Especially after Jenny and Angela threatened to, ah,
"withhold their affections." So there I sat in a studio,
day after day, sulking on a stool next to a table loaded
with silly fruit. What made it all the worse was that
Benny got really into the project.

When he finished, I took one look at the damn thing
and flat refused to accept it. What an utterly slanderous
portrayal! Jenny and Angela couldn't budge me an inch.
Benvenuti just shrugged and put the stupid thing on
the market where, to my outrage and disgruntlement,
it brought in an astonishing price. Eventually, I heard,
it even wound up in some hoity-toity museum.

A Study in Melancholia, indeed!

Nonsense. What was involved here was my reason,
not my emotions. Logic, pure and simple. Greyboar
could sneer at my rude, crude, lewd and uncouth
intellect. Crap. I knew cause and effect when I saw
it.

If Greyboar hadn't taken up philosophy, we never
would have gotten involved in *l'affaire Prygg.* If we
hadn't gotten into that mess we never would have
gotten into that other idiot business in Blain and
Greyboar never would've gotten hooked up with
Schrödinger's Cat. If he hadn't gotten the hots for a
crazy woman, he never would have dreamed of mixing

it up with an *artiste*. If he hadn't mixed it up with high-falutin' artist types, he wouldn't have gotten soul-sick with the realities of a perfectly reasonable trade. If he had developed what he started calling *weltschmerz*, we never would have looked twice at doing jobs for out-of-town eccentrics. If he hadn't been out of town doing a weird job for a heretic abbess, his girlfriend wouldn't have run afoul of Church and State. If his lady love hadn't managed to get herself into the silliest scrape you ever heard of—you'll hear about it, hold your horses—he wouldn't have made an even sillier attempt to rescue her. If he hadn't tried to rescue her, we wouldn't have gotten involved in the dwarf business. If we hadn't gotten mixed up with the dwarf business, his sister Gwendolyn wouldn't have developed a soft spot in her heart for the clown. And if Gwendolyn hadn't decided maybe Greyboar wasn't the absolute pure scum of the earth, after all, she certainly wouldn't have—

Never mind. I'm getting ahead of myself. Just take my word, for the moment. Without philosophy, our life would have stayed on an even keel. Instead, like being sucked into a whirlpool, we wound up where we are today.

You'll see.

Chapter 10.
Worse Than the Worst

The job started off bizarre, and then got weirder as it went along.

First off, we were hired by means of a letter, delivered through the post just like we were the proper haberdasher or respectable jeweler. Not your normal method of employment for a strangler, don't you know?

But there it was, big as life, a letter requesting our professional services. Just a note, really.

> *Dear Mr. Greyboar:*
>
> *I find I have need of a professional strangler. Having made inquiries in the proper quarters, I have been assured that you are the very finest practitioner currently active in the trade. Would you be so good as to come to my Abbey? The work will need to be done here.*
>
> *I shall, of course, reimburse you for all travel expenses, as well as paying your standard fee. I might*

> *mention that a very handsome bonus will be pro-*
> *vided as well, upon satisfactory completion of the*
> *choke.*
>
> > *Sincerely yours,*
> > *Abbess Hildegard*
> > *Abbey of the Sisters of Tranquility*

"The Abbess Hildegard!" exclaimed Greyboar. "What in the world could she possibly want with me?"

His puzzlement was understandable. Of course, we knew who the Abbess was, at least in a general way. She was famous—notorious, more precisely. The Twelve Popes had excommunicated her years earlier. She'd ignored them, just as she ignored every pronouncement coming from the Temple of the Ecclesiarchs. Rather irritated they got, the Popes, to put it mildly.

First, they talked the Queen of Sfinctria, Belladonna III, into sending the Seventh Cavaliers to raze the Abbey and deliver Hildegard over to the Inquisition. Then, after the Seventh Cavaliers disappeared in Joe's Favorite Woods (that's the forest which surrounds the Abbey), the Queen sent the whole Third Royal Regiment to do the job. After they disappeared, she gave it up. Got in quite a tiff with the Ecclesiarchy about the whole thing.

So, finally, the Ecclesiarchy pulled out all the stops and ordered the gentle monks of the monastery of St. Shriven-on-the-Moor into action. The gentle monks murmured and muttered amongst themselves, working up their usual pogromist fury. But then, to everyone's astonishment, they settled down and told the Popes they couldn't do it. Seems they'd gotten a vision from the Old Geister himself, the gist of which was that falling on the Abbey of the Sisters of Tranquility would be a really stupid move.

The Popes weren't happy about it, but they didn't

get where they are by being fools. Not even the Ecclesiarchy in full regalia was about to get into a serious quarrel with the gentle monks of the monastery of St. Shriven-on-the-Moor. Take their visions seriously, the monks do.

The point is, any old lady who'd been able to handle all of that without—so far as anybody could tell—even working up a sweat, well, what would she need a strangler for? What I mean to say is, your average chokester's employer is the type who can't handle their own rough work. We really didn't get much business from people who could make whole armies vanish.

I wasn't keen on taking the job, myself. The Abbey was a fair ways off. Sure, and the Abbess Hildegard said she'd reimburse our travel expenses, but so what? While we were out of town, who knows what lucrative Greyboar-acceptable "ethically correct" choke might come up. Besides, promenading through the countryside sucks. Wafting down a river on a luxury barge is one thing; traipsing through a primeval forest is another story altogether.

Greyboar was of the same opinion, so I figured that was that. Until he mentioned the letter to the Cat over dinner that night.

The Cat had made one of her periodic reappearances early that morning. As soon as they heard, Jenny and Angela came over and invited us all to their house for a big dinner. With all the fancy trimmings. Then charged off with me in tow. They said they needed someone to carry all the provisions they were going to buy.

I was still complaining when we got back to their house. Partly from the labor—a *lot* of provisions—but mostly from responsible financial concerns. "This cost a lot of money," I whined. (Oh, sure. Did you think

I let *them* pay for it? A man loses his pride, he's got nothing. Especially a little man.)

Jenny was on tiptoe, hauling one of the big pots down from its hook on the kitchen wall. "You've got money, Ignace," she retorted. "Plenty enough to afford a modest little feast."

"Sure do!" added Angela. "And we didn't ask you to pay for it, anyway." She was doing something with dough and a rolling pin over at the counter, flour up to her elbows. " 'A man loses his pride, 'e's got nothing,' " she mimicked, giggling.

Jenny slammed the pot onto the stove. "I'm amazed Greyboar doesn't roll right off his bed, as much loot as you've got stashed under it."

"Business is slow," I whined.

Jenny's hair had grown so long it hung down to her waist. She started doing that incredibly complicated and quick-graceful thing that women with long hair do when they coil it up out of the way that I love to watch when it's Jenny doing it. Smiling like a cherub all the while.

"Bullshit," she retorted. "Business is *exclusive*. As in: *top drawer*."

"That's right!" piped Angela. She'd finished whatever she'd been doing with the dough and was washing her arms. Then, snatching up a towel and starting to dry herself, she marched out of the kitchen. A moment or two later she was back, clutching a thick book in her hands.

I recognized it, and couldn't stop myself from wincing.

"The latest edition!" she announced. "Jenny and I bought it not two days ago." She plopped the tome onto the kitchen table and started rifling through the pages.

"I know what it says," I growled. I'd bought a copy of it myself, the day before. A professional has to stay

abreast of developments in his field, don't you know?
And *Jane's The World's Perps* is the definitive record.

"Here it is, right at the beginning of the section on
stranglers. 'Greyboar. Category: Professional. Class:
Super-heavyweight. Rating: AAA.' And there's—"

"I know what it says!"

"—even an addendum. And I quote: 'Our AAA
rating may well be obsolete, as by all accounts the
chokester often known as "The Thumbs of Eternity"
perhaps requires his own AAAA rating. With the possible exception of Ozar's Pythoneus—' "

"That twerp!" I grit my teeth. "That poseur! No way
he's—"

Angela blithely drove over me: " '—no other strangler currently in practice can be considered in the same
league.' "

She closed the book with a flourish. "So there!"

While she'd been talking, Jenny had left. Now she
came back into the kitchen, clutching another book.
A very slender volume, with the kind of loose-leaf
binding where you can remove the separate pages.

I recognized that one also, of course, and didn't
know whether to laugh or cry. Or scream.

I settled for growling. "You shouldn't be spending
money on that kind of useless stuff."

"We earn enough from our sewing!" snapped Jenny.
She plopped the book onto the table next to the other.
A mouse next to an elephant.

"This is the one we'd *really* like to see you guys in,"
said Angela, softly. "You'd even get mentioned yourself, Ignace, right there in the text, instead of just being
a footnote."

I curled my lip. "Yeah, sure I would. For about a
month." I marched up to the table and flipped open
the new book. Then, pointed to the binding.

"You wanna know why it's loose-leaf?" I demanded.

"That's because the thing is obsolete the day it comes out of the printers. Half of everybody in it is already dead. Or crippled or maimed or locked in a lunatic asylum or being exorcised on account of they're possessed by demons."

I gave the book my very finest sneer. "*Jane's The World's Heroes, Champions, Knights-Errant, Paladins, Gallants, Chevaliers, Lion-Hearts, Valiants, Exemplars, Beau Ideals, Paragons, Non-Plus-Ultras, Shining Lights, And Other Loose Screws And Goofballs.* Ha! Fat chance!"

Angela shook her head fiercely. "It's different! Greyboar could do it!"

"So could you," murmured Jenny. Her finger stroked the open pages. "You'd be real good at it, Ignace. Really you would, if you put your mind to it."

"That's right!" chimed in Angela. "And you guys could survive too!"

"Survive *what?* Monsters and mayhem and murtherous demons? Maybe." I planted my hands on the table and gave them my superb man-of-the-world stare. "Did you look at the *companion* volume? The one that takes a wheelbarrow to haul around?"

Silence. But they were still glaring at me. Unreasonable women!

Again, my magnificent sneer. "Oh, sure. *Jane's The World's Toast.* Last edition I saw was up to four thousand pages. And guess what's listed as the cause of death, more often than not?"

Still glaring. As bad as Gwendolyn!

"Starvation, that's what! Or falling under the talons of a chicken due to weakness from beriberi and dysentery!" I really put the sneer into overdrive. "I can see it already. Me and Greyboar staggering through the Flankn, with signs around our necks. 'Will derring-do for food.'"

Still glaring!

"*You* could do it," insisted Jenny. Her voice was soft, but firm for all that. "You *could!*" chipped in Angela. More tempestuous, as usual.

The silent standoff that followed lasted for maybe a minute or so. Then I turned and stalked out of the kitchen. Once in the little living room, I plunked myself down in a chair and glared at the wall, my arms crossed over my chest.

After a while, Jenny and Angela drifted into the room. I ignored them for a bit, until Angela plopped herself in my lap and gave me a big kiss. That was hard to ignore. So were Jenny's hands, rubbing my shoulders.

"S'okay," murmured Angela. "We love you anyway. And you're a hero to us, even if you're a perp to the rest of the world."

"It's not fair," I muttered. "Pay's good. Work's steady."

Jenny kissed the top of my head. "And what else do you ever get in this world?"

"Not fair," I repeated. "I never asked for any damned philosophy."

By now they were pretty much impossible to ignore, and I discovered I wasn't trying anymore. Rather the opposite, actually. Sometime later, Jenny went back to the kitchen to do something or other. After a bit, Angela followed. Before she left, she kissed me and whispered: "You guys could do it. Jenny and I know you could."

Not fair!

It was a very nice feast. Even if I wasn't in a good mood. Over the brandy afterward—I bought it, without anybody even pestering me—the Cat rose and made a toast.

"Here's to adventure!"

I kept my mouth shut, shut, shut, shut. Greyboar, of course, slurped down the toast and so did Jenny and Angela.

Then the Cat continued: "I think you should definitely take up the Abbess' invitation."

I groaned. Silently, I think. I'm not sure, because the minute the Cat made that announcement Jenny and Angela were chattering like magpies wanting to know what it was about. As soon as they found out, they immediately joined in with the Cat pushing the silly idea on Greyboar. I squawked and protested, but it was no use. Greyboar caved in right away. I swear, the man was an absolute patsy in the hands of women!

Then, naturally—I saw this coming a mile away—Jenny and Angela wanted to go along. The Cat said she couldn't herself, on account of looking for Schrödinger, but she thought it was a great idea. Then, naturally, Greyboar caved in again.

Then, naturally, Jenny and Angela wanted to travel to the Abbey on horseback. Fastest way to get there, they said. But at least here Greyboar put his foot down.

"Not a chance," he said. "First of all, you girls have never ridden a horse in your lives. Second, the critters always get surly, having to carry me. And Ignace doesn't see eye to eye with the beasts, either. They take one look at him and figure why should they take orders from this character who isn't much bigger than a lump of sugar." (I resented that, even though it was true.) "So we'll hire a coach. A big one. What the hell? The Abbess said she'd pay the travel expenses."

A big one, I thought sourly. *Translation: expensive.*

But I didn't say anything. Although my tone was probably surly when I said I'd go out and rent one. The one bright spot in the whole thing was that I figured I could hire Oscar and his gang to drive the great thing. Sure, they were all a bunch of kids, who usually hauled people around in their home-built rickshaws. But even at his age—eleven, he was then— Oscar was as good as a professional teamster.

The following day, around lunchtime, I went out looking for Oscar. I found him in the stable where he and his boys usually hang out, not far from The Trough.

And discovered that my "bright spot" had become a conflagration.

I'd always known Hrundig was probably as strong as a bull. But "knowing" in the abstract is one thing. Having your arms clamped to your chest and his iron-bar forearm ready to crush your throat is something else entirely.

I think I may have gurgled. Not sure. My vision was getting blurry and I could barely see anything in the dark interior of the stable. Just enough to see Olga Frissault and her daughters huddling fearfully in one of the stalls. Oscar and his lads were huddling in another. They didn't look fearful. They looked terrified.

I heard a grunt behind me, and the pressure left my chest and throat. "Sorry, Ignace," Hrundig muttered. "Didn't realize it was you."

I took a couple of steps forward, gasping for breath. "Who'd you think it was?" I complained, massaging my throat. "How many red-headed, freckled footpads are there, less than five feet tall?" I suspect my tone was, ah, peevish.

By now, Hrundig had padded around to stand in front of me. He had that thin, merciless grin on his face.

"None, that I know of. But there's probably a thousand informers in the city fit your description. Close enough, anyway."

My eyes flicked back and forth from him to the

Frissault women. I didn't understand anything of what was happening, mind you. But I am:

1. Not stupid.
2. Pessimistic.
3. A student of the wise man. Among whose saws, of course, is the classic: "Never try to think of the worst thing that could happen. It's bound to be worse than that anyway."

"No," I groaned. My mind raced like wild horses, trying to think of the worst. "Olga and the girls are Joeist heretics, fleeing from the Inquisition."

Hrundig grinned. "Dead on the money. But it's worse than that, Ignace. They were found out and arrested two weeks ago. Judge Jeffreys set their bail at two hundred thousand quid, no doubt on the assumption that nobody could come up with that kind of money. I wracked my brains trying to figure out a way to spring them, but it was impossible. You know what the Durance Pile is like. Take an army to break into it."

My mind raced like the wind, trying to think of the worst. "Somebody figured out a way to do it. You? Must have robbed the Royal Treasury."

Hrundig shook his head again. "Worse. Benvenuti came up with the bail money. Got them out yesterday before Jeffreys got wind of what was happening, and turned them over to me."

My mind raced like a hurricane, trying to think of the worst. "He defrauded a noble client," I croaked. "The Queen herself."

Hrundig's grin widened. "Worse. He defrauded the Church. Cardinal Megatherio in particular, but the whole Church is in a frenzy because he—ah! Never mind the details."

My mind raced like a meteor, trying to think of the worst. "He's on the run. All the forces of Church and State are out looking for him. And the Frissaults too."

The headshake was inevitable. "Worse. They already caught him. He led them a merry chase, but he figured he could draw the pursuit away from me and Olga and the girls long enough for us to find a hiding place. Which he did. But now he's in the hands of the Inquisition."

My mind raced like—like—

Hrundig laughed. "Relax, Ignace! You take the wise man too seriously. Benvenuti won't be spilling his guts yet. He told me he was sure he could hold out for at least a day before he started lying. Another day before they untangled his lies, and another before he'd have to spill the truth. Which gives me two days to figure out a way to get Olga and the girls out of town. I'll have to leave too, of course. No way to keep my involvement a secret."

He moved his eyes away from me, and looked over at Oscar and his friends. "I brought us here because I knew Oscar and the boys could be trusted. And since it's a stable, maybe we could jury-rig some way to get us out of town without being spotted."

His smile was no longer in evidence. "It's not looking good, though. None of the vehicles in this claptrap place are anywhere big enough. Not for all of us. But I'm hoping I might still get the girls out. Olga and I will take our chances."

I started choking. Hrundig cocked a quizzical eye.

"The hell I take the wise man too seriously!" I snarled. Then, feeling lightheaded, I squatted down, crossed my arms over my chest, and glared at the straw-strewn dirt of the stable floor.

" 'Never try to think of the worst thing that could happen,' " I mimicked in a mutter. " 'It's bound to be worse than that anyway.' "

The worst!

"What's your problem?" demanded Hrundig.

"It's not fair!" I exclaimed. "I never asked for any damned—"

I bit it off. What was the point? Sighing heavily, I came back up to my feet. "Never you worry, Hrundig. I'll get you out of here."

I crooked a finger at Oscar and the boys. "Come on, lads. I'll need you to pick out the right one."

Not fair!

Chapter 11.

Not Fair!

We left early the next morning.

The worst of it was having Jenny and Angela hugging me the whole time, like the world's most wonderful teddy bear. Well. Okay, *that* part wasn't bad. It was that I knew Hrundig would be able to hear all the gibbering nonsense they were babbling.

No way he couldn't, after all. He and the Frissault women were hidden in the fake compartment which Oscar and the boys had jury-rigged in the largest coach we'd been able to find. Right under the seat where Jenny and Angela and I were perched. With every single trunk and valise we'd been able to buy, filled with every piece of clothing we owned and a lot more we'd bought and all of Jenny and Angela's seamstress supplies. Even the cavernous interior of *that* coach was packed to the gills. In order to search the whole thing, the porkers would have to work like coolies.

I'd never hear the end of it! I could see Hrundig's

cold grin already, and hear the derision. *Hero, is it? Man of their dreams, no less!*

"Don't get any ideas," I snarled, for maybe the hundredth time. "This is just an exception!"

"Our hero," whispered Jenny, kissing my cheek. "Man of our dreams," murmured Angela, running her fingers through my hair.

I glared at Greyboar, sprawled on the opposite seat. He returned my glare with what you could call an insouciant shrug, if the term "insouciant" can be applied to someone with shoulders like a buffalo.

Insult was added to injury. "What the hell, Ignace?" he drawled. "It's entropy, that's all."

Truth to tell, the lunatic escapade went off pretty much without a hitch. There was a spot of trouble at the Northwest Gate. By then, the authorities in the whole city were on a rampage, and even the lazy guards at the gate were on what passed for an "alert." So they stopped the coach and started making noises about a search.

Not much of a hassle, really. Greyboar climbed out of the coach and explained to the guards—there were six of them—that he was really in a bad mood that morning, on account of how his breakfast hadn't agreed with him, and that if they didn't open the gate in five seconds he was going to turn them into Queen's Guard au gratin. He shredded their pikes by way of illustration.

The guards made the deadline. On our way through, Greyboar leaned his head out of the window and suggested that the guards might find it healthy to forget the incident. His suggestion was accompanied with the whole recipe for *purée d'imbécile officieux*. But it's a short and simple recipe. I'm sure the guards had no trouble remembering all of it.

It was a nice outing, actually, at least for the first day. I'm not normally the type who enjoys the great outdoors, as I believe I've mentioned. Smell of the wildflowers, all that rot. My idea of a proper backpacking expedition is struggling my way from one smoke-filled room into another, hauling a full pot of ale.

But still, it was nice. Autumn had arrived, and the leaves were turning color. And, if nothing else, outwitting the authorities always put me in a good mood.

Quite a nice inn where we spent the night, too. Very comfortable lodgings, and the ale was surprisingly good. Not up to Trough standards, of course, but I've led a rough life, learned to survive in the wilderness. And once we saw how lazy the innkeeper was, we realized we'd be able to smuggle Hrundig and the Frissault family into our rooms, so they'd even be able to get a good night's rest.

The next morning we set out for the Abbey. Since we would soon be entering Joe's Favorite Woods, we had to find a guide. Whatever their skills as teamsters, Oscar and his partners were city kids. They'd get lost in a cornfield, much less a primeval forest. But it didn't take me long to find a local peasant who was willing to ride along and show us the way.

By midafternoon, we were well into Joe's Favorite Woods. I was wondering if the peasant would squawk at that, since Joe's Favorite Woods had been declared forbidden territory by the Queen. Violation of whose edict is a crime punishable by etc., etc., etc., etc.

But it soon became clear that the Queen's edict didn't seem to faze the native folk any. Our peasant guide never blinked an eye when I told him our destination. And, along the way, I saw many a local lad in the forests with bow in hand. Made sense, of course—who was going to stop them from poaching the Queen's game? Game wardens had been banned, too.

The only problem with the whole trip came at the end. Late in the afternoon, when—by my estimate—we weren't but a few miles from the Abbey, our guide ordered Oscar to stop the coach. Greyboar and I climbed out to see what the problem was.

"This is as far as you can go," he pronounced. "Across that little bridge"—he pointed to a span over a small creek, just a few yards ahead—"and you're on Abbey land. Can't take a coach on Abbey land."

Greyboar frowned. "What's the problem? You've already broken the Queen's writ, coming this far."

The guide sneered. "Piss on the Queen's writ." He thought a moment, added: "Piss on the Queen." He thought a moment more, added: "Piss on the whole Royal Family."

"Then what's the problem?" I asked.

"It's the horses," explained the guide. "They'll bolt if you try to get them to cross the bridge. On account of the snarl scent."

"*Snarls?*" This came from me. I've met a snarl close up, I have. And while the great monster was pleasant enough, once the wizard's apprentice quieted her down, it was still one of those experiences you'd like to keep in the "once in a lifetime" category.

"Sure, snarls," said the peasant. "The Abbey's land is packed with 'em. Forest snarls, to boot. They don't never bother the local lads, mind you, as long as they keep their poaching off the Abbey's land. But woe betide the man who crosses that line!" Here he launched into a long and gruesome tale regarding the various fatal mishaps encountered by local yokels over the years who'd made the mistake of trying to fill their larder on the Abbey's land.

"O' course," he concluded, "the snarls got a little sloppy about enforcing the rule, after the Seventh Cavaliers went in. And after the Third Royal

Regiment—well! For a few weeks there, you could poach anywhere to your heart's content. Skin a deer right under a snarl's great snout, you could, the monsters were so fat they couldna hardly walk. But they've slimmed down since, and the rule's been back in place for years."

"What about us?" I demanded. "How are we supposed to get to the Abbey, mobbed by forest snarls?"

"Oh, you won't be bothered, long as you stay on the road. Lots of local folks been up to the Abbey, over the years. They make most of what they need for themselves, do the Sisters of Tranquility, but still and all, there's always the odd tidbit now and then. But whenever we make a delivery, it's always got to be on foot. Horses'll panic as soon as they cross the bridge. Mules and ox teams, too."

Well, there was nothing for it. I paid the guide and he ambled off, back down the road. As soon as he was out of sight, we gave Hrundig the signal. After he and the Frissaults climbed out of their hiding place, we started unloading the luggage we'd actually need for our stay at the Abbey. Most of the stuff we left with Oscar and his friends. I also gave them enough money to buy whatever food supplies they'd need while they waited for us to return. I wasn't even my usual tightfisted self about it.

That done, we set off toward the Abbey. Within a minute or two, we'd crossed the bridge and were into the heart of the forest.

Not happy, I wasn't. Not happy at all. The road wasn't bad, actually, for a dirt road. But still and all, it was a two-hour hike. And I believe I've made my sentiments regarding this sort of mindless exercise clear enough.

But the worst of it was the snarls. Sure, and you didn't really see them much. Masters of camouflage, your snarls. It's amazing, really, you'd never think creatures of their size could keep themselves so invisible. But they can, except for the odd glimpse of a vague motion, a rustle in the woods, and so on and so on and so on and so on and so on and so on. Lots and lots of rustles, there were.

"How can they survive, as many as all that?" demanded Greyboar.

"Probably starving by now," opined Hrundig. It was a thought I wished he'd kept to himself, especially after the sun went down. It was incredible, the number of snarls there must have been in that forest. You could see dozens of pairs of their great eyes, shining in the dark. Looking at us.

Olga and her daughters stayed very close to Hrundig and Greyboar the whole way. For their part, Jenny and Angela were walking huddled against me, their arms wrapped around my waist. I enjoyed the closeness, of course. But, to be honest, I enjoyed their newfound trepidation even more.

Adventure—ha!

I would have made a sarcastic remark or two. But Jenny told me if I made a sarcastic remark or two that she'd bite my ear off (or two) and Angela muttered sullen phrases about the relationship between discretion and valor and I decided to forgo the pleasure.

You can believe me, I was never so happy in my life as I was when we spotted the lights of the Abbey up ahead. I would have broken into a run, but I was determined to maintain my dignity in front of the womenfolk, cost me what it would.

At least we weren't kept waiting out there in the dark. I had just started to rap on the great door to the Abbey—rapped very, very firmly, I did, you can be sure of it—when it opened wide. Before us stood a Sister of Tranquility.

I was startled by her appearance. Of course, I knew that the Abbess Hildegard advocated a most unorthodox theology. But I'd never really given much thought to the ins and outs of it. Theology's not really my forte, don't you know?

Not that the Sister's clothing wasn't eminently proper, mind you. They aren't given to Dionysian deviations, the Sisters of Tranquility. Their theology was, I soon discovered, offensive to the Ecclesiarchy in much more fundamental ways. It's just that I'd had a mental image in my head, on the way to the Abbey, of what the Sisters would look like. You know. Withered, dried-up faces, pale as ghosts (what little you could see of them under the great black robes), severe frowns, lips tight as a banker's heart, you know, the usual.

So I hadn't expected this very attractive, very cheerful middle-aged woman, dressed in a snug green outfit that looked like a combined jacket and pants. Wearing a garland on her head, which didn't begin to cover the long sun-bleached light brown hair. And I certainly hadn't expected the dimples.

"May I help you?" she asked pleasantly.

Greyboar replied, "I'm Greyboar. I believe I'm supposed to meet with the Abbess Hildegard."

"Oh, yes!" exclaimed the Sister. "She'll be delighted to see you. We really hadn't expected you for another day or so."

Greyboar started to make a fumbling explanation for the presence of the others in our party, but the Sister was already striding away.

"Just follow me," she commanded. "The Abbess is in the salon with the composers." Greyboar and I looked at each other, shrugged, and did as we were told. The others came after us, with Hrundig closing the door. A very casual setup, they seemed to have here!

The Sister led the way through a labyrinth of corridors and rooms. Big place, the Abbey. Quite well lit, and very—how can I put it?—well, sort of much more spacious and airylike than I'd expected. Not at all the gloomy, cramped quarters I'd always imagined an Abbey would look like, on the occasions I'd thought about the subject in the past. On the rare occasions I'd thought about it. Well, the one or two occasions when the thought of what an Abbey would look like had crossed my mind. For maybe the odd second or two.

As we went down the final corridor, heading toward a big set of double doors at the end, we began hearing piano music coming from beyond. By the time we got to the doors, the music was very loud. And very beautiful.

"That's one of the Grump's intermezzos," said Olga. "Love that piece. It's being played beautifully, too."

The Sister looked at her like she was crazy. "Well, of course the Grump can play his own music beautifully!" she exclaimed. She opened the door and strode through.

Following her, we found ourselves in a very large room. There were maybe a dozen people seated on chairs toward the center of the room, in a semicircle around a grand piano. At the piano, playing, sat a short, pudgy man with a great beard.

"I'll be damned," I whispered to Greyboar. "It's the Grump." I recognized him, of course. Years back, he'd come into The Trough more than a few times, before he shook the dust of New Sfinctr off his feet for good.

"That's not the least of it," whispered back Greyboar. "Gramps is here too. So's the Blockhead. And—I don't believe it! Look! It's the Big Banjo!"

Sure enough, it was the Big Banjo, sitting in a chair. His back was straight as a ramrod. He was watching the Grump play with that hawk-faced intensity which would make him stand out in any crowd even if you didn't know who he was.

"The Fallen Woman's with him," whispered Olga. She almost sounded awestruck. "I've always wanted to meet her. But, you know, she hardly ever leaves their villa."

Soon enough, the music ended. The Sister approached the group.

"Pardon me, Hildegard," she said. "I hate to interrupt, but Greyboar's here."

"So soon?" came a voice clear as a chime. A figure arose.

I'd been so surprised to see the Big Banjo that I hadn't really looked at any of the other occupants of the room. But now my attention was drawn completely to the woman who was advancing toward us, smiling broadly, her hands outstretched in a gesture of warm welcome.

Quite a striking woman she would have been, anyway, what with her beautiful white hair and a face that positively radiated intelligence. She wore a very nice outfit, too, much like the other Sisters but with a certain elegance of the cut that was quite noticeable.

But mainly, it was her size. She was at least seven and a half feet tall! I realized then that I hadn't noticed her sitting down because I'd assumed she'd been standing.

She wasn't built along the same lines as Greyboar— none of his obscene massiveness, you'll understand— but she still seemed to dwarf him, stooping over and clasping him like he was her long-lost brother. And when she got to me—well!

The damned woman picked me up! Like I was some kind of toddler! There I was, held up in her huge hands, while she inspected me.

"And this must be Ignace! Why, he's such a sweet-looking little cherub of a man! All those freckles! Doesn't look at all like the evil imp Gwendolyn described."

Right then, alarm bells started going off in my head. I knew it! I knew it! I knew there was something fishy about this job!

We'd been suckered!

Not fair!

Chapter 12.
The Trouble With Sisters

"Gwendolyn?" asked Greyboar, his jaw sagging. "My sister?"

The Abbess looked at him. "Of course, Gwendolyn. How else would I have gotten your name and address?" She frowned. "Surely you don't think I keep a list of the world's great chokesters in my study? After all! I *am* the Abbess of the Sisters of Tranquility."

"Gwendolyn?" he repeated. "My sister?" His jaw was now down to his chest.

The Abbess' frown grew deeper. "Oh, dear," she said, "Gwendolyn told me you were a stupid jackass. But I just thought she was being harsh and unforgiving, like she usually is. I didn't realize she meant you were actually retarded."

Greyboar's jaw snapped shut. He glowered.

"That dirty, rotten—" He stopped, but the glower didn't.

"Oh, what a relief," sighed the Abbess. "It would

have been difficult, the job ahead, with a moron for a chokester."

Time for the agent to take center stage. "And just exactly what is this job you—"

But she cut me off with a gesture. "Oh, not tonight! Tomorrow we'll have plenty of time to discuss the job. Actually, we'll need most of the day to get everything prepared. We really weren't expecting you so soon. But no business tonight! Tonight is for music."

Her gaze now moved to Olga Frissault, who was listening to the music with rapt attention. "I'm afraid I've not been introduced to your companions," the Abbess said pleasantly.

Greyboar and I both flushed. Well, he did. So I can only assume that I did also, since my skin is about as fair as any redhead's ever gets.

"Sorry," I muttered. Then, I hesitated. On the outs or not, the Abbess was still part of the Church. I wasn't at all sure how she was going to react to the presence of outright heretics—especially Joeists!—even if Olga had insisted that there wouldn't be any problems.

As it happened, Olga herself took the plunge.

"I'm Olga Frissault, and these are my daughters," she announced quietly. "I'm the widow of—"

"*Dreadful!*" exclaimed the Abbess. "Absolutely dreadful!" She reared up to her full towering height, glaring furiously. I braced myself for a ruckus.

"Bad enough the Inquisition should treat anyone in that manner!" the Abbess snapped. "But to have done so to one of Grotum's greatest artists! Dreadful!"

A moment later she was giving Olga that giantess embrace. Then, the girls. As huge as she was, Hildegard managed to hug all three of them in one swoop.

My jaw was probably hanging loose. The Frissault woman was the widow of an *artist*? A famous one, to boot? Plump, cheerful, unassuming *Olga*? The same Olga who had a thing going with a rude and crude *barbarian*?

What was the world coming to?!

Then I remembered the way Olga had browbeaten the lackeys in that exclusive lodge, and all those weird little ways in which Hrundig didn't fit the image of a proper Alsask. And then—finally—the name registered.

Frissault? *That* Frissault? One of the few artists I'd ever actually heard of?! One of Grotum's most famous national martyrs?! *Olga's* husband?!

I was probably muttering to myself. I *hate* being caught unawares, like some kind of country bumpkin. However, while I was staggering to catch up, things were progressing apace.

"You'll be seeking asylum, of course," the Abbess announced. "In the Mutt, eventually, I should think. But, for the moment, welcome to the Abbey. You'll be quite safe here, until whatever arrangements you need can be made for your further travels. Or, if you prefer, you may stay here indefinitely."

Olga was smiling now. Then, chuckling. "You *do* understand, Abbess, that we are Joeists. So we're in the odd position of seeking asylum in a Church institution from—ah, from—"

"The Lord Almighty Himself," finished Hildegard. "I fail to see the problem. Really! Sauce for the gander, sauce for the goose. It would be quite unethical for the Old Geister to insist on being made an Exception to His own rules, now wouldn't it?"

My brain groped with the peculiar logic involved with that last remark. I'm no theologian, to put it mildly, but I always thought the whole point of the exercise was that God *was* the exception to the rules. But Hildegard didn't leave me any time to flounder.

She had already embraced Hrundig and Jenny and Angela, and was turning away, motioning all of us to follow.

"Come," she commanded. "Let me introduce you to the others."

When we were introduced to the Blockhead, he gave us a polite but distant greeting. A fierce-looking man, he was. I was awestruck, myself. Everybody says he's the world's greatest composer. Except when they say that Gramps is the world's greatest composer, and he was the one we were introduced to next. Now Gramps was another kettle of fish entirely. He was one of the nicest and friendliest old gents you'll ever run into, whether or not he or the Blockhead is the world's greatest composer. Which is what everybody argues about except when they're arguing that the Deadbeat is the world's greatest composer, and he was the one we were introduced to next. Huh! Maybe he is the world's greatest composer, I wouldn't know. But he was certainly a silly little chap. Vulgar, too.

But the truth is, like most lowlifes, my taste runs to opera. And so the big thrill of the evening was being introduced to the Big Banjo and his old lady.

We'd met before, actually, but under the circumstances at the time I was sure he wouldn't have noticed us in the crowd.

I was wrong. He interrupted the Abbess halfway through the introduction.

"I am already acquainted with the gentlemen, Hildegard," he said. "In point of fact, I am deeply in their debt. These two were among the stalwarts who defended me at The Sign of the Trough upon that occasion when the Ecclesiarchs' lackeys set upon me in the streets of New Sfinctr. Outraged, they were, at the implications of my latest opera. Fortunately, 'twas close to the Flankn, so I was able to effect my escape.

Even so, it would have been sticky had it not been for the proper Trough-men."

"Wasn't just us," rumbled Greyboar modestly. "Whole Flankn turned out, once the word spread. Gave the bootlickers quite the drubbing, we did." Greyboar actually blushed a little. "Nothing really, for the national hero of Grotum."

About the only thing that would arouse Greyboar's very, very, very faint tinge of pan-Groutchery was the Big Banjo's music. The chorus, sure, like everybody else, but he actually knew most of the other operas, too. Fortunately, he didn't sing them.

The Big Banjo studied Greyboar intently. "Gwendolyn's brother, are you not?"

Mutely, Greyboar nodded. The Big Banjo cocked his head a bit. "You wouldn't, by any chance, have any of your sister's vocal talent?"

I choked. Greyboar grinned. The Big Banjo sighed.

"Pity," he mused. "I've written the most splendid opera especially for her voice. She sang a few arias from it, when she and that marvelous Benvenuti fellow arrived in the Mutt some time ago. Months and months, it's been now."

He shook his head ruefully. "But—you know Gwendolyn! She spurned all my pleas. Said she'd only return to singing after the revolution triumphed."

Greyboar wasn't grinning anymore. I looked down at the parquet floor. Scowling fiercely, I imagine. Of all my memories of Gwendolyn, her voice probably hit the sorest spot.

Especially when she sang. No woman in the world had a voice like Gwendolyn's. Sure as hell not when she was cutting loose with it. A *contralto profundo*, you could call it—and strong enough to shake whole buildings.

When we were kids, we always figured she'd wind

up in the opera house. That was our dream, actually. I'd be her manager and Greyboar'd be her bodyguard. Then—

Sigh. Then one of the pogroms hit. A family of dwarves scurried into our ramshackle little house, begging for mercy and shelter. There was a small mob pounding on their heels, led by a handful of monks.

Greyboar and I hesitated, but Gwendolyn was out the door with her cleaver before the dwarves got more than two sentences out. Sixteen years old, she was then, but she'd already reached her full size. The monk at the head of the mob got his head split before he screeched two words out. "Split," as in pumpkin.

Then the rest of the mob started swarming Gwendolyn, and the issue of hesitation was a moot point. By the time it was all over, what was left of the mob was in what they call "full retreat." Between them, Greyboar and Gwendolyn must have mangled a good dozen, including all four of the monks. I did for a couple of the pogromists myself. Small as I was, even at that age I knew how to use a knife in close quarters better than just about anybody except maybe your best muggers.

Sigh. That's when all our plans went right off the cliff. Because Gwendolyn wasn't satisfied with just rescuing the dwarves. She insisted on escorting them to the nearest refuge, and before you knew it she was involved with the Underground Railroad herself, and before she knew it she'd joined up with the revolution and The Roach, and before you knew it—

Sigh.

Fortunately, an interruption arrived to break the mood of the moment.

"The heart of the Flankn, is *The* Trough," came a new voice. It was the Grump, extending his hand.

"I am also acquainted with the gentlemen," he said,

"an acquaintance I shall enjoy renewing. It's the one thing I still regret about leaving my hometown. Best ale in the world, The Trough's."

That lightened things up quite a bit, talking about ale instead of Gwendolyn. And, as it turned out, it really was a great evening once we got over our shyness at being in such august company.

Really august company, you understand. Kings and nobles and bishops be damned, Greyboar and I sneered at 'em once we took their money. These were composers! Really pretty much like average blokes, once you got to know them. Especially Gramps. He was like everybody's favorite great-uncle that they wished they had but didn't.

The next morning we had a wonderful breakfast. The food was great, but what was even better was that we were serenaded by a small ensemble playing one of the Deadbeat's divertimenti. With the Deadbeat himself conducting! He seemed much the more pleasant individual in the morning. I decided to write off his gaucheries the night before to too much drink. A terrible thing, too much drink. I know whereof I speak.

A leisurely pace, they had at the Abbey. It wasn't until midafternoon that Greyboar and I were summoned to Hildegard's study by one of the Sisters. The invitation didn't actually include Jenny and Angela, but they came along anyway and the Sister didn't make any objection.

The Sister led the way, in and around and back and forth and up this flight of stairs and down that one and back around and back up another flight of stairs—etc., etc. I was totally lost after three minutes. It really was a huge place, the Abbey. Much bigger than it had looked the night before in the dark.

But finally we were ushered into Hildegard's study.

It was quite a room, that study. Enormous, it was, with floor-to-ceiling bookcases covering two of the walls. A great bay window on a third wall opened onto the Woods beyond. The last wall was only half a wall, because there was a huge alcove leading off, filled with what looked at first glance like tombstones, oddly enough. Then I saw small flames flickering amid the stones, and decided it must be some kind of peculiar fireplace.

In the center of the room, just slightly off toward the window, was the Abbess' desk. Like everything else in the room, the desk was built to large scale. Beautiful desk, made of maple or cherry or some kind of fancy wood. Covered with papers.

All this, however, I noticed later. Upon first entering the room, my attention was immediately drawn to the floor, which was completely covered by a thick rug.

Most of which rug was not actually visible, because it was covered in turn with a gigantic snarl.

Our eyes, you can well imagine, were focused entirely on the snarl. Well, my eyes and Greyboar's. Angela and Jenny were huddled behind us, pressed close. Although I'm sure they were peeking within seconds. Curiosity always overrode everything else with those two, even outright terror.

The first time I'd ever seen a snarl close up it was lunging at me with its great maw agape, roaring and bellowing with rage. Bit sticky that would have been, even with Greyboar on the scene, if it hadn't turned out that the wizard Zulkeh's apprentice—a dwarf kid named Shelyid, I believe I've mentioned him before—was a snarl-friend. If you're wondering what a snarl-friend is, just stick around. You'll find out soon.

This snarl presented quite a different image. It was lying there—she, to be precise, and it pays to be precise when it comes to snarls—for all the world like a tabby cat. Lying on her side, stretched out, dozing. When we came in, the monster awoke from her snooze, raised her head, eyed us once, yawned (horrible sight, that, really is), and went back to sleep.

"Do come in!" exclaimed Hildegard, looking up from her desk. She was apparently in the middle of writing a letter.

Greyboar coughed. "Wouldn't want to disturb the snarl, we wouldn't."

"What?" asked Hildegard. She looked down at the monster. "Oh, nonsense, you won't disturb her. Quite difficult to disturb a snarl, actually. Especially Rose, she's really the most even-tempered snarl I know."

"I didn't think they could be tamed," I mumbled.

The Abbess frowned. "Oh, dear. Gwendolyn told me you were a wicked little man, but I actually got the impression that you were quite bright. I must have misunderstood her."

She pursed her lips, thinking, then continued:

"Oh, well. I suppose it won't be much of a problem, having a moron of an agent present. Although I would have thought someone in your occupation would need more brains than a rabbit."

The odd thing was, I wasn't even offended. The Abbess had this way of being offensive without—I don't quite know how to put it—without there being anything personal in it. You got the impression that the fact she thought you were an imbecile wasn't meant as a slur on you, it was just a fact that had to be taken into account.

Offended or not, I set her straight. "I'm as smart as a whip!" I exclaimed. "And I know snarls can't be tamed. I should know! Didn't I have to listen to an endless lecture by the wizard Zulkeh on the subject? Complete with footnotes and bibliographic citations! It's just that—"

She rose to her feet with excitement. "You've met Zulkeh? When? Where? I've been trying to reach him for months!"

I shook my head, trying to clear it. The Abbess seemed to have this thing about going off on tangents. Greyboar answered her.

"We met him in Prygg. Last year. After—well, after concluding some business with him there, we traveled together with him for part of our way back to New Sfinctr. He and his apprentice, Shelyid. We parted company with them in Blain. They were headed south to the Mutt."

"The Mutt?" She frowned, then sighed. "Of course, of course. On his way to see Uncle Manya, I suppose."

She wasn't dumb, that was sure. Tangent-brained, maybe, but not dumb.

"That's right," rumbled Greyboar.

"Oh, dear. Oh, dear. I suppose it's too late now, then."

"Too late for what?" I demanded.

She looked at me for a moment, as if deciding something.

"Well, I suppose there can't be any harm in telling you. You must already know, anyway. You see, Zulkeh's gotten himself mixed up in the Joe business."

I knew it! I knew we should have passed up this job! Anything involves Gwendolyn, it's going to get you into the Big Soup Pot, sure as sunrise.

"That's why I was trying to reach him while he was still in Goimr," continued the Abbess. "I sent him a letter, warning him to steer clear of the thing. I knew if he dug into it, Zulkeh would break open the Joe problem before the world was ready. He's a terribly talented mage, you know, but without the sense of a chicken. Sorcerous bungling raised to the level of genius."

She eased herself back into the chair, chuckling rather ruefully. "Not that he probably would have heeded me. He's as stubborn as he is maladroit. But, it's all a moot point anyway. The message apparently never reached him. It was returned to me."

Here she frowned fiercely. "Impudent rascals! Look at this!" She dug into a desk drawer and drew forth a letter. The letter had been torn open, then resealed. A crude outline of a black hand had been drawn on the outside.

"My letter was opened by the authorities in Goimr. They sent it back to me, with an accompanying note saying that the wizard Zulkeh was under death sentence in Goimr—there's some new regime there now, it seems—and warning me to avoid any further contact with him. Can you believe the cheek? Even threatened my life, the silly fools. Warned me of the 'wrath of the Black Hand of Goimr.' "

"What's the 'Black Hand of Goimr'?" asked Angela, finally able to overcome her fear of the snarl.

Hildegard shrugged. "Who knows? Who cares? Just another ridiculous little death squad, I assume. Probably be sending assassins to the Abbey, I don't doubt, like all the others." She smiled, like a saint. "Hope so, really, it keeps the snarls from getting too hungry."

As if to register her own agreement, the snarl lying on the rug cracked her eyes open a bit and yawned. A ghastly great red tongue licked a gruesome great pink maw. Horrible sight, really.

But I had other things to worry about than a mere snarl. "We don't want no part of any Joe business!" I shrilled. "Got enough of that in Prygg! You didn't say nothing about Joe business in your letter!"

Jenny piped up. "I don't understand what this is all about. Who's Joe?"

Everyone stared at her. Then, at Angela, after Angela

piped up: "Yeah. Me too. I've heard his name mentioned before. But who *is* this guy, anyway?"

I was surprised, until I remembered that most people don't know about Joe. Which really *isn't* surprising, of course, when you consider that Joe is the ultimate heresy and even whispering his name in the wrong place can get you burned at the stake. What's left of you.

The Abbess was frowning. "I declare! What kind of education are they giving children these days?" She planted her hands on the desk in front of her and leaned forward a bit.

"Joe, my dear girl, is the man who invented God. Way back in the ancient times."

She hesitated, pursing her lips. "Well, I suppose I shouldn't call him a 'man,' perhaps. The scholars are in dispute over the matter. Those of them who've managed to avoid the Inquisition, anyway. He was one of the Old Groutch, you know, those ancient cave dwellers in Grotum who were possibly our ancestors. Or possibly not. As I say, the scholars are still wrangling ferociously over the thing. 'Leaky' Sfondrati-Piccolomini claims they were, but Johansen Laebmauntsforscynneweëld insists they were a collateral branch who went extinct with no issue. And there are other theories. A host of them! For instance—"

She broke off, seeing Angela and Jenny's jaws agape.

"But, my dear girls—surely you can't be surprised! *Somebody* had to invent the Old Geister, after all. Why shouldn't it have been a caveman named Joe? I assure you the theological reasoning is impeccable."

Jenny was almost spluttering. "But—but—He's *God.*"

Hildegard frown deepened. "Of course He's God. The Lord Almighty, and all that. What of it? Somebody still had to invent Him."

She waved her hand, as if brushing aside a fly. "But

that's really a minor issue. The big question, of course, is whether God actually destroyed Joe afterward, as the myths always claim." She snorted derisively. "Silly things, myths. No, no, my dear girls. You can be quite sure that Joe will be coming back. Quite soon now, I imagine, especially with that exasperating Zulkeh stirring the pot."

Jenny and Angela were utterly befuddled by now. I wasn't, myself. Just moderately fuddled. But I was determined to get off the subject. The quickest way to perdition I know is to meddle with the Joe business. By now, I trust, the reason is blindingly clear.

"Just exactly what do you require from us?" I demanded brusquely. "And I repeat—we're *not* doing anything that involves the Joe stuff."

"Well, of course not!" exclaimed Hildegard. "What possible reason would I have to hire a strangler for *that?* No, no, my dear Ignace. I should have thought the matter was obvious. I need Greyboar's assistance to obtain the score for the Harmony of the Spheres."

Yeah, that's it—her reply to the question, word for word. Didn't make any sense to me, either.

"Come again?" asked Greyboar.

Hildegard frowned. "Strange, really. Your sister's such a smart girl. Well, so be it. We'll just have to do the best we can with the human material available."

She laced her fingers and began speaking, in much the same tone that one speaks to a child. A slow-witted child.

"It's the Harmony of the Spheres, is the problem. Now that Joe's coming back, the Old Geister's on His way out. Pity, really. He was such a promising young Deity, in His early years. But I'm afraid there's no hope for Him now. The Man's—well, He's not really a Man, you know, but since He insists on using the masculine pronoun, He can't very well complain—anyway, He's just gotten hopelessly set in His ways, the past few millennia. Become a complete Pighead, actually, much as I hate to say it."

I was beginning to see why the Ecclesiarchs were miffed with her.

"I've tried to warn Him, needless to say. There's still a chance for a harmonious resolution, if He'd mend His ways and try to set things right before Joe gets back. Joe will be peeved with Him, of course, under the best of circumstances. But I've tried to explain to the Old Geister that Joe isn't the vindictive sort, so if He can at least show that He's made an attempt to get everything back on track there's every reason to believe that Joe will decide to let bygones be bygones. Of course, He'll have to give up all of this Lord Almighty foolishness, but that'll be for the best, anyway—even for Him. *Especially* for Him, as a matter of fact. Megalomania has always been the worst occupational hazard for a Supreme Deity. If He had the sense of a Pigeon, He'd see it right off, but I'm afraid He's gotten so swell-headed over the ages that—"

"Hold it! Hold it! Hold it!" I had visions of the Inquisition's chambers dancing in my head. Vivid, vivid, vivid images. "I said no Joe business, lady! And what do you do, right off? You go into it like the wizard Zulkeh wouldn't dream of on his worst days!"

"In addition to which," added Greyboar, "you're nuttier than a fruitcake."

The Abbess stared at him. I got the impression that she was puzzled by his words, rather than offended.

"What on earth do you mean, young man—'nuttier than a fruitcake'?"

Greyboar snorted. "What do I mean? All this ridiculous chatter about how you've been trying to warn the Old Geister about Joe, that's what. I mean, look, your Abbess—"

"Hildegard, please! I detest formality."

"—Hildegard, then. Sure and I've heard of people claiming they talk with God, but they're either weird mystics squatting on a mountain somewhere or they're fruitcakes chained up in an asylum."

"Well, of course!" exclaimed Hildegard. "No sane person would try to talk with the Old Geister. It's impossible—and don't believe anything those silly mystics tell you, either. You *should* be able to talk to Him, of course, but the Man's an absolute Fanatic about following proper channels. Insists that you have to correspond with Him through the post. I don't mind so much myself—I've always rather enjoyed writing letters, actually. But it makes it so difficult for the poor people. It's hard for them to write to Him, you know, suffering from illiteracy the way they do. And then, even when they do manage to block out a simple note, the Old Geister will refuse to read it, like as not. I hate to say it, but the truth is He's a fearsome Snob. Won't even look at a letter unless it's written in a fine hand, and then He insists the text has to be in the ancient cipher of the Order of the Knights Rampant. It's such a nuisance! I know the cipher, of course, but there aren't more than a handful of people in the world who do—outside of the Godferrets, naturally—and, besides, even for someone who knows it, the cipher is an absolutely beastly script, absolutely—"

"No Joe business, I said!" I started hopping up and down with agitation. Then stopped as soon as the snarl raised her head and gave me a look I didn't much care for. So I calmed down a little, and continued:

"Look, Abb—Hildegard, I'll say it again for the last time: *no Joe business*. Especially, I don't want to hear about the Godferrets. Heard enough about them back in Prygg. If it scared the wizard stiff, it's nothing Greyboar and I want anything to do with, that's for sure."

Hildegard was still frowning. "But, my dear little man," she said, "I was simply responding to Greyboar's remark about my alleged lunacy."

"Hildegard," said Greyboar, "I wasn't saying you were a madwoman because I thought you said you were *talking* to God. I don't care how you claim to do it— through the Royal Mail or carrier pigeon. You're nuts."

She drew herself up stiffly. "Well!" she exclaimed. "I can certainly understand now why Gwendolyn isn't pleased with you. A stupid jackass, just as she said!" She sniffed. "Thinks the world isn't any bigger than the bag of oats stuck on his nose."

She rose from the desk and walked over to the alcove. She turned and crooked a finger.

"Come hither, then, man-who-thinks-like-a-jackass. Examine the oats for yourself."

I swear, the woman was just too weird to get angry with. Greyboar and I looked at each other, shrugged, and went over to the alcove.

Chapter 13.
Remedial Theology

Well, I hate to admit it, but the next few minutes rather shook my long-standing hardheaded view of the world. Turned out, all those slabs I'd noticed in the big alcove weren't tombstones, after all.

They were stone tablets, covered with lettering. Written in fiery flame.

Yep. God's letters to Hildegard.

"It's an insufferable nuisance, really," she complained. "Why can't He use paper like everyone else? Part of His growing senility, I'm afraid. Always tends to manifest itself as grandiosity, you know, when Supreme Deities start reaching their dotage. My share of our correspondence fits very nicely into a simple drawer. But His side! I had to have that alcove built especially just to store them. Frightful waste of space. And it heats the room up terribly, during the hot spells in summer."

She sighed heavily. "In our early exchanges it wasn't so bad. His tablets were written in pleasant letters of lambent gold. But for the past few years—well, perhaps the last twenty years—it's always those horrid fiery flames. He's irritated with me, of course. But it can't be helped. It's my duty as a pious woman to tell Him the plain and simple truth about Himself. He doesn't want to hear it, naturally."

She moved back toward her desk. "I hate to say it, I really do, after having devoted my life to His service. But I've finally come to the conclusion that there's just no hope for Him. I had wanted to avoid unpleasantness when Joe comes back, but I see now that it's inevitable. A terrible scene Joe's going to make, you can be sure of it, when he sees what a mess the Old Geister's made of everything."

I was too dazed to object to the Joe business. Matter of fact, I was too dazed to do much of anything except be dazed.

"I can see why the Ecclesiarchs aren't too fond of you," croaked Greyboar.

As she resumed her seat, Hildegard snorted. "Those shriveled-up old toads! Nasty things! Can't even call them men anymore. I'm quite fond of men as a rule, even if their natural handicaps frustrate me at times. But it never fails—once you load a man down with power and wealth, he turns into a toad. Every time." She ran her fingers through her thick white hair. "Well, I should be fair. Vast majority of women turn into toads, too, when you load them down with power and wealth."

I'll say this much for Greyboar—he's nowhere near as smart as I am, but he recovers from shock a lot better. He scratched his head, and asked the Abbess:

"Just out of curiosity, Hildegard, how do you get away with it? Pissing in the face of every power in the world, starting with the Lord Almighty himself. Pardon my language."

Hildegard grinned. Really a great grin she had, that old woman. Cheerful, friendly, a bit devilish.

"Oh, I don't mind a little vulgarity. Don't use such language myself, of course. Wouldn't be proper—after all, I am the Abbess of the Sisters of Tranquility. But you can't spend as much time as I have with the wise old women of the Sssuj and retain your girlish prudery. Earthy lot, they are."

"I thought the Sssuji ate everybody who goes into the swamp," said Greyboar. "Especially, you know, missionaries."

"What nonsense!" The Abbess frowned fiercely. "That's a foul lie spread by disgruntled imperialists. They're just sour, you know, because the Sssuji eat all the *armies* they send into the swamp. Very diet-conscious, actually, the Sssuji. I was deeply impressed by that aspect of their culture. They refuse to eat missionaries, for instance, despite everything you've ever heard. They say the sanctimony in the veins spoils the meat. The swamp snarls absolutely adore missionary, on the other hand, so it all works out nicely."

"Then why didn't they feed you to the snarls?" asked Angela timidly.

Hildegard was clearly puzzled. "Why would they do that? I didn't go there to preach to them. I went to ask questions. Spent several years there, as it turned out. It was marvelous, really. And to get back to your question, Greyboar, it was the wise old women of the Sssuj who told me how to—as you put it—'get away with it.' By which expression I take it you mean be able to expound the true faith without being pestered to death by God and the Inquisition and that sorry lot of Ecclesiarchs."

"So what's the secret?" asked Greyboar.

"It was obvious, once they explained it to me. 'Just build your Abbey in Joe's Favorite Woods,' they said. So obvious! I should have seen it myself."

Greyboar frowned. "I don't see why that would do it."

Hildegard looked at him, shook her head sadly. "So odd, it really is. The same parents, there's no question about it. You look just like her, except Gwendolyn's quite pretty in a huge sort of way. Strange how genetics works itself out, the sister being so intelligent and the brother such a dumbbell."

"Would you mind just answering the question," growled Greyboar. "I'm getting a bit tired of these comparisons between my sister and me."

"But it's obvious, my good man! Why is this forest called 'Joe's Favorite Woods'?"

"Well—"

"Because it was his favorite woods, that's why! And why was it his favorite woods? Because it was filled with snarls. Forest snarls, too, who were always Joe's favorites even though he denied it and tried to pretend he loved all his snarls the same."

Greyboar was hopelessly lost. So was I.

"So, since I'm a snarl-friend, once I set up my Abbey here I could go about my business without worrying about a lot of fretful old men. The forest's still full of snarls, you know. Highest density of snarls in the world, actually."

The light finally dawned. There aren't many snarl-friends in the world, at any one time. Hildegard was the second one I'd met in my life. Shelyid was the first. And that little dwarf had—well, never mind the details. The point is, I'd seen what one enraged snarl could do. I shuddered to think about an entire forest full of hundreds—thousands?—of the monsters. It's no wonder the gentle monks of St. Shriven-on-the-Moor got a vision from God!

"But come," said Hildegard, "I'm afraid we've wandered away from the purpose of our meeting. I don't believe the Old Geister is going to be around much longer, sad to say. So I have to make sure to obtain the score of the Harmony of the Spheres before Joe gets back. He's quite a nice man, Joe is. According to all the legends, at any rate, and I've no reason to believe his personality will have changed. But the fact is, the man had apparently no ear for music. Such, at least, I have to assume since there's no record that he invented music."

She leaned back in her chair, again planting her hands firmly on the desk in front of her. "No, there's no question God's been much the better influence in that regard. But it would be just like the Old Geister, on His way out, to take the Harmony of the Spheres with him. Purely out of malice, of course—it's not as if the Harmony would do Him any good where He's going! So I've got to get the score, before it's lost."

By now, Greyboar and I had given up trying to make sense out of anything the Abbess said. It's not that we doubted her, mind you. Rather difficult to argue with a woman who corresponds with God and has His old letters to prove it, don't you know? It's just that we couldn't begin to follow her reasoning. So we gave up. As the wise man says: "I hate to be the one to break the news to you, General, but you're a foot soldier."

"So how do we do that?" asked Greyboar. "And where do I come in?"

"Well," explained Hildegard, "we'll have to get the score from one of the fallen angels. It doesn't matter which in particular. Any of them will do—they all know the score. The Old Geister made them memorize it, of course. He makes His angels memorize everything He says."

"Fallen angels?" I squeaked. "You mean—devils?"

Hildegard frowned again. "And you claimed to be the smart one! Well, I should make allowances, I suppose. No doubt you had a rotten education. You have the air about you of a dog who was beaten too often as a puppy. Can't mistake it—that certain perpetual scowl at the world; it's unmistakable, really."

Abbess or not, I was starting to take exception to her attitude. But she cut off my exception before I got a chance to express it. Started right in lecturing again, just like a schoolmarm in a class for the mentally handicapped.

"Devils, you see, are independent creatures of the Darkness. Same with demons, daemons, imps—that whole wretched bunch that dwells in the infernal regions. Fallen angels are something else entirely. They're figments of the Lord's imagination, which He created and brought to divine life for no good reason except that He's such an Egotist that He doesn't really want to talk to anyone except Himself. So the Old Geister created angels in His image, so He could carry on a conversation with Himself. Kept them within limits, of course. He didn't want any backtalk, you understand, just an audience who'd listen to His every word like it was Holy Writ and say 'Yes, God' and 'You're absolutely right, God' and so forth. The problem, naturally, is that, like every egotist you've ever known, the Old Geister's as vain as a Peacock. Sooner or later one of the angels doesn't fawn over Him as quick as He likes, so—off you go, bum! It's to the netherworld with you! Eventually, He lets them back upstairs, but the fallen angels hate the whole thing. It's not that it hurts them any, you understand. It'd do them some good, actually, a stint in the netherworld, if they'd learn anything from the experience. But since the angels are created in His image, naturally they never learn anything, since they think they already know it all. But while they're down there they become quite frightful. It offends their self-esteem, you see, being snickered at by devils and such. They become exceedingly nasty, after a while. Very hard to tell them from proper devils, if you just happen to run into them without knowing the trick of it."

"Which is what?" I asked.

Hildegard got a very prim look at her face. "I don't believe there's any need to get into *that* subject. It wouldn't be proper for me to talk about it."

Greyboar was back to scratching his head. "I think I see where you're going. We have to descend to the netherworld, somehow—"

"Goodness, no!" gasped Hildegard, clutching her throat. "Why, the very *idea!* My good man, I *am* the Abbess of the Sisters of Tranquility! It's a shocking idea, positively shocking! You should be ashamed of yourself! A devout woman like myself, consorting with devils and demons. Shocking!"

"But then, how are—"

"We shall summon the fallen angel here, of course!" exclaimed Hildegard. "It's the only proper way to proceed."

Like I said, it was impossible to follow the woman's logic. Just keep foot soldiering. Greyboar apparently felt the same way.

"Fine, fine," he said hurriedly. "No problem—we'll bring the character up here. I assume you know how to do that? I certainly don't." Seeing the frown gathering on Hildegard's brow, he hastened on: "Yeah, yeah, of course you know how to do it! After all, you are the Abbess of the Sisters of Tranquility! So, anyway, the idea is you haul the bum up here and I choke the answer out of him."

The strangler looked down at his huge hands. Cracked his knuckles. The snarl raised her head, gave him a speculative look—sort of, *Hmmm, this guy might make for an interesting little set-to, not like those squealing soldiers what just jump into your maw like rabbits.*

"I've never tried to put the squeeze on a fallen angel," mused Greyboar. "What the hell, why not? It'll be an interesting challenge."

Hildegard had that look on her face again. The one I was beginning to detest heartily. The one that expressed the idea: *How does this guy manage to feed himself, anyway, with a brain like a cabbage?*

"My dear man," she explained in that patient tone, "how in the world do you propose to strangle an angel? Didn't I just get through explaining that an angel is nothing but a figment of the Old Geister's imagination? They're utterly immaterial, angels are— fallen or not."

Greyboar threw up his hands with exasperation. "Then what am I doing here? I'm a damned strangler, not a theologian! I do manual labor, lady, I'm not a philosopher!"

I couldn't help it—I giggled. Greyboar glared at me.

"Well, of course you're a strangler, my dear man. That's why I engaged your services. I'm not one of those silly people who thinks they can substitute their amateur fumbling for the trained skills of a craftsman. In fact, for the task in front of me, I not only need a professional, I need the best in the field. It won't be easy, I can assure you. If I may be so immodest, I believe you'll find this the most difficult choke in your career."

"Is that right?" demanded Greyboar. He's normally quite cool-headed, the big guy is, but I could tell the Abbess was starting to get his goat. "So who am I supposed to strangle?"

"Why—me, of course," replied Hildegard. "Who else?"

$\approx$ $\approx$ $\approx$

At that point, my brain went on strike. Total walk-out, picket lines up, the whole shot. Greyboar gaped.

Of course, Hildegard just kept chugging along with her lesson in Remedial Theology.

"Since they're immaterial figments of the Old Geister's imagination," she explained, "the only way you can force an angel—fallen or risen, by the way, the principle's the same, it's just that you can't summon a risen angel down to earth—to do anything is to squeeze their spirit. And the way you do that is by demonstrating your utter indifference to their existence. Hate that, angels. It tortures them no end, the idea that someone not only isn't overawed by their presence but would just as soon die to get away from them. It's an ancient trick, first perfected by the swamis of the Sundjhab. Great austerities. Does it every time."

She pursed her lips. "Of course, the trick's gotten more difficult over the millennia. In the old days, you could coerce a fallen angel just by practicing the traditional austerities: fasting, scourging, suchlike. But I'm afraid that just won't do, anymore. The Old Geister's gotten tougher as time goes by. Like old Shoe Leather, He is now. His angels just laugh at fasting, today. Scourging will still make them wince, of course. But to force a fallen angel to cough up the score of the Harmony of the Spheres, well, for that I'll need to practice a truly great austerity. I considered the problem at some length, let me tell you, trying to figure out what would be the greatest austerity I could come up with. And then—like a bolt out of the blue!—it came to me: I'll have myself strangled by the world's greatest chokester. If that doesn't do the trick, nothing will."

She smiled. "Is it clear now?"

I had my own opinion as to who in the room suffered from mental deficiency, but I kept it to myself.

Didn't need to say anything, anyway. I knew Greyboar would turn the job down flat.

"Not a chance," he growled. "I don't choke girls. Abbess of the Sisters of Tranquility or not, you're still a girl as far as squeezing's concerned. You'll have to get another chokester. Even if he isn't the best in the world."

Hildegard nodded her head. "Yes, yes. Gwendolyn told me you'd be stubborn on this point. So I had her give me a note. I have it right here." She rummaged around in a drawer, brought out a letter.

"It's for you," she said, walking around the desk and handing it to Greyboar.

The strangler opened the letter and read it. After reading it twice, he handed it to me. Here's what it said:

> *Dear brother:*
> *I don't have time now to write a long letter. Things are getting sticky here, and I have to go underground again. Hildegard explained her problem to me, and I told her to hire you. I hate the fact of it, but there's no question you're the world's best professional strangler. And if she's to do what she needs to do, she'll need the best help she can get. I know you've always kept the promise you made me about not choking women. I'm not going to say I'm proud of you for that. You're still nothing but a damned thug. But I am pleased. Sort of. Anyway, you have my permission—this one time—to break the promise. In fact, I'm telling you to do it. Mind your sister! Go ahead and choke Hildegard.*
> *Gwendolyn*

It was her letter, all right. I recognized her handwriting, and besides, you couldn't mistake the sentiments—talk about self-righteous!

"Well, I guess it's all right, then," said Greyboar.

"It's not all right!" I exclaimed. "I've said it once, I'll say it again—no Joe business! And this job has Joe business written all over it."

Greyboar shook his head. "Doesn't matter, Ignace. Normally, I'd agree with you. But you saw what it said in the letter. Gwendolyn didn't just give me permission to do the job, she told me to do it. That means it's important to her, for whatever reason. I've disappointed her once in her life, I'm not going to do it again. Not for something like this, anyway. What the hell—we've already gotten mixed up with Joe business."

It'd always been a sore point with me, as an agent, the way Greyboar stuck his nose into deciding which assignments we took. That was my job, dammit! He provides the thumbs, I provide the managerial skills. I admit, he was usually pretty good about it. But, I swear, the man was an absolute pawn in the hands of women. I ask you—what's the point of being the world's greatest strangler if you're going to let every Tina, Diane and Harriet push you around?

Chapter 14.
Great Austerities

After that, things moved pretty quickly. Hildegard rose and ushered us out of her study and down to the music salon. There, we found that all the great composers were already set up at tables scattered against the various walls, pens in hand and blank composers' sheets spread out in front of them. It suddenly dawned on me why they had all come to the Abbey.

There was a single chair sitting in the middle of the big room, with a small side table next to it. The only thing on the side table was a little bell. The kind that looks like a cow bell only it's smaller. Hildegard marched up to the chair and took a seat, her head lifted high and her back ramrod straight. She motioned Greyboar to come around and stand behind her.

Jenny and Angela and I stayed off to one side, near the table where the Big Banjo was sitting. Despite my better judgment, I found myself getting interested in the affair. Never been part of such an operation before.

I'd made it a point, in fact, to keep my distance from angels—fallen or otherwise.

The main thing that surprised me was how simple and straightforward it all was. I'd rather expected a much more elaborate affair. Drawing of pentacles, guttering torches, bell, book and candle, long incantations in an unknown tongue, naked witches leaping about. (The only part I'd been looking forward to, that last. Except I was a little nervous that Jenny and Angela would insist on participating.)

Instead, Hildegard stuck two fingers in her mouth and whistled. Very loudly. When my ears stopped ringing, there was the fallen angel. Squatting in the middle of the floor.

"What took you so long?" demanded Hildegard.

The fallen angel sneered. "For you, I should hurry?"

Horrid ugly thing, it was. If this creature was an angel, I definitely didn't want to meet a devil, I'll tell you that. Colored a kind of nauseating yellow. A twisted face like a giant bat. Horns, cloven hooves, barbed tail, the works. Actually, I found out later that fallen angels take on the appearance of devils. Part of the punishment. Only difference, actually, is that fallen angels don't have—well, bit delicate, this—but let's just say that the Old Geister, being as He is a righteous God, doesn't believe it's proper for His angels (even fallen ones) to have, you know, sexual organs. Real devils have them, of course—that's why they're called devils, don't you know? Hung like moose, your real devils. Which is probably why they get into so much trouble.

Other than that, however, this fallen angel was the spitting image of a devil. All the way down to his temperament.

"Which one are you?" demanded Hildegard.

"Ralph," responded the angel, looking like his feelings were hurt.

"I can never tell," said Hildegard. "Angels all look the same to me. It's ridiculous, anyway, giving you names. You're all just figments of the Old Geister's imagination." She shook her head regretfully. "And He's got such a limited imagination."

The angel snarled. "You better watch your mouth, lady! You're already on the Boss'—well, you know what."

"I'll not stand for vulgarity from the likes of you!" snapped Hildegard.

"Is that so?" sneered Ralph. But he did seemed a bit cowed. Don't blame him, actually. When she's in the mood—which she was—Hildegard could be called The Schoolmistress From Hell.

"I don't have to take any guff from you, lady," he whined. "You've been excommunicated by the Popes."

Hildegard snorted. "And so what? I'm still the Abbess of the Sisters of Tranquility. Who cares what those shriveled-up old geezers think?"

"They're God's chosen authorities on Earth!" shrilled Ralph.

"And so what? Is that my fault? I told Him to get rid of the Popes. Dozens of times, in fact. The Popes are going to infuriate Joe when he gets back, leave aside everything else."

"Joe's dead and gone!" shrieked the angel. But he couldn't meet Hildegard's gaze. Like a bar of iron, that gaze.

"The Boss says you've been excommunicated," groused Ralph. "So that's that."

"What cheek!" exclaimed Hildegard. "It's just like Him to make a mess of things and then blame me for it. No better than a six-year-old Brat trying to stick His little sister with the punishment."

"You can't talk about the Boss that way!" protested Ralph. "I won't stand for it!"

Hildegard laughed. It was a beautiful clear laugh, like a chime, except that no chime you've ever heard could produce that sound of total contempt.

"And how do you propose to stop me?" she demanded. The fallen angel glared at her, but said nothing. I'm no expert on the fine points of theology, but even I could figure out that if the Lord Almighty couldn't shut the woman up, His stooge sure as hell wasn't up to the job.

"What d'you want?" growled Ralph. "You didn't summon me here to chat. Not that I mind, of course"— here he ogled Jenny and Angela—"the view's nice."

Angela blew him a raspberry. Jenny sneered: "Dream on, dickless."

"I summoned you here in order to obtain the score for the Harmony of the Spheres," said Hildegard.

The fallen angel collapsed to the floor, howling with laughter.

"What a chump!" hooted Ralph. "What a silly old biddy!" Hildegard kept quiet, but she bestowed upon him the look which all schoolmarms bestow upon their least favorite pupil.

Eventually, Ralph composed himself enough to sit back up. Wiping tears of laughter from his eyes, he said: "And just how do you propose to get that out of me? Going to practice great austerities, are we? Oh, how wonderful! How was I so blessed, to be allowed to watch while the great Abbess Hildegard starves and beats herself?"

He convulsed to the floor again. "Be still my trembling heart!"

"Impudent rascal!" snapped Hildegard. Then she turned to Greyboar. "Are you ready?" she asked. Greyboar shrugged.

Hildegard plucked the bell off the side table. "I will remain seated here at my desk. You will stand behind me to apply the choke. Whenever I ring the bell, you will tighten the choke. Is that clear?"

Greyboar scratched his head. "Well, sure, except for one thing. How will I know when you want me to let go? You won't be able to say anything. Believe me, you won't."

Hildegard looked at him, once again, as if he were a moron. "But, my dear man, it's obvious! You will release the choke when Ralph coughs up the Harmony of the Spheres." She frowned briefly, then added: "Actually, to be on the safe side, you'd best wait until he repeats it. Even the world's greatest composers will have difficulty recording this harmony, and it's essential that we get every note down properly."

Greyboar was still frowning.

"Oh, stop worrying, young man!" snapped Hildegard. "You'll have no difficulty recognizing the score of the Harmony of the Spheres! You've never heard it before, of course. No mortal has. But it's quite unmistakable, really it is. And besides, we've all agreed that the Big Banjo will announce when the score is completely recorded."

Greyboar threw up his hands in frustration. "You are the most impossible woman!" he bellowed. "I'm not worried about that! How will I know when you want me to let up because you're about to die? That's the problem!"

Hildegard's look now conveyed the certainty that Greyboar was dumber than a moron.

"My dear man, the question simply won't arise. I intend to have the score, and that's that. Now, please! I'm a tolerant woman, but you are, after all, my employee. Do as you're told!" The Schoolmistress From Hell, like I said.

Greyboar exhaled a deep breath. Then, stepped up and stood just behind Hildegard. Meanwhile, Ralph had been following the exchange with a look of growing confusion on his bat's face.

"What's going on here?" he demanded. "And who's this big gorilla?"

"Name's Greyboar," rumbled the strangler.

The fallen angel looked suddenly interested. "Is that so? Well, I'll be damned. Never knew what you looked like—although I should have guessed. Know who you are, of course, even though you don't send much business our way."

He paused, pondered, then: "Actually, I don't think you've ever sent any business our way. But the devils are tickled pink with you. Talk about you all the time. 'Best supplier in the business,' they say."

"Glad to hear it," said Greyboar pleasantly. He placed his hands around Hildegard's throat. As huge as they are, his hands barely went all the way around. She was such a feminine woman, Hildegard, that it was easy to forget what a giantess she was. Most people's necks, even on great muscular bruisers, look like pipe-stems in Greyboar's hands.

Ralph was now totally confused. "Hey, what gives? What's the—"

The ringing of the bell cut him off. Greyboar started squeezing. Well, not really. I know what a real Greyboar squeeze looks like, and this was just a faint imitation.

Hildegard began ringing the bell impatiently, like she was a ranch woman summoning shepherds to the dinner table. And kept ringing. And kept ringing.

Greyboar's shoulders slumped. He really wasn't enthusiastic about the job, I could tell. Then he shrugged, took a deep breath, and really went to work.

Hildegard's face turned bright red. Her tongue popped out of her mouth. Yet—I swear it!—her face mostly conveyed deep satisfaction. She even stopped ringing the damned bell.

Ralph winced. "Boy, that's a horrible sight," he muttered.

But he was a tough fallen angel, I'll give him that. He took a deep breath and stared right at Hildegard's face, without even blinking. And there it remained for the next five minutes, Hildegard and Ralph staring each other down. The woman must have had lungs like a whale, I thought to myself.

After five minutes, Hildegard started ringing the bell again. Greyboar tightened up further. He was scowling fiercely, his great shoulder muscles bunching up, the tendons in his forearms like so many steel cables.

Hildegard's face was now bright purple. Her tongue was out a mile. Her eyes began protruding like a toad, except a toad's eyes don't show that horrid network of bright red veins in the eyeballs.

Ralph wasn't looking much better. His complexion was now gray. His horns were starting to curl in. His cloven hoofs were crossed. Drops of oily sweat were pouring down his bat's face.

Five more minutes went by. Hildegard rang the bell again. Greyboar went into overdrive. His shoulders hunched up like a bison's. The enormous muscles in his arms were rippling like a nest of anacondas. His own face was red, and sweat was pouring off his forehead.

I was flabbergasted. Only once before had I ever seen Greyboar throw this much into a choke. That was three years before, at the Barbarian Games, when he faced the Terrible Talon in the finals. Been champion at the Games for six years running, Greyboar had— ever since he started competing, in fact—and the Terrible Talon was the only one ever really gave him a run for the title. Would have made a great rematch. Of course, rematches are unheard of in the choking event.

Even the Terrible Talon hadn't lasted but a minute, once Greyboar hit his top speed. But Hildegard! After two minutes, the crazy woman rang the bell again! By now her face was black, her tongue was writhing like a huge worm, her eyes were almost completely out of their sockets.

Ralph quit. He looked almost dead himself. He started spasming, as if in a seizure. His hideous bat mouth opened, and out came—

The Harmony of the Spheres.

Yeah, Hildegard was right. Like nothing you've ever heard. It's impossible to describe, and you can't begin to imagine what sort of instruments could produce such music. But you can't mistake it.

All the composers were now scratching away furiously in their sheets, their expressions combining concentration and awe.

Hildegard wasn't just crazy, she was absolutely insane. She kept ringing the bell until the fallen angel had run through the entire score three times.

Finally, it was over. After the third run-through, Hildegard stopped ringing the bell and the Big Banjo, after glancing around quickly and seeing the nods of his fellow composers, told Greyboar to let go. The strangler staggered back and crouched over, his hands on his knees. He was gasping, for all the world like he was the one who had been choked. Hildegard leaned forward in the chair, rasping for breath, massaging her throat.

I think she recovered faster than Greyboar did. She certainly recovered faster than Ralph! The fallen angel was truly a fallen angel—flat on the floor, wailing like a lost soul. Don't blame him, really. Later, Hildegard told me the Old Geister was so furious with Ralph that he turned him into a devil, permanent. Probably worked out for the best, though—at least the guy got a pecker out of the deal.

"Marvelous!" cried Hildegard, when she got her voice. "Oh, just marvelous!"

She turned in her chair and bestowed a look of great approval on Greyboar.

"You were simply splendid, young man! Simply splendid! Gwendolyn was certainly right—I can't imagine a finer choke. There'll be quite an excellent bonus for your work today, you can be sure of it." My spirits perked right up, hearing that. "And I shall certainly not even think of hiring another chokester, should the occasion ever arise again." She frowned slightly. "Though I can't imagine it will. I am, after all, the Abbess of the Sisters of Tranquility."

She turned back and bestowed a very different look on Ralph.

"You may go," she announced haughtily. A split second later, the fallen angel vanished.

Chapter 15.
Aesthetics and Reason

After it was all over, Hildegard announced that she was going to need a bit of rest before she did anything further. I didn't doubt that in the least. I was amazed that the woman was still alive, much less that she didn't really look any worse than someone who was completely exhausted.

So Greyboar and the girls and I spent the rest of the day, and the evening, enjoying an excellent meal and many hours of musical entertainment. And I'll say for the record that there are worse fates than being in a secluded Abbey with most of the world's greatest composers having what lowlife musicians call a "jam session."

The next morning, Hildegard summoned us into her office. After a day's rest and a night's sleep, she was looking quite a bit better. Although I noticed she was wearing a scarf around her neck, probably to hide the bruises.

As soon as we walked in, she greeted us with a big smile. So did the snarl on the rug.

I was so preoccupied with keeping an eye on the snarl that I didn't even notice the size of the casket that Hildegard hauled up from the floor and plunked on her desk. Not until she opened it and my eye caught a glint of the world's most splendid color. Gold.

All fretting thoughts on the subject of snarl smiles vanished, then. In fact, all thoughts of any kind vanished. I was awash in the bliss that mystics talk about, when they babble about pure emotion transcending the petty limits of apparent reality.

Of course, your mystics always shoot for what you might call the more ethereal emotions. But, me, I've always found that plain old everyday stuff works just fine. Greed, for instance.

To be sure, some feeble still-flickering portion of my intellect was probably fumbling around, trying to estimate the actual value contained in that casket. But I had no time for sordid arithmetic, at the moment. I was just awash in the transcendental experience of realizing:

We're rich! We're rich!

"As I promised," Hildegard said, "an excellent bonus for your excellent work."

Greyboar muttered something decorous, I believe. I tried to follow his example, but the words sort of got lost in the drool. Then Hildegard shoved the casket across the desk toward us and I, ah, advanced to take possession.

Greyboar claims I trampled the snarl on the way, but I think that's nonsense. I mean, wouldn't the beast have gobbled me or something? Greyboar claims the only reason it didn't was because I don't weigh enough to really disturb a dozing snarl, even stepping on its great hairy ugly flanks. In fact, he claims the snarl purred, as if my footsteps were like so many little petting strokes.

Could be, I dunno. I suppose things might have gotten stickier if I'd trampled the snarl on the way back, what with being weighted down with the casket. But I couldn't lift the thing, anyway, so Greyboar had to come and do the crude muscle work. He claims he carefully avoided the snarl in the doing. I dunno. Maybe. It's true that he doesn't have any of my sense for the true worth of things.

The next three days or so are pretty vague in my memory.

Greyboar and the girls were gone most of the time, down in the salon with the composers listening to music. Me? Ha! Sure, and I love music. But a man has to have a clear sense of priorities. Art and entertainment come a long way second after the really important stuff. Counting your money being pretty much at the top of the list.

It was *so* strenuous. A lot of people don't give much thought to the matter, you know, but a connosoor like myself understands that money-counting (when there's enough money) is an art form all in itself. You always want to start with racking up the total, of course. But after that, the variety of styles is almost endless. Stack coins by size, then by content of actual precious metal. Arrange them in a lot of short stacks, a few tall ones. Then, of course, the whole world of truly creative work opens up as you stack and restack them in the multitude of wondrous shapes available to the intelligent mind in full flower. Castles, pyramids, bridges, you name it.

One of the happier times of my life, it was. Even though I don't remember much of it because I was lost in such a state of artistic frenzy. But that's the way creative work always is, I'm told.

～　～　～

On the morning of the fifth day after our arrival, Greyboar interrupted my plans for the day with a most outlandish proposal.

"Hildegard said she wanted to talk to us today, Ignace. So let's go."

"Ridiculous!" I protested. "I'm halfway into my next creation! A perfect replica in coin stacks of the Leaning Tower at—"

No use. Greyboar picked me up, tucked me under his arm, and hauled me off to Hildegard's office. Once there, he plunked me into a seat.

I was so disgruntled that I didn't start following the conversation for a couple of minutes. When the words finally penetrated, however, I started *really* paying attention. And within a few seconds was participating in a lively fashion.

"Ridiculous!" I protested. "You're nuts, lady! Give up a perfectly respectable trade—pay's good, work's steady, what else do you ever get in this world?—for a lot of airy-fairy theological gobbledygook? Ridiculous!"

Hildegard responded to my sensible words with a look which combined amusement at the antics of a child with that "more in sorrow than in anger" business that amusement at childish antics always brings in its wake with a certain brand of individual. You know the type. Policemen, workshop owners, slave drivers. Parents. Abbesses.

"But my dear Ignace," she said, "surely you don't deny the existence of an immortal soul—"

"Surely I do!"

"—and even if you do, you must surely recognize the necessity of maintaining a proper psychological balance in life—"

"Surely I don't!"

"—and even if you don't, you can't deny the simple claims of morality."

I maintained a stubborn silence.

"Which, no matter how you slice it, are sorely tried by your current occupations as a serial murderer and his accomplice. Accomplice, did I say? It might be better to use the terms: aider and abetter; instigator; organizer of the mayhem; miniature butcher; diminutive monster; bantamweight fiend—oh, I could go on and on!"

"No doubt," rumbled Greyboar. "And it's not that I haven't got a certain sympathy for your argument, Abbess. It's a dirty rotten trade, no doubt about it. But—" He shrugged his massive shoulders. "The truth is, I don't believe in any of that stuff much more than Ignace does. And in the meantime the food's got to be put on the table. As he says, the pay's good and the work's steady and what else do you get in this world?"

For a moment, his eyes got a little hard. "Fine for you, Abbess—meaning no disrespect—to spout fine sentiments. You weren't working in a slaughterhouse from the time you were a kid, earning barely enough to keep alive just enough to stagger into the slaughterhouse again the next day." His eyes got very hard. "So screw it."

Hildegard sighed. "You are determined, I see. Very well. I simply thought I'd bring the subject up, for your consideration. My duty, you know, as a pious woman of the Church. Do please think about it, from time to time, will you? And you might want to consider that the world is teetering on the brink of a Great Change. Joe's return will surely trigger off a cataclysm. Interesting times, as the ancient curse goes. During which, of course, nothing is needed more than heroes."

Greyboar nodded. So did I, after a moment's sulk. No point in refusing to humor someone who's just paid you the biggest commission of your life, don't you know?

As soon as we got out of her office, of course, I said something sarcastic to Greyboar. But he didn't seem to be paying any attention to me. His mind was off in a cloud, somewhere.

Then he started muttering about the conflict between entropy and the search for lucre, and I realized right off that it was time to get out of that Abbey. Money-counting is a high art, sure. But you've got to keep your priorities straight. Unless you *keep* the money you've got no art to practice.

"We're outa here," I growled. "I'll tell the girls. Pack up your stuff. We're leaving right after lunch."

We left an hour later. Hrundig came along with us, but Olga and her daughters stayed behind. I guess the plan was that they'd wait until the hunt for them died down before making their way south to the Mutt. In the meantime, Hrundig was going back to New Sfinctr to see if there was anything he could do to help Benvenuti. Wasn't much chance of that, of course—not with Benny in the Durance Pile—but I guess Hrundig felt an obligation.

We had a little encounter on the road out of the Abbey which stiffened my determination to get clear of the place. We had to stand aside while the mailman came by on his rounds. The poor bastard was sweating like a dog, pushing a wheelbarrow in front of him. Whatever was in it must have weighed a ton. But I couldn't see because there was a tarpaulin of some kind covering the contents.

When he came abreast of us he set down the wheelbarrow and heaved a sigh of relief. Then, straightening up and massaging his back, he gave us a polite smile.

"G'd afternoon, folks."

"What's in the wheelbarrow?" asked Angela.

The mailman sighed. Then, grimacing ruefully, he flipped off the tarpaulin. Nestled in the barrow was another of those stone tablets. The letters inscribed on it were practically shooting jets of flame. The heat drove us back a step or two.

"Really pissed today, He is," announced the mailman. He pointed to the lettering. "I can't read but a bit of it, you'll understand, on account of the cipher is that Order of the Knights Rampant stuff. But I can recognize some phrases, well enough."

His finger moved about, indicating the most fiery clauses in the message " *'Fry in hell,'* that one. This is *'eternal damnation.'* Over there's a bit about the *'tortures of the netherworld.'* The real big lettering at the bottom says: *'BURN, BITCH, BURN!'* "

The mailman clucked his tongue. "He really shouldn't talk that way to an Abbess, I don't think. Even if He is God Himself."

I took Jenny and Angela by the arms and started hustling them down the road. "We're *outa* here!" I hissed.

By late afternoon we were off Abbey land and back into the coach which Oscar and the boys had kept ready. I started to relax. Left to himself, without an Abbess sticking her nonsensical notions into the works, Greyboar's silly fiddling with "ethical entropy" wouldn't lead to anything more annoying than laziness. Philosophy's a pain in the ass, sure, but left to its own devices it's really pretty harmless. It's when it starts getting filled with all that moral content business that it starts getting really dangerous.

So, at least, I told myself. But it was all a fool's paradise. For, just as Greyboar had said, the fact that a sane man doesn't recognize philosophy does not prevent philosophy from recognizing him.

Or, to put it in more mundane terms, you can play around with cause and effect all you want. Doesn't change the fact that effects are caused by causes, and that causes are caused by people fiddling around with the damned things. Then, as sure as effect follows cause, you're in that one-way tunnel to disaster that philosophers call "the logic of events." Which sensible fellows like me preferred to think of as "what happens when you mess around with stuff you had no business messing around with in the first place."

Or, as the wise man puts it: "If you want to stay out of trouble, don't trouble yourself."

But that's the way it works. One thing leads to another. A small problem turns into a big one, which turns into an unholy mess, which turns into a crisis, which leads to a disaster, which ends in calamity.

I'd seen it coming, sure enough. But what I didn't know, as we made our way back to New Sfinctr, was that the crisis was already upon us.

Chapter 16.
Twenty Bob on th'Lady!

We heard the story from Leuwen as soon as we got back in town. He was normally close-mouthed, Leuwen, like any good Flankn barkeep. For sure and certain, he didn't want to tell this particular story. Especially to Greyboar. Really especially, not to Greyboar. I could tell—the lack of color in his normally ruddy cheeks, the shifting eyes, the twitching fingers, the fat body poised for desperate flight, the sweat pouring down his face, the gulping voice. As the wizard Zulkeh would say, these are the classic symptoms of the bearer of sad tidings in the grip of *le terreur d'étrangler en plein fureur*, as described in the ancient writings of the great physician and scholar Hippocrates Sfondrati-Piccolomini.

Indeed, indeed, Greyboar was in a rare rage, and it was plain as day that Leuwen would rather be anywhere else at that moment than behind the bar at The Trough telling his story. He'd started off hemming and hawing, moaning about his bad memory and all, but

after Greyboar told him, and I quote: "You either spill
your guts or I do it for you," Leuwen got right into
the tale like a bard of the olden days. Positively
babbled, he did.

The Cat was in trouble. Big trouble.

It seemed—nobody really knew how it got started—
that she'd attracted the admiration of the Goatmonk
after we left for the Abbey. Probably ran into him while
she was wandering around looking for Schrödinger.
Anyway, his interest aroused, the Goatmonk had apparently followed her back to The Trough.

"The first I knew about it I swear the very first time
was when the Goatmonk come in the door and Fergus
said we had trouble and I looked and sure enough it
was him and I swear he went right to the table where
the Cat was sitting where she always does and I swear
it all happened so fast I didn't have time to move and
I swear I don't even know how he could've spotted her
so quick because you know how dark it always is in
this place that's how the customers like it and the lights
were just as dark as always I swear on my mother's
grave but he spotted her right away I don't know how
he could have—"

Simple, that was. The Goatmonk had ELP—
extra-lecherous perception. Every time he went off on
one of his country outings the farmers hid their wives
and daughters (and their mothers) in special bunkers.
They'd try to hide the sheep, too. Father Venery, they
called him.

Anyway, I'll just tell the story from here on, as I put
it together from Leuwen's babbling. Bit difficult to
follow his own petrified grammar, don't you know?

The Goatmonk hadn't come into The Trough in
quite a while. The one and only time he did The Roach
took a dislike to him. Instant dislike, in fact—the
Goatmonk didn't even make it to a chair. Unfortunately,

The Boots just missed him by a hair, and the Goatmonk made it out the door before The Roach could send him to the Big Cell in the Sky. Pity, that.

The Roach's voice—quite the voice it is, too—followed Father Venery down the street, informing him in The Roach's inimitable style that if the stinking priest ever showed his face in The Trough again he'd be so much stomped parson. Not scared of much, the Goatmonk wasn't, but like most people he had a real fear of The Boots. Not that I blamed him. Over the years I must have turned down a hundred jobs from The Roach's ex-employers, wanting to hire Greyboar to choke "that booted, bearded ruffian," as they usually called him.

First time we got an offer, I consulted with Greyboar, but the big guy said not a chance. "I like The Roach," he'd explained, "even though he doesn't approve of my 'idle ways,' as he calls them. Then, there's the fact that my sister thinks the world of him—'old friend and comrade-in-arms,' she calls him, when she isn't calling him 'the champion of the toiling masses.' Wouldn't want to antagonize Gwendolyn, surely wouldn't. And besides," he concluded, scratching his head thoughtfully, "I'm not actually sure how it would all turn out, trying to choke The Roach. Bit dicey, job like that, bit dicey. Fearsome they are, The Boots."

But the Goatmonk must've heard The Roach was out of town, so he followed the Cat into The Trough. The trouble started right away. The Goatmonk sat himself down at the Cat's table. She told him to get lost. Then Leuwen swore (a hundred times) that he tried to stop the whole thing before it got started but he swore (a thousand times) that the Cat told him to shut up, she didn't need any help. He was probably telling the truth, it'd be just like the Cat. What they call an independent woman. It was one of the reasons she and Greyboar were so tight—they gave each other plenty of room.

So anyway, the Goatmonk didn't take the hint. Started groping, he did. So the Cat whipped out her sword and started chopping. Father Venery was not easily discouraged, however, and responded by swinging away with his priestly staff. Figured he'd pound the woman into a pulp and then get on with the seduction, I imagine. Wouldn't be the first time he'd used that particular technique, no sirree.

It must have been a hell of a fight; I wish I'd seen it. Huge, the Goatmonk, built like a hippo. A lot of it fat, sure, but he was still as strong as a bull. And he always carried his staff. "To bless the poor," he'd say, laughing like a sewer. Six feet long, that staff, two inches thick, made of solid oak—the Old Geister knows what it weighed. Capped with iron ferrules at both ends. Father Venery could handle it like a normal man could handle a twig. Once, in the marketplace, I saw him split an ox's head with one blow of the staff. Just for the fun of it. Split the owner's head, too, when the peasant started yowling at him.

The Goatmonk started off aiming for the Cat's legs. Wasn't trying to kill the lady, just change her mood, don't you know? But soon enough it dawned on him that he'd gotten himself into something a lot trickier than it looked, and after that he started fighting in earnest.

Really wish I'd seen it. You wouldn't think it'd be much of a contest. The Cat was big for a woman, but she was no giantess like Greyboar's sister. True, she was quick on her feet, and her sword was three feet long and sharp as a razor. But she was also half blind. And the truth of it is, she hadn't any real idea of how to use a sword. She'd just grab hold of the hilt like it was an axe and start chopping.

But I'd seen the Cat in a fight before, that time in Blain, and I would've put my money on her in a minute.

You see, the woman's strange. Really strange. Sure, and you always hear that women are unpredictable, but the Cat took it to extremes.

Oh, I would've given a lot to have been there! I could see it in my mind. Father Venery roaring like a bull, his staff slashing right and left. And the Cat here and there and up and down and back and forth, cutting and chopping and hacking and hewing at anything at all that happened to be in the area. I almost felt sorry for the Goatmonk. Whenever he thought she was one place, she'd be someplace else. And whenever she was moving, it was either faster than he thought or slower than it looked or just plain in the opposite direction from where she was going. It's impossible to describe the Cat in action. I know, I've seen her. You can figure out where she is, or how fast she's going, but you can't do both at the same time. And sure, she was practically blind, so she couldn't see the Goatmonk either, but did the Cat care? Not a fig. She just chopped away at whatever was around, playing the percentages. Innocent spectators be damned.

Made the Cat's fights quite exciting for would-be bystanders, I can tell you. Oh, do I wish I'd been there! It makes me laugh just to think about it!

The Trough was packed. It'd been a busy night to begin with, and once the word hit the streets everybody came running. The Trio in B-Flat came charging in just as the Cat's sword went whizzing through the doorway. They were down in a flash. Good reflexes, those boys—best thieves in the Flankn. Naturally, they fell to quarreling.

"Twenty bob on th'lady!" cried McDoul.

"You're on!" came Geronimo Jerry. The Weasel held the bet. The money was in his hand before they hit the floor.

Yeah, the Cat was all over the place. It was a good thing for the spectators that she was still using her sword instead of the lajatang she'd been training on. One second she'd be chopping up the counter, the next a table in a corner, then swinging at some poor slob who was just trying to watch. She was hacking at anything that moved—anything that didn't move, for that matter.

And the patrons! Scrambling for cover under tables one minute, climbing on each others' shoulders for a good view the next. It's not like they couldn't have left if they were worried about their skins. Naturally, nobody did, except old Sylvester, and he never heard the end of it. "A proper Trough-man'd rather die than miss a good fight." He's heard that sneer a thousand times since, if he's heard it once.

A great fight! Best fight in years! Everybody agreed on that after it was all over. Of course, it always helps to have a local favorite, and it goes without saying that everybody was cheering for the Cat. Even the ones with their money on the Goatmonk, which was almost all of them.

A great fight! Went on for quite a while, too. After a good ten minutes, the Goatmonk hadn't landed once on the Cat. Didn't sound like he even came close. And the Cat? Well, it's true, the first ten minutes she hadn't made a real mark on Father Venery, either. But she'd nicked him more than once, and in the meantime she'd turned half the furniture into kindling and put a few hundred serious ale drinkers through a crash exercise program that must have dropped eight tons, collective gross.

The end was inevitable. One moment the Cat was

over in a corner, making toothpicks out of a chair. The next thing anybody knew she was standing right in front of the Goatmonk, caught him smack off guard.

Sssstttt. Plop. The moment of truth.

When Leuwen got to that part of the story, I couldn't stop laughing for five minutes. Even Greyboar cracked a smile, mad as he was.

Don't let anybody tell you there's no such thing as poetic justice.

The Cat never even noticed. *Sssstttt*, plop, and she's on her way, hacking up a table down the room. But everybody else saw it. Total silence. Father Venery was just standing there, eyes popped out, couldn't even move.

The Trio broke the spell. They convulsed to the floor.

"Goatmonk no more!" howled the Weasel.

"We'll call 'im Monkmonk f'r sure!" came McDoul.

Yeah, that's where the name started, and it's stuck ever since. The Monkmonk. Father Chastity. You still see him around, now and again. Look for a very fat monk lying in a gutter somewhere, clutching a bottle of cheap wine, sobbing and wailing and crying out to the Lord. In a high-pitched voice.

A great story, and under other circumstances Greyboar would have been the first to relish it.

But at the moment, things were a bit sticky. Because the Goatmonk, you see, was beloved by the Church authorities in New Sfinctr, especially Luigi Carnale, Cardinal Fornacaese, his drinking buddy. And the Queen! Belladonna III thought the Goatmonk was a holy man, listened to every word he ever drooled. Main reason Father Venery had survived as long as he had, seeing as how half the fathers and husbands of the Sfinctrian aristocracy would have cut his throat in a minute.

So naturally it wasn't but a few hours later that the Praetorian Guard came pouring into The Trough to arrest the Cat. Wasn't any problem for them, the arrest itself. The Cat was sitting in a corner, sharpening her sword, paying no attention to anything. Totally ignored the Guard when they grabbed her and hustled her into the paddy wagon. Off in her own world, like she often was. Strange, strange woman.

But first, of course, the Guard had to get through The Trough. Packed solid, mind you, with proper Trough-men. Took a bit of time, that did. Time and trouble. A few months later, a friendly Guardsman I met in a tavern told me it was worse than the Second Battle of the Bundy.

For the moment, however, the problem was that Greyboar was not entirely satisfied that the patrons had quite put up the good fight. I'll grant you, his demands were a bit unreasonable.

"Two hours?" he roared. *"Two lousy hours?"* The Trough-men in the room blanched. Greyboar continued bellowing.

"When they came after Lefty Davidovich we stood 'em off for four hours! Long enough for Lefty to make his escape!"

"Those was just Stullens," whined Fergus.

"And what about the Big Banjo?" demanded Greyboar. "When they came after him, we held 'em off for a whole day! They quit trying!"

"Them was just porkers and such," whimpered Angus.

"An' besides," sniveled Danny Boy, "the Big Banjo's hero of the people, the whole Flankn turned out that time."

"Was just us this time," blubbered Scotty, "and you wasn't here, nor The Roach neither."

But, like I said, Greyboar was in one of his rare

unreasonable moods. He glared around the room. Everybody hung their heads. Then he cracked his knuckles, like the doom.

"I am not pleased," he announced.

Now and then, you'll sometimes hear it called The Running of the Bellies Through The Streets of New Sfinctr. Other times, The Great Flankn Stampede. But mostly, people call it The One Day The Trough Emptied Out.

Casualties were minimal, however, thanks to O'Neal. Don't think it wasn't appreciated, either. Never been a day since somebody doesn't buy the poor fellow an ale pot and politely listen to him croak a word or two.

Naturally—I believe I've mentioned before that O'Neal was not quite bright?—this was the time O'Neal chose to stand his ground.

"And besides," he'd grumbled, just as the stampede got started, "she's only a woman. Shouldn't even be hanging around in here at all, she shouldn't, 'tisn't ladylike. So why should—" His last words spoken in a normal tone of voice, here faithfully recorded for posterity.

I tried to tell Zulkeh the story, years later, but the wizard cut me off before I hardly even got started.

"Bah!" he oathed. "Am I an ignoramus, to be told of The One Day The Trough Emptied Out? 'Tis the classic illustration in the literature of the theory of natural selection! Darwin Laebmauntsforscynneweëld himself devoted an entire chapter to the episode in his *Evolution of Common Sense in Man*."

So it was O'Neal who saved the day. Kept Greyboar preoccupied while everybody else made their escape. The strangler even lingered over the job, not at all like his usual "give-'em-one-quick-crunch-and-move-on-to-the-next." He was bound and determined, it seemed, to prove that the euphemism "wring his neck" was not a euphemism. O'Neal even survived the experience, unlike his vocal cords. By the time Greyboar went after the rest, they had a good head start. And as quick as he is with his hands, Greyboar's not really built for a long stern chase, don't you know. Like I said, light casualties.

Eventually, Greyboar came back to The Trough. I was there, perched on a barstool, chatting with Leuwen. Only customer in the place. (Not counting O'Neal, who didn't regain consciousness for hours.) Leuwen paled when Greyboar came in, but he stayed put. Couldn't have outrun the big guy anyway, as fat as he was.

"I can't take sides in a brawl, Greyboar," squeaked Leuwen. "I'm a barkeep. Professional ethics, you know?"

Greyboar glowered at him, but he let it go. Had a great respect for professional ethics, the strangler did.

Quick as a snake, Leuwen put a pot of ale in front of Greyboar. "On the house," he squeaked.

Greyboar took a drink.

"And where was the Trio in B-Flat?" he demanded. "I was looking for those boys especial, looking to wring their mangy necks. I've been hearing Geronimo Jerry claimed to be my cousin last time he was in the Pile, so's the guards would treat him good. Was going to let it pass, but—!" He glowered. "Mangiest dogs in the Flankn, the Trio."

"Actually," I responded, "if you hadn't been so all-fired eager to throttle the collective throat of the ale-house world, you'd have done the intelligent thing like I did and stuck around and let Leuwen finish the story."

"Trio's in the Pile," said Leuwen, his voice sounding more like its usual self. "They was the last row, you know, between the Cat and the Guard. Fought on, the boys did, longer than anyone. Kept the Guard at bay all by themselves, the last minute or so. Pissed off the Guard so much they was the only ones besides the Cat herself what got arrested as well as beat up."

Greyboar frowned, took another pull of ale. Then—I loved it!—said: "Good lads, the Trio. Always said so."

"Cat's trial is tomorrow," I told him.

Greyboar sat up straight. "We'll go! Stand by her side!"

"Don't be stupid!" I snapped. "Think they'll let lowlifes like us—you especially!—anywhere near the Royal Court? Much less get inside! Leuwen's been telling me the Queen's ordered the whole Guard out for security at the trial. Not just the Guard, either. The Fifth Hussars are being brought into the city for crowd control. The Black Grenadiers've been assigned to patrol the city limits, keep out the peasants."

"Supposed to be a whole column of peasants marching on the city tomorrow," commented Leuwen. "Got icons and everything, going to petition the Ecclesiarchs to declare the Cat a saint."

"But I've got to see her!" cried Greyboar. "Got to figure out a way to get her out of this mess." He glared at his alepot like it was the cause of the problem. Then—surprise, surprise—he turned to me.

"You're supposed to be the brains of the team, Ignace," he grumbled. "Think of something."

Bite the tongue, bite the tongue, bite the tongue. That's what I had to tell myself, so's I wouldn't do something really stupid—really fatal, probably, given the mood of the moment—like make sarcastic remarks about self-professed philosophers.

"What do you want me to do?" I complained. "I can't even figure out how we could get into the courtroom, much less rescue the Cat."

"You'll never be able to spring her right now," said Leuwen. "You wouldn't believe the security! The

Queen's in a rare fury, curse her soul. Have to wait till the trial's over, and the Cat's been sentenced. Then maybe things'll ease up a bit."

"Cat'll be dead by then!" cried Greyboar. "Executed!"

Leuwen shook his head. "Not a chance, Greyboar. The Cat's not for an early grave, that's sure. The Queen ordered Judge Rancor Jeffreys be put on the bench for the trial."

Greyboar paled a little. Some of that was relief, sure, because with Jeffreys on the bench there wasn't any chance the Cat was in for a quick execution. But it wasn't much relief. Jeffreys didn't believe in quick hangings, except when he ordered judges hanged who didn't hand down enough death sentences.

No, no, not the good Judge Rancor Jeffreys. Said it once, he'd said it a million times: "Quick hanging's no deterrent to your lowlife miscreant. Sneer at it, the scum do. Their lives are worthless to begin with, so what do they care about a quick and easy snap of the neck? No, no, lords and ladies of the court! A thousand times no! Death by torture—that's the trick! Slow, horrible, lingering death—there's the ticket! Prolonged agony, endless torment—aye, the very thing!" And he prides himself on the ingenuity of his sentences, does the good Judge Rancor Jeffreys.

"What you've got to do," mused Leuwen, "is find someone who can get into the trial. They can report back to you, tell you what happened. Especially, they can let you know what the Cat's sentence was. Then you might be able to figure out some way of rescuing the lady."

Greyboar snorted. "And who do I know could get into the Royal Court? All my friends are lowlifes, and look the part."

"One of your customers, maybe?" asked Leuwen. "Mostly noblemen, them. They could get in."

"Are you nuts?" demanded Greyboar. "Sure, most of my customers are nobles. So what? I'm their strangler, not their bosom buddy. Wouldn't give me the time of day, they wouldn't, if they didn't need somebody choked."

"Then what about them two girls show up here now and then? Never actually come into the place, I think they're too shy. But they've peeked in here a few times, looking for Ignace. Raised his prestige no end, I might add."

"Angela and Jenny?" I asked.

"That's the ones," said Leuwen. "Sure, why not have them get in? They could do it, too, I bet, if they wore the right kind of hoity-toity clothes. Guard wouldn't look at 'em twice, as cute and innocent looking as they are."

Well, I thought the idea was terrible and I said so more than once, and quite forcefully and in no uncertain terms either. Imagine! Dragging two sweet young girls into something like this!

But Greyboar thought it was a great idea. And when they heard the idea from Greyboar later that evening, Jenny and Angela thought it was a great idea too.

"Oh, that'll be wonderful!" said Jenny. "Sure we'll try to help you spring your lady!" said Angela. And before you could say a thing, they were hauling out cloth by the yard and planning out their fancy dresses.

I was still against the whole idea, but nobody was paying the slightest attention to me. Greyboar and Jenny and Angela plotted it out while they were working on the dresses. I contributed the voice of sanity, but nobody was listening to my protests. I especially started protesting when I got roped into the scheme.

Angela's doing, that was. After they'd finished the dresses, her face fell, and she started shaking her head vigorously.

"It'll never work," she said. "It'll never work, just
me and Jenny. You never see two young noble ladies
out by themselves. They're always with a chaperone.
We need a chaperone."

At first, I was smiling like the sunshine. She was
right, bless the little darling! And Greyboar and I didn't
know any sour-faced old women; at least, not any who'd
go in on this scheme!

Greyboar said as much. *And that's that*, I said to
myself.

"But it doesn't have to be an old woman chaperone,"
said Jenny. "Lots of times it's an old man, a tutor like,
a little tiny guy all shriveled up, looking like he's worn
out and worried about everything."

All eyes turned to me. I was outraged.

My first sentences, expressing my total disagreement
with the idea, were possibly not coherent. But I was
soon able to demolish the scheme.

"It's impossible!" I sprang to my feet, spread my
arms wide. "Look at me! I'm the picture of health!
Straight as an arrow! Vigorous! Handsome! Look at my
face! Cheerful! Debonair! Look at the rakish goatee—
the suave mustachioes!"

"He's right," said Angela. And the two hoydens from
hell got out the scissors and started cutting. Greyboar
held me down.

"It's really a great idea!" squealed Angela. "He's so
tiny already he won't even have to stoop! Just put him
in a big coat and everybody'll think he's worn out by
a lifetime of teaching stupid little girls!"

I made several remarks concerning stupid little girls.
Jenny chucked me under the chin and cooed: "We
don't care if you're a shrimp, Iggy. We think you're
cute."

Then, after I'd been shorn of my hair and bundled
into a greatcoat, I tried again: "It still won't work! I

just don't have the right air about me! I ask you—do I look worn out? Exhausted by life's cares? Ridiculous!"

All three of them stared at me. Then Jenny and Angela looked at Greyboar and smiled sweetly.

"Greyboar, why don't you come back tomorrow morning?" suggested Jenny.

"Not too early," added Angela.

Chapter 17.
The Cat in a Box

When Greyboar showed up the next morning, the girls brought me out, all bundled up. I've got to admit, the costume they designed was perfect. And I could hardly stand up.

"There's still the one big problem," said Angela, frowning.

"That stupid grin he's got plastered all over his face," complained Jenny. "It just doesn't go with the image we're looking for."

"No problem," rumbled Greyboar. "I'll take care of that."

Not more than ten minutes later, the girls and I were on our way to the courthouse in a carriage Greyboar had hired. By now, I had to admit, the plan just might work. I was dressed the part, I probably did look like I was exhausted to the point of death, and I certainly bore on my face the look of a man worried about everything. Of course, I wasn't worried about everything. I was worried about just one thing. The Thumbs of Eternity. Greyboar had been most explicit.

"You choke, I choke. So don't blow your lines."

Believe it or not, it worked like a charm. Angela and Jenny were perfect. They looked like the sunshine to begin with, and dressed in their finery—I mean, who could possibly have taken them for lowlifes bent on undoing the Royal Justice?

And me? Well. Ahem. Ahem. Ignace the Great Thespian, at your service!

Actually, it was easy. On the way over to the court-house, I figured it all out. All I had to do was act like a complete pedant. And hadn't I—not so long before, either!—spent days and days in the company of Zulkeh of Goimr, physician? Sure and he was probably the greatest sorcerer in the world, but there was no question at all that he was the world's pedant *par excellence*.

And so it was we breezed right through the guards into the courtroom.

"Blessed beyond measure are you, unworthy children!" I lectured Jenny and Angela in a loud voice, wagging my finger, as we walked down the corridor. "Thus to have the privilege of observing in person the great Judge Rancor Jeffreys! In full regalia—like unto the jurists of old! Why, did not the great Solon Laebmauntsforscynneweëld himself, in his classic *Justice Begins With the Rope*, compare Judge Jeffreys to the legendary—though, I admit, 'tis true that Hammurabi Sfondrati-Piccolomini has, in a recent monograph in the *Journal of Avant-Garde Torture*, advanced the argument that Jeffreys lacks—well! No need to wallow in Hammurabi's pathetic reasoning. Nay, fie upon such witless notions! The man has absolutely no grasp of the dialectic. And his epistemology! Scandalous, scandalous, there's no other word for it! Unless, perhaps, the word be disreputable, or infamous, or contemptible, or ignominious, or execrable, or peccant, or opprobrious, or—"

Well, you get the idea.

Before you knew it, we were ushered into the galleries reserved for the aristocracy. Only challenged once, by an officious usher. But he fled before the torrent of my polysyllabic indignation.

Quite interesting, actually, the whole experience. Not, of course, the first time I'd been in the Royal Courtroom with Judge Rancor Jeffreys on the bench. But on all previous occasions I'd been seated down below. In the docks for the accused, to be precise.

And here came Judge Rancor Jeffreys, seating himself at the bench. Just as I remembered him. He was really a difficult man to forget, don't you know. It wasn't so much the stony face, the gleaming eyes, the lips like a vise, the nose like a hatchet, the chin like a spade, the jaws like the very crunch of fate. No, it was the way he dressed. Not the gloomy black robes, of course—you expect that on a judge. No, it was the great necklace of finger bones, the earrings made of babes' skulls, the hangman's noose for a necktie, the scalps woven into his wig, the tattoo of an Iron Maiden on his forehead, the gavel in the form of a miniature headsman's axe. A disheartening sight he was, to the defendant in the dock. The cup of blood from which he refreshed himself throughout a trial didn't help much, either.

Then they brought the Cat out and hauled her into the dock.

I won't bore you with a recital of the charges. They were long, long, long. And mostly silly, although I liked the one about "interfering with a cleric in his pursuit of the Lord's work." And I thought "altering the voice of piety" was a very nice touch.

Best part was when the Cat was allowed to speak.

This was usually the point where the accused threw themselves on the mercy of the Court. Never did any good, of course, but pleading innocence was always worse. Infuriated Judge Jeffreys, pleas of innocence did.

But the Cat wasn't having any of it. A strange, strange woman. But she had a will of iron, and she just didn't give a damn.

She started off by peering at Jeffreys through her bottle-bottom spectacles, inspecting him like he was a side of wormy meat.

"Boy, do you look like a side of wormy meat," she said. "Why don't you wash those scalps once in a while? They're collecting flies. But it probably wouldn't do any good—I'm sure you stink like the pits of hell all by yourself."

She had a great, loud, piercing voice, the Cat, on the rare occasions when she wasn't speaking softly. That day she wasn't speaking softly. Oh no, not at all.

Jeffreys started to bellow with rage, but the Cat's voice cut right through it like a foghorn.

"You have got to be the sorriest slob I ever saw," she continued. "Why don't you do the world a favor and tighten your necktie? And where did you get those babes' skulls hanging from your ears, anyway? Did you fight off the mongrels in the garbage pit for 'em? No, can't be that—you couldn't scare off a puppy. Of course! I know! Must have been your own tots—died laughing at your dick when you waved it in their faces. And what's with the blood-drinking business, anyway? I know! You need it to—"

That was as far as she got, before the guards chained her and gagged her. I'm glad Greyboar wasn't there. Cool as he usually was, he would have lost it then. I'll grant you, he would have taken plenty of guards with him, but he'd still never have made it to the front of the courtroom. Not even Greyboar could have fought his way through all the troops they had in the place.

Jeffreys was in a rare humor, let me tell you! Fact is, he was so apoplectic that he couldn't think of a suitable sentence. The Church came to the rescue. Luigi Carnale, Cardinal Fornacaese, asked leave to address the bench. Jeffreys garbled something the Cardinal took for an assent, and he said:

"May I recommend to the Royal Justice that the defendant—whose horrid crimes have now been compounded by contempt of court—deserves nothing less than the ancient sentence of immuration, so sadly unused in these excessively liberal modern times."

Oh boy, I thought to myself, that was about the worst thing I could think of to do to the Cat. The woman absolutely hated being confined. And this—*immuration*.

Naturally, Jeffreys was ecstatic.

"Of course! Of course! Perfect!" And so he pounded his gavel—actually, he only pounded it once because he swung so hard the little axe got stuck in the bench, but never mind—and sentenced the accused to immuration. The guards started to haul the Cat away—quick, your Royal Justice in Sfinctria—but the Cardinal stopped them.

"A moment, Your Honor! I believe—well, I'm afraid the Church must insist—that the felon should be immured in that portion of the Durance Pile set aside for offenders against God. Is not her crime equivalent to heresy? What greater scorn could she have shown for the Lord Above than to have so foully disfigured His beloved servant?"

Well, Jeffreys wasn't going to argue the point, so the Cat was sentenced to immuration in the heretics' quarter of the Pile, and that was that. She was hauled off, and we slid out of there with the crowd.

～　～　～

"Immuration," groaned Greyboar. "You know how the Cat hates being cooped up, it'll kill her."

"Well, yes," I said, "that's the whole idea. You wall up the condemned in a sealed room, buried under a pile of rock, and leave them there to die. Not too quick, of course—there'll be a separate room full of dried food, enough to keep you going for years if you ration it proper. And a water supply, just a trickle, but enough to keep you alive forever. And that's it. There you are, alone in a room dark as death, forgotten by the world. Eventually you die, but no one will ever know when. It's an old sentence, immuration, hasn't been used hardly in centuries. There's people in rooms in the Durance Pile were immured a thousand years ago. Nobody's ever opened their crypts."

"But at least she'll be alive for a while," said Jenny. "And they haven't really hurt her or nothing."

"So we've got time to figure out how to rescue her!" piped up Angela.

I glared at her. "What's this 'we' business?" I demanded. "I mean, you've been a great help, even if I didn't like the idea and still don't, but that's it. From here on you girls are out of it."

Jenny and Angela glared right back.

"You can go jump in a lake!" said Jenny.

"That was a lot of fun, what we did," added Angela. "Never done anything like that before, we haven't. Felt good, sticking it to the high and mighty, instead of the other way around like it's always been for us."

I would've continued the argument, but Greyboar cut me off.

"This is all counting chickens before they're hatched. First we've got to figure out a way to rescue the Cat. Then we can argue about who's in on it and who isn't." The strangler gave me one of his patented stares. Chill a volcano, that stare. "And if the plan needs two girls what've got more spunk in 'em than any ten average cutthroats," he added, "then they're in."

Jenny and Angela squealed with delight. "Let's come up with a plan!" they cried in unison.

Greyboar was scratching his chin. "First thing we've got to do is find out everything we can about the Durance Pile," he said. "Ignace and I have been in it ourselves a few times, but they always keep us in a special cell, so we don't really know much about the whole layout." He looked over to me.

"Who knows the most about the Pile?" he asked.

"The Trio in B-Flat, who else? They've held the record for incarceration for—what is it now?—yeah, four years running. Don't even have any real contenders, any more. Hook Harvey made a pretty good run at the title two years ago, but then—you remember, that heist went bad?—he—"

"Yeah, yeah, I remember," interrupted the strangler. "All right, so we'll have to bring the Trio in on it. They owe me a favor anyway," he added, flexing his hands, "seeing as how I let 'em live after using my name like they did to cozzen the guards."

A great guy in his own way, Greyboar, don't get me wrong. But for somebody who claimed to be a philosophy student, he had the thickest skull in creation. I tried to break it to him gently.

"You stupid jackass," I snarled, "the Trio are in the slammer their own selves! How are they going to help? What are we supposed to do, march up to the warden and tell him pretty please we've got to talk to the Trio so's we can figure out how to spring your star inmate? Overmuscled moron. What was it the wizard called you? Oh yeah—the mentally retarded mesomorph!"

Greyboar didn't even scowl. I hate to admit it, but my attempts at constructive criticism never did have much impact on the big loon. The big loony, I should say, because naturally he added:

"So first we'll have to spring the Trio."

I threw up my hands in despair. "That's great! That's great! In order to spring the Cat we've got to first spring the Trio! And in order to do that—what's your plan? No, tell me—it's great to watch a genius at work! Don't hide your light under a bushel! Who have we got to spring in order to figure out how to spring the Trio, so's we can spring the Cat. And who do—"

I was interrupted by a knock on the door. Jenny and Angela jumped in their chairs.

"Who could that be?" asked Jenny. "We haven't actually opened our shop yet."

"Nobody comes here except you guys," added Angela. There was a trace of apprehension in her voice. "You don't think it could be some—well, you know, another assassin like you were supposed to be?"

Greyboar chuckled. "I really doubt it, girls. The Baron's in no position to hire any more assassins. And just in case there might be some friend or relative who gets ideas, I had Ignace pass the word around that I would take it hard if any harm should come to you. Real, real hard." He looked at me. "You did pass the word around, Ignace?"

I laughed. "Sure! I started with Reilly—he's the top specialist in wayward girl jobs, you know? Explained to him that even though you've always been a stickler about doing a proper choke, anything happened to Jenny and Angela you'd like as not lose your professional aplomb and revert back like an animal to your days in the slaughterhouse. Described in detail, I did, how you used to debone steers with your bare hands on account of you'd get impatient with all that slow knifework. When I got to how hard it'd be for him, bellying up to the bar to order a pot of ale, what with no spine and all, he started puking."

There was another knock on the door.

Jenny got up, looking less nervous. "Well, I'd better see who it is." She disappeared into the little vestibule which led to the front door. We heard the sound of indistinct voices for a minute. Jenny returned, looking puzzled.

"It's three gentlemen—well, they really look more like three ruffians—well, actually, more like absolute scoundrels—who say they're the Trio in B-Flat and they're looking for Greyboar and Ignace. They say Leuwen the barkeep told them you might be here."

"The Trio!" exclaimed Greyboar. "But how did they—well, let's hear it from them. Show 'em in, Jenny, if you wouldn't mind."

Chapter 18.
The Trio's Tale

A moment later the Trio filed into the room. It was them all right, in the flesh. Erlic the Weasel, McDoul, and Geronimo Jerry—that's what everybody called him, anyway, that or just "G.J." He had some fancy official moniker which ran on about three sentences, full of "de" thises and "y" thats; claimed to be descended from a long line of Grenadine landholders. But nobody believed that story, not even G.J. himself.

They were looking a mite apprehensive. I could tell— the twitchy feet alone gave them away. Not to mention the sidelong glances at the door, oh, maybe eight times a second, like they were sizing up the escape route. Fat lot of good it'd do them! Well, McDoul could have probably outrun Greyboar, he could scurry faster than any hunchback I ever saw. And Erlic might have had a chance on the flat, if he could avoid tripping over his potbelly. But Geronimo Jerry couldn't have escaped a pack of wild turtles. The man was built like a two-legged pumpkin.

And, of course, they were bowing and scraping and tugging their forelocks.

"Quite th'onor, this, y'Gripship sir," babbled the Weasel, "bein' admitted t'ye presence 'n all."

"Aye!" and "aye!" came from McDoul and G.J.

"Cut it out!" snapped Greyboar. "What am I? Some snooty count you're fawning all over so's you can figure out the quickest way to get to his purse?"

Erlic—he was more or less the leader of the gang, emphasis on the less—cleared his throat and said:

"N'doubt, n'doubt. Aye an' I've long admired y'philosophic acumenation, y'Squeezeness—Greyboar, I mean t'say!—idna 'at true, lads? 'Aven't I—th'million times at th'least!—spoke'd like th'true dev'tee of th'uncanny intelligence of y'Lord 'o th'Larynx? 'Aven't I? 'N now y'can ken for y'selfes the—"

"CUT IT OUT!" roared Greyboar.

It was a great act, really. Best thieves in the Flankn, the Trio, there was no doubt about it. The most craven lackeys in the world's grandest throne rooms couldn't hold a candle to them when it came to lickspittling and kowtowing. Big part of the reason for their success. There was many the fine gentleman been found in an alley, his throat cut and his purse gone, with that unmistakable look of utter astonishment on his face that told you the Trio did the job.

The Weasel cleared his throat again.

"Well, it's like this, Greyboar. We just got out o' th'Pile and natural we right off headed down to th'Trough fer a brew, when what'd ye know but what Leuwen explained t'us as to what ye was inquirin' as t'our whereabouts, an' so—" He cleared his throat again. "—an' so we's consulted 'mongst ourselfes an' decided as to what would prob'bly be best t'come see you right off, rather then wait an' all until y'found us on y'own an' all." Another throat clearing. "What wit' y'blood in y'eye."

And then, of course, they fell to quarreling. The Weasel and McDoul swore on the graves of the mothers they never knew that it had all been Geronimo Jerry's idea to claim Greyboar as his cousin so that the porkers in the Pile would pay back the money G.J. lent to them at his normal usurious rates. Geronimo Jerry swore on the graves of a long line of fictitious Grenadine landholders—hidalgos one and all, to hear him say it—that he'd been talked into it by the other two on account of their insatiable lust for the little finer things of life what make a long stay in the dungeon tolerable and which can only be gotten from bribing guards and how are you supposed to bribe guards in the first place when you're broke and so what better way to do it but lend them money at 200% the weekly interest—don't ask me where they got the seed money, I couldn't follow it—and then of course the problem is getting the great surly sadistic brutes to pay back the money and how else to do it but claim the world's greatest strangler as your cousin what dotes on you and it was all McDoul's idea in the first place. That was a nice little touch, that last twist, because before you knew it the lineup was shifting and now it was Erlic admitting as to how, well, yes, and it had been McDoul who'd thought it up first and Erlic and G.J. had just gone along because sure and McDoul swore as he'd talked it all over with Greyboar before they'd gotten pitched into the Pile. And then—your great chancellors and ministers haven't got a thing on the Trio when it comes to treacherous alliances and *realpolitik*—the wind started veering again when McDoul demanded as to how he could have spoken to Greyboar and gotten permission ahead of time when everybody knew Greyboar had been in Prygg hiding out from the porkers and wasn't it actually—this to Geronimo Jerry—Erlic who'd claimed he'd gotten a letter from

the great strangler in Prygg graciously giving his nod
to the impersonation and of course he and G.J. had
taken the Weasel's word for it since wasn't it true that
Erlic always handled the Trio's correspondence on
account of McDoul and G.J. were wretched orphans
what had never learned to read and write—a bald-faced
lie, that; any one of the Trio can distinguish in the blink
of an eye between the denominations of every known
currency in the world—being as they had been forced
to work in the sweatshops since they was tots. And
then—

Well, I was enjoying the whole thing, I love to watch
masters of a trade at their work, but Greyboar was in
one of his impatient moods so he cut it short. He could
always cut through long-winded argumentation,
Greyboar. Three quick squeezes and the Trio fell as
silent as the tomb.

"I don't care about you claiming to be my cousin,"
he grumbled, after he resumed his seat. "I would have
let it go, anyway." He chuckled. "Kind of amused me,
actually, cozzening the porkers like that."

Then he gave them a sour look, and said: "I hate
to admit it, but you three worthless hounds happen to
be in my good graces at the moment. On account of
how I heard you fought to the last gasp when the
Guard came to arrest the Cat."

"Ye wunnerful Cat!" hacked Erlic.

"Natural we did'r best to defen' th'Lady o' the
Flankn," choked McDoul.

"Th'Light o' Sfinctria," gasped Geronimo Jerry.

"Speakin' o' last gasps an' all," said Erlic, massaging his throat, "ye wouldna 'appen t'ave th'odd pot o'
ale lyin' about now, would ye? Thirsty work, bein'
throttled an' all."

Jenny went to get some ale, and soon enough the
Trio were sitting about on the floor drinking their pots

and cheerful as could be. Not surprising, this was one of the few times they'd ever enjoyed Greyboar's good graces.

"How did you get out of the Pile, anyway?" I asked. "For that matter, how'd you get out the time before that?"

The Trio grinned in unison.

"We informers," Erlic announced proudly.

"On th'highest levels, no less," added McDoul.

"Report direct to th'Queen's Inspector General, we do," said G.J.

"An' to the Cruds!" cried Erlic. He was positively beaming.

"Been interviewed by th'Angel Jimmy Jesus hisself," boasted McDoul.

"Come all th'way from the occupation in Prygg, 'e did," bragged G.J., "just t'question us personal."

Well, I believe I'll just summarize the story. Always enjoyed the Trio's dialogue myself, but I admit it gets a tad difficult for the uninitiated to follow. And I'll say it now, before I even begin, that you have to hand it to the Trio—nobody else could have pulled this one off.

They'd been in the Pile for some crime or other. I don't remember the details, but it must have been a doozy because Jeffreys had sentenced them to the lowest dungeons. Then, as it turned out, the artist Benvenuti wound up in the very same cell, after he got convicted of defrauding the Church.

Greyboar interrupted them at that point, wanting to make sure they were talking about the same Benvenuti. But it only took the Trio a minute to satisfy him. It was Benny all right. The description was perfect.

(Weird coincidence, I thought at the time. Later, in light of ensuing events, I realized that it was the inexorable workings of fate. Shit happening, like it always does.)

Getting back to the Trio's tale, what did you know but what the great lawyer Jauncey Utterwert Muroidea IV was the next one pitched into the cell with them. He'd somehow fallen out of momentary favor with the Queen, which is not hard to do. Greyboar and I recognized the name, of course, since Muroidea was one of the scummiest lawyers of Sfinctria (i.e., the Scum of Scum). Known as "the bonestripper" in the slums of the city, Muroidea. You could satisfy your regular lawyer with a pound of flesh nearest the heart, but not Muroidea—he always got the full measure.

Muroidea didn't survive but a few minutes in the cell. The Trio would have slit his throat on general principles anyway, but beyond that—well, no need to go into the grisly details. Let's just say that they saw to it that there were no remains of Muroidea and leave it at that.

Then, no sooner had they disposed of Muroidea when who should pop up into their cell, out of a tunnel he'd dug from below, but the famous Underground Artist of New Sfinctr, Vincent van Goph? The great painter sketched a triptych on the walls of their cell. Then, just as he'd finished, the porkers came into the cell looking for Muroidea, who had just been pardoned by the Queen and named her new Royal Adjudicator. (The Queen's favor is fickle—you can fall into it as fast as you can out.)

Vincent van Goph made his escape down the tunnel, along with the artist Benvenuti, but the Trio hadn't managed it because G.J. had gotten stuck in the hole. Again, Greyboar interrupted, to make sure that Benvenuti had actually made his escape. The Trio assured us that he had. But . . .

Being lost in the labyrinth of tunnels beneath the

dungeons of New Sfinctr didn't really qualify as much of an "escape." The tales about those tunnels were enough to terrify a demon. But that was the last they'd seen of Benny. Disappearing down the hole.

So there they were—caught red-handed in an escape attempt right after vanishing a lawyer who'd just been appointed the Queen's Royal Adjudicator. A dark moment, you'd think, in the life of desperate criminals.

Not them. Sure, and your average felons would have been for the high jump. But they were always quick-witted, the Trio.

So right away, after being hauled before the Queen's Inspector General, they started in spinning a tale of how they had been cowering in the cell, listening to Muroidea and that other beast, what's-his-name, planning to cut their throats before the lawyer and his cohort made good their escape so that the Trio wouldn't be able to warn the Queen of the coming attempt on her life.

What coming attempt on her life? Why, the one Muroidea boasted about. Rubbing his hands with glee, he was, cackling at the thought of the poor Queen sprawled on the throne, her life's blood pouring out of a hundred wounds. A horrible plot! Masterminded, of course, by the Dark Duke.

What Dark Duke? Muroidea's boss, the archvillain of the conspiracy. Well, no, the Trio didn't know exactly who it was, but it was plain as day from listening to Muroidea talking with that other vicious assassin, what's-his-name, that the Dark Duke had to be one of the great nobles of Sfinctria. The Trio would have figured that out anyway, because nobody else but a great nobleman could afford to have a thousand assassins on his payroll.

What thousand assassins? Why, the ones Muroidea told the other scoundrel, what's-his-name, that the Dark

Duke had gotten infiltrated into every level of the Sfinctrian government. Hundreds of 'em in the Praetorian Guard alone.

Every level of the Queen's government? Naturally, on account of how this Muroidea and his fellow cabalist—what's-his-name—were the trickiest plotters you ever ran into. Why, hadn't Muroidea even fooled the Queen herself into appointing him the Royal Adjudicator? Of course, when he heard the porkers coming into the cell, natural and he'd had to take it on the lam, even forgetting to slit the Trio's throats, on account of how he must have figured the Queen's men were on to him and of course he couldn't afford to be caught and tortured where he might spill his guts because didn't Muroidea know every detail of the whole plot, even including the identity of the Dark Duke's mole in the highest levels of Ozar's greatest espionage agency, the Commission to Repel Unbridled Disruption?

And, of course, that was the masterstroke. Because as soon as the Crud adviser who was sitting in on the Trio's interrogation heard that, he screeched like a castrated pig and demanded that the Trio be held for questioning by the Angel Jimmy Jesus himself, the Director of the Cruds. And, sure enough, as soon as he got the news the Angel raced in to interview the Trio.

From then on, of course, they were in the gravy. The Angel Jimmy Jesus was undoubtedly the world's champion paranoid, and he'd been saying for years that the Cruds had been infiltrated by moles, and now—at last!—he had proof. Mind you, nobody in their right mind would have believed the Trio if they'd said the sun rose in the east and set in the west. The porkers tried to tell that to the Angel, but he wasn't having any of it. Then again, nobody had ever accused the Angel Jimmy Jesus of being in his right mind.

So there they were. Released from prison, now informers for the Cruds, hot on the trail of the Dark Duke.

"A master criminal, 'e is, th'Dark Duke," intoned Erlic solemnly.

"'As 'is treach'rous fingers in ev'ry pie, 'e does," added McDoul piously.

"'Specially 'mongst lowlifes like what 'angs around y'rotten dives sech as th'Trough," continued Geronimo Jerry, shaking his head sadly, "which, o' course, is what necess'tates us t'spend so much o' our days there, knockin' down one pot 'o ale after 'nuther, which we couldna afford 'cept for th'Cruds is payin' fer it an' all, so's we can ferret out th'treacherous plot of th'Dark Duke."

And that explained, naturally, why they'd been forced—much though it pained them to raise a hand against the Queen's finest—to form the Cat's last guard in the brawl at The Trough. Keep their cover, don't you know? And it worked like a charm. Not only did they get released, but they even got a raise out of the Cruds.

Chapter 19.
A Plot Is Hatched

Once they finished their tale, Greyboar explained to them what we wanted. The Trio pondered the problem deeply—three ale pots' worth apiece.

"Th'information regardin' th'layout o' th'Pile, now," mused Erlic, "aye an' that's no th'problem."

"Get it from Vincent, we will," explained McDoul. "Aye an' there's not a thing th'lad dinna know about th'plan o' th'Pile."

"Will he help us?" I asked. "I mean, why should he?"

So the Trio explained that after they'd been pitched back into their old cell, where they waited for the Angel Jimmy Jesus to arrive, who should pop up again but Vincent van Goph? It seemed the artist hadn't been fully satisfied with some of the detail work on his triptych. While he finished it up, the Trio struck up a conversation with him.

"Disgruntled, 'e is," said Geronimo Jerry, "at th'sorry state o' th'Queen's art stocks, which o' course ye'll be understandin', is where 'e obtains 'is own supplies. Quite th'proper thief 'e is ins'own right, Vincent."

Then they began quarreling as to the precise position occupied in the pantheon of thievery by the Underground Artist. But Greyboar brought them back to earth. The gist of what came out of it was that Vincent had offered, if the Trio would provide him with some good quality paints, to sketch their portraits on some appropriate wall in the dungeons. Not really thinking they'd ever follow through on the deal, the Trio had made certain arrangements for leaving a note for Vincent in the event they should obtain his supplies. In a corner of the ale cellar under The Trough, as it happened.

"No wonder Leuwen's been grumbling about somebody stealing his ale stock!" exclaimed Greyboar. "Must be this Vincent fellow, burrowing into the cellar from below and making off with the odd keg."

The Trio nodded their heads, their expressions showing great disapproval of the sorry moral state of the thief Vincent van Goph.

"Inexcus'ble conduct on 'is part, 'o course," intoned McDoul piously, "but ye canna 'ardly blame th'lad. Says th'Trough's ale is th'best in th'world."

"That it is," agreed Greyboar. "So you think if we provide him with good paints he'd find out for us the exact location of the Cat's cell? Well, let's try it."

Then Greyboar told me to go out and buy plenty of good artist's paints. I was tempted to argue the point—cost us a pretty penny out of the stash I'd been storing up, don't you know?—but I decided to let it pass. "Never try to reason with a love-struck man," the wise man says, "when he's got hands the size of bulldogs."

Within two days the Trio had made the contact with Vincent, and it took but two days longer for Vincent to return with the needed information. Interesting tidbits he'd picked up, too.

"That scumbag!" roared Greyboar, stomping around the room. "That lecher! That—that priestly vulture!"

The focus of the strangler's ire was upon Luigi Carnale, Cardinal Fornacaese. For, it now turned out, the Cardinal had apparently had an ulterior motive in demanding the immuration of the Cat in the heretics' quarter of the Pile. An ulterior motive, let me say, which cast a definite shadow on the Cardinal's vows of chastity. Admittedly, casting a shadow on Cardinal Fornacaese's vows of chastity was a bit like casting a shadow on a solar eclipse.

Vincent had reported that the Cat had been immured in a cell buried deep in the heretics' quarters. That much was expected, of course, although it was nice to have the artist's exact pinpointing of the cell's location. The more interesting tidbit, however, was that the Cardinal was having a tunnel dug from his own chambers—his bedchamber, to be precise— to the Cat's cell. True, his motives in so opening a line of communication with the Cat were unknown. Perhaps he simply wanted to be able to take her confession, so she could die in a state of grace. The various means of restraint which he was simultaneously having attached to his great bed, however, argued otherwise. Not to mention his long-standing reputation as one of the world's legendary satyrs. Not to mention his not-so-long-standing but not-so-recent-either lust for the body of the Cat.

"He was ogling her back in Blain," growled the strangler. "I should have choked him then."

The rest of us kept silent. Best policy around Greyboar in a snit, don't you know? Eventually the big guy calmed down and we started trying to work out a plan.

"How about Vincent?" asked Jenny. "Would he help us—you know, dig us a tunnel to the Cat's cell?"

Still on that "us" business, the two little imps. I'd tried to get our meeting place changed, so as to get the girls out of the picture, but Greyboar insisted that it was best to hatch our plots at their house. Less chance of being overheard by slobs who'd squeal to the porkers for a penny. The Trio had readily agreed, mainly—I suspected darkly—because Jenny and Angela made their depraved hearts go pitter-patter. And that was another thing I didn't like about the whole business!

I tried to warn the girls of the horrid reputations of the Trio—especially that goat McDoul—but they treated me like I was retarded.

"Now, now, Iggy," cooed Jenny, chucking me under the chin, "you know Angela and I aren't interested in any men."

"Except you, Iggy," cooed Angela, grinning like a hussy, "and that's 'cause you're just the cutest little thing."

Anyway, the Trio poured cold water on Jenny's proposal. As they explained it, Vincent wouldn't be any help except as a source of information. This, for two reasons. Point One: Vincent was practically a midget, so his tunnels weren't big enough for what the Trio called "normal-sized" men—translation: beer-bellied slobs. This part made me wince, because naturally Jenny and Angela started squealing with pleasure and right off proposed that the two of them and me carry out the rescue, since we were all small and could fit in the tunnels.

Fortunately, that plan fell through because of Point Two: Vincent was also a temperamental artist with his head in the clouds and wouldn't be bothered with digging any tunnels that weren't necessary for his art.

Quite the rugged individualist, Vincent, as the Trio portrayed him.

So we were back to square one. And, now that it's all over, I'll admit that maybe it wasn't such a bad idea to bring the girls in on the plotting and the scheming. Fact is, even though they were young as the morning and fresh as the dew and innocent as the lambs of the field, they had fiendish good brains. So it was Angela who actually came up with The Plan.

"You know," she said, peering at McDoul closely, "you look a lot like the Cardinal. He used to come over to the Baron's house now and then and I've met him up close. I mean, if you cut your hair decent and shaved off that horrid great beard you've got growing on you like moss on a tree. And even though the Cardinal's not a hunchback, he always walks all stooped over like he was being crushed by the weight of his sins, which he probably is, so if we cleaned you up and dressed you right, we could pass you off as the Cardinal and maybe that's how we could rescue the Cat."

McDoul was delighted with the plan. It appealed to his conceit, his much-vaunted (him doing all the vaunting, naturally) perception of the social graces. All of it except the barbering and shaving part, I should say, but his objections here became moot after Greyboar held him upside down and the girls went to work with their scissors. Then it didn't take long before the girls had a full set of Cardinal's robes made up, which fit McDoul like a glove.

"Not bad," mused Greyboar, inspecting the final result. "Not bad at all. He'd never pass a close inspection, of course, but we're fortunate there that the Cardinal always favors a cowl. To hide his guilty face from the righteous, no doubt. As long as McDoul moves fast, he should be able to get past the guards." Then he scowled. "Unless he gets questioned and has to talk. That'll blow the whole thing, that gutter accent he's got."

"I beg your pardon, my man?" came a strange, haughty voice from beneath the cowl. Greyboar was startled. I wasn't myself, I've heard McDoul impersonate the upper classes' accent before. He was really quite good at it—claimed it derived naturally from his unfailing perception of the social graces.

"Say that again!" demanded Greyboar.

McDoul drew himself up in the very image of *Great Prelate of the Church, deeply offended.*

"I'll have to insist you abandon that tone, my good man! I'm a forgiving soul, but still!"

"That's quite a trick," admitted Greyboar. "This just might really work."

"And what do you plan for him to do?" I demanded. "Just waltz on into the Cardinal's mansion? And then what? Suppose he gets past the guards at the front door—then what's he supposed to do? Finish digging the tunnel to the Cat's cell and carry her out past the guards? And all this in three hours, which is maybe about the most time he'll have before the Cardinal finds out there's something fishy going on!"

"Oh, he won't be alone," said Greyboar. "You and I'll be going in with him—and these other two thieves, as well."

Erlic and G.J. did not seem overjoyed at the idea, and began to say so in no uncertain terms. But Greyboar stilled their protests with a look. Yeah, *that* look.

"It'll work like a charm," he rumbled. "I figured it all out while Jenny and Angela were getting McDoul dressed up in his ecclesiastical finery. Oh, that reminds me—we'll be needing a couple of servant outfits for Erlic and Geronimo Jerry, and Inquisitors' robes for me and Ignace. And cut the Weasel's long oily ringlets while you're at it, will you, girls? They don't go with the image of your Cardinal's lackeys."

No sooner said than done. Jenny and Angela started working on G.J. and the Weasel immediately, ignoring the latter's complaints.

While they were working, Greyboar explained the plan. I was impressed, I've got to admit. I usually had to do the fine-filigreed plotting and such, but the strangler'd come up with as clever a scheme as I'd ever heard. Maybe all that philosophic rumination was oiling up the rusty gears in his head, after all. But more likely it was the image of the Cat wasting away in her cell which made him think better than he usually did.

Not meaning to make fun of the great brute here, mind you! If I could bend steel bars with the fingers of one hand, I imagine I would have let my brain cells wither on the vine, too. But built like I am—well, let's just say that I had to rely on wit rather than brawn to get by. Helped having Greyboar for a client and friend, I admit.

But I don't want to get too carried away, here. There was still a great gaping hole in his scheme, big enough to drive a wagon through. The Trio spotted it at once.

"An' what'll th'Cardinal be doin' all this time?" demanded Erlic. His voice was sulky, caused, I've not a doubt, by the sight of his beloved oily ringlets lying on the floor. "E'en wit' th'four o' us t'do th'work, it'll still take th'day or two t'dig the Cat out. Vincent said th'tunnel t'her cell was still th'good ten feet away."

Greyboar scratched his chin. "Yeah, yeah, I know. I still haven't figured that out. Somehow or other, we've got to get the Cardinal out of the picture for a couple of days. I'm stymied on that part of it, I admit."

"Oh, that's easy!" exclaimed Jenny, smiling like a spring day.

"We'll take care of the Cardinal!" shrieked Angela, clapping her hands with delight.

I tried to cut them off, but it's hard to advance the cogent voice of reason when you've got Greyboar's hand the size of a dinner plate wrapped around your mouth.

Smart girls, dammit. Didn't take the little rascals but three minutes to lay out a whole plan to keep the Cardinal out from under foot for as long as we needed. The plan was a good one, too. But I was thinking quick myself, so during the same three minutes I thought up two cogent lines of reasoning. Then I started mumbling as loud as I could.

Jenny looked cross. "Oh, let him talk, Greyboar," she snapped. "We'll have to listen to it sooner or later, anyway."

"Fusses over us like a hen over her chicks, Ignace does," added Angela. She glared at me.

My voice back, I laid it out:

"One. None of us'll be here to help you tie up the Cardinal. Even with him out of the way, we'll still be pressed for time. The rest of us will have to get into His So-Called Grace's mansion as soon as he leaves. You'll be alone with the monster! Helpless! At the mercy of his unbridled lust!"

"Pooh," said Angela. Jenny stuck her tongue out at me. Then they refuted my argument.

"He's just a wretched old man!" snapped Jenny.

"Can't hardly walk!"

"Think we can't handle him?"

"Sure we're not big, but he's not so big either!"

"And there's two of us!"

"And we're real strong for our size!"

"We really are! We're really healthy and energetic and full of vim and vigor!"

Then, the unkindest cut of all, coming with a pair of evil grins:

"You should know, Ignace," smirked Angela. "You never last more than an hour."

"That's why we always start with you," cackled Jenny, "and finish with each other."

I ignored the vulgar snickers coming from Greyboar and the Trio. Pressed on, undaunted, head bloodied but unbowed.

"Two. Sure and the Cardinal'll come running with his tongue hanging out. But what do you think he'll do when he sees this house? Not his type of place, don't you know? Man of refined tastes, the Cardinal. Not that he'll have any objection to sating his fiendish lusts on the bodies of two working-class girls, mind you—especially young and pretty ones. In a pinch, the man'll hump a goat. It's true—he keeps one in his basement for the odd rainy day. I heard it once from one of his servants. But he'll certainly not agree to doing the dirty deed here, in the slums. He'll insist you come back to his mansion. And then we're in the soup!"

Ha! That did it! Wiped those evil grins right off their faces.

Until Greyboar put them back on, oh, maybe two seconds later.

"No problem. We'll just have to rent some fancy townhouse in the hoity-toity part of town, that's all. Plenty of 'em available at the moment. Half the nobility's out taking the waters at the spas."

"Know jest th'place," interjected McDoul.

"Th'finest townhouse on its block," added Erlic. "Aye an' 'tis y'proper snooty block. Not far from th'Cardinal's mansion, to boot."

"We've been casin' th'place," explained G.J.

Another dagger in my heart!

"But that'll cost money!" I fear my voice was shrill. "Lots of money!"

"We've *got* lots of money," said Greyboar. "There was

enough in Hildegard's bonus to take care of everything
we need. I know you've got it stashed away. So now's
the time to cough up."

Well, I quit arguing at that point. As the wise man
says: "You've got to know when to hold them, and when
to fold them, and when you haven't even got enough
to ante up."

Chapter 20.
A Plot Goes Awry

The next day—after spending more money to buy myself fancy clothes and hire a fancy carriage, so I'd look like a gentleman—I rented the townhouse from the agent handling the property. Very nice place, too, the Trio were right about that. But it wouldn't have done them any good since the place was completely empty. It turned out the owners had moved to a country estate and the townhouse was up for sale. So that meant spending still *more* money to provide us with minimal furnishings, and two extra days to obtain it.

But the lost time was probably a blessing in disguise. By the time the townhouse was ready, the costumes were done to perfection and McDoul had had plenty of time to perfect his accent. Angela was even able to remember enough of the Cardinal's voice to get McDoul to a fair imitation of it.

Then we all got some sleep, so we'd be rested up for the long two days and nights ahead of us. Well, I didn't get a lot of sleep. Angela and Jenny saw to that. After they'd worn me out, they kissed me on both cheeks and said, "We love you too, Ignace." Then it was an odd thing, really. I cried for the first time since I was a kid. But I slept better than I had since then, too, even if it was only for a few hours.

The next morning, the game began.

Not long after sunrise, Greyboar and the Trio and I were lurking in the bushes next to the Cardinal's mansion. Oddly enough for someone with his vices, Fornacaese was one of those weird early-to-bed-and-early-to-rise types. Was but a moment later that the Great Man of the Cloth emerged from his mansion. Eager to spend the day doing the Lord's work, no doubt. But he hadn't taken three steps before Jenny and Angela popped up from somewhere, calling out to him.

They really looked stunning, there wasn't any two ways about it. Somehow they'd designed their dresses so they conveyed an impossible combination of demure innocence and barely repressed lust. Wasn't two seconds after they came up to the Cardinal that His Grace's tongue was hanging out.

We could hear their voices as clear as bells.

"Oh, Your Grace, we're in such a horrible situation," moaned Jenny.

"We thought—it's forward of us, we know it is, you being such a great holy man and all, but—" This from Angela.

"Speak, my children," slavered the Cardinal. "Unburden your troubled souls."

"Well, you see, our parents have gone off to the spa."

"Left us all alone."

"Instructed us to behave properly."

"But we're troubled by the devils."

"They come to us in our dreams."

"Filling us with—with—with—"

"Speak, children, speak!" I swear, even from where I was hiding I could see the foam on his lips.

"—with thoughts of lust and depravity!" moaned Jenny.

"So we were wondering, Your Grace," murmured Angela sweetly, "if you might come to our house and pray for us today—and maybe even through the night."

"We don't live far," Jenny hastened to add. "Just a three-minute walk."

Well, to sum it up, the Cardinal agreed that he would meet them at their house in a quarter of an hour. Anything to save two young and innocent souls, don't you know?

Jenny and Angela left, sauntering down the street. The Cardinal raced into his mansion. Practically bowled over the doorman on the way in. Wasn't but five minutes later that he came charging back out—and this time he *did* bowl over the doorman. And there he went, scuttling down the street like a crab, a holy book in one hand and two bottles of wine in the other.

We waited until he disappeared around the corner before we made our move. Then we went up to the front door. McDoul was in the fore, dressed identically to the Cardinal. Greyboar and I came behind, clothed in the red robes of the Inquisition. Erlic and G.J. brought up the rear, dressed like servants, bearing on their shoulders an enormous chest. They were huffing and puffing as if the chest were full of who knew what, instead of being almost empty.

The door opened. McDoul pushed his way in, with Greyboar right behind so as to pin the doorman against the wall with his shoulder.

"Your Grace!" gasped the doorman. "But—but—you just left but a moment ago!"

"Knave!" hissed McDoul, his face hidden in the cowl. "How long have you been in my service now?"

"Six years, Your Grace."

"And you could be fooled by that impostor? He's my double, you idiot!"

The doorman's jaw was agape. "Your double, Your Grace?"

"Of course, my double! The enemies of the Church must be kept off guard! Imbecile!"

McDoul's act was pretty much wasted. Because Greyboar had transfixed the doorman with The Stare, and after that the poor man was lost. McDoul hissed some vague nonsense about dark plots and foul machinations, and instructed the doorman to forget everything he'd just seen. By that point, I think the fellow had forgotten his own name.

Then McDoul pointed to Erlic and G.J. "Show these varlets to my bedchamber," he hissed. And to them, he hissed: "Drop that chest and you'll answer to the Inquisition!"

So the doorman led us to the bedchamber. The man's wits were so addled that it never occurred to him to wonder why the Cardinal couldn't lead the way to his own bedchamber. Answer to that, of course, is that we had no idea where it was. That mansion was gigantic. It was nestled up against the Pile, the great ugly crag which overlooks New Sfinctr and most of whose interior is filled with the cells and tunnels of Grotum's most notorious dungeon. As it turned out, the bedchamber was all the way in the back, on the third floor, carved right into the stone of the Pile itself. Figured.

The whole thing really went as smoothly as you could ask. Of course, we must have run into a dozen other servants along the way. But they took one look at the terrified expression on the face of the doorman and disappeared in a flash. Not known for his kindly ways, the Cardinal wasn't. And it was as clear as daylight that every lackey in the place had long ago memorized the most profound of the sayings of the wise man: "Don't ask. Just don't."

So there we were, at last. In the Cardinal's bedchamber. McDoul hissed some final instructions to the doorman, to the effect that he would be occupied for some time with urgent business of the Inquisition. He did *not* want to be disturbed.

Disturbing the Cardinal, clearly enough, was the last thing the doorman intended to do. He was gone in a flash.

"All right, let's get to work," said Greyboar. He watched Erlic and G.J. slowly lowering the chest, grunting and groaning.

"Oh, cut out the act!" snapped the strangler.

"What act?" demanded the Weasel.

"Great crate weighs th'ton," gasped G.J.

"Filled as it is wit' th'needed supplies for our labor," explained Erlic. And so saying, he opened the chest.

Well, the plan had called for an empty chest, except for two shovels, a pick, and a lantern. The tools were there, all right. But the rest of the chest was full of ale pots.

Greyboar was not pleased, but he let it go after I pointed out that the Trio hadn't ever been known to do anything, not even steal, until they were full of ale. So we started inspecting the bedchamber, looking for the entrance to the tunnel which the Cardinal had been digging to the Cat's cell.

Didn't take us long to find it. The entrance was concealed in the floor of a closet. We lifted the trapdoor. A ladder led down to a landing below. Bringing the digging tools and the lantern, we climbed down, Greyboar leading the way.

And ran right into an unexpected complication. It was obvious, in retrospect. In fact, we all felt like total idiots.

Who had been digging the Cardinal's tunnel? Not the Cardinal himself—not the great prelate of the Church! No, he'd gotten hold of three dwarves somewhere, and made them do the work. And there we found them, chained up to the wall of the tunnel.

The poor little guys were scared out of their wits. But once they understood we weren't the Cardinal's men, they were ecstatic. They'd always known the Cardinal would have them killed after they finished the work, so they'd gone as slowly as they could. That had cost them plenty of whippings, but a whipping's better than the Big Cut.

Now they pleaded with us to let them escape. The Trio started making noises to the effect that "dead men tell no tales—dead dwarves neither." But one glare from Greyboar was enough to scotch that idea. The truth is, Greyboar had a soft spot in his heart for dwarves ever since he met Zulkeh's apprentice, the dwarf Shelyid. Actually, I'll admit to the same soft spot. Really a great kid, Shelyid. He was a little on the lippy side when we first met, but after I slapped him down he turned out all right. He and I got to be pretty good friends, actually. Greyboar and I spent quite a bit of time with the wizard and his apprentice on our way back from Prygg. Greyboar hung around the wizard, naturally, talking about who-knows-what philosophical nonsense. Me, I found Shelyid's company much more congenial.

So doing away with the dwarves was ruled out. On the other hand, we couldn't just let them go either. They'd be bound to raise the alarm trying to sneak out of the mansion. In the end, we struck a deal with them. If they'd help us dig out the Cat, we'd figure out some way to take them with us when we escaped.

Then, as it turned out, they did all the digging. Greyboar offered to help, but the dwarves turned him down.

"Shoulders like yours," explained one of them—Eddie, his name was—"be good for breaking rocks out in the open, where you've got room to swing a hammer. But this here's close-in work, like. You'd just get in the way."

Then Greyboar offered my help, and that of the Trio. But the dwarves turned him down again.

"By the looks of 'em," sniffed another—Lester, he was called; the last one, for the record, was named Frank—"they haven't done an honest day's work between 'em in the last five years."

I let it go, but the Trio were deeply insulted.

" 'Aven't *never* done no 'onest day's work," groused the Weasel.

"Aye an' do we look like idiots?" demanded G.J., red in the face.

"Not since we's little 'uns, anyhow," grumbled McDoul. "Not since we's sprung usselfs from th'sweatshop, after knifin' the o'erseer."

In the event, finding the dwarves turned out to be a blessing. Now that they were motivated to work as fast as possible, instead of stalling, they cut right through the rock. Work like moles underground, dwarves could. Not surprising, really, most of them did a stint in the mines sometime in their lives. It was one of the few jobs people would give to dwarves. And while the work was brutal, at least the poor little bastards didn't have to worry about pogroms as long as they were underground. Your average lynch mob had a fear of hunting dwarves down there. The tricky little devils had this way of making the tunnels real narrow. Not to mention the cave-ins that always seemed to inflict the few vigilantes who were stupid enough (or drunk enough) to chase dwarves below the surface.

So the dwarves did all the digging. Greyboar stayed down there almost the whole time, fussing and fuming and driving the poor little guys crazy. The Trio and I, on the other hand, being sane and rational men, spent the time up in the Cardinal's chamber. Good company, the Trio, especially with plenty of ale to keep their stories coming.

And there was another upside to the whole affair— a *big* upside. The Trio started prying up loose boards, more out of habit than anything else, and discovered the Cardinal's secret stash. A whole chest full of gold coins, gems and jewelry. All of it obtained illegally, no doubt, so the Cardinal could hardly report the loss to the authorities.

On the spot, we arranged a satisfactory split. A third for me, a third for Greyboar, and a third for them. It took me an hour to get the Trio to agree to it. Fifty-nine minutes of ferocious debate with me, them advancing the ludicrous proposition that we should split it evenly—a fifth apiece. One minute for Greyboar to come up and reason with them.

It only took the dwarves a bit more than half a day to break into the Cat's cell. Without them, it would have taken two days. And the cell was right where Vincent had told us. Yes, everything was working just according to The Plan. Except for one little problem.

The Cat wasn't in the cell.

We wasted two hours while Greyboar inspected the cell about ten thousand times. Stupid, stupid, stupid. The cell wasn't more than five feet by seven feet by four feet tall, with a small alcove added on where the hardtack was stored. And every surface was faced with hard rock, so there was no way to dig out if you didn't have tools. There wasn't any sign of digging, anyway.

The point here being that all it took was two minutes to figure out the Cat wasn't there and hadn't dug her way out. But still the big lummox spent two hours at it before he gave up.

Oh, she'd been there, all right. There wasn't any doubt about that. Every surface of the cell was covered with handwriting, scratched with a sharp stone. You couldn't mistake the Cat's hand—she wrote with big bold letters, probably because she was half blind.

You couldn't mistake the language, either. Pure Cat. The Trio were positively awestruck.

"Never seen sech command of y'profanity," marveled Geronimo Jerry.

"Genius, genius, th'Cat," whispered Erlic, in tones you usually hear in a church.

" 'Tis not alone th'mastery o' the curse," admired McDoul, "but th'beauty o' th'anatom'cal depictions— an' th'lass ne'er repeated herself the onc't! Imposs'ble, o' course, th'most o' th'acts ascribed to th'Judge—but th'imagination! Ne'er could've thought o' th'half o' them, m'self."

It was true enough. They'd gagged the Cat at the trial, but she'd wiled away her time in the cell completing her speech. He'd chosen the wrong time to say it, but you couldn't deny that O'Neal had been right. The Cat was not ladylike.

So, she'd been there, all right. But where was she now? It was a complete and total mystery.

It took me two hours, but I finally convinced Greyboar that we didn't have any choice but to leave. The Cat was gone, the Old Geister knew where, when or how, and that was that. Wouldn't do any good for us to linger around and get caught.

So we left, not without the strangler moaning and

groaning and running back, oh, maybe two hundred times, to make sure the Cat hadn't magically reappeared. Once in the Cardinal's bedchamber, we waited while the dwarves sealed up the entrance in the closet so as to leave no trace of the tunnel. Then, the three of them crammed themselves into the chest—that was how we'd planned on taking the Cat out, of course— and we left the mansion.

Getting out was a piece of cake, even with us carrying the extra chest with the treasure. During our stay in the Cardinal's quarters, the servants had had plenty of time to terrify themselves with speculation about whatever horrid consultations were going on between the Cardinal and the Inquisition. As soon as they realized we were coming out, they disappeared. We marched through the mansion totally unobserved. We even had to let ourselves out.

Less than a day had passed. Sunrise was still just a hint on the horizon, so we made our way through the streets without being observed by anyone. Five minutes after leaving the Cardinal's mansion we were going through the front door of the townhouse we'd rented. And discovered again that the Cat was a strange, strange woman.

Chapter 21.
Justice and Injustice

Because there she was, big as life—sitting in a chair in the main room, casual as could be.

Greyboar charged over and clutched her like a drowning man clutches a life preserver. It was a touching scene. Or at least, it would have been, if the Cat hadn't been furious with him.

I believe I've indicated she had quite the command of the earthier aspects of the language? Well, we were all given another demonstration.

The gist of her displeasure, stripped of the rhetoric, was: *What was the big idea, you ape, this stupid rescue attempt? Have I ever asked for any help? No, and you'll never see the day I do, either. I am not pleased. Indeed, I am displeased. Most displeased. Most extremely displeased.*

It wasn't often you got to see the strangler groveling and apologizing and begging for forgiveness, let me tell you. He was usually on the other side of the equation, don't you know? I loved every minute of it and so did the Trio. Not that we didn't keep a straight face, mind you. If Greyboar'd seen us grinning ear to ear, he wouldn't have done anything about it. Not at the moment. But the Trio and I were students of the wise man, not the least of whose saws is: "Idiots never remember the fatal word—*later*."

Eventually, the Cat was appeased. She even relented enough to give Greyboar a big kiss. Naturally, the big dummy immediately blew it.

"But how'd you get out of the cell?" he asked.

That started another round of the Cat's—what can I call it? Swearing doesn't begin to do the woman justice. Whatever, the gist of it was: *You unspeakable* (actually, this part was full of speech) *great baboon, you know I hate being cooped up. Think there's a box in the world can keep me in? That's what Schrödinger thought, too. I left, that's how I got out. You stupid* (well, and then on and on and on).

So, how'd she get out? Beats me. I'm not stupid. I never asked.

After the Cat wound down, I decided it was safe to introduce the voice of logic and common sense.

"Shouldn't we be figuring out the future instead of the past?" I asked. "We're not done yet—we've still got to deal with the Cardinal."

"Where is the rotten slimy bastard?" roared the strangler, his huge hands making various motions which boded ill for the aforementioned man of the cloth.

"He's upstairs," said the Cat. "Jenny and Angela tied him up in their bedroom."

Growling like an animal, Greyboar stalked toward the staircase.

The Cat blew her stack again. The gist of it: *You arrogant moose, what do you think you're doing? Think I'd need any help chopping a sorry worm like the*

Cardinal? Think I'd wait around for the big strong gorilla to do the job for me? You conceited jackass. You egotistical peasant. You puffed-up peacock. You over-weening slob. You—etc., etc., etc., etc.

"You already killed him, huh?" mumbled Greyboar, after the storm passed.

The Cat was still glaring at him. Quite a glare, too—the combination of those incredibly blue eyes magnified by the inch-thick lenses on her spectacles. Then she snorted.

"Didn't have a chance. He was already dead when I got here. It was the girls did him in."

"The girls?" I demanded. "But they wouldn't—oh, no! He must've struggled!" I was frantic with worry. "Are Jenny and Angela okay? Are they hurt?"

I started my own charge for the stairs.

"Relax, Ignace!" came the Cat's voice. A penetrating voice, I believe I've mentioned. Stopped me dead in my tracks. I turned around. The Cat was bestowing a look on me that did not indicate any great favor.

"You're just like him!" she snapped, indicating Greyboar with her thumb. "Another swell-headed male, thinks women are lambs." Definitely an unfavorable look. "Men!" she growled.

She took a deep breath. And then, like a sunburst, she smiled. Nobody in the world had a smile like the Cat, when she put herself into it. It was blinding, really.

And now she was laughing her heart out. She had some kind of laugh, too, the Cat. Great to hear, sort of, if it weren't for that maniacal tinge. Like a she-wolf mocking the world.

When she stopped, still chuckling, she nodded toward the stairs. "Go on up and see for yourselves," she said. "You'll love it. But be quiet. The girls are asleep. All tuckered out, the poor things."

So we tiptoed up the stairs and went into the

bedroom. I was the first one through the door. As soon as I saw the scene, I insisted everybody else had to wait outside until I had the chance to cover up Jenny and Angela. Naked they were, sprawled on the bed in each other's arms, exhausted contentment on their sleeping faces. I wasn't about to let leering slobs like the Trio get a look at them!

Then everybody came in, and we all circled the bed, gazing on the most-definitely-deceased corpse of the Cardinal. He was still in his robes, tied to the bedpost at the foot of the bed. His complexion was bright purple, his eyes were bugged out like veined eggplants, his gray tongue was hanging out about eight inches. He looked like the aftermath of one of Greyboar's chokes—except there wasn't anything wrong with his throat and neck.

And, besides, the cause of death was obvious.

We woke the girls up, then. Didn't mean to, but the howling laughter which filled the room would have awakened the dead. They were startled at first, rubbing the sleep out of their eyes, but soon enough they were joining in the gaiety.

"Isn't it perfect?" giggled Angela.

"We didn't mean to do it, really we didn't," protested Jenny. Her grin did not, let me say here, indicate deep remorse.

And it really was the perfect way to do in the Cardinal. Even Greyboar and the Cat, itching as they'd been to do the job themselves, admitted as to how it had all worked out for the best.

The Plan had gone perfectly. Too perfectly, in fact. As soon as the Cardinal had come into the house, the girls had overpowered and tied him up. That hadn't taken but two minutes. Truth is, the girls were right—a shriveled-up old lecher had been no match for them. Then, they decided the best place to keep him was in the bedroom. One of them could watch him at all times, while the other one got some rest.

So they hauled him up into the bedroom. They tied him to the bedpost because it was the handiest place available. And then—

Well, then it started getting boring. They hadn't counted on that, a boring adventure. But the truth of it was that after doing their part—to perfection, too!—they really didn't have anything to do for the next two days or so except keep the Cardinal tied up.

Jenny and Angela didn't take well to tedium. Much, much, much too full of vim and vigor and youthful energy.

"And besides," said Angela, "he was such a pain in the ass, cursing and threatening us the way he was doing."

So, partly because they were bored, and partly to get the old goat's goat, they started doing what the two of them did often and very, very well whenever they had the time (they always had the energy). Later, they swore they'd only intended to tease the Cardinal a little, but—but, the truth of it is, Jenny and Angela were crazy about each other and either of them alone had enough pep to keep a whole factory going for a week if you could bottle it up somehow, and both of them together, when they were in the mood—which they usually were, and certainly were that day—could—how shall I put this? Well, let's just say they violated several of the Commandments for hours and hours and hours, naked as the day they were born, and in their usual freewheeling style.

Not five feet away from the tied-up-but-not-blindfolded person of Luigi Carnale, Cardinal Fornacaese, lecher and pedophile *sans pareil*.

"We're not exactly sure when he croaked," giggled Angela. "Couldn't even place it to the hour."

"We weren't paying him any attention at all," cackled Jenny.

Judge Rancor Jeffreys couldn't have devised a better means of execution himself. Death by torture. Slow, horrible, lingering. Prolonged agony. Endless torment—especially that, endless torment.

Going to be a bit tricky for the Cardinal—sweet-talking his way through the pearly gates, that is. Likely to frown, the guardian angels, when they pondered the manner of his passing.

Bad enough for a Cardinal to die unshriven. But in his state! The Lord in His Heaven hath long decreed that Envy and Lust are mortal sins, each of them alone, not to speak of the two combined. And that's what Cardinal Fornacaese died of—terminal Envy, complicated by Lust.

The whole affair turned out to have a number of beneficial side effects.

First, it got the Trio another raise from the Cruds. As soon as they sized up the situation, they raced to the Cruds with dire warnings of a plot by the Dark Duke—uncovered by perilous spy-type derring-do on their part!—to kidnap Cardinal Fornacaese. The authorities charged over to the Cardinal's mansion to foil the plot. Alas, too late! The Cardinal gone! Never to be seen again! Mysterious, the whole thing, very mysterious. The servants were unable to shed any light on the situation. Even under the Inquisition, they could only babble about some unknown party of Inquisitors who had been in the presence of the Cardinal on his last known day on earth.

So the Trio—excellent timing those lads had, they calculated to the second when the servants would started babbling about Inquisitors—raced to the Cruds with the breathtaking news that they had just uncovered—through the most thrilling spy-type adventures!—the Dark Duke's scheme, now well under way, to infiltrate the Inquisition with his agents. They got another raise. They even got a medal from the Angel Jimmy Jesus—unnamed and unmarked, of course, just a blank piece of metal. Very security-conscious, the Angel Jimmy Jesus. What was better yet, the Inquisition started inquisiting itself. Never quite the same, after that, the Inquisition in New Sfinctr.

At first, we were worried that things were going to get sticky for the Cat. The Cat wasn't worried about it, of course. The woman didn't worry about anything except finding Schrödinger. But the rest of us were fretting that she'd be arrested again, wandering around the streets like she insisted on doing. But our fears were unfounded. The porkers tried to arrest her, but Judge Rancor Jeffreys wouldn't hear of it. Hadn't he ordered the Cat immured? Yes. Hadn't she been immured? Yes. Then that was that. Whoever this other woman was, she was—by definition—an impostor. The porkers tried to talk the Judge into opening up the Cat's cell, just to make sure she was still there, but Jeffreys blew his stack at the idea. The whole point of immuration, don't you see, is to wall away the criminal from the world forever and forever. What would be the point, if the authorities dug them up? So the porkers gave up, especially after the Judge ordered three of them hanged for attempting to undermine the law.

There was a downside, of course. There always is. For wouldn't you know it but what Jenny and Angela had developed a taste for the fine life, staying in that swanky townhouse. So they started wheedling Greyboar into buying it.

"It'll give you so much more fashionable a place to live, instead of that bear's den you've got in the Flankn," insisted Jenny.

"You'll get more clients," argued Angela. "Especially the ladies, who are afraid to go into the Thieves' Quarter."

"And it'd be great for us, too!"

"Much better location for our dress shop."

"Much higher class of clientele."

Of course, the little monsters didn't try to wheedle me, they know better. But I wasn't worried. Greyboar didn't have the sense about money that I did, but he wasn't a fool either—his grip was tight more ways than one.

Until the Cat stepped in. I swear, the big gorilla was an absolute patsy in the hands of that woman. Didn't have any of the masculine firmness that I had in my dealings with Jenny and Angela.

All it took was for the Cat to stare at him with those telescope blue eyes and sneer: "What a cheapskate." Two seconds later, Greyboar's ordering me to spend our hard-earned money to buy the house! I couldn't believe it! Of course, I knew better than to argue with him when he was in one of his the-Cat-wants-it moods.

The whole thing turned out pretty good for Eddie, Lester and Frank, too. They'd been staying in the house, hiding out in the cellar. It wasn't at all safe now for a dwarf in the streets of New Sfinctr. When they heard we were going to buy the house, they approached Greyboar and asked him if they could stay on—as hired hands, or something—cooks, maybe, or—or, whatever. Well, the truth is, the dwarves really didn't have any of the skills of a house servant, and besides, Angela and Jenny wouldn't hear of the idea. What were they, anyway? Snotty little rich girls, what didn't know how to look after themselves? They weren't against the idea of the dwarves staying, mind you. They thought it was a great idea, seeing as how Frank, Lester and Eddie were such sweet little men and all. But they thought it was ridiculous to actually hire them as something or other. Why not just let them stay? So that's how it ended up.

I wasn't too pleased with the idea, myself. Not that I had anything in particular against the little guys. Very nice dwarves, they were. But if you let dwarves move in with you, you'll sooner than you know it have all the dwarf business with it.

"They'll build a stop for the Underground Railroad," I complained to Greyboar. "You know they will, as sure as the sunrise. Dig one right down through the cellar."

Greyboar shrugged. "Sure, I know. So what? I never have liked the way dwarves get treated in this world, you know that. You should be against it, too—self-preservation, if no other reason." I was quite offended at the evil grin that he gave me at that point. "Easy to mistake you for a dwarf, in the dark."

Then he made that firm-type gesture with his great ugly hand which I hated—it meant: *the question's settled.*

"Let 'em stay. And let 'em build their stop on the Railroad. Nothing else, maybe that'll put me back in Gwendolyn's good graces, just a bit. She's been a topside organizer of the Railroad for years. Has strong feelings on the subject, strong feelings. So when she hears, maybe she'll decide I'm not quite the complete worthless scum of the earth, after all."

So the dwarves stayed, and, sure enough, it didn't take them long to build a stop on the Railroad. Then, before you knew it—almost overnight, it seemed like—our cellar became the main stop for the Railroad in New Sfinctr. Dwarves sneaking in and out all times of the night. I was surprised at first, but after reflection it made sense. A lot of it was Angela and Jenny. Pretty soon the girls got so involved in Railroad work that they stopped even talking about opening their dress shop.

Mostly, though, it was Greyboar. Biggest problem the Railroad always had was keeping the porkers from discovering and busting up the stops. Never a problem, that, with our stop. The first time the porkers came by, poking and prying and asking questions, Greyboar went out to talk to them. He gave them The Stare, and that was that. They never came around again.

But, like I've said a thousand times, it's the natural state of life to be unjust. As the wise man says: "Every silver lining has a cloud."

Because, you see, Gwendolyn did find out. And, sure enough, she did come to the conclusion that maybe her baby brother, the cold-blooded murderous thug, was—just maybe—not such a totally worthless piece of human garbage, after all.

And, of course, if you want to get yourself into big trouble—Big Trouble—there's no quicker way to do it than to get into Gwendolyn's good graces.

PART III: *SYNTHESIS*

Chapter 22.
Disaster Strikes

It was bound to happen. The signs had all been there, gathering like clouds. Good deeds done, promises kept, righteous behavior maintained, the lot. I could feel disaster coming, like hearing thunder over the horizon.

Now that we were flush, it was impossible to get Greyboar to work at all. Hildegard's bonus, on top of the Cardinal's treasure, had elevated us into the ranks of the "idle rich." Which is a splendid place to be, of course, but not when it leads to delusions of grandeur. The fact is that your true idle rich can stay that way because they've got *other* people slaving away to keep them in that blessed state. All we had was a hoard that would be gone soon enough, and the pitiful earnings which Jenny and Angela brought in from the dresswork they did on the rare occasions they weren't totally preoccupied with the Railroad.

Live on the interest, you say? Huh. Not familiar with the practices of Groutch bankers of the day, I see. Fees for this, fees for that. Not to mention the charming practice of charging you 4% of the existing balance every month in recompense for the time and labor involved in calculating your 4% interest. No slouches, they.

Fie on all respectable financial institutions! My bank is the bottom of a mattress. Which is safe enough when you've got Greyboar snoring away on top, but it's still withering away.

But—

No use. Greyboar refused each and every job I turned up. His criteria for "philosophically acceptable" chokes got more ridiculous by the day. I tried to point out the contradiction involved between demanding an advance in entropy while simultaneously maintaining ethical standards that no genuine beatified saint could ever have matched, but—

No use. Every day, the same thing. Practice his "Languor," study his "Torpor," daydream about the eventual bliss of eternal "Stupor." Except for whenever the Cat floated back around, at which point all of that philosophical nonsense went right out the window in favor of, uh, what you might call "empiricism." As in, pleasures of the flesh. At those times, I always had to make sure I'd extracted whatever moneys we needed before Greyboar and the Cat had finished with their first clinch and gone upstairs. Never get to the mattress thereafter.

Yes, I could feel it coming. *Disaster.*

I started getting twitchy. Moving from one window of the townhouse to another, scrutinizing the streets below, watching for the first signs. Muttering under my breath. Eating sandwiches while on guard, instead of joining the festive little crowd at the dinner table.

Angela and Jenny were peeved with me, needless

to say. Accused me of being a paranoiac. At one point, they got annoyed enough to put me on a regimen of abstinence for a week. I'll admit that jolted me out of it, for a time. Terrible thing, abstinence. I'd always thought so, even in the good old days before I'd fallen madly in love like some fairy tale dunce.

Didn't last, though. Soon enough, that immensely pleasant state which the upper crust likes to call "post-coital tristesse" turned into genuine distress. Staring up at the ceiling, expecting a meteor to come through any minute.

So Jenny and Angela would boot me out of the bed and I'd go wandering through the house in the dead of night. Afraid even to light a candle lest some lurking danger spot me in the darkness. A ghost before my time. A specter, I say! In my own home!

Stupid, of course, all of it. A total waste of time and effort. I should have remembered the sayings of the wise man: "Don't bother looking for trouble. It'll find you all on its own." Or: "When troubles come, they come not in single spies but battalions." (I think he stole that one; doesn't really sound like him.)

Or, of course, the classic: "You want to relax? Drop dead."

But, still—

The way it happened was *so* unfair.

"You've got guests," announced Angela.

I jumped, and spun around from the peephole in the front door. "Who? Where?"

Angela was standing in the entrance to the front parlor, grinning like an imp. Jenny's face was perched over her shoulder.

"Lots of them," added Jenny. Grinning like an imp.

I peered at the pair suspiciously. I didn't like the expression on their faces. Not one bit. Not at all.

Partly that was from bitter experience. Partly it was simple indignation. No girls that young and fresh and good-looking should be able to imitate denizens of the underworld.

But mostly it was because another of the wise man's sayings was clanging in my mind: *When the cat looks like it's swallowed the canary, start chirping.*

"Who?" I demanded again. "Where?" I repeated. "No one's come near the house. I've been watching!"

The faces got impier. You know that look. The one where the guilty party wallows in their guilt. Basks in their sin. My stomach felt like lead. I looked down at the floor.

"Through the Railroad, of course," chirped Angela. "How else?"

"*From be . . . low . . .*" quavered Jenny, in a tone of mock doom. She and Angela burst into laughter.

Not fair!

Chapter 23.
A Crazy Proposal

Angela and Jenny led me into the "salon," as they liked to call it.

Disaster, sure enough.

Not just one calamity, either, but a whole collection. There they were:

Zulkeh, the pedant from perdition.

Shelyid, the dwarf from disaster.

Hrundig, the mercenary from—never mind. (And just what the hell was he doing in that company, anyway?)

Magrit, the proper witch. And her familiar—the salamander Wittgenstein.

Finally, of course, Gwendolyn.

Greyboar was already there, standing in one of the other doorways leading into the salon. The Cat was pushing her way past him, drifting her way into the room.

" 'Lo, Gwendolyn," I heard him mumble.

The chokester seemed in a bit of a daze. He looked around for a place to sit, but there wasn't any. The couch and the two chairs we had were already taken by the guests. (I kept a tight lid on frivolous expenses, you understand.)

" 'Lo, brother," came her response. She wasn't quite frowning—you've never seen a real frown until you've seen Gwendolyn's, let me tell you—but she certainly didn't seem overjoyed to see her long-lost brother. Tense as a coil of steel.

The ice was broken by Shelyid. The dwarf sprang off his chair and raced over to Greyboar, squealing his happy greetings. A moment later, he was hugging the strangler's right knee.

Greyboar winced. You wouldn't think it, looking at the little guy, but Shelyid's as strong as an ogre. Strange dwarf. Ugly as sin, for one thing. Hairier than a musk ox, for another.

"Hey, take it easy, Shelyid."

"Oh! Sorry." The dwarf released Greyboar's leg and grinned up at him. Greyboar grinned back. He's really very fond of that dwarf.

So am I, actually. A bit to my regret, then, because Shelyid raced over and gave me the same hug. I thought my ribcage was going to go, but I was surprised at how happy I was to see him.

Then Wittgenstein piped up and I wasn't surprised at how much I hadn't missed the slimy creature. "Isn't that sweet, Magrit? Midgets meet again."

"Shut up, Wittgenstein," growled the witch. "We're supposed to be on our best behavior."

"That *is* my best behavior," groused the salamander. "What am I supposed to do? Be polite?"

Greyboar nodded to Magrit. "I see you escaped the Cruds. I was a little worried when we heard the Ozarines had invaded Prygg."

The witch sneered. "Those chumps? They couldn't have caught me even if I hadn't had the Rap Sheet."

I made frantic little waving motions with my hands. You know the ones: shuddup, shuddup, shuddup.

Magrit's sneer deepened. "And what's your problem, Ignace? Don't want any mention of the Rap Sheet in your presence?"

Very frantic waving motions: *shuddup, shuddup, shuddup.*

"You remember the Rap Sheet, don't you? You ought to, Ignace. You helped steal it."

"Absolutely!" shrilled the salamander perched on her shoulder. Wittgenstein reared up like a herald. "Ignace was deeply involved! Totally! Integrally!"

SHUDDUP, SHUDDUP, SHUDDUP.

Jenny and Angela were staring at me, wide-eyed.

"*You* stole the Rap Sheet?" gasped Angela.

"Is *that* what you were doing in Prygg?" demanded Jenny. She stared at Greyboar. "So that's why you won't ever talk about it!"

I clutched my head. *The whole world would know!*

"Shut up!" I cried.

"Whatever for, Ignace?" demanded Wittgenstein. As always, the high pitch of the familiar's voice grated on my ears. "Since when have you become so modest?"

Wittgenstein swiveled his neck and peered intently at Jenny and Angela.

"Yes, yes, ladies! You are in the presence of terrible desperadoes! The very men who were complicit in the theft of Ozar's Rap Sheet which drew down the wrath of that mighty empire upon poor, downtrodden Grotum. Responsible, I say, for the invasion of Pryggia and the ensuing horrors and atrocities."

He rose to his full height and pointed at me. "*J'accuse!*"

"Oh, stop it," said Magrit.

Wittgenstein snickered. "But it's all true, Magrit! You know it is. You were there, after all." Snicker, snicker. "It was your plot in the first place."

Wittgenstein's beady red eyes rolled back to Jenny and Angela. Again, that nasty snicker. "From subtle hints, I'd say the two of you have formed a romantic attachment to this Ignace fellow. Dummies."

Jenny and Angela nodded. Gwendolyn frowned. Magrit sneered. Shelyid looked confused. Zulkeh didn't.

Wittgenstein snickered again. Then, hissed: "Cradle robber. *Bigamist* cradle robber."

"He is *not* a bigamist!" snapped Jenny.

Angela giggled. "More like a trigamist." She put her arm around Jenny, and smiled seraphically. "As for the charge of robbing the cradle—well—"

"It's true," pronounced Jenny. "We are but lambs, led astray by this lustful beast." She put her arm around me and rubbed her hip against mine. The motion involved was not, uh, lamblike.

For the first time, the wizard Zulkeh spoke.

"Do I understand correctly? Is it true that this wight has engaged in carnal intercourse with both of you hoydens? Who have, in your turn, transgressed the well-established bounds of heterosexual propriety?"

Jenny and Angela nodded happily.

"Like I said," piped up Wittgenstein. "A bigamist cradle robber." The salamander goggled the girls. "And dykes, to boot."

"Bah!" spoke Zulkeh. The wizard stroked his beard. "You would do well, Magrit, to silence that unnatural beast. Its ignorance is beyond belief. The charge of bigamy is utterly specious, inasmuch as bigamy presupposes the sundering of lawful bonds through subterfuge, whereas we have, in this instance—I misdoubt me not—neither lawful bonds to be sundered nor any subterfuge utilized in not so doing. This—" he continued, while everyone was trying to catch up with the tortured logic—"being due to the fellow Ignace's well-known disdain for all moral precepts."

He waved his hand in judgment.

"As well accuse a wolf of moral turpitude for being a carnivore. Now, as to the charges of cradle robbing and perversion, it seems to me, at first glance, that we have to deal with more substantive matters. I would remind all present, in regard to the first, of the well-known precepts of Nabokov Laebmauntsforscynneweëld. Then, dealing with the problem of perversion, we can begin with the texts of Sappho Sfondrati-Piccolomini, in whose execrable verses are clearly—"

"*Enough!*" bellowed Magrit. She planted her hands on the arms of the chair and swiveled her ample figure toward Zulkeh. Her plain and modest long dress fit her middle-aged matronly appearance. But the scowl on her face was as ferocious as you'd expect from one of the world's down-home, no-fooling, proper witches. "Enough already!"

The wizard glared at her. I expected another of the mighty wrangles between the two of them which I had gotten used to—sort of—while we were in Prygg.

But Greyboar interrupted. "Why are you here?"

Silence fell. All eyes turned to Gwendolyn.

"Oh, no," I moaned. (Very softly, mind.)

Sure enough: "I need your help, brother."

The words were choked out, as if she were trying not to say them. The next words, even more so: "And yours too, Ignace."

She wasn't even looking at me when she said it. Just slumped in her chair, staring at the floor.

My temper started to rise. "What's this? All of a sudden I'm not the little scuzzball what ruined your brother's moral fiber? All of a sudden—*urfff!*"

Angela's elbow hit me like a rocket, right in the wind. An instant later, Jenny's hands were clapped over my mouth.

"Just ignore him," she said to Gwendolyn, very sweetly. "Keep talking. Please."

Gwendolyn raised her head. When she caught sight of the three of us, she barked a laugh. "What a picture! My congratulations—Jenny, isn't it? And you too, Angela. I was never able to shut him up that quick."

I snapped back a hot retort. "Grrrmrrgrnrrbrr!" Jenny's hands clamped down, and I fell silent. Not so much from the pressure, but from the sight of Angela's elbow. Cocked, and ready for another shot.

Gwendolyn shook her head ruefully. "You are a piece of work, Ignace. Only person I know who gets angrier when he gets a compliment than an insult."

She ran the fingers of her left hand through her thick mass of long, black hair. It was a gesture which I remembered well, from the years back. As always, her fingers got a bit tangled up. Gwendolyn's hair wasn't quite as kinky as her brother's. But, then, she had a lot more of it.

The gesture drained away all my anger in an instant. I felt myself slumping a little. Damn woman! I never had been able to maintain a proper spite against Gwendolyn. Not when she was in my presence, anyway.

"The reason I need you too, Ignace," she said softly, "is because Greyboar's always a little lost without you. You and your fussing, and your mother hen routine."

She emitted a chuckle that was more in the way of a sigh. "Missed it myself, tell you the truth, all these years."

She stared at me for a moment, as if she were studying something. Then, sighed again and squared her shoulders, turning her head toward Greyboar.

"You heard about Benvenuti?"

The strangler nodded. "Yeah. Not much. He got caught, and then seems to have escaped."

Gwendolyn shook her head. "Not exactly. He escaped from the *dungeons*, yes. But after that—" Her hand waved about, vaguely. "We're not sure what happened. I asked my dwarf friends to see if they could find out anything. They were able to pick up his trail, eventually. He must have gotten lost in that labyrinth under the Pile, and kept going downward. But—"

She fell silent, tightening her lips. Then: "The dwarves tracked him to one of the entrances to the netherworld. Further than that, they wouldn't go. Dwarves stay clear of those depths. Always."

"And rightly so!" exclaimed Zulkeh. "Dwarves are expressly forbidden any congress with the netherworld. Both in Holy Writ and in all the prophetic commentaries. 'Tis because they are damned in the Lord's eyes, of course."

I tried—failed—to follow the logic. But Zulkeh was steaming right along.

"The Lord's decree, needless to say, is rigorously enforced by the powers in the netherworld. As a result, your average dwarf is firmly convinced that he can under no circumstances survive a journey into the infernal regions. Superstitious dolts! The truth, of course, is quite otherwise. I have studied the problem extensively, and I can assure you—"

"Enough!" bellowed Magrit. "Let Gwendolyn finish, for the sake of all creation, before you bore us all to death!"

Gwendolyn spoke hurriedly. "I finally asked Zulkeh for his opinion. He consulted—something—and said that Benvenuti apparently had some trouble with the devils—"

I couldn't suppress a sudden hysterical laugh,

gurgling up past Jenny's fingers. *Apparently had some trouble with the devils! Gee, no kidding?*

"—and wound up getting pitched out of the infernal regions altogether. Into—into—you know."

My humor vanished entirely. Half in a daze, I heard Greyboar's rumble.

"The story's true? There *is* a Place Even Worse Than Hell?"

"Bah!" oathed Zulkeh. " 'Tis a truth known to savants in swaddling clothes! Indeed, the most recent scholarship leads us to the conclusion that there are any number of transfernal territories. The Place Even Worse Than Hell being only the first in line of descent. Beyond—'tis certain, this!—there is the Snowball's Last Laugh and Can You Believe This Shit Is Really Happening? Past those regions, our knowledge becomes less precise. The currently accepted hypothesis, of course, is that—"

A miracle! Zulkeh shut himself up! He cleared his throat noisily; and then muttered: "But perhaps for a later, less pressing time. For the moment, Sirrah Greyboar, rest assured that I was able to ascertain the artist Benvenuti's whereabouts. He is, indeed, in the Place Even Worse Than Hell. And, I regret to state, has fallen into Even Worse Hands. The soul-wracked demonic specter whom I conjured up and whose soul I wracked still further was quite specific on the matter."

Again, he cleared his throat. "And I dare say he was telling the truth. I wracked his soul quite thoroughly, if I say so myself."

"Nasty bugger was squealing like a pig by the end," piped up Shelyid cheerfully. "The professor had him begging for mercy. Well, sort of. Actually, he was begging for eternal damnation. But with soul-wracked demons that's pretty much the same thing."

I was *very* light-headed by now. Almost fainting, to

tell you the truth. I could see what was coming a mile away. But I made one last desperate attempt to restore sanity to a world gone mad. I started mumbling and muttering fiercely, trying to get words out past Jenny's hands.

"Oh, let him talk, Jenny!" snapped Angela crossly. "We're going to have to listen to it sooner or later anyway."

Jenny snorted, but she released her grip.

"S'nuts!" I gasped. "Fer pity's sake, Gwendolyn! I know he used to be your boyfriend and all, but that's ancient history. I mean, I'm sorry things turned out badly for the guy—nice guy, I'll admit it, even if he was so disgustingly good-looking—but, hey—it's over! You gotta get on with life, you know. Let bygones be bygones. Put it all behind you and—"

No use. Tears started welling up in Gwendolyn's eyes and I felt my throat closing. Damn woman. I never could bear to argue with Gwendolyn when she started crying. Probably because she almost never did, even when she was a little girl.

Damn woman.

"I never stopped loving him, Ignace," she whispered. "Not for one second. Even though it was I who insisted we break it off."

"Why did you, then?" asked Greyboar quietly. His eyes lurked under the overhang of his brow like two black mice studying a morsel of food.

Gwendolyn pinched the tears from her eyes. "Oh, come on, brother. D'you really need to ask? *You*?"

She managed a chuckle that even had a bit of humor in it. "Benvenuti's an artist. It's what he lives for, nothing else. Me—" Again, she shrugged. "You know me, brother. Ignace. My whole life is devoted to the revolution. There's no place in there—not for either of us—for some damned fairy-tale romance. And I knew if we stuck with it, Benvenuti would sooner or later run into trouble with Church and State."

"Which he did anyway," snorted Magrit. "And managed to piss off the Devil so much in the bargain that he got booted out of Hell. Silly girl! You shoulda—"

"Magrit!" barked Gwendolyn. "Do you *have* to second-guess everybody about everything?"

Magrit smiled sweetly. "Just trying to help, that's all."

Gwendolyn scowled, but let it go. She took a deep, almost shuddering breath, and fixed her eyes on Greyboar. Then, on me.

"There's still no future in anything between Benvenuti and me. But I can't bear the thought of him where he is. So I'm going to try to rescue him. Me and Hrundig. Zulkeh and Shelyid agreed to help, and so did Magrit."

"I didn't!" snapped Wittgenstein. "But—*nooo*—does a witch's familiar ever get any say in these things? Fat chance! If you ask me—"

"Salamander soup," grunted Magrit. "I got the recipe right here in my pocket." Wittgenstein blinked; shut up.

Gwendolyn took another of those deep, shuddering breaths. "But Zulkeh says we really don't have much chance at all, without you along. Even then, it's going to be touch and go."

"To say the least!" piped up Shelyid, as chipper as could be. "Actually, the professor said it was a desperate and foolhardy adventure which he strongly recommended against except for the fact that it's the only chance anyone's ever had to study the Place Even Worse Than Hell at first hand so of course it was imperative that we do it."

Then the tears started leaking out of Gwendolyn's eyes again. The next thing you know Greyboar's got his sister enfolded in his arms and he's whispering promises and assurances.

Disaster!

Naturally, it went downhill from there.

"Oh, that sounds like fun!" cried Jenny.

"Sure does!" agreed Angela. "Let's get Eddie, Lester and Frank in here. They'll be a big help!"

I started protesting right off—not about the dwarves, but the role which Jenny and Angela obviously foresaw for themselves in this madness. But the two girls ignored me and charged out of the room.

"Who are Eddie and Lester and Frank?" asked Magrit suspiciously.

Still embracing Gwendolyn, Greyboar turned his head and explained. Wittgenstein goggled.

"You let *dwarves* stay here with you? For no good reason except the so-called milk of human kindness?" The nasty little salamander whistled. "Boy, are you a sorry excuse for a strangler!"

"Shut up!" snarled Gwendolyn, glaring over her brother's shoulder. Wittgenstein snapped shut its mouth and scurried into Magrit's blouse. A moment later, the witch hauled the creature out and tossed it onto the floor.

"Get away from my tits, you miserable amphibian."

"She'll beat me," whined Wittgenstein. "She'll twist my tail off."

I was impressed. I'd never seen Wittgenstein intimidated by anyone before. Then I thought about Gwendolyn's temper and studied her.

Greyboar's sister hadn't changed in the slightest. She looks a bit like Greyboar, what with her eagle nose and her dark, kinky hair and her black eyes. Except that Gwendolyn's kind of beautiful—in a scary, Amazon kind of way—while Greyboar's almost as ugly as Shelyid.

Don't let her good looks fool you. For a woman, she's a giant. Over six feet tall and built like a tigress. Well . . . if a tigress had a build. And she's got incredible reflexes for someone as big as she is. Better than Greyboar's, even. I suspected that Wittgenstein had discovered that the hard way. The thought cheered me up a bit.

Jenny and Angela charged back into the room, with the three dwarves in tow. Eddie and Lester and Frank were kind of confused, at first. But after the situation was explained to them, the confusion vanished.

"Can't be done," pronounced Eddie.

"Impossible," agreed Lester.

"Out of the question," concluded Frank. "Even if you were willing to get anywhere near Even Worse Hands, you couldn't get near them in the first place. They're in the Place Even Worse Than Hell, you know."

I beamed. "Well, that's that. Sorry, Gwendolyn, but you just heard it from the experts. Miners, you know, all three of them. Know the tunnels like the back of their hand."

"Shut up, Ignace," snarled Magrit.

"Yes, do!" snapped Jenny.

Angela made an apologetic shrug to the crowd. "Don't mind Ignace. He's not really a coward. He's just so greedy that he can't bear the idea of doing something for free."

"And that's another thing!" I cried. "Greyboar's got a professional reputation to maintain! The Standards Commission won't—"

"Shut up, Ignace," growled Greyboar.

Shelyid gave me a wounded look. "You helped steal the Rap Sheet for free, Ignace."

A stab to the heart. But I rallied. "That was in another country. And besides, the Crud is dead."

My protests, alas, were ignored. Greyboar plowed right over them.

"Why do you say it can't be done?" he asked Eddie. "Doesn't sound all that difficult to me. From what you've told me before, all those tunnels link up sooner or later. Sure, it might take awhile. But if we plug away at it, we ought to be able to find him eventually."

The three dwarves shook their head in unison and began to speak, but the wizard cut them off.

"I fear not, sirrah Greyboar. Indeed, 'tis the very impossibility of the task which has led us to your door."

Greyboar looked to Zulkeh. The mage spread his hands apologetically.

" 'Twas my recommendation, that, when Gwendolyn approached me in the Mutt with her proposal. She had thought it would be a simple matter of continuing down the tunnels past the place where the dwarves broke off their search. But I was forced to open up to her understanding certain inauspicious realities of tunnelics and cave lore. Not the mundane aspects of the science"—here, a dismissive wave of the hand—"which any miserable engineer can handle, but the more arcane branches of the study. I speak, of course, of monstrology and beastics. Subterranean devilism, and the like."

An apologetic cough. "Not to mention the more abstruse problems posed by the Joe relics we might possibly encounter. Which, of course, explains to a degree my own willingness to assist her in this otherwise ridiculous affair of the heart."

Another apologetic cough. "So, naturally, I thought of you at once. I was quite impressed by the talents which you displayed in the course of our adventure with the Rap Sheet. In an adventure such as this, one really does require more than a modicum of brawn."

"Why?" demanded Greyboar. "What's in those tunnels?"

As one dwarf, Eddie and Lester and Frank shuddered.

"For a start," explained the mage, "we may encounter tunnel snarls."

"I'll take care of that!" exclaimed Shelyid. Proudly: "I'm a snarl-friend."

Greyboar eyed him skeptically. "How sure of that are you, Shelyid? Rock snarls, yes. I know you've dealt with such. I was there. But—"

"And forest snarls!" piped the dwarf. "I met them when we went through the Grimwold."

His face scrunched, injured. "*Any* kind of snarls, Greyboar," he said in a hurt little voice. "You shouldn't doubt me. It's not right, you shouldn't."

Greyboar smiled. "All right, Shelyid. I'll take your word for it."

He looked back to the wizard. "What else?"

The mage stroked his beard furiously. "What else? Say better: what else is there *not?* In terms of monstrology, we are certain to encounter any number of noxious specimens. Devils, too, of course. If I misdoubt me not, our expedition will most certainly require penetrating into divers of the divers regions of that diverse realm known to the ignorant as the Inferno, but more properly titled—"

Greyboar interrupted, frowning. "I've never tried to choke demons and devils."

"Bah!" oathed the mage. "Your talents shall not be needed with that tripe. I shall deal with any such who might make so bold as to confront our puissant presence. Besides, I have a stratagem in mind which may enable us to circumvent the problem of the passage through the Inferno, and even many of the other horrors of the underworld. But stratagems—even my own—do go awry from time to time."

If I hadn't seen him in action, I would have laughed

right there. Zulkeh's not only the world's greatest pedant, he *looks* the part. Picture a middle-aged scholar, then imagine a caricature of one. That's Zulkeh. Oh, yeah—don't forget the ridiculous robe covered with obscure signs and runes, the tall pointy wizard's hat and the staff.

But—fact is, I *had* seen him in action. A truth: when it comes to real actual *sorcery*, there probably isn't a better thaumaturge in the universe than Zulkeh of Goimr, physician. Except for maybe God's Own Tooth, the dreaded master of the Godferrets.

"No, no," continued the mage, "your physic skills will be required to deal with the less ethereal denizens of the underworld. I speak, of course, of the deadly Worm of the Deep—"

As one dwarf, Eddie and Lester and Frank wailed.

"—the dreaded Beast from Below—"

Another wail.

"—the Slathering Sanguine Skulker—"

A great wail, there.

"—the Creeper from the Crevasse—"

A pure howl.

"—the Undulant Umbellant from Under—"

A shriek.

"—and, of course, the It and the Thing and the Them and the They."

A cacophony of pure terror, from the dwarves. Shelyid piped up cheerfully:

"You forgot the Torrid Terror, professor. And the Kankr Connection and the Flaying Crutchman and the Minions of the Minotaur—and the Minotaur himself, come to think of it—and—"

"Enough, my loyal but stupid apprentice!"

Less cheerfully: "And the Switches."

"I say—enough!"

Not cheerfully at all: "And the Nun."

"Desist, diminutive wretch!"

Gloomily: "Attila the Nun."

Suddenly, the Cat spoke up. As often, I had forgotten she was there. The woman had a way of disappearing without actually doing it.

"Any chance Schrödinger might be down there?"

The wizard frowned. "Of course. Schrödinger might be anywhere."

"Who's Schrödinger?" asked Magrit.

"Who are you, for that matter?" shrilled the salamander. "You got a name, lady? Or should we just call you Four-Eyes?"

That was the only bright moment of the whole day. An instant later Wittgenstein was clutched in the Cat's hand, its eyes popping, its tongue bulging out.

"Schrödinger's supposed to be a slimy sort of creature," muttered the Cat. She inspected the salamander from a distance of two inches, peering at the wretched amphibian through her telescope lenses.

Greyboar cleared his throat. "That's actually not Schrödinger, love. Its name's Wittgenstein."

Wittgenstein tried to splutter. The Cat drew her sword.

"Maybe he's in disguise," mused the Cat. Magrit tried to say something, so did Greyboar. I just grinned.

The Cat chopped off Wittgenstein's tail. The deed done, she dropped the salamander and inspected the tail. Closely, as only she can do.

"Nope," she concluded. "It's not a disguise. Real tail."

Wittgenstein was scurrying about, cursing a blue streak. "Of course it's a real tail, you fucking idiot blindwoman! It *was* a real tail, I should say!"

Wittgenstein inspected his stub mournfully. Everyone else in the room started laughing.

Then the laughter died, and disaster finally struck.

"Sure we'll do it," rumbled Greyboar. Gwendolyn started crying again and he took her in his arms. Then she even kissed him on the cheek and I knew we were lost.

And that's how it happened. A slimy salamander, inspecting his lost tail. An honest chokester's agent, inspecting his ruined life. His wrecked world.

Chapter 24.
The Gripster in the Grotto

If you've never participated in one of these insane adventures, you probably have all kinds of weird ideas about how they get started. Solemn councils, plotting strategy; sage advice proferred, modified, adapted; tactics developed; preparations made; re-made; re-made again. Then, a great ceremony when the heroes depart on their quest.

Crap. That's the way it *should* have been, of course—and you can be sure that I so advised, every step of the way. *Lengthy* councils, I advocated. *Well-planned* strategies, I called for. *Elaborate* preparations, I counseled. And re-counseled. And re-counseled.

I might as well have been talking to the wall. The only one who listened to me was the wizard, and even Zulkeh demurred.

"As a general rule, my dear Ignace," allowed the sorcerer, "I am inclined toward your approach to these matters. But in this instance, alas, time presses."

"Why?" I demanded. "Benny struck me as a

competent chap. I'm sure he'll manage well enough
until we can get there."

Zulkeh stroked his beard, shook his head. "I fear not.
Regardless of his competence—and we should remember, in this regard, that the man is after all an artist,
a breed not noted for their practic skills—he has no
chance of survival if we do not rescue him from Even
Worse Hands within a fortnight. The oscillation of the
galactic plane, you understand."

"The *what*?"

Zulkeh stared at me as if I were a moron. "Is such
ignorance possible?" he demanded.

"Just answer the question," I growled. (I didn't take
offense. I'd dealt with Zulkeh before.)

The mage stroked his beard furiously. "But, my dear
illiterate, the matter's obvious! As our solar system
rotates through the galaxy, we move slowly up and
down across the galactic plane. The cycle time is
thought to vary between sixty-two and sixty-seven
million years. I myself, of course, opt firmly for the
latter figure, inasmuch as the Law of Gravity—properly
so named only by myself, as I am its discoverer despite
the preposterous claims advanced by—"

"Yes, yes!" I cried. Let Zulkeh get started on the
"Law of Gravity, properly so named only by himself,"
and you'll die of old age. "Continue!"

"Well! As I said, well—in the event, we are even
now approaching the equinox of our oscillation. Within
a fortnight, our solar system will cross the exact center of the galactic plane."

He fell silent, exuding scholarly self-satisfaction.

I waited. Waited. Finally:

"So?"

The wizard glared furiously. "So? *So?*" He stretched
his hands to the heavens. "Is such cretinism possible?"

"Just answer the question!"

"The thing's obvious, Ignace! The moment we cross the exact center of the galactic plane, the entire planet will undergo a momentary shuddering in its geologic equilibrium. The tremors, needless to say, will emanate outward from the precise center of the core. Everything will be stirred up!"

A wave of his hand. "Oh, to be sure, the denizens upon the surface will note little beyond a slight haziness in the sky. Minute dust motes, agitated upward from the soil. But in the interior! Oh, no, a different matter altogether. The most ancient creatures will be stirred to sullen life!"

He frowned, stroked his beard.

"Troglodytes, of course—both of the Mesozoic and earlier branches of that noxious order. 'Tis the more evolved Mesozoic breeds which are to be feared. The primitive specimens can be handled with a few cantrips from H.G. Sfondrati-Piccolomini, the which should suffice to cast them back into the abyss of time from which they emerge."

Again, he dismissed the matter with a wave.

"But even the more advanced troglodytes are a trifle for my science. No, the difficulty will lie with other specimens stirred from their antediluvian slumber. I speak of such terrors as the Malevolent Magnetic Monopoles, driven to nihilistic fury by the transference of polar magnetism which is sure to accompany the planet's passage across the galactic plane; the insensate Thing From Beneath—not to be confused, mind, with the related but less disheartening Thing From Below—which, in its turn, must be distinguished from the more-distantly-related and yet-less-fearsome Thing Which Came From Below—which, in its turn—"

"And what else?" I demanded.

The wizard goggled. "What else? *What else?* Say better—what else will there *not* be stirred up?"

He frowned. "I fear, my dear Ignace, that the timing is not good for our expedition. A perilous adventure at the best of times! But to essay the penetration of the earth's interior on the very eve of the crossing of the galactic plane—well! Perilous in the extreme, that. But barely possible, so long as we depart at once."

He turned away. "At once, I say! At once! For, even as I explicate to an ignoramus, time wanes!"

So, we were off.

What a crew! The mage led the way. Cowardly, Zulkeh is not. He's not brave, either. It's just—oh, you'll see. As the wise man says: "Never stand between a scholar and his subject. Stampeding buffalo would be trampled."

Following the mage came Shelyid. The dwarf staggered about under the burden of the wizard's sack. Except for Greyboar, Shelyid's the only person that I know strong enough to carry that sack. You couldn't see anything but his little legs twinkling beneath the overhang.

What's in the sack? Everything the wizard Zulkeh had ever collected in his long and lore-lust life:

Instruments, scrolls, thick leather-bound tomes of great weight, clay tablets, stone figurines, vials, beakers, jars, jugs, amulets, talismans, vessels, bowls, ladles, retorts, pincers, tweezers, pins, bound bundles of sandalwood, ebony and dwarf pine, bags and sacks of incense, herbs, mushrooms, dried grue of animal parts, bottles of every shape and description filled with liquids of multitudinous variety of color, content and viscosity, charms, curios, relics, urns of meteor dust, cartons of saints' bones and coffers of criminals' skulls, and all the other artifacts of stupendous thaumaturgic potency crammed into every nook and cranny of every niche, room, closet and hallway in the abandoned death house in Goimr where Zulkeh and Shelyid used to live, not excluding the heavy iron engines in the lower vaults.

Still—

"It looks a little smaller than I remember," I commented to Shelyid.

"Oh, it is!" came the dwarf's little voice, from somewhere below the sack. "We dumped all kinds of stuff out of it while we were on the sled trying to make it to the Mutt. The Godferrets were chasing us, you know."

No, I didn't know, but I wasn't surprised. Bound to draw the attention of Godferrets, mucking around with Joe business.

"I tossed the Great Newt of Obpont, too," came Shelyid's self-satisfied voice. "Nasty bugger!"

After Shelyid came me and Jenny and Angela. Eagerly charging off to adventure.

Oh, sure, I tried. I hate to admit it, given my reputation for firmness with womenfolk, but they hadn't paid my protests any attention at all.

Then came Hrundig and Magrit and the Cat. The mercenary was as grim as ever—he still hadn't said a word. Magrit was her usual foul-mouthed self. Wittgenstein rode on her shoulder, making occasional comments on the plight of salamanders in a human-dominated ecosystem.

"Hadn't been for that fucking comet," I heard him mutter, "we'd still be running the show. Wouldn't be any of this derring-do nonsense, let me tell you. Just loll about in the swamp, gobbling insects."

The Cat, as often, was off in her own world.

Finally, Greyboar and Gwendolyn brought up the rear. They weren't talking anymore. Just walking alongside each other, holding hands.

Lester and Eddie and Frank came along, too, for

the first part of the trip. It turns out that you can enter
the labyrinth of tunnels beneath the dungeons of New
Sfinctr from any of the main branches of the Underground Railroad.

So our adventure started right there in our own
basement. Lift the hidden hatch to our stop on the
Railroad, down the ladder, and off you go!

The first problem we faced was plowing through the
mob of dwarves down there. I knew Jenny and Angela
had turned our house into the main Railroad station
for the whole city. But I hadn't ever gone down there
myself. So I wasn't prepared for the population density.

"There's half the miserable dwarves in Grotum down
here!" I cried, surveying the scene.

Dwarves, dwarves, dwarves. All over the place.
Crammed into every nook and cranny of every little
grotto and room carved into the bedrock. Papa dwarves,
mama dwarves, baby dwarves. All wrapped up in blan-
kets and rags and gathered about little pots of food.
(I didn't inquire about the food, and who paid for it.
I didn't want to know.)

"Well, of course there's a lot of dwarves!" snapped
Jenny.

"What did you expect?" demanded Angela. "You
know the pogroms are getting worse!"

Well, yes, I did. But it's none of my business, that.

Gwendolyn spoke up. "There's also the new secret
camp which the Ozarines are building in the Baronies. Project Nibelung, they call it. They're rounding up
dwarves all over the subcontinent and shoving them
into that hellhole."

I maintained a discreet silence, here. I happened to
know about *that* little business, on account of—well,
never mind. Let's just say they don't call Shelyid "The
Dwarf From Disaster" for nothing.

In the end, I shut up. Jenny and Angela tended to

tolerate my own little quirks (rational self-interest, I call them), but they did get testy on the subject of dwarves. And those callous souls—rational men, I called them—who ignored their plight. Hey, look, I was sorry the little buggers got such a raw deal. But a guy had to look out for himself, push comes to shove. You started standing up for dwarves and, before you knew it, you were in the crapper yourself.

Eventually, we made our way through the mob and started down one of the Railroad's branch lines. The one leading to Blain, I think. There wasn't much to see, even if the lighting had been better than the occasional lantern on the wall. Just a narrow tunnel carved through rock, with a couple of wooden rail lines running down the center. At one point, a train came through, and we all had to press ourselves against the wall. The adult dwarves hauling the carts paid us no attention at all. The little dwarves riding in them stared at us like apparitions, but they remained silent.

Okay, okay, dammit. I admit the dwarves got a *really* crappy deal. As bad a taskmaster as Zulkeh was, Shelyid was probably better off sticking with the wizard than being on his own.

Finally, we stopped. Eddie and Lester and Frank did some odd things at a section of the wall that looked like any other section, and within moments the wall opened up. A narrow passageway appeared, leading off to no place I wanted to go.

"That's it, then," announced Lester.

"The way to the infernal regions," added Frank.

"As far as we go," concluded Eddie. No fools, they.

For a moment, hope flared in my heart. There was no way Shelyid was going to fit that enormous sack through that opening, and I knew from experience that the wizard would rather die than be separated from his "necessities of science," as he called them.

Alas. Somehow—don't ask me, it was geometrically impossible—Shelyid squeezed the sack through.

So down we went. Down, ever downward. That's not a figure of speech, although it certainly fit my mood of the moment. The tunnel we had now entered did, in fact, slope noticeably downward.

I didn't notice at first, lost as I was in gloom. But then—it *was* gloomy, lit only by lanterns held by Gwendolyn and Hrundig—I tripped on some outcropping and fell flat on my face.

Hrundig hauled me up. "Watch your feet," said the mercenary.

"Found your voice, did you?" I grumbled.

Hrundig smiled thinly. "Never lost it," he rasped. "Simply had nothing worth saying."

Still don't! I almost snapped. But I held my tongue. He's not actually a good man to irritate, Hrundig isn't. So I settled on social pleasantry.

"And what are you doing here?" I asked. "The Frissaults have already been rescued. I'm sure by now you got them off safely to the Mutt."

Hrundig chuckled. "Oh, my. Aren't we testy? What's the matter, Ignace? Does the presence of a hard-bitten old mercenary on this damn-fool expedition upset your *weltanschauung?*"

Yeah, his very words. I tended to forget sometimes, looking at Hrundig, that he wasn't stupid. He wasn't even ignorant. Unusual, that, for an Alsask barbarian. But, for all his harsh demeanor, Hrundig was generally a placid-enough sort of fellow. So he deigned to explain:

"You know perfectly well why I'm here, Ignace. Two good reasons. First, I owe Benvenuti for rescuing my family. And second, he's a friend of mine. I don't have all that many friends that I can afford to lose one."

I was a little touched, to tell the truth. I even started

to utter some inane pleasantries on the subject of glorious friendship, but was brought short by bumping into Shelyid's sack.

"Watch where you're going!" I chided the dwarf.

"Watch where *you're* going," rasped Hrundig. "We've stopped."

So we had. I hadn't seen it, because Shelyid's sack had obscured the view, but we had entered a rather large grotto. Shelyid now moved forward, slowly. More of the grotto came into view, lit by the lanterns.

I proposed an immediate retreat. An immediate, *hasty* retreat.

Large subterranean grottoes filled with bones call for that tactic, to my mind. Cracked, splintered bones; sucked dry of marrow; heaped about in piles. Crushed skulls; teeth scattered about like grains of corn.

Greyboar lumbered past me.

"What's the problem?" he asked. Jenny and Angela pointed mutely. (Pleased I was, too, to see that their earlier insouciance had disappeared. Wanted adventure, did they? Ha!)

"What do you think, professor?" he now asked Zulkeh. "Is Ignace right? Should we try another route?"

The wizard had advanced to the very center of the grotto, and was now poking at a pile of bones with his staff.

"Bah!" oathed the mage. "Do I hear me aright? Has the proposal been advanced to thwart me in my forward progress because of a pile of bones?"

"Lots of piles of bones," I protested. "Cracked, broken bones. Fresh bones, some of 'em. Sucked dry of their marrow."

"Anthropophage of Reason!"

(I wasn't offended. For Zulkeh, that's a mild expletive. Sort of like "drat" to the average man.)

"Base cur of low degree!"

(He was warming up.)

"Dullard dunce of—"

"Professor!" interrupted Greyboar.

Zulkeh fell silent, still glowering at me. Then he made a disgusted gesture with his staff.

"These—*trifles*—are no cause for alarm. Merely the typical residue of that loathsome creature known to the unwashed masses as the Great Ogre of Grotum—"

Jenny and Angela gasped. (So did I.)

"—thereby, in their gross ignorance, seeking to distinguish the beast from its lesser cousin, the Lesser Ogre of Grotum, but which detestable creatures are properly known by their scientific cognomens as—"

"When will it come back?" interrupted Greyboar. (Let the mage go on, and you'll get an entire lecture in natural history.)

Zulkeh frowned. "Do you trifle with me, sirrah? 'Tis well known that the Great Ogre of Grotum never leaves its lair for any reason."

He thrust out his staff, pointing to a dark corner of the grotto. "Indeed, the miserable monster lurks yonder."

Everyone had now entered the grotto. Everyone gasped. Everyone stared where the staff pointed. Gwendolyn and Hrundig held up the lanterns.

A voice came from the dark corner. A horrible, dry, croaking kind of voice.

"Don't hurt me," it whined.

"Show yourself!" commanded the mage.

"Don't hurt me," repeated the voice.

The mage pounded his staff into the floor of the grotto. "Show yourself!" he commanded anew.

"Don't hurt me."

Smoke and lightning issued from Zulkeh's ears. (I'm serious. It astonished me too, the first time I saw it happen.) The wizard began stalking about the grotto, staff in his left hand, his right fist clenched above his head.

"Oh, boy," said Shelyid. "You're in for it now, you Great Ogre of Grotum! That's the famed and dreaded *peripatis thaumaturgae.*"

So it was. I'd seen it before, in the chamber at Prygg where we—never mind. It's quite a distinctive tread, the *peripatis thaumaturgae*—counterclockwise, eleven steps to the circuit, with, of course, the semi-hop following each third completion of the circuit to throw off what demons might be tailing behind in the astral plane.

"I'm coming! I'm coming!" squealed the voice from the corner. A moment later, the Great Ogre of Grotum scuttled into the light.

I gaped. So did everyone. The damn thing wasn't more than two feet tall! Oh, sure, it was horrid looking, what with those bat ears and the bat fangs and the talons and the knobby limbs. But still—

"Ah, excellent," spoke the mage. He turned and bestowed a cheerful smile upon us. "You are most fortunate, my fellow adventurers. Not often does one encounter such a perfect specimen of this breed!"

Here the wizard began another impromptu lecture, pointing out the diverse features of the little monster which—to his mind—made it such a singular model of the famed Great Ogre of Grotum.

Again, Greyboar cut him short. "But it's so little!" he protested. "Why's the thing got the reputation it does? It can't be more than two feet tall."

Zulkeh spread his arms wide, exuding satisfaction. "Did I not say it was a perfect specimen?" he demanded. "Nowhere more than in this, I might add— that it demonstrates that absolute mastery of disguise which is the diagnostic trait of the Great Ogre of Grotum to all scientific taxonomists."

Greyboar frowned. "What disguise?"

"Its size, naturally. Marvelous, marvelous. I was familiar with the phenomenon, of course, from the literature. But not even the excellent monographs of the Grimm Brothers Laebmauntsforscynneweëld had truly prepared me for the wondrous—"

"How big is it?" cried Jenny.

"Yes!" added Angela. "Really, I mean?"

Zulkeh examined the little ogre carefully. The ogre returned his gaze with a fearful scrunch of its beady red eyes.

"I estimate—" The mage pondered. Then, with his usual sureness: "Eight feet tall. Possibly nine."

"Nine and a half," said the ogre smugly. A moment later, the disguise vanished and the great slavering monster sprang upon the wizard.

Or would have, if Shelyid hadn't lunged forward and interposed the sack. The Great Ogre bounced off like a rubber ball and sprawled to the side. But it was back to the attack in less than a second.

The next few minutes were a whirlwind. Greyboar met the monster's charge with a roar and a choke. More precisely, a neck grip. The Great Ogre was so huge that even Greyboar's hands couldn't fit around its throat. Think of a baby strangling a mastiff and you've got the general picture. A very strong baby, to be sure. But at a certain point the exercise gets a bit ridiculous.

Still, Greyboar was able to stop the monster. And while I didn't think he'd be able to actually choke the thing, he was certainly keeping its attention concentrated.

This was wizard's work, as far as I was concerned.

"Zulkeh!" I shouted. "You stirred this damn thing up—so deal with it!"

"Bah!" oathed the mage. "Think you a pitiful Great Ogre of Grotum can withstand my powers? Bah!"

He turned to Shelyid. The dwarf had already unlaced the sack and was climbing into it. "What'll it be, professor?" he asked cheerfully. "Quick Yerkil's *Disgorement Made Easy*? Angemar the Clear-Minded's *Insta-Quick Talisman*? Suleiman the Modest's *Simple and Surefire Cantrips*?"

"Bah!" oathed the wizard. "Am I a novice? An apprentice fumbling at lessons? Get me Gastro's *Iliac*, insolent dwarf! The Gravid translation, mind you—I have no truck with the others."

I had a bad feeling even before Shelyid's face fell. "But, professor," whined his apprentice, "that'll take—"

"Do as I command!" bellowed the mage. Shelyid ducked and vanished into the sack.

I started to argue with the sorcerer, but a glimpse of Jenny and Angela hurling themselves on the Ogre distracted me. Completely.

"*What are you doing?*" I shrieked.

The girls paid no attention to me at all. The next thing I knew, Jenny was perched on the horror's left shoulder and was biting one of its great bat's ears. The Ogre squealed and tried to swipe her off with a paw. But Angela was already on the other shoulder and met the paw with a swipe of the kitchen knife she'd brought with her.

The knife bounced off the Ogre's knuckles and went sailing. A second later, so did Jenny. Angela shrieked and started biting the other ear. The paw swiped again, and off she went. Both girls wound up in a heap on one side of the grotto.

"Are you hurt?" I wailed, racing over to them. "Are you hurt?"

They bowled me over on their way back to the fray. I went sailing myself, head over heels.

By the time I untangled myself, they were back up on the Ogre's shoulders and were resuming their

ear-biting. Again, the Ogre broke off its grappling with
Greyboar and started swiping at them. Ear-biting
wouldn't kill the great monster, but I guess its ears were
pretty sensitive.

This time, however, Gwendolyn was up there with
them. She was clad in that leather get-up that she'd
always favored for what she called "real work." Leather
jacket, sleeveless leather vest, tight leather pants
tucked into knee-high leather boots. It's quite an
outfit, especially filled with Gwendolyn's Amazon figure. She could have made a fortune as a professional
dominatrix.

She was straddling the creature's great back, with
her legs around its rib cage. Gwendolyn's legs were just
long enough that she'd been able to reach all the way
around and lock her ankles together. If the Ogre had
been inclined toward bondage and discipline, it would
have been in sheer ecstasy. Even if the boots *didn't*
have high heels.

Alas, it wasn't. But its swipe at Jenny was met with
Gwendolyn's cleaver this time, and that was a whole
different kettle of fish. Gwendolyn could split logs with
that thing. She *did* split a knuckle, right down to the
bone.

The Ogre howled and swiped at her. Another *chunk*
of the cleaver, then another. One of the Ogre's talons
fell off.

Hrundig and the Cat, meanwhile, were hacking at
the creature's legs with sword and lajatang, trying to
hamstring the brute. They didn't seem to be having
any luck, although they'd turned the legs into a mass
of green ichor.

The Ogre was staggering around the grotto now,
bellowing with fury. Greyboar's hands were still locked
onto its throat, like a pit bull on a mastiff three times
its size. I saw that he'd left off trying to crush the

thing's windpipe and had both his hands sunk into the sides of the Ogre's neck, trying to close off the jugular veins. From the dazed look on the creature's face, it looked like the project was starting to yield fruit. As they say.

As terrified as I was over Jenny and Angela's situation, I gave up any thought of trying to haul them off the Ogre. It was clear enough from the way they were chewing on its ears that both girls had adopted the ancient motto of the midget in a brawl: *You may get a meal, bigshot, but I'm damned well gonna get me a sandwich.*

Besides, they weren't in any immediate danger. I could figure out what was coming next. As stupid as it was, the Ogre must have finally realized that Greyboar was the real danger. It stopped trying to swipe at the women and grabbed Greyboar's head in its talons. Then, gaping like the entrance to the Pit, its huge maw descended to bite off the chokester's head.

My first dart sailed into its mouth and sunk into the soft tissue inside the maw, which should have been pink instead of that nasty, nasty blue-green dripping with saliva. Three more followed, in the blink of an eye, before the horror snapped its jaws shut. The Ogre blinked and gave me a reproachful look.

"Nasty stuff, ain't it?" I shrieked. I shook my fist at the monster, hopping around with glee. "Try swallowing *that*, you—you—"

The monster belched and spit out all four darts. "*Yech!*" it roared. Again, that reproachful look. "You tried to poison me, you little squirt!"

The Ogre started lumbering toward me, intent on revenge. Clearly enough, it had forgotten all about everyone else. I discovered, then, a secret about poisoned darts that I'd never known. Even if you can't actually kill something that big, you can sure as hell infuriate it.

Under other circumstances, of course, I would have been terrified out of my wits. Having a nine-and-a-half-foot-tall Ogre chasing you around a subterranean grotto will do for that. Take my word for it.

But, at the time, I was practically delirious from joy. As long as the brute was concentrating on me, it wasn't trying to go after Jenny and Angela. Or Greyboar and Gwendolyn, for that matter.

And, besides, it wasn't the first time in my life I'd been chased by something bigger than me. If there was one thing I knew how to do, it was scramble-duck-and-dodge.

Oh, I led it a merry chase, if I say so myself, for at least a minute. Then it got sticky, when I slipped on a loose stone and fell flat on my face. By the time I scrambled back to my feet, the Ogre was right there, reaching for me with its talons.

But there weren't actually that many talons left, just a bunch of bleeding stumps. Gwendolyn's cleaver-work, that. And with Greyboar still hanging on in the front, the Ogre had to stoop to reach me with its gigantic maw.

Which it did, Greyboar flip-flopping around on its belly. But my two throwing knives went into the gullet, which seemed to discombobulate the monster for a moment. And then—I don't know where he came from—Wittgenstein was perched right on its snout pissing into its eyes.

Horrid stuff, salamander piss. Especially Wittgenstein's. The Ogre squawled and forgot all about me. Eyes squeezed tight shut, it was frantically pawing at its snout. But Wittgenstein was long gone by then. The familiar scampered off the monster and scuttled through my legs.

"You owe me, Ignace," it hissed along the way. "Breakfast in bed, twice."

I wasn't about to argue the point. Fact is, my long-standing dislike for the surly little creature had completely disappeared. Let's hear it for unnatural amphibians!

I started scrambling away myself. Then, behind me, I heard a great thud. I turned around and saw that the Ogre had collapsed to its knees. Hrundig and the Cat must have finally worked through to the sinews.

The Ogre's eyes were open again, but they seemed empty of any emotion beyond dull confusion. I realized that Greyboar's death grip was taking its toll. His huge hands were sunk completely into the monster's neck. If the damned thing wasn't so stupid it would have been unconscious by now.

The Ogre's maw was gaping wide again, but this time it was purely a grimace. A moment later, Magrit waddled up and tossed a handful of some kind of powdery stuff down its throat.

"Hold your breath, girls!" she called out cheerfully. "One of my special concoctions—you *don't* want any part of it."

Some of the stuff, whatever it was, must have drifted onto Jenny and Angela. Both of them reared back from the Ogre's ears—what was left of them—and started hacking and coughing.

"Oh—*yuch*!" squeaked Angela. "That's even worse than the ear!" Jenny didn't say anything. She just looked purely nauseated.

So did the Ogre. Its eyes bulged. Then Gwendolyn released her scissor lock and hoisted herself higher onto the monster's shoulders. An instant later, she plunged her cleaver hilt-deep into the Ogre's left eye. Two seconds later, did the same for the right.

And that, as they say, was all she wrote. The Ogre

swayed back and forth on its knees for maybe five seconds, and collapsed right on top of Greyboar. The strangler *still* had his hands locked in place. Gwendolyn and Jenny and Angela spilled off onto the floor of the grotto.

Hrundig took one last vicious hack at the monster's heel tendon—what was left of it—and danced away. He looked as fresh as a daisy, despite the rigors of his swordplay. I would have been amazed, except I knew that Hrundig made a religion out of endurance training.

The Cat seemed more worn out, but not much. Just breathing heavily.

"I take it all back," she said, her chest heaving a bit. "That stuff about silly exercises."

Hrundig grinned. "Stamina, woman. I told you. It's the soldier's best friend."

The Ogre's body lurched and rolled over onto its back. Greyboar pried himself out from under and stumbled to his feet.

He was *not* in a good mood. His head swiveled, bringing the wizard under his hot gaze.

"Zulkeh!" he roared. "What was the big idea, stirring this thing up?"

His words triggered off my own temper. "Yeah! And where were you all this time, you—"

I choked off the words. The mage was ignoring us completely. He was hopping back and forth on one leg, with a huge tome clutched in his hands, reciting from it aloud.

"—*and thus, by the power of the wine-dark sea, do I smite thee with my rosy finger!*"

He pirouetted, lifted his right hand from the tome, and pointed his forefinger at the Ogre's corpse. The finger, I noticed, was indeed rosy. A bolt of something like wine-colored lightning sprang from the fingertip and smote the dead monster in the chest.

"*Yuch!*" squealed Jenny and Angela. Pieces of Ogre were splattered all over the grotto.

"That's great, Zulkeh," growled Greyboar, wiping a fragment of grue from his face. "You just killed a dead Ogre."

The wizard frowned, examining what was left of the monster. Shelyid took the tome from his hand and tucked it away in the sack.

"I tried to talk him out of it," he said apologetically. "Sure and the rosy finger's a doozy, but before you can use it you gotta wade through all that stuff about the wrath of what's-his-name and all that squabbling over the girl and that silly business where everybody's racing around in chariots getting in the way of the gods who are doing all the real stuff and—"

"Silence, dwarf!" barked Zulkeh.

"Silence yourself!" snapped Magrit. She waddled toward the wizard, shaking her plump fist. "You damn near got us all killed and then didn't do a damn thing except—"

Zulkeh didn't seem to be listening. The mage had his head cocked, as if he were listening for something.

"Silence!" he hissed. "There has been too much noise already!"

Magrit wasn't about to let Zulkeh shut her up, of course, so she kept squawling her displeasure. But the wizard's obvious disquiet transmitted itself to everyone else.

"Silence the creature, Greyboar!" hissed Zulkeh. His usual arrogance seemed entirely absent. He waved his hands frantically, urging silence upon everyone.

Greyboar grunted, and clapped a hand over Magrit's mouth. The witch looked furious, but she seemed to settle down a bit.

Silence. The strangler removed his hand and frowned. "What's the problem, prof? Why are you—"

"Silence!" hissed the wizard again. Zulkeh was almost dancing with agitation. "Silence!"

A sound was heard. A deep, faint sound. Like—rocks moving, maybe. Or crunching.

"As I feared!" cried the mage. "Come! We must be off—and quickly!"

Matching deed to words, Zulkeh strode across the grotto to the tunnel entrance opposite the one from which we had entered. Shelyid followed.

Another sound. Much louder. Definitely like rocks moving. Or crunching.

We all hastened into the tunnel after Zulkeh and his apprentice. Behind us, the sound grew into a crescendo. It sounded like a rock slide—coming from the bottom up.

"Make haste! Make haste!" cried Zulkeh from ahead. We made haste.

"What's making that noise?" asked Angela. "Another Ogre?"

"Bah!" oathed the mage. "Do you think a pitiful Great Ogre of Grotum can rip apart the very roots of the mountains? Fie on such witless notions!"

The noise behind us now sounded like a volcano.

"Nay, nay!" cried Zulkeh. "The Great Ogre of Grotum is a trifle. Alas, the brutes are doted upon by their—"

"Oh, shit!" cried Magrit.

"Good move, guys," groused Wittgenstein.

"That's just a myth!" protested Hrundig.

The noise behind us now made a volcano sound tame.

"The Great Ogre of Grotum's Mother," concluded Zulkeh. "No myth, sirrah! And what is worse is the very real possibility—"

The volcano behind us was suddenly joined by an earthquake.

"As I feared! The Peril More Dire Still!"

Racing down the tunnel, led by the mage's voice: "Fly for your lives!"

Volcano and earthquake were now joined by a tidal wave of rippling rock.

Again: "Fly for your lives!"

Chapter 25.
(Too disgusting to title)

Well, we escaped. Barely. As time passed, the rumble and crumble of collapsing passageways behind us faded slowly into distant thunder. But by the time the wizard got done leading us down about a million twists and turns in the labyrinth, we were hopelessly lost.

Or so I thought. Zulkeh claimed otherwise.

We finally stopped in another grotto. A very small one, dank and damp. Nervously, I inspected the moisture-glistening walls in the lantern light. Except for an oval-shaped door on one side—what sailor types call a hatch—and a tunnel maybe fifteen feet from it, the grotto seemed empty.

Zulkeh was standing in front of the hatch, inspecting it closely. After a moment he straightened, exuding satisfaction. "Just as I planned!" he proclaimed. "My stratagem bears fruit."

I must have snorted loudly enough for him to hear. He turned a baleful eye upon me.

"You doubt my words?" he demanded. "Lost, you say? At wit's end, I presume?" Zulkeh rapped the hatch with his staff. The rusty iron rang hollow. "Stymied by this unexpected obstacle in the course of my science, you claim?"

He was genuinely pissed, I could tell. Not hard, that. Zulkeh was usually genuinely pissed about something.

"You shouldn't doubt the professor, Ignace," complained Shelyid. A moment later, the huge sack gave a little heave and whumped softly on the floor of the grotto. Shelyid's furry little face stared up at me reprovingly. " 'Tisn't right."

"What, kid?" I demanded. "Are you still standing up for the tyrant? I thought we cured you of that habit in Prygg. Gave you a labor contract and everything!"

The dwarf rummaged in one of the pockets of his tunic. "Teach your grandmother to suck eggs," he muttered. A moment later his hand emerged, clutching a well-worn and dog-eared little booklet. I recognized the thing. It was the labor contract which Les Six had negotiated for him in Magrit's house, after the full extent of Shelyid's position had become clear. Most indignant, they'd been—and rightly so. True, Les Six are notorious malcontents, even by the standards of the Groutch proletariat. But there wasn't much doubt, by anybody's standards except outright slavers, that Zulkeh's concept of "conditions of apprenticeship" was, ah, quaint.

Shelyid's little fingers flicked through the pages with practiced ease. "Here it is!" he piped. " 'Part IV, Section B, Paragraph 3, clause (a): It shall be the responsibility of the short-statured-but-fully-qualified apprentice to rise to the defense of the sorcerer when said mage's sagacity is questioned by ignorant louts.' "

The nerve of that kid!

"I know how to read contracts myself, you know!"

I flicked a finger dismissively, curling my lip. "Read the *next* clause, why don't you?"

Shelyid didn't bother to consult the booklet. He was already returning it to his pocket. "Clause (b)," he intoned. " 'Except when the mage is making a damn fool of himself.' "

He gave me a half-reproachful, half-derisive look. "Which he didn't, in this case, because this *is* exactly how he planned the whole thing."

"Well said, my stupid but loyal apprentice!" spoke Zulkeh.

My lip curled mightier still. I daresay my mustachios flourished.

"It's true!" insisted Shelyid. "It all happened exactly like the professor said!" He hesitated. "Well. He gave it an eighty-seven percent probability. But that's awful close!"

The dwarf pointed back at the tunnel through which we had entered. The rumbling sounds of collapsing passageways had almost faded away completely by now.

"He said we were bound to meet a Great Ogre of Grotum before too long. And then it was almost a sure thing that somebody would screw up and alert the Great Ogre of Grotum's Mother and the Peril More Dire Still."

He gave the sorcerer an apologetic glance. "It's true the professor predicted it would be somebody else who'd blow it. Instead of himself."

Zulkeh started to bridle. So did Greyboar and Gwendolyn. So did Jenny and Angela. Fortunately, Magrit—of all people!—intervened before tempers got further aroused. "Cut it out, all of you!" she wheezed.

The witch huffed and puffed. Magrit's on what they call the matronly side, which is a polite way of saying middle-aged and plump. The long race through the corridors had clearly put a strain on her.

But she's a tough cookie, Magrit, no doubt about that. Under all that heft there was plenty of muscle. Not to mention probably the most sarcastic soul in the world, except her familiar. Which, since she's the one who conjured him into sentience, explains Wittgenstein. Like witch, like witchee.

"And he's right, anyway," she huffed, jabbing a finger at Shelyid. "I heard the old fart say it myself. Then blather on about how the inevitable ensuing destruction of a portion of the labyrinth would disguise our entry from malevolent monsters while he led us to a secret alternate route into the Infernal Regions." Sourly: "Scheming like he always does, even if he calls it thaumaturgical guile."

Zulkeh started to say something, but Magrit cut him off.

"So—okay, genius! We're here. Now what?" She nodded at the hatch. "You *did* notice that the 'secret alternate route' has got no handle to open it, I trust. And by the looks of the thing, we're certainly not going to break it down. So how are we supposed to get in?"

"Bah!" oathed Zulkeh. He pointed with his staff toward the tunnel not far from it. "Some of us shall simply take that route, circle around, and open the hatch from the other side." He cleared his throat. "Greyboar and Ignace, to be precise."

A torrent of protest erupted.

"Why only them?" demanded Angela.

"Yeah—we should *all* go!" yelped Jenny.

"And how will they keep from getting lost?" added Gwendolyn.

"We're *already* lost," groused Wittgenstein. "Don't believe all this wizardly folderol. Probabilities, my ass!"

"I think we should—"

"*Enough!*" thundered the mage. "Is my science to

be questioned at every step? My reason doubted at every fork?"

Again, he jabbed at the tunnel. "Some of us, I say, because *all* of us may not go. *Imprimis*, because Gwendolyn and Hrundig are needed to stay behind, in the event some sullen brute insensate to my sorcery should happen to stumble upon us in this grotto. One *does* require mighty thews upon occasion in these adventures, even when guided by such a puissant mage as myself. *Secundus*, because it is no fit place for ladies."

Here, he managed a gracious bow at the "ladies." Magrit snorted. Jenny and Angela stuck their tongues out. The Cat just gave him her patented bottle-glass gaze, followed with: "You're not a lady. Neither's the runt."

Zulkeh cleared his throat. "Indeed not. But, if you will allow me to continue, madam: *Tertius*, because Shelyid is needed to carry my sack and, as you can plainly see, the sack will not fit into that pitiful entryway."

The Cat's cold, unforgiving eyes were still upon him. "Still leaves you."

Bless the woman! She's nuts, but she's no fool.

Zulkeh straightened indignantly. "My dear young lady! Surely you don't expect me to advance into danger without my instruments? My scrolls! My tomes! My talismans! My—"

Wittgenstein blew a raspberry. Zulkeh broke off his expostulation and glared at the salamander. "None of which reasoning requires this odious amphibian to remain behind. Indeed! He would make a splendid addition to the party soon to be advancing into yon tunnel!"

Wittgenstein blew another raspberry. "Do I look like one of these primate morons? Think I can't smell what's down that tunnel? Ha!"

Zulkeh, for just a fleeting instant, almost looked

abashed. One of the few times I'd seen the wizard even come close to being embarrassed about anything. When you've got an ego as big as he does, "chagrin" and "mortification" are pretty much *terra incognita*.

None of which, of course, prevented me from smelling a rat myself. "What's in that tunnel?" I demanded.

Zulkeh cleared his throat. Said nothing. Cleared his throat again.

"It isn't a 'tunnel,' dimwit," sneered Wittgenstein. "It's the entrance to a sewer."

"I don't like it," rumbled Greyboar.

"The needs of science!" cried Zulkeh. "The requirements of our quest!"

"I *still* don't like it," grumbled Greyboar.

"Shuddup!" I snarled. I probably liked it even less, but—

As the wise man says: "Cheap shots are life's bargains."

So, with a perfect sneer: "You've got to learn to be philosophical about these things."

Oh, joy. The pure glare on the chokester's face registered the bull's-eye. Greyboar started to snap back some—feeble, feeble—retort, but his eyes bulged and he lunged to the side. Pressing himself against the rough, curved stone wall, he goggled at a very large object floating by.

At first, I thought it was a dead body of some sort. But then, as the object floated further into the light shed by my lantern, I recognized it and started to choke. Disgust, sure, but—oh, joy! Another cheap shot!

I sneered again. Perfectly.

"What did you expect to see in a sewer, big guy? *The philosopher's stone?*"

This time, alas, the shot missed. At least, no glare

erupted on the strangler's face. Instead, he just frowned mightily as the object went its way. Didn't even wrinkle his nose.

"What in the world," he mused, "could have produced that thing? D'you see the size of it, Ignace? Like—"

"I did."

I froze. The voice, coming from the darkness ahead of us, thundered down the sewer like an oxcart racing over cobblestones.

"Who spoke?" demanded Greyboar. His basso voice was like a twittering bird compared to—

Again, the thundering oxcart: **"I did."**

"Show yourself!" demanded Greyboar. Forgetting all squeamishness, the strangler surged into the very center of the sewer, arms and hands spread wide.

"Show yourself!" he commanded.

"No, don't!" I cried, interjecting the voice of sanity. "Stay right where you are!"

Alas, too late. In the gloom ahead, a greater darkness began to congeal. A figure took form, advanced. Ahead of it, a bow wave surged through the stinking water.

Now it was my turn to press myself against the rough stone wall. Very rough, that wall, very stony, and wet with slime. But I clutched it like a baby clutches his mother's breast.

Even Greyboar was shaken, a bit. "By the bones of Saint Agnes," he whispered. "I always thought the damn thing was a fairy tale. It's the Ogre of the Sewer!"

The rumbling voice: **"I wish you wouldn't call me that."** A plaintive tone filled the voice, contrasting oddly with the rumble: **"I really wish you wouldn't."**

"Don't call him that, Greyboar!" I snapped. "It's so impolite. You should be ashamed of yourself!"

I smiled my best smile at the advancing monster.

"I apologize for my friend—acquaintance. He really has no manners at all."

"Don't smile at me like that."

Smile vanished.

"Nasty little smile."

The horror was close enough to discern features, now. It was—well, another ogre. But there was no disguise about this one. The creature was even bigger and nastier-looking than the Great Ogre of Grotum! Gray, lumpy skin. Beetling brow. Huge, flapping ears. Small, red, piggish eyes. And all the rest, of course. You know—tusks. Talons. The lot.

The piggish red-fury eyes transferred their glare from me to Greyboar. **"There's no such thing as the Ogre of the Sewer. It's a fairy tale!"**

Greyboar looked puzzled. The monster's eyes became flaming slits.

"Just because I'm ugly!"

Greyboar suddenly laughed. "Ugly, be damned. It's not your looks, it's your diet. Every kid knows that if you jump into a sewer to go exploring, the Ogre'll get you. That's why kids don't—"

He stopped. Frowned. "Though, now that I think on it, I don't imagine too many kids—"

"Last kid got lost exploring the sewers was Tommy Wingle. Eight years ago. He stills comes down, now and then, brings me chocolates."

It eyed us hungrily. **"Got any chocolates?"**

Greyboar was still frowning. As usual, I had to do the quick thinking.

"No, we don't, sir, sorry about that," I piped up. "But we've got a loaf of bread. And some cheese." I unhitched the backpack from where it had been riding on my shoulders. (*High* on my shoulder, needless to say; only proper way to carry a backpack in a sewer.) Started rummaging through it.

"What kind of bread?"

I pulled out the bread, stared at it. "Uh, I don't really know. I'm not a baker. It's good bread though! I swear! Really really good—"

It's odd, if you've never heard it. A sort of rumbling, gigantic, disdainful sniff:

"It's rye." SNIFF. **"Crappiest bread there is. Even worse than pumpernickel."**

I prepared for the worst. Just about the very absolute worst I could imagine. I'd never thought I'd die of old age in a bed, mind you. But still! Being devoured by an ogre in a sewer was a bit much.

Suddenly, the monster sniffed again. Then again. I realized it had detected the odor of the cheese in the knapsack. Nasty, gooey stuff, it was. Jenny and Angela had scrounged it up just before we left. Neither Greyboar nor I had touched the crap, after taking one look at it. I cringed.

"Camembert!" squealed the horror. **"And I've got just the wine for it, too! A nice little *pinot noir* I've been saving!"**

"Delightful," purred Maurice, daintily dabbing his lipless maw with a talon. "And such a wonderful change from baby alligator!"

The not-ogre cast a reproachful glance at Greyboar. "You'd crap some giant turds too, if all you had to live on was baby alligator."

The chokester nodded politely. "I'm sure I would."

The not-monster stuck out his tongue with disgust. It looked like a giant, purple leech.

"Nasty things, baby alligators. All bones and teeth and tail and scaly hide. And it takes at least five or six of them to make a decent meal." A heavy, heavy sigh. "Fortunately, people keep buying the stupid things and dumping them after they start growing up. When they discover they've got a big, stupid, nasty, man-eating reptile on their hands. Some pet!"

Maurice craned his head around—had to turn his whole body to do it; no neck—and glared at a huge pile of baby alligator bones in a corner of his grotto. He snorted. "Wouldn't find a troll doing something that stupid."

To back up a bit, Maurice—that was the monster's name, as you may have deduced—had explained, with quite the air of injured *amour propre*—that he was not an ogre, but a troll. A bonafide troll, yessirree. A member in good standing of the species *Trollus sapiens*.

I managed to keep a straight face, after he clarified the point. Not easy, that—not even with the sight of Maurice's tusks and talons to keep me civil. It was a bit too much like a murdering fiend insisting he was really a homicidal maniac.

Greyboar, of course, had no trouble at all keeping a straight face. Naturally, he got interested in the distinction, and started asking questions. So we had to sit there for an hour in that cold, dank, stinky, dimly-lit grotto while Maurice blathered on. It seems—

Oh, yeah. I suppose I should pause in order to give you a proper description of what they call the "locale." Hm. A bit difficult, that. Let's do it this way:

Close your eyes and try to imagine a troll's lair. Try real hard. Got it?

Add raw sewage.

Okay, moving right along, Maurice insisted on giving us a long-winded discourse on the fine distinctions between:

1) Ogres and trolls. This mainly involves—you're getting the troll version, mind—an extra little bone in the ankles, certain minute and subtle differences in the shape of the talons, and a vast difference in cranial

capacity. I.e., they look exactly alike except trolls say they're smarter.

2) *Trollus horribilis* vs. *Trollus sapiens*. This mainly involves the same picayune differences (see above). If this does not make sense to you, join the club.

3) *Trollus sapiens*, civilized and couth, vs. *Trollus sapiens, au naturelle*. This mainly involves dietary habits, along with a fine distinction in ecological niche. To wit: *Trollus sapiens au naturelle* eats anything, anywhere, anytime. *Trollus sapiens*, civilized and couth, on the other hand, eats anything, anywhere, anytime— so long as in so doing they do not disturb the ecological balance of their habitat. And cheese and chocolates, of course. And whole wheat bread, bean sprouts and something called tofu.

Finally done with this tedious tripe, Maurice got around to asking us what we were doing in the sewer. Greyboar explained, more or less. The troll got an uncertain look on his face (I think that's what those furrowed wrinkles signified, anyway) and scratched his jaw with a talon.

"Dunno," Maurice muttered. "Not supposed to let anyone through that hatch."

"Says who?" I demanded. My voice was perhaps a bit more shrill than the circumstances warranted. I wouldn't normally get peevish with a giant troll in his lair. But I *really* wanted to get out of that place. If I needed to explain why, you wouldn't be reading this book. You couldn't read, period.

"The CEO of the Infernal Regions, that's who!" Maurice snapped. He hesitated. "Well . . . I suppose I shouldn't boast. I've never actually had the honor of meeting the Top Devil in person. The Lord of Evil communicates with me through channels, you understand."

The horrid face got more horrid still. I realized I was looking at a troll version of a scowl.

"Kind of resent it, actually. He always sends imps up here with my orders, instead of proper devils. He really ought to show me a little more respect." Now, the monster was practically whining. "This is an important post, you know. The only thing standing between the Infernal Regions and possible invaders is that hatch."

I refrained from pointing out the obvious—*what idiot is going to invade the Infernal Regions?*—and went for the main chance. "Time for some working-class action, then! A slowdown, by G—by the Devil!"

Greyboar nodded solemnly. "Ignace's right. A work-to-rule campaign. We slid by on account of you were all tied up carrying out your multitude of other responsibilities with meticulous precision. Obviously, you need some help. A couple of imps, maybe, to serve as your flunkeys. A promotion!"

Maurice growled. Growled again. "Got that right!" he snarled. A moment later, he was heaving himself erect.

"This way," he commanded. "We'll show the bosses what's what!"

After he opened the hatch and saw who was waiting on the other side, Maurice changed his tune.

"Zulkeh!" he bellowed. "*You swine!*"

The troll glared at me and Greyboar. "You didn't tell me that *he* was on the other side!"

I didn't know what to say. Greyboar shrugged. "You didn't ask," he pointed out, reasonably enough. "But if you had—"

Maurice was not mollified. He started to shake a huge fist in Greyboar's face. But the wizard distracted him.

"Come, come, my dear troll!" reproved Zulkeh. "Surely you're not still peeved over that monograph?"

"Peeved?" roared Maurice. He stooped and stuck his head through the hatchway, spitting in Zulkeh's face. "You slandered me! And after all the hospitality I showed you, too!"

The sorcerer immediately matched the troll's umbrage with his own. "Slander?" he cried. "Do I hear me aright? *Slander?*"

Zulkeh was practically spitting himself. He *was* hopping about in a funny little dance. You know the one: *the scholar, critiqued and disputatious.*

"No slander in the least! Preposterous! Opprobrious! My research was meticulous, my logic impeccable, my conclusions foregone!"

"You tricked me!"

Zulkeh was apparently prepared to argue that point too, but Shelyid interrupted him.

"Uh, he's right about that last part, professor. You *did* tell him you were doing an article for *Subterranean Life.* Not the *Review of Contemporary Monstrosity.*" The dwarf looked up at the troll. "Sorry, Maurice. I couldn't say anything at the time because—"

"Be silent, miserable dwarf!" commanded Zulkeh.

"—I wasn't working under a proper labor—"

"Silence, I say! Degenerate imbecile!"

"—agreement like I am now." Shelyid frowned at the sorcerer. "And you shouldn't call me those names, professor. That's a clear violation of the contract, and you know it."

I braced myself, sighing. I'd seen Shelyid and Zulkeh mix it up over a contract dispute. Tedious, tedious—lengthy. The mage's temper full-matched by the dwarf's stubbornness. Temper, as in volcano; stubbornness, as in Mule God.

To my relief, Shelyid broke away. The next thing I knew, he was rummaging in the huge sack. "But I always planned to make it up to you, Maurice! Honest!"

A moment later he emerged, clutching a package. "Look! Chocolates!"

Well, that did it. A word to the wise: if you're ever faced by a huge and murderously furious troll, make sure you've got some chocolates on you. I can recommend caramel creams.

After Maurice had gobbled down the whole box, he belched and retreated from the hatchway. "Go on through," he muttered, waving a huge paw. "I'll wish you luck, all of you except Zulkeh."

The troll leered. "Bet you didn't tell *them* either, did you? The truth, I mean."

Greyboar frowned. "*What* truth?"

Maurice's leer was a sight to behold. "About what's coming next. Bet the lousy mage just said all you had to do was get through this hatch and you'd have a clear shot at the Infernal Regions. Didn't he? Boasted and bragged about how he knew a shortcut that'd avoid all those nasty Things From Below and It Came From Unders. *Didn't he?*"

All eyes now turned to Zulkeh. "Yeah, as a matter of fact," muttered Magrit. "He just got through spending the last twenty minutes bragging about it."

The sorcerer drew himself up stiffly. "And 'tis true!" he exclaimed. Cleared his throat. "As far as it goes."

All eyes were now squinting. As in: *hostile suspicion*.

"There *is* the matter of the Guide," added Zulkeh. In as close to an abashed mumble as I've ever heard issue from the wizard's lips.

"Oh, swell!" shrilled Wittgenstein. The salamander

reared up on Magrit's shoulder. "You're talking about Virge, aren't you? The Little Snotnose from Hell!"

Zulkeh *was* abashed. "Well . . . Well. The poetry's not *that* bad."

"It is too!" shrilled Wittgenstein. The creature swiveled his beady little red eyes onto the rest of us. "You'll see!"

Chapter 26.
It Gets Worse

"There stands Jackie grotesquely, and he snarls,
    examining the unworthy at the gate;
        he judges and dispatches, tail in coils.
"He it was, cursed beast, who judged me so
    on the earth above, in earlier life,
        and said I was worthless every time.
"Never choosing me to be on his team!
    Never! Not once! Sneering me and jeering,
        Saying I was nothing but a clumsy shrimp!
"You see now his punishment—isn't it grand?
    Condemned to choose for ever and ever
        between nothing but losers and fumblers."
The intrepid guide, the young but wise Virge,
    now led us through a hideous portal
        into a vast and echoing cavern.
Men and insects alike trembled aghast
    at the murky, unformed, endless reaches
        of that grotto of abomination.

Naked forms of nubile adolescents
 swept past as if caught in a mighty gale,
  a torrent of pale, pimply visages,
Their eyes streaming tears, their mouths wide open,
 their arms outstretched, a look of hopelessness
  horrid on each and every girlish face.
"Ha! Ha!" cried young Virge, pointing to one girl.
 "You see there that one? Pleading and begging?
  Ha! Ha! That's Judy Winfield herself,
"Who laughed at me when I asked her to the prom,
 sneering and jeering, calling me a geek.
  Who's getting turned down now, Judy?
"Tell me that! Ha! Ha! Look at her whirl away!
 Condemned to everlasting rejection!"
  So spoke the doughty lad who was our guide.

Not that bad, sayeth the mage! Ha!
Judge for yourself, why don't you?
And if you're whining already, tough. We had to
wade through the whole journey to the heart of the
Inferno in that fashion.
Here, have some more:

We were now in the third circle, a realm
 of cold and rain, a cursed and dreary place,
  where an endless line of condemned sinners
Trudged past, hopeless, their sinuses swollen,
 coughing and hacking, wheezing and sniffling,
  Blowing their noses, endlessly groaning.
"And who are these piteous souls?" asked the strangler.
 "I note they are ladies of mature age,
  their faces filled with care and concern."
"Not so!" cried young Virge, who suddenly sprang
 at one figure slogging by, kicking her
  and reviling her with youthful vigor.

"They deserve their fate, each and every one!"
    shouted our guide. "These here are the mothers
        who made their little children go to school
Even when the poor kids were sick abed!
    There! You see that one?" asked wise young Virge,
        pointing to a careworn gray-haired woman.
"That's my mother, the foul rotten creature.
    Hey Ma! How's the weather today? Ha! Ha!
    Listen to her sniffle, the poor old cow!"

Sweet, isn't it?

Sure, taking the Guide's Route gives you immunity from the perils of the Inferno, even from the CEO himself. But is it worth it? Just to avoid having to battle a million demons and devils and whatnot?

Think so?

Here, then! See if this changes your mind . . .

And then we started down a fourth abyss,
    making our way along the dismal slope
        where all the evil of the world is dumped.
Along the slope, strewn about like boulders,
    rested a multitude of condemned ones,
        shackled to heavy chairs, their mouths agape.
About them, clutching horrible iron
    implements of fell and fearsome design,
        capered horned devils and barb-tailed imps.
"This place is the doom reserved for dentists,"
    explained the wise young Virge. My own dentist,
        the swine, moans somewhere here.
"But we cannot tarry, though it tempts me.
    We must press on." And so saying, our guide
        Hastened his steps and led us ever down.

Enough!

Wittgenstein was right. The poetry *was* that bad.

Circle after circle of it. On and on, just like that. A
pimply-faced adolescent's Guide to the Infernal Regions.

We couldn't do anything about it, either. That was
the downside of using Zulkeh's clever little "alternate
route." Once you go that way, you have to follow what
the little snotnose brat who led us called the "Guide's
Rules."

I whined at Zulkeh, but the wizard confirmed the
bad news.

" 'Tis inescapable, I fear," he stated gloomily. "On this,
Ignace, whatever may be their other points of conten-
tion, all the savants agree. I refer you in particular to
the universally acknowledged masterwork of the literature, Alighieri Sfondrati-Piccolomini's *Once is Enough!*
Whomsoever enters the Infernal Regions by utilizing the
Guide's Route must agree to the Guide's Rules."

And that's that. So don't ask me to describe what
we passed through on our way down to meet the CEO
of the Infernal Regions. I can't do it. Not unless you
want more of that crap which "the wise young Virge"
calls "terser reamer" or something like that.

It doesn't get any better, either, not until we get past
the interview—if you'll allow me to use the term—with
the Chief Evildoer himself. (And, yeah, that came as
news to me too. I'd sort of assumed we'd be sneaking
past him or something. Turns out if you take the Guide's
Route you can't. Marvelous, huh? Imagine my reaction
at the time! That damned Zulkeh! Never trust a mage!)

Anyway, after what seemed an endless time listening to "the wise young" Snotnose droning on and on,
we finally debouched onto the lowest level. It's not the
ninth, by the way—that's a myth started by that
Alighieri fellow in order to get tenure. The truth is,
he had no more idea than we did which level it is, but
I guess he couldn't very well put that in his doctoral
dissertation. The Infernal Regions don't follow the same

numbering rules which the rest of the universe does. Something to do with Chaos, the way I understand it.

You can imagine my sigh of relief.

Sigh. No dice. Once you buy into the Guide's Rules you're stuck with them, even after the Guide himself bows out of the picture. Which "the wise young Virge" did as soon as the CEO loomed into sight. You can say what you want about the Prince of Darkness, but he ain't all bad. At least he doesn't tolerate lippy teenagers.

So "the wise young Virge" scuttled away and I thought we were home free. Not a chance. The next thing I knew, the whole area was resounding with the chatter of about a jillion imps, all prattling away in what the bedamned scholars call a "classical chorus."

I groaned. Hrundig grinned.

> *"You think   this is bad?*
> *You ought   to see the*
> *Guide's Rules   in my homeland's*
> *version of   eternal damnation."*

I groaned again.

Since you might be interested—heh—and since I'm a firm believer in the wise man's saw that "misery conscripts company," here's what happened then:

THE CHORUS OF IMPS: *They come! They come!*
                    Arrivistes!

CEO OF THE INFERNAL *Whence come ye, mortals?*
REGIONS: *And by whose leave?*

ZULKEH OF GOIMR,   *From above, Foul One.*
PHYSICIAN: *And our leave is sufficient,*
                    The will of my own intellect.

CEO OF THE INFERNAL REGIONS:	*For what purpose then?* *And by whose fell design?*
THE CHORUS OF IMPS:	*By whose fell design?* *Speak! Speak!*
ZULKEH OF GOIMR, PHYSICIAN:	*For the purpose of discovering* *All secrets of Joetry.* *As for the design,* *From far Pryggia it comes,* *Dispatched by Magrit's hand,* *Whose withered veins and* *Talons held the might to cast* *Her mission unto decrepit* *Goimr, tumored city of* *Once-proud kings,* *Now overthrown, their dynasty* *Brought to ruination,* *Whose wretched hovels huddle* *By the very woods whose shade* *Once dappled fair Gwendolyn,* *The long hours she strode,* *Her keen eyes searching* *Every shadow for sign of peril* *Whilst her mind wandered,* *Pondering the newfound love* *Discovered in the unexpected* *Form of the hated intruder* *From haughty imperial Ozar.*
THE CHORUS OF IMPS:	*Cut to the chase!* *Cut to the chase!*
ZULKEH OF GOIMR, PHYSICIAN:	*Now the bone fought over by* *Miscreants mad and military* *Who sought in vain to*

> *Forestall the shrewd acumen*
> *Of the mage Zulkeh,*
> *That is myself, who, now*
> *Apprised of Magrit's vision,*
> *Seeks to wrest from all*
> *Powers, be they high or low*
> *The truth concerning the fell*
> *Dream of the dotard king.*

THE CHORUS OF IMPS:
> *Get to the point!*
> *Get to the point!*

ZULKEH OF GOIMR,
PHYSICIAN:
> *Bah! Impudent imps!*
> *Foul Vizier of Vileness!*
> *I demand the truth, all*
> *That is known in Hell*
> *Anent the ancient Joe,*
> *Who invented everything.*

CEO OF THE INFERNAL
REGIONS:
> *Not a chance, Zulkeh.*

THE CHORUS OF IMPS:
> *What a clown!*
> *What a clown!*

ZULKEH OF GOIMR,
PHYSICIAN:
> *Bah! Impudent archdevil!*
> *Desist, Lord of Lies.*
> *I am impatient, for even as*
> *I pontificate in epic meter,*
> *Time wanes.*

CEO OF THE INFERNAL
REGIONS:
> *I'm dying here. Dying!*
> *Of laughter. Not a chance,*
> *Zulkeh of Goimr. Ask me*
> *Something serious.*

ZULKEH OF GOIMR, PHYSICIAN:	*Since you insist!* *Where is fair Gwendolyn's* *Former squeeze?*
THE CHORUS OF IMPS:	*Ha! Ha! Ha! Ha!* *Hee! Hee! Hee!*
CEO OF THE INFERNAL REGIONS:	*Gasp! Choke! Wheeze!* *Gigglegigglegiggle.* *He's in Even Worse Hands* *Than me! Gasp! Choke!* *Thattaway.*

So off we went, before the CEO of the Infernal Regions and his minions could stop laughing. True, he'd pointed us to the door himself, so by all rights he could hardly object to our following his directions. But they don't call him the Archdevil for nothing.

According to the Guide's Rules, I can't describe the door itself which led to the Place Even Worse Than Hell, but the inscription over it is within the guidelines:

> Abandon All Hope
> Ye Who Enter Here
> And This Time We're Not Kidding

I was so relieved when the door closed behind us that I practically collapsed. I paid no attention to my surroundings. Some kind of huge grotto, glittering with light from what seemed like thousands of veins of peculiar minerals, glowing from within.

"Wonder what faces us next?" mused Greyboar.

"Don't care!" I gasped. "At least it'll come at us in prose!"

Chapter 27.
Moments, High and Low

But my gasping didn't last for long. Not two seconds later I was right in the wizard's face. Clutching the lapels of his sorcerer's robe in my hands and shaking him the way a terrier shakes a rat. Well. Small terrier; big rat. The terrier actually does most of the moving around part.

"*What's the big idea, Zulkeh?*" I demanded. "What are you doing getting into a wrangle with the CEO of the Infernal Regions—the Archdevil himself!—over this damned Joe business? You were just supposed to ask him about Benny!"

Oh, I was hot—*hot*.

"Bad enough we get hauled down here in the first place! For any reason! But at least Gwendolyn's family so we got that excuse!" I took the time here to bestow a share of my furious glare on her. "Such as it is. Screwy, you ask me, chasing after an *ex*-boyfriend."

Gwendolyn glared back. Normally, that would have

shut me up—she's *such* a scary woman—but not this time.

Hot—*hot.*

"That damned Joe business! I'm sick of it! Want no part of it! None, d'you hear? *None!*"

Alas, browbeating a wizard is easier said than done. Before I'd even finished, Zulkeh was spluttering his own outrage.

"Do I hear me aright? Is this midget jackanapes presuming to question me on the pursuit of my science?" Spittle, spittle. "Outrage! Impudence!"

Fortunately or otherwise, Greyboar interposed himself between us. It was *so* undignified. Greyboar's version of "interposing himself" involves scruffs of the neck and large hands and sundry hoisting operations. I leave the coarse details to the imagination.

I tried to keep hollering even suspended in midair— so did the wizard—but Greyboar gave us both a little shake and that pretty much brought silence. Hard to holler when your teeth are clattering together.

"Shuddup," he growled, after he set us down. "Both of you."

To add insult to injury, Greyboar's ensuing reproof was all aimed at *me.*

"And you're supposed to be the brains of the outfit!" he snorted. "What in the world did you *think* Zulkeh was doing on this little expedition, numbskull? You think the mage came along because he gives two fiddles about a revolutionary agitator's artist ex-boyfriend?"

"Preposterous!" spoke the mage. "Offensive—nay, insulting! Would any scholar allow himself to be diverted from his science for such a paltry and mundane purpose? Much less such a savant as myself?"

I goggled at him. Then, cursed myself.

What an idiot I was! *Of course* Zulkeh wouldn't have come along on this insane expedition for the normal reasons that grip your workaday lunatic. Ever since he decided that the weird dream of a now-dead king of Goimr portended some awful and unknown disaster for civilization, he's been a monomaniac about that damned quest of his. And since he was a maniac to begin with, you can just imagine what he was like once he got rolling.

That realization brought another. I swiveled and bestowed my glare on Magrit.

"And what about *you*?" I demanded. "What's your angle on this thing?" Here, a big sneer. "And *don't* bother telling me that you're doing this as a favor to Gwendolyn. You wouldn't cross the street to piss on a man dying of thirst unless he paid you in solid coin or—"

I stumbled to a halt. Magrit grinned. Wittgenstein spun around on her shoulder and mooned me. Disgusting, really, the way a salamander moons.

"What a dimwit," snickered the vile little creature. "Good thing he's built so low to the ground. Any taller, and the drop or two of blood which reaches his brain wouldn't be enough to keep him from passing out."

"You're swapping favors with her," I croaked. "You help Gwendolyn find her ex-squeeze and she owes you."

Magrit kept grinning. Wittgenstein snickered again. I could feel the emptiness of eternal destiny yawning wider and wider beneath my feet.

"And you count favors like a miser counts pennies. She owes you, you'll insist she pay you back. With a favor. And since Gwendolyn's in no position to do anything for you herself—she's on the run from every porker in Grotum—she'll have to put the screws on her brother—"

Light-headed now with growing horror, I stared at Greyboar. Even since we'd started on this insane trek, Greyboar had spent most of his time with his sister.

In a *tête-à-tête*, I believe the sophisticated crowd calls it. I hadn't thought about it much, at the time. Sibling reconciliation, you know. Slobbering sentimental stuff; babble, babble, babble.

"Tell me it isn't true," I whispered.

Greyboar cleared his throat. "Ah. Well. Actually, Ignace . . ."

At that point, I believe I wailed. Not sure. My memory gets a little fuzzy. Sheer terror, I'm told, will do that to a man.

Then, it got worse. My wail was cut off by a hand placed over my mouth. Two hands, actually. Not Greyboar's dinner-plate mitts, but two little hands belonging to Jenny and Angela.

One from each. They're not hard to distinguish between. Angela's hands are small, well-shaped and beautiful. Jenny's hands are exactly the same, except her fingers are longer. I could tell them apart in my sleep. I *have*, actually, not to put too fine a point on it. And if that comes across as a lecher's remark, think again. It's got nothing to do with that. They comfort me differently, that's all. Can't explain how, exactly, but they do.

I love those hands. Just as I love the faces that were staring at me.

Um. Squinting at me, to be precise. As in: exasperation, discontent, contumely. That sort of thing.

With ever-growing shock, I realized that Jenny and Angela had *also* been spending a lot of time with Greyboar and Gwendolyn since the journey began. *Tête-à-quatratête*, so to speak.

"We think it's a great idea," snapped Jenny. "You would too if you ever paid any attention to what we told you about what's happening to the dwarves."

Angela sneered. "Ignace? Pay attention to anything

in the world except what's going to make him a few quid? Ha!"

They were *exceedingly* disgruntled, now. I could tell. I tried to mumble something but the hands on my mouth just tightened down.

"Oughta cut him off for good, we should," growled Jenny. "Him and his tight fist for a heart. Put him on a *real* budget."

Angela snickered. "Great austerities. Be good for the midget. His heart wouldn't be the only thing shrunk down to a walnut."

To add insult to injury, Zulkeh added his advice.

"Splendid idea! A stratagem worthy of the ancients! Should you need guidance, damsels of dubious virtue, I shall be delighted to provided you with a copy of the classic treatise. Lysistrata Sfondrati-Piccolomini's seminal—if you will pardon the expression—*Do It Yourself, Big Shot; You're a Man, Aren't You?*"

By now, I suspect I was whimpering. Jenny's frown got crosser still.

Angela's was even worse. "We *are* going to rescue the dwarves at Operation Nibelung. One of these days, when the time's right. Magrit's still figuring out the plan. Greyboar's already agreed, and so have we. So's the Cat, for that matter."

My eyes rolled wildly in the direction of the Cat. The woman was standing not too far away, giving me her own cold-eyed stare.

"*Et tu?*" I managed to mumble through the fingers.

The Cat shrugged. "Sure. Why not? And Gwendolyn says Schrödinger may be there."

"Bastard's one of the 'top scientists,' according to one rumor," Gwendolyn snarled.

It was hopeless. Everybody was against me. An outcast in my own land, you might say.

So I did the only rational thing, of course. I capitulated.

"Okay," I mumbled. "I'll help. When the time comes."

Jenny and Angela's squints were now so suspicious that their eyes were mere slits. But they moved their hands off my mouth.

"S'true!" I protested. "Give you my word."

Squints. *Squints.*

Support came from an unexpected quarter. Gwendolyn, to my surprise.

"That's good enough, girls," she rumbled. (Oh, yeah. Gwendolyn talks in a rumble just like her brother. Different tone, of course. *Contralto profundo*, you might call it. Her voice is just like she is: beautiful in a way that's hard to describe. Think of a very feminine avalanche.)

"Good enough," she repeated. Gwendolyn moved up alongside Jenny and Angela. "He's a little scoundrel, true—greedy as a sponge and with about as much concern for moral standards. But he's no liar. Never has been."

I stared up at Gwendolyn. Her hawk face loomed over me. A lot like Greyboar's, that face. She's got the same dark complexion, same black eyes, same kinky mass of hair—except hers is a glorious mane instead of a bramble—same raptor beak of a nose. How she manages to look gorgeous instead of just scary is a mystery to me, but she does. *And* look scary at the same time.

Suddenly, Gwendolyn's face burst into a smile. *Her* smile, which is not quite like anything else in the world. Not a whole lot of warmth in it, mind you. Gwendolyn's not what you'd call the sweet-and-sentimental type. But it's such a *real* thing.

I found myself getting choked up. It had been so

many years since I'd seen that smile. It was my first memory of Gwendolyn. My first memory of either one of them, actually, because it was Gwendolyn who had introduced me to Greyboar.

Happened way back when I was a kid, growing up in one of the slums near the Flankn. Six years old, maybe seven. I'd gotten cornered in an alley by half a dozen bigger kids. Bunch of sullen snots, if you know what I mean. Was it *my* fault they couldn't take a joke?

Really a humorless lot, no doubt about it. Had chains and clubs and everything. But just when things were looking dicey they started flying every whichaway. The ones who didn't land on their asses took off running like rabbits. And the next thing I knew this really *big* girl was smiling down at me.

"Hiya, shrimp," she'd said. "I thought it was a pretty good wisecrack, myself. But you might want to work on your timing."

"Hiya, shrimp," Gwendolyn said.

"Long time," I croaked back.

The next thing I knew—just like it'd happened all those years ago—I was clutching her. Bawling my eyes out, if you can believe it.

"S'okay, Ignace." She squatted down. Her powerful arms gathered me up and held me tight. So tight, so real, just like I remembered. "S'okay. I never really stopped loving you either. Even if you were a crook, I knew you weren't dishonest. A rotter, yes. Rotten, no."

"Faint praise," I mumbled sourly, my face still pressed into her neck.

Gwendolyn's big shoulders heaved. One of those chuckling kind of shrugs, I would have thought, except that I could feel her own tears leaking into my hair.

"What else do you ever get in this world?" she whispered.

That brought the high moment of the day. Because Wittgenstein made a wisecrack, and, like me, his timing was off.

"Idn't dat sweet?" he sniggered, from his perch on Magrit's shoulder. "Weeping willow meets blubbering bantam."

The Cat was there, somehow, clutching Wittgenstein in her hand. Didn't even see her move.

"Wonder if salamanders can grow new heads?" she mused, hefting the lajatang.

The Cat's not given to idle speculation. She proceeded immediately with the experiment.

"You fruitcake!" howled Wittgenstein. Hissed, I should say. It's hard to actually howl, when your head's no longer connected to your lungs.

Everybody else was really howling, now. With laughter, except for Magrit.

"You fruitcake!" She charged up, shouldering the Cat aside, and stooped over to pick up Wittgenstein's head. "You got any idea how hard it's going to be to fix him back up?"

The Cat shook her head. "No. Can I watch?"

Chapter 28.
Consolation Prize

In case you've never witnessed the operation, recapitating a salamander is a time-consuming affair. It would have taken even longer if the Cat hadn't been there to give Magrit a hand.

"Quit squirming around, Wittgenstein!" Magrit was trying to hold the creature still while she positioned the head in the right place. She snarled at the Cat: "If he twitches one more time, start cutting something else off."

"My pleasure." The lajatang weaved over Wittgenstein's form, like a dragonfly looking for food. The salamander was suddenly as rigid as a board. Even his eyes stopped rolling around, except for following the movement of the blade. Very closely.

"That's better," grumbled the witch. Then she pulled a sewing kit out of her witch's bag and went to work. The process took quite a while on account of the teeny little stitches Magrit was making, and all the incantations she droned over each and every one. At one point,

377

Wittgenstein lost enough of his fear of the Cat to start whining, but Magrit shut him up right quick.

"You wanna look like Wittgenstein—or Frankenstein?"

She and the Cat started howling. The salamander's eyes bugged even further, and he hissed with outrage. "That's Frankenstein's *monster*, you ignoramus!"

An instant later, he was squealing. Magrit shook her head sadly. "Oh, look. You made me drop a stitch."

Magrit and the Cat went off into another round of maniacal cackling. Thereafter, the wretched little beast maintained his own counsel.

After a while, I lost interest and started studying the surroundings.

A "grotto," I believe I called it. Well, forget that. Now that I had a chance to really examine the place, I saw that the space we were in was much too big to be called anything except a "cavern." The Mother of All Caverns, to be precise.

Huge—in every dimension. The reason I'd been fooled by those first glimpses was simply because there were peculiar columns all over the place. Those drippy-stone things—you know, what they call something like catamites except there's no pedophilia involved. And the columns were all veined with that inner-glittering gold-fire substance.

My greed would have been aroused except that even I could tell this wasn't real gold. Not even fool's gold. Even from a distance, the stuff had a nasty look to it.

The wizard confirmed my suspicions immediately. He was over by one of the columns poking at the stuff with his staff. Shelyid was standing by his side, leaning against the huge sack.

"No doubt at all, my loyal but stupid apprentice. 'Tis indeed the fell mineral known as overthebrimstone." He poked it again, his lips pursed with distaste. "A dreadful substance. Magrit will be delighted."

Magrit must have overheard him. "I want no less than three pounds of it, Zulkeh! That was part of the deal!"

Shelyid sighed. The mage didn't even have to give him the order. The dwarf opened the sack and disappeared within. A minute or so later he reemerged, clutching a large stoppered jar—what sorcerers call an amphora—and a rock pick. Soon enough he was hard at work, chipping pieces of the stuff into the jar.

Moved by some odd impulse, I wandered over to give him a hand. But Shelyid waved me back.

"Don't come no closer, Ignace," he hissed. "Really is nasty stuff. Saps your moral fiber like nothing you ever ran into. And since you don't have much to begin with, you wouldn't last more than a few seconds."

I retreated hastily. *Chip, chip, chip.* Shelyid muttered: "What does she want it for, anyway?"

Zulkeh had moved back a few feet himself, but was still in hearing range. "Bah!" he oathed. "The vile harridan is the mistress of foety, apprentice. You should know that by now! There is none on earth can match her skills at revenge-work."

The sorcerer pointed at the jar with his staff. "Not more than a few flakes of that horrid substance, ground into powder and mixed with an enemy's food or drink, will do the trick. Transform their venial sins into mortal ones, their mortal sins into no mere turn of phrase. Within a fortnight, the glutton will be dead of gluttony, the miser of starvation, the envious of a burst spleen. Dire stuff, indeed!"

Still sewing, Magrit cackled. "And you should see what it does to lechers! According to the books, anyway. Never used the stuff before, myself. Can't get it anywhere except here, in the Place Even Worse Than Hell. Half the reason I agreed to come."

That reminder of how dangerous the place was made me look for Jenny and Angela. To my relief, they weren't nosing around like they usually would be. Instead, they were sitting cross-legged next to Greyboar and Gwendolyn, chattering away like magpies.

That sight didn't bring much relief, however. Gloomily, I was quite certain that they were exchanging stories about me with Gwendolyn. You know the kind of stories. The ones women swap about their menfolk, running along the theme of: Yeah, He's No Good But There's Hope For Him And We'll See To It, We Will.

Sigh. I could see it coming, a mile away. The Great Ignace Rehabilitation Project. The cheerful eager smile on Greyboar's face confirmed it, along with the way he was nodding his head like a witless orangutan. You know the one. The smile reformed sinners get around their womenfolk when the ladies are chattering away on the theme of One Down, One To Go.

Sigh.

Hrundig interrupted my thoughts of gloom and doom.

"Gloomy place," he remarked. "Makes me think of doom."

"Thanks a lot," I grumbled. "Just what I needed to hear."

His cold grin was back in place. "What's the matter, Ignace? Contemplating the Fate Worse Than Death?"

I snarled. "You've got a lot of nerve, making jokes about mending your wicked ways!"

The barb bounced right off. He just shrugged. "I did that a long time ago, to tell you the truth. After Olga's husband was murdered and I got her and the girls out safely, I sort of took stock. As you might say."

I stared into his ice-blue eyes. Hrundig is one of those deadly-looking men, if you know what I mean. I don't mean "dangerous." I mean—*deadly*. It's always a shock, with someone like that, when you realize they actually have a soul. Just like people.

I'd learned some of the story. Hrundig had been hired in Prygg by Olga's husband, after the Alsask retired from the Legions. The artist had gotten so famous that he needed a bodyguard just to fend off the adoring aesthetes. When Frissault got arrested for heresy, Hrundig hadn't been able to save him from the tender mercies of the Inquisition and the Godferrets. But he did manage to smuggle the widow and the daughters to safety. Along with enough of Frissault's paintings to set the family up in a secret villa in New Sfinctr. Then, I guess, kept them afloat with the money he made from his *salle d'armes*.

Odd thing to do, for such a man.

I guess he must have seen the question in my eyes. He shrugged again, in a gesture so economical it might be called "minute."

"I wrestled with it. Long time. The truth is, it really bothered my conscience. I'd fallen in love with the woman within a week after I was hired. I tried to save her husband—did; tried hard as I could—but—"

"The Inquisition," I jeered. "What were you going to do? Must have been a hundred Godferrets swarming all over him, after he was exposed."

Hrundig took a little breath. "A hundred and six, to be precise. I counted. Headed up by none other than Godferret Superior #3."

He broke off for a moment, his eyes scanning the reaches of the cavern. The glittering gold-fire reflecting in the blue irises reminded me of nothing I wanted to be reminded of. For a moment, I almost felt sorry for Godferret Superior #3. Nobody in the world can feud like an Alsask, and they never forget a vendetta.

"Anyway," he continued softly, "it was a struggle. On the other hand, I was glad the man was dead. Not that I ever had anything against him. Damn good employer, to tell the truth. But Olga was a widow, now. So—"

He brought his eyes back to me. "So, in the end, I decided I could make it good by making it good. If you understand what I mean."

I tried not to, but I did. And, needless to say, sighed again.

"I *hate* righteous living," I grumbled.

Hrundig gave me that patented mirthless grin of his. "Oh, it really isn't that bad, Ignace. Of course, it *does* require you to get acquainted with the foulest, most rotten, most disgusting four-letter word in the universe."

I nodded gloomily. "*Work.*"

A moment later, Magrit hollered: "Done! You're as good as new, Wittgenstein."

Then, a moment later, Shelyid trotted up and handed her the jar full of overthebrimstone.

From there, things went like a mudslide. Greyboar and Gwendolyn and Jenny and Angela were up and about, raring to go. Wittgenstein was back on Magrit's shoulder while the witch cheerfully went about packing up her bag. The salamander's red eyes were glaring at everything and everybody except, of course—

—the Cat, who was drifting around here and there, apparently studying nothing in particular.

Worst of all, though, was Zulkeh. Because while I was chatting with Hrundig, Shelyid had hauled the wizard's brazier out of the sack and Zulkeh was busily burning nasty stuff in it while muttering some kind of incantations.

Oh, yeah, it looks silly when you see it. Idiot sorcerer in his idiot robes, making idiot noises while he goes through idiot motions. Ha. Most wizards, of course, really are idiots. But the problem with Zulkeh is that despite his grotesque ways he really isn't an actual idiot. Fact is, he's what they call the genuine article. So when *he* starts—

Sure enough. A giant form was taking shape in the cavern. Think of a huge, roiling blackish-gray sort of cloud, with quick glimpses of lightning flashing somewhere in the dimly-glimpsed interior. Except these didn't look like bolts of lightning so much as cobra fangs.

Cheery.

Shelyid had drifted back and was now standing next to Hrundig and me. "The professor really knows his stuff," he piped. "Aren't more than three, maybe four mages in the whole world know the cantrips of Schwarzchild Laebmauntsforscynneweëld."

The thing taking shape in the cavern was changing even as the dwarf spoke. The cloud form was now starting to firm up into something even more shapeless, if that makes any sense. Kind of like a huge black hole that you really can't see at all but you know it's there.

"Only way anybody can go any further," added Shelyid cheerfully. "Now that we're past the Infernal Regions and into the Place Even Worse Than Hell." He pointed his finger at the thing. "The Evil Horizon, the professor says it's called. Once you go past it you can't ever get out."

A faint ray of hope began to flicker in my heart. Shelyid quenched it immediately. "Unless you mend your wicked ways, of course. But you have to have really really wicked ways to mend, and you have to really really mend them. Big time. Nobody else has a chance."

His voice was loud enough to be heard by everybody. All eyes turned to Greyboar. Then to me.

"Wonderful," I growled.

"Ain't so bad," chuckled Hrundig. "I might be able to qualify too. Maybe."

"Wonderful," I growled. "We've been suckered *again*."

Chapter 29.
Beyond the Evil Horizon

"This is *really* why Greyboar and I had to come along on this damn-fool expedition, isn't it?" I glared at Hrundig; then, realizing the futility of that enterprise, at Shelyid. "You needed us to get through that thing."

Shelyid shook his head vehemently. "Oh no, Ignace! This is just *one* of the reasons. We also needed you on account of the Even Worse Hands which are lurking *beyond* the Evil Horizon."

The dwarf peered at me dubiously. "I thought you were a student of the wise man," he complained. "Didn't you even hear his famous saying that you shouldn't try to think of the worst thing that could happen because—"

"It's bound to be worse," Hrundig chuckled. He clapped me on the shoulder. "Ignace knows that one. I'm sure he does!"

I started to say something sarcastic, but Jenny and Angela distracted my attention. They charged up to Zulkeh and started arguing with him.

"We're going too! We're going too!" they shouted in unison.

The wizard scowled. "Nonsense! Utter nonsense!"

They kept hollering. In fact, they were hopping up and down in front of Zulkeh, shaking their little fists in his face.

"Are too! Are too!"

Zulkeh smote the floor of the cavern with his staff. "A Distinction!" he cried. "I demand a Distinction! The Sinners from the Wicked! The Repentant from the Unrueful!"

The vast formless form seemed to quiver a bit. A sound like a huge, distant snicker emerged from the thing. Zulkeh smote the cavern floor again, swiveling his head and glaring furiously at the Evil Horizon.

"What means this insolence?" he demanded. " 'Tis an outrage!" A moment later he was striding right up to the monstrosity, waving his staff about. The sheer, pure *evil* emanating from it didn't seem to faze the mage a bit.

"Mock me, will you?" he demanded. Again, he smote the cavern floor with his staff. "So be it! Wretched ultimate evil! Base cur of low degree!"

He turned his head and glared at the dwarf. "Shelyid! Fetch me the Codex of Evaporation!"

"Right away, professor!" The dwarf started unlacing the top of the giant sack. Ready at an instant—it was obvious to all—to climb into its cavernous interior and retrieve whatever object the mage was demanding.

Zulkeh, meanwhile, was back to shaking his staff at the form of ultimate evil. I swear—I saw it, I tell you— he even took a two-handed swipe at the thing.

"Defy me in my quest, will you?" he shrilled. "We shall see about that, pitiful wretch! Once I begin my intonation of the dread formulae of Hawking Sfondrati-Piccolomini—"

The Evil Horizon suddenly blanched. Weird, that—seeing a black hole turn white as a ghost, for just a nanosecond. But it did. Word of honor.

"Aye, indeed!" spoke Zulkeh. "Indeed! By the first verse, ye shall begin to wither. By the second—"

The Evil Horizon emitted another sound. Like a huge, distant yelp. An instant later, it made a sound something like a belch. Out popped a wizened old demon-sort-of-thing, clutching a ledger and a quill pen.

"Easy, easy!" squealed the demon-sort-of-thing. "Easy, now! We can straighten all this out in a moment!"

There was another belching sound, and a table came flying out. Along with a stool. Another belch, and out came four more demon-sorts-of-things, even more wizened than the first.

The first demon-sort-of-thing hastily arranged the table and stool and set itself up behind it, ledger open and quill pen in taloned hand. The other four ranged themselves in a row off to one side.

"Now, then," it said. "What seems to be the difficulty?"

The mage stepped forward to the table. "We demand passage through the Evil Horizon—*with* a guarantee of safe return."

"I see," muttered the demon-sort-of-thing. It poised the pen over the ledger, preparing to write. "And you are?"

"Zulkeh of Goimr, phy—"

He didn't even have a chance to finish before the little gaggle of other demon-sorts-of-things started chanting in unison.

"Petition denied! Petition denied!"

The demon-sort-of-thing at the table finished scratching Zulkeh's name into the ledger and then immediately scratched a line through it. "Absurd," it muttered. "Even if the saints hadn't spoken, I would have denied the petition myself."

The "saints"? I stared at the four demon-sorts-of-things. And noticed, for the first time, that a faint halo flickered over the head of each one. *Very* faint halos, mind you—and sickly-looking, to boot. But halos, no doubt about it.

My confusion must have shown on my face. Wittgenstein hissed at me: "No private parts, dummy. That's how you can tell fallen angels from real devils."

His words made me realize why Hildegard had been so reticent on the matter. I stooped and peered under the table, examining the private parts of the demon-sort-of-thing sitting there. Sure enough. He didn't have any private parts either.

"You aren't a demon-sort-of-thing," I complained. "You're a fallen angel."

The fallen angel got a sour look on its face. "Bah!" oathed Zulkeh. "Say better: a plummeted angel. Or, best of all: a diver into the ultimate deeps."

He cocked his head so far over I thought his pointed wizard's hat would fall off. Then, after finishing his examination of the fallen angel, pronounced: "Harry, if I am not mistaken. The one mentioned in the Book of Tribulations, verse seventeen. You recall, Ignace? The one who told the Old Geister—"

"That's not how it happened!" groused the fallen angel. "And I'm not Harry, anyway. He works midnight shift. I'm Jack."

"Which one?" demanded the mage. "The Jack mentioned in Exasperations II? Or the Jack—"

"Never mind!" snapped the fallen angel. "Just Jack!"

I suspected he was probably the one in Exasperations II, judging from the exasperated way he scratched two more lines through Zulkeh's name. "Petition denied! And don't bother protesting, mage! Your reputation is a byword and a hissing. You're a sinner, sure, but you've no intentions at all of giving up your wicked quest. You know it as well as I do."

"Certainly not!" exclaimed Zulkeh. "The needs of science—"

"Next!" shrilled Jack-the-fallen-angel. "Move aside, Zulkeh! You're blocking the line."

Zulkeh might have kept arguing, but Gwendolyn was next and she just picked him up under the armpits and set him off to one side, as easily as a normal woman would have moved a toddler.

"I'm Gwendolyn Greyboar," she announced, "and I'm also requesting—"

"*Petition denied! Petition denied!*" chorused the saints.

Jack must have been *really* exasperated now, because by the time he finished writing in Gwendolyn's name and crossing it off there was nothing left in the ledger but a huge blob of ink.

"Is this some kind of joke?" he shrilled petulantly. "The second-most-notorious revolutionist in Grotum claiming she's mending her wicked ways and giving up all riotous agitation 'gainst lawful authority?"

"I said no such thing," growled Gwendolyn. "But I *still* want—"

"Step aside! Step aside!"

Well, nobody except Greyboar could have moved Gwendolyn aside by picking her up, and Greyboar—the last faint trace of sanity, here—was still loitering in the rear of the line with me and Hrundig.

Then my heart seized, because Jenny and Angela were pushing their way past Gwendolyn eagerly.

"Us! Us!" they cried. "Jenny and Angela! We wanna go too!"

Jack-the-fallen-angel squinted at them suspiciously. Then, slowly wrote their names into the ledger and swiveled his head to look at the line of saints. The saints, for their part, were studying Angela and Jenny intently.

My heart was frozen, I swear it was. Not beating at all. Then—

"Petition denied! Petition denied!"

I could breathe again. Whatever else happened, my girls weren't going into that—that *thing*.

"Why?" demanded Jenny. "Yeah—why?" echoed Angela. In a rush, together: "We swear to mend our wicked ways, honest!"

Jack sneered. "So what? The ways aren't wicked enough in the first place."

"Are too!" shrieked Jenny. "We're dykes and everything!" Angela cocked her head and gave me the eye. "Even worse than that," she snickered. "*Fallen* dykes."

Jack's sneer never even wavered. "Big deal. You think the Lord Almighty loses sleep over stuff like that?"

Jenny and Angela's mouths dropped. "We've been denounced by priests and monks, even," whined Angela. "Lots of times," added Jenny.

Jack rolled his eyes and cast a sour look at the saints. The saints started cackling. Weird sound, they made, as dried up and shriveled-looking as they were.

"Priests and monks," giggled one. "Leave it to a bunch of sophomores!"

"Gotta make allowances," wheezed the one next to him. "Bigotry 101 and Introductory Prejudice really doesn't prepare you for postgraduate work."

Jack looked bored. "Make an official Sorting, would you? I'd like to get to lunch before they close the cafeteria."

"Insufficient sin! Insufficient sin!" intoned the saints. Before they'd even finished, Jack had scratched out their names. "Denied," he droned. "Next."

Jenny and Angela stumbled away, looking both shocked and upset. They stared at me, faces pale. I fell in love with them all over again, and knew it was forever and ever. Which, given my prospects at the moment, wasn't too far off.

Then Greyboar nudged me and I took a breath. Then another one.

There was still a last gasp. I nudged Magrit, standing at my side. "How's about you?"

She snorted. "Me? I ain't getting anywhere near that thing. This is as far as I go, Ignace. That was my deal with Gwendolyn."

"And I'm with her, runt," hissed Wittgenstein.

I sighed and started forward. But Hrundig held me back.

"Wait, Ignace. Let me go first. I may need a bit of help here."

I was willing enough. Hrundig stepped up to the table and gave his name. Jack scribbled it in and turned, once again, to the saints.

This time, the saints spent more than a second or two pondering the matter. A full minute, maybe. Before:

"Petition denied! Petition denied!" They didn't wait for Hrundig to demand an explanation before giving it: "Excessive prior atonement! Preexisting condition of soul-searching and mortification!"

Hrundig must have been expecting it, though, judging by the cold little smile on his face. And I guess he must have gotten some advance coaching from Zulkeh, because he immediately demanded the right to give what he called "non-extenuating circumstances."

Now Jack got a *really* sour look on his face. But apparently Hrundig was following the red tape properly, because the fallen angel removed the pen from the ledger and muttered: "Okay. Let's hear it."

Hrundig squared his shoulders, clasped his hands behind his back, and started bellowing:

> *"My name is Hrundig   Fjalkerson*
> *And I am accounted   the fiercest berserk*
> *Of my district.   One day I met*
> *Wart Giddle at the   river crossing*
> *And he refused to   give me passage*
> *So I took out my axe   and killed him.*
>
> *Then his brother   Thord Herjolfson*
> *Who is the son of   Herjolf Kollson*
> *Who was the brother   of Hallgerd who*
> *Was married to   Hoskuld the Fat*
> *Took umbrage. He   had many thralls and*
> *Neighbors who owned   lots of pigs."*

"And horses!" I shouted. "*Don't forget the horses! And the sheep!*"

> *"And lots of horses   and sheep too.*
> *One horse was called   Red-foot Swiftsure*
> *And she was . . ."*

Well, this went on for some time, since Hrundig took care to specify by name all the offspring he sired on Fat Hoskuld's mares and ewes and sows until the saints started wailing that Hrundig was stalling and so Hrundig veered back on to his other sins:

> *"So I smote Fat Hoskuld   in the eyeball*
> *With my spear which got   stuck in the socket*
> *So I drew my sword and   smashed Hoskuld's*
> *Two nephews in the head   but the sword*
> *Bent over the head of   the second nephew*

Who was called Ingemar the Dimwitted
Before I bent my sword over his head.

Afterwards he was called Ingemar the
Dimmerwitted. But because my sword bent,
Fat Hoskuld's nephews went at me with
Their axes and I was forced to duck and dodge
While I took a rock and hammered the sword

As straight as I could while I was ducking
And dodging. Then I bent it again over Gunnar
The Low-Browed who was called Gunnar
The No-Browed afterward. But my sword bent again
And now Gunnar's uncle Ulf the Unwashed came at me
So I dropped the sword and used my own axe—"

"Which one?" I demanded. "You've got to say which
one, Hrundig!"

"That is true. I mean the axe which I got
From Golf the Fearless when I met him at a
River crossing and he would not let me pass
So I struck him with my spear and took his
Axe after he died after I pushed his head
Under water after my spear bent.

I took the same axe and smote Golf's
Brother Ragnar at another river crossing
When Ragnar wanted weregild but I would
Not pay it. Instead I cut off his leg with the
Axe but Ragnar hopped back to his horse
And took up his own axe and came at me but I
Cut off his other leg but Ragnar crawled back

To his horse and took his spear and crawled
Back so I hit his head but the axe bent

> *Even though his head   bent also. So I took my*
> *Own spear and spilled   Ragnar's guts but he*
> *Writhed to his horse   and took up his mace and*
>
> *Hauled himself back   along his own guts and I*
> *Cut off his arm but he   wriggled back to his*
> *Horse and took up his   dagger in his teeth*
> *And squirmed like an   eel back toward me but I*
> *Broke all his teeth   with my spear but the*
> *Spear bent when he   had two molars left.*
>
> *So Ragnar chewed on my   boot but I took up my*
> *Other boot and struck   him on the head again*
> *Many times until his   head bent further*
> *But so did my boot but   then he—"*

"*Enough! Enough!*" shrieked the saints. "Petition granted! Petition granted!"

Hrundig stepped aside. "Does it every time," he smirked, as he sauntered past me.

I couldn't stall any longer. I gave Gwendolyn a glance. She was staring at me, her dark face almost pale. Her lips trembled, as if she were on the verge of whispering something.

She wouldn't, of course. Not Gwendolyn. But I knew what she wanted to say. *Please, Ignace. Do it for me.*

Sighing, I took Greyboar by the elbow and stepped up to the table with him.

"He's Greyboar the strangler," I muttered, "and I'm—"

But Jack was already scribbling my name into the ledger right after Greyboar's. "Piece of cake, this one!" he cried. "Can still make it to lunch!"

He swiveled his head. The saints were squinting at us. Jack got a sour look on his face. Very sour.

"Oh, come *on*," he whined. "What more do you want? A professional serial killer and his accomplice ain't good enough for you?"

The saints sniffed. "Possible duplicity," muttered one. "Not about the sins, of course," added another, "but about the mending of wicked ways."

A moment later they started that damned intoning business again: *"Need insurance! Need insurance!"*

Jack sighed and rubbed his face. "All right," he grumbled, swiveling his head back toward the Evil Horizon. "Send out a bonding agent!"

Another belch, and out came a rotund little creature looking not so much like a fallen angel as one who'd never risen in the first place. The butterball rolled to his talons and trotted forward cheerfully.

"Only take a minute!" he cried. "Relax, Jack—you can still make lunch. Don't want to miss it, either. Chipped virgin on toast, today."

Once he was standing in front of Greyboar and me, the newcomer assumed as dignified a stance as a beachball-shaped demon-sort-of-thing can.

"I'm Fred, by the way. You can read all about me in Logarithms II, Verse Three. The business about not eating armadillos with cranberry sauce. Now. Repeat after me: 'I solemnly swear . . .' "

This nonsense went on for some time, while Greyboar and I swore to abandon all evil and wickedness and devote our remaining days to righting wrongs and blather blather blather.

And *still* the saints weren't satisfied.

"New profession!" they intoned. "New profession! Need new professional ethics! Only thing can be trusted!"

"Quite right!" agreed Fred. "What'll it be, gents? Professional Flagellants? Career Whipping Boys? Mercenary Village Idiots? Or—" Here, a great sneer rippled his face. "Professional Heroes?"

I gagged. What a choice!

But Greyboar didn't hesitate. "Hero," he growled.

"Third, Second, First Class—or Excelsior?" demanded Fred.

My agent's instincts did us in, there. Because—not understanding the new rules—I immediately piped: "Excelsior! Greyboar's the best!"

The saints and fallen angels snickered. I got a sinking feeling in my stomach.

"Good move, Ignace," hissed Magrit from somewhere behind me. "Third Class only has to tackle stuff like local bullies."

"And you even get to charge a fee," cackled Wittgenstein. "Just a token, of course, but it beats the rules for Professional Hero, Excelsior, which are—"

I didn't hear the rest, though, because Jack was already gleefully stamping our names with some kind of official-looking seal and Greyboar was hauling me toward the Evil Horizon.

"Let's go," he said. "May as well get it over with."

"What about the Cat?" I whined. "She hasn't had her turn yet."

Greyboar started running toward the Evil Horizon. For all practical purposes, he was carrying me in one hand. I could see Hrundig pounding after us. Along the way, Gwendolyn tossed him a bag holding something lumpy-looking.

"That's why I'm in a hurry!" he snapped. "She already went through."

I must have been gaping. Greyboar chuckled. "What? *Rules?* You know anything can keep the Cat out if she feels like going through?"

The Evil Horizon was looming over us. I could feel the tidal pull in my soul. And if you don't think *that's* a weird and scary feeling, think again.

"I just want to get there before she gets herself hurt," he muttered.

The Horizon was upon us! I was being torn in half! (Spiritually speaking.) Greyboar picked me up and we went through in a leap.

Chapter 30.
Into Even Worse Hands

When we landed on the other side, my senses were still befuddled. It didn't help any that Greyboar must have jumped through leading with his shoulder so we arrived all discombobulated and tangled up. He tripped, but at least he had the good grace not to land on top of me.

I bounced off, while he scrambled out from under, trying to get my bearings. Things weren't helped any when Hrundig came through and avoided tripping over me by *stepping* on me!

But I wasn't so disoriented that I didn't understand what Greyboar was shouting. My heart froze. Just the words I most *didn't* want to hear.

"We're just in the nick of time!"

Trust me on this one. If you ever go adventuring, always try to find the situation where the appropriate words are: "Damn! We're too late! The villain hath done his villainy and decamped to parts unknown!"

Beats *just in the nick of time*, let me tell you. *Parts*

unknown is the best place for villains, in my book. As the wise man says: "The only scientific definition of evil is that you can't ignore it."

I raised my head and stared at the scene in front of me. We were in another cavern, also lit by the same glittering gold-fire, but this one was built on a smaller scale. The ceiling was especially low, not more than twenty feet above our heads. But I didn't spend much time looking at anything except the person we had come to rescue. Benvenuti Sfondrati-Piccolomini himself, in the flesh.

It was *so* trite. I mean—really! You'd think the Place Worse Than Hell would have more of an imagination. I'd been hoping that Benvenuti was being subjected to some kind of spiritual torment, don't you know? The sort of ethereal agony that Greyboar and Hrundig and I could have spent hours standing around scratching our heads wondering what bruisers like them and a sensible sinner like me could possibly do about it. While we enjoyed a quiet lunch and maybe a flask of whiskey.

Nope. Instead—

Benvenuti was stripped naked except for a loincloth, suspended upside down from the ceiling by a rope tied around his ankles, his head not more than five feet above a huge iron kettle full of boiling oil set over a bronze brazier. The rope ran through some kind of pulley arrangement and was tied off on a post set in the stone floor of the cavern maybe ten feet from the kettle. Ready at an instant, obviously enough, to lower him to his doom. Which, judging from the various flaying instruments sitting upon a giant tray next to the kettle, was intended to be protracted.

Apparently—judging from the rope marks still on his flesh—his arms had also been bound up. But somehow he'd gotten loose from those ropes and had even

managed to shed the manacles on his wrists. One of
them, anyway—the set of manacles was still dangling
from his left wrist.

At first, I thought the Cat might have cut them loose
with her lajatang. But then, seeing the freewheeling
style with which she was wielding the thing against her
enemies, I realized that couldn't have been it. As sloppy
as ever, in a fight, the Cat would have hacked Benny
himself to pieces.

No, I found out later that Benny had done it himself, as soon as he saw the Cat waft into the cavern.
Turns out one of the many things his multitude of
uncles had trained him in was the secrets of what they
call "escapology." He'd been saving it up as a last resort
while he held off Even Worse Hands with the secret
lore of suspended insults and shackled derision in which
his uncles had *also* trained him. He'd managed to stall
the Even Worse Hands for days that way. Got them
so infuriated they held off from flaying him alive until
they could rummage up the kettle and enough oil for
boiling.

(Benny was an orphan, you see, and had been raised
by his artist and *condottieri* uncles. And if you're
wondering why I hope I never meet those uncles,
figure it out for yourself. The nephew is plenty bad
enough, getting-you-into-scrapes-wise. Why would his
uncles know all that stuff if they didn't *need* it? Huh?)

Greyboar, of course, was rushing off to the Cat's
rescue. As slippery as she was, Even Worse Hands had
her pretty much cornered against a wall of the cavern. She was flailing the lajatang around like you
couldn't believe—way better than she'd ever used a
sword. Hrundig, I now realized, was every bit as good
a weapons trainer as his reputation. But while her
enemies bore the marks of several slashes, they could
obviously shrug off the injuries easily enough.

Knuckle them off, I should say.

I suppose this is as good a time as any to describe Even Worse Hands. Picture two gigantic hands, each one about the size of a bull. Great, gnarled, ugly things, with calluses all over them and the worst manicure you ever saw. Fingers more like talons than fingers, and fingernails so long and scraggly they were almost claws.

Okay? Got the picture?

These were Even Worse.

They were prancing around on their fingertips, like giant tarantulas. (Oh, yeah. *Of course* they were hairy.) Lunging back and forth, working together like—well, like a pair of hands—one of them trying to feint the Cat out of position while the other one got itself around her. After that . . . it'd be all over. As huge and powerful as Even Worse Hands were, either one of them could have crushed the Cat in seconds.

Greyboar flew through the air and landed on the right Hand. A moment later he had the thumb in a half nelson and was giving it the old hip roll. The hand went skittering across the cavern. Greyboar followed, like a hound after his hare.

The Cat was still backed up against the wall, flailing away at the other Hand. "Thanks a lot!" she snarled. "The damn thing's a leftie!"

Greyboar skidded to a stop and came rushing back. "I'll get him! I'll get him!" He pointed his finger at the right Hand. "Hrundig! Ignace! You take care of that one!"

Hrundig paused just long enough to toss the bag he was carrying up to Benvenuti. "A present from Gwendolyn!" he shouted. "She said you'd know what to do with it!" Then he drew his sword and charged at the right Hand.

Benvenuti snatched the bag with his left hand and upended it. A bullwhip slid out into his right.

"She remembered!" he cried gleefully. "What a woman! Nonpareil!"

Honest. That's what he said, hanging upside down over a kettle of boiling oil. *Nonpareil*. Crazy artist. He seemed as ecstatic over a bullwhip from an ex-girlfriend as he would have been if she'd presented him with a negative pregnancy test.

A moment later, I discovered why. I knew Benvenuti was accounted an expert swordsman. What I didn't know was that his skill with a bullwhip was even greater. His weapon of choice, as it happens, being as he'd been trained in its use by his uncle Larue Sfondrati-Piccolomini.

Good thing they don't allow bullwhips in dueling, all I've got to say. Still hanging upside down, Benny cracked the thing once and the bullwhip parted the rope holding him by the ankles like it was a thread.

On the way down—I believe I've mentioned his grotesque physical condition—Benny not only managed to twist himself around so he was falling feet first, but he did some kind of bizarre little quick rubbing motions with his feet like he was trying to take socks off and shed the rope altogether. His feet now free and unfettered, he landed right on the rim of the kettle. Balanced there perfectly, for an instant, before springing to the ground and racing off to the Cat's rescue.

Moments later, he and the Cat and Hrundig were battling away with the right Even Worse Hand while Greyboar and the left were scrabbling around in a melee that would give delirium tremens to a drunken wrestler.

And me? What was I doing?
Thinking, of course. What else?

∼ ∼ ∼

Give me a break. I stand four feet, eleven inches tall when I climb out of bed in the morning. By nighttime, I'm probably an inch shorter. Soaking wet, with a full meal in my belly, I claim a hundred pounds.

That's a lie. Jenny and Angela once forced me onto a scale after a feast. Ninety-eight and a half pounds. After I whined, they poured a basin of water over me and weighed me again. Ninety-nine pounds.

So. We've got two gigantic hands each of which outweighs me by what your mathematician types call an order of magnitude. Not even going to talk about relative strength. Each of them—not to mention both together—are so vile and insensate and ferocious and wicked that Whoever Decides These Things had relegated them to the Place Even Worse Than Hell.

Nor was Whoever Decides These Things any kind of dummy, either, let me tell you. Outnumbered two-to-one, Even Worse Hands was holding its own against:

The world's greatest strangler;

The world's most unpredictable female slasher;

The world's second-most-accomplished artiste with a bullwhip; and,

Hrundig of Alsask, Barbarian Master-at-Arms.

And you want to know what Ignace was doing?

Thinking, that's what. It's a tough job, but somebody's got to do it on these asinine adventures.

I set my pack down and squatted beside it. Then, dug out a flask of whiskey. And a corned beef sandwich. A bit on the stale side, maybe, but it was the best I could manage.

Munch, munch; take a sip; think.

The first thing I considered were the darts I still had on me, which I'd retipped with poison after the scrape with the Ogre. But I discarded that idea right away, because it was obvious at a glance that the dosage

was hopeless. Even with all the blood pouring out of
the right Hand from the various wounds the Cat,
Hrundig and Benny had managed to inflict on it, the
thing was still going as strong as ever. While I watched,
a jab of the thumb sent Hrundig flying and Benny
barely managed to avoid a murderous flick of the pinkie
by a prodigious leap in the air that would have had
the audience at the ballet bringing down the rafters
with applause. Especially the women, what with
Benvenuti's physique so exposed to view. All of it, for
practical purposes. That loincloth was pretty much a
joke.

I spent even less time thinking about my throwing
knives. Might as well try to bring down an elephant
with tavern darts.

Munch, munch. The sandwich really was pretty stale.
At that moment, the smell of the boiling oil hit me.
Olive oil, by the Old Geister!

"Say what else you will," I muttered happily, rising
to my feet, "but at least Even Worse Hands have a
decent sense of cuisine."

I ambled over to the kettle and dipped the sandwich into the oil. Just a quick dip, enough to soften
up the bread and give the dry beef a bit of flavor. As
I munched on the now-much-improved sandwich, I
contemplated the problem further.

A solution was going to be needed pretty quickly,
so much was obvious. No sooner had I dipped the
sandwich than I saw Greyboar go sailing through the
air. The left Even Worse Hand had a pretty mean half
nelson of its own. Fortunately, Greyboar was back on
his feet and met the scuttling charge with a roar and
a grapple.

Still, things were not looking good. Hrundig's right
arm must have been badly bashed up—maybe even a
greenstick fracture—because he was now wielding his

sword left-handed. Benny had picked up so many bruises that he looked like a leopard. The Cat had a black eye and a gash on her arm, probably from one of those horrid fingernails.

To make things worse, all of them—even Hrundig—were starting to show the first signs of fatigue. Whereas if Even Worse Hands were feeling weary at all, I couldn't spot it. Something was going to have to be done quick, or the conclusion of this brawl was, as they say, foregone.

Thinking, thinking . . .

My eyes fell on the tray on the opposite side of the huge kettle. The one holding all the implements for flaying Benvenuti's hide.

It was a huge tray, of a size to match the kettle. Necessary, of course, to hold all those implements—which were themselves of a size to fit Even Worse Hands.

Fit Even Worse Hands . . .

One of your big-and-burly-type adventurers would have shrieked "Eureka!" at that point. Assuming they could manage a word with three syllables. But when you're my size, the first thing you learn is "couth." So I daintily finished up the sandwich—okay, I wolfed it down, but it was a suave kind of gulping—and raced around the kettle to the other side.

To my delight, the tray was one of those folding things. You know, the sort where the legs have hinges and can be tucked away for storage. (Though why anyone would need to store something in a cavern is a mystery. It's not as if, judging from the detritus, Even Worse Hands was what you'd call a meticulous housekeeper.)

Just to make things perfect, the tray was a tripod. With the third leg being the one away from the kettle.

Ah, the joys of quick thinking! It didn't take me three seconds under the thing to figure out how the mechanism worked. Pop this; push in that; give the hinge a good kick.

Down it came, the whole side of the tray, spilling the flaying implements onto the cavern floor. When everything settled down, the lip of the tray was still leaning against the kettle, held there by the two legs still solid.

Only it wasn't a "tray," now. It was a ramp.

I stuck my fingers in my mouth and whistled. I've got a damn good whistle, if I say so myself. Not in Abbess Hildegard's league, maybe, but pretty close.

And I was probably—hate to admit this, since it casts a poor light on the state of my suave couth at the moment—what they called "hopped up." So the whistle penetrated even the din of the battle.

Hrundig looked up. Using a few words and some gestures, I indicated my plan. (Well. Okay. Hopping up and down and shrieking like a maniacal monkey, I indicated my plan.)

As I've said before, despite appearances Hrundig is no dimwit. An instant later he was bellowing his own directions.

Benvenuti got the gist of it right away. Before you knew it, he had the middle finger of the Even Worse Hand snatched up in the bullwhip and was dragging the Hand toward the kettle.

Trying to, anyway. One of the Even Worse Hands doesn't drag easily, even for a man as big and strong as Benvenuti. Hrundig tried to help him along by driving his sword into the meat of the Hand's thumb and pushing. But another jab of the thumb sent him flying again.

Fortunately, the Cat stopped flitting around in her usual whimsy and got with the program. Uttering a she-wolf shriek, she drove the lajatang like a spear right through the skin and sinews on the back of the Hand. The lajatang was now sticking out from both sides, as if the Hand had been pierced by a huge pin.

Quick-witted as always, Hrundig scrambled back onto his feet and grabbed the other end of the lajatang, just below the ferocious blade. A moment later, he and the Cat were each heaving up and half-carrying the Hand toward the kettle while Benny kept dragging it.

And so it went, according to plan. Of course, in the real world these things never work as neatly as they sound. The Hand was squirming back and forth, and Hrundig and the Cat had their own hands full to keep from getting slashed to ribbons by the blades of the lajatang. Before too long, both of them were bleeding from several nasty gashes. Nothing bad enough, fortunately, to put them out of the action.

Then, things got a bit awkward when Benny bumped against the kettle while he wasn't looking because he was concentrating on his drag-work. The kettle was almost as hot as the boiling oil inside it. So Benny got a really nasty burn on the bare skin of his back.

But, although he let out an operatic-quality yelp, he didn't let go of the whip. And, being so incredibly quick and well-coordinated (is there *no* justice?), he managed to scuttle around to the other side of the kettle without once even allowing any slack in the tension of the whip holding the Hand's finger.

The finale was a great series of grunts and a muddle. Up the ramp, up the ramp went the Hand, jittery as a nightmare. At the end, I got so excited I even pitched in for the final heave.

Over it went, plop, into the oil. With a great flourish and "huzza!" Benny did something tricky with the whip and managed to disentangle it. The Cat, almost as smooth, yanked the lajatang out of the skin. Fortunately,

Hrundig saw it coming in time to get his hands out of the way of the blade.

Oh, sure, the Hand still put up a fight. Nasty looking, it was, trying to scrabble out of the boiling oil. Imagine a tarantula trying to claw its way up a jar.

Ptah!

Advantage—heroes. Even something as huge and nasty as one of the Even Worse Hands can't survive long when its flesh is peeling off and its tendons are going soft as butter. The Cat and Hrundig and Benvenuti took turns holding it under with the lajatang, pinning the horrid thing to the bottom of the kettle. Meanwhile, I stoked the coals in the brazier.

Five minutes later, it was all over.

And, in the meantime, what about Greyboar?

Well, what about him? Haven't I told you a thousand times he's the World's Greatest Strangler?

Still was, too, even though he'd officially abandoned the trade.

At first, of course, the Cat and Hrundig and Benvenuti were all for racing off to his aid. I tried to restrain them with reason, but it was soon enough obvious that was pointless.

The problem, you see, was that they were suffering under what's called a "misapprehension." Even in the midst of their own melee, they'd gotten enough glimpses of Greyboar and the other Even Worse Hand to get the idea that Greyboar was in what's called "desperate straits." Barely "holding his own," as they say.

Heh. This is what's called: *Doesn't have a clue.*

I knew the truth. The real problem was that Greyboar had been preoccupied with the Cat's plight. (Well—and a bit with Hrundig's and Benny's, sure; but mostly the Cat's.)

So he hadn't really had his mind on what he was doing, you see. Half the time he was looking over at the Cat, worrying and fretting and fussing, trying to deal with the left Even Worse Hand as quickly as possible so he could Come To The Rescue Of His Beloved.

Everything, in short, which the world's greatest professional strangler wouldn't normally touch with a ten-foot pole.

But, now—

Again, I whistled. "*She's safe!*" I hollered. "So are the rest of us!"

I saw Greyboar's head pop up between two of the Fingers and stare at us. I gave him the thumbs-up. (If you'll pardon the expression.)

Greyboar grunted. Then—

Something seemed to heave inside the palm of the Even Worse Hand and the next thing you knew the monstrosity was sailing through the air. *Whump!* against the stone wall of the cavern; then, collapsing into a heap at the bottom. Like a stunned tarantula.

Greyboar shook himself like a wet dog and started advancing upon it. In—

The Stance.

Not too many people had ever seen The Stance. And precious few of them were still around to talk about it. Greyboar never bothered with it for the average job, you'll understand. The Stance was pretty much reserved for the Finals at the Barbarian Games, and such jobs as the famous burke he put on the Comte de l'Abattoir and his entire party of knight-companions.

Hrundig and Benvenuti, once they saw The Stance, had enough sense to leave off any further idea of "rescue" and concentrate on finishing off the Hand in the kettle. Even the Cat, after bouncing around the cavern a bit, settled down and took her turn at the chore.

Of course, everyone couldn't stop watching. Annoyed the hell out of me, that did, since it meant I had to concentrate on keeping their minds on The Task At Hand.

So I didn't get to see much of it myself, since I had to keep my eyes on the Hand at hand and keep the others steady at their work. Which annoyed me even further, until I realized that it really didn't matter whether I could give a detailed and accurate report to the Records Committee since Greyboar and I were no longer members in good standing of the Professional Stranglers' Guild anyway.

Which *really* annoyed me.

So, here's how it went, as best as I can tell you:

Crunch, crunch. That was the pinky, going first at both joints. I could tell it was the pinky from the—comparatively speaking—delicate sound. I knew then that the Even Worse Hand was in for that they call a "Bad End," because Greyboar doesn't normally trifle around with curlicues. This was one of the rare occasions when his temper was up.

But even when he's pissed Greyboar doesn't really let his professionalism lapse. So the next thing he did was take care of the middle finger—CRUNCH; broken in half—and the index finger. YERK! Torn out of its socket, no doubt about it.

From there it was all denouement. There was a lot of *crunching* and *yerking*, and a stretch of about a minute or so with a lot of *thumping* when Greyboar put the Hand through a series of what they call "body slams" when it's an actual body instead of a giant Hand.

Then, silence—except for the sound of Greyboar's heavy breathing and something which, for lack of a better term, we'll call a *scrinnnch.*

At that point, I risked a look. And saw what I expected to see. The Hand itself was nothing more than a pulpy mass, now, and Greyboar was going in for the Final Big Squeeze on the Even Worse Thumb.

Horrible thing to watch, it really is. The Final Big Squeeze, I mean. But I didn't tear my eyes away until the very end, when Greyboar—

He doesn't usually do this kind of thing, honest. It's not like him at all. But the Even Worse Hands had attacked his girl, you see, and even Greyboar can get kinky about stuff like that.

So he finished by tearing off the Even Worse Thumbnail and brandishing it like a trophy. (He's still got it, too. But at least he keeps the damn stinky thing packed away in a chest somewhere in the cellar.) Then, after the Cat wafted over and steadied him down a bit, he hoisted the Hand's corpse (is that the right term?) onto his back and brought it over to the kettle.

Plop. Bubble. And it was all over.

"Hand stew," I announced. "Anybody hungry?"

And that's another thing about heroes. No sense of humor at all. They even took away my flask and drank all that was left in it.

Said I hadn't done enough to deserve a drink!

Chapter 31.
Marvelous

There was a spot of trouble getting Benvenuti back through the Evil Horizon. The first time he tried the leap, the Horizon bounced him right back out. Fortunately, Hrundig was there to catch him before Benny went sailing into the kettle of oil.

Greyboar and I had already made the leap, so we weren't aware of the problem right away. Greyboar was preoccupied with reassuring Gwendolyn that we had, indeed, found Benvenuti and that he was, indeed, in splendid condition. I was preoccupied, of course, with giving Jenny and Angela the same reassurances concerning myself. Deeply distraught, they were.

"Sure, and it got a bit dicey before I took care of the first Hand what with the way it was advancing on me and all, but after I told Greyboar to distract the lefty while I—"

"Ignace!" barked Greyboar. I turned and saw that the Cat had appeared and was jabbering away in the strangler's ear. (For the record, he's *still* "the strangler" as far as I'm concerned. I'll use "the Hero" for official reports, but not here where I'm telling the straight truth about everything.) "Benny's having some kind of problem! Go see what it is, will you?"

Of course I dug in my heels right there. Until I found out just what the perks and requirements were for my new job as "Professional Hero, Excelsior, Management," I wasn't about to let any precedents get established. Not for nothing does the wise man say: "Lackey once, you'll lackey forever."

"Do it yourself!" I snarled. "What? Am I supposed to be some kinda—"

Sometimes it's a real pain in the ass trying to have a rational discussion with Greyboar. For a guy who claims to love philosophy, he's got an astonishing lack of appreciation for the dialectic. He picked me up and pitched me through the Evil Horizon.

Having, on occasion, undergone this lowbrow form of debate with him, I landed in a roll and came up to my feet without injuries or too much, even, in the way of damage to my dignity.

"What seems to be the problem?" I asked, dusting myself off casually. "Greyboar asked me to look into it."

Hrundig shrugged and jabbed a thumb at the Horizon. "Damned thing won't let Benvenuti through. We just tried again."

Benny was standing next to him, looking exceedingly disgruntled. His sculpted physique was starting to look much the worse for wear. That might have assuaged my primitive envy, except that his loincloth was looking worse still. Not to put too fine a point on it, he'd have been more modest if he were stark naked.

But the truth is I'd grown pretty fond of the guy, despite his handicaps. And I reassured myself that, first,

Gwendolyn was on the other side to keep him preoccupied; and, second, that he really didn't seem to have
much of a poaching inclination; and, finally, that neither Angela nor Jenny had ever been the least
impressed by standard notions of male pulchritude. Any
kind of male pulchritude, actually. (Except me!)

So I didn't hesitate more than two seconds before
setting the whole matter straight.

"Evil Horizon!" I hollered. "Cut the crap!"

The Evil Horizon might have flickered, maybe. Good
enough. I told Benny the way was clear and he leaped
into it and came bouncing back and suffered a bit more
wear and tear. The loincloth was pretty much nonexis-
tent, now.

"Guess not," I mused. I scratched my head, not sure
what to do.

Then, the Evil Horizon flashed soundless shrieks of
lightning and started getting real fuzzy around the
edges. A moment later, Zulkeh came stalking through
the damn thing. As casually as if he were taking an
evening stroll, except for the ferocious scowl on his face
and the way he was waving his staff around.

"Impudent metaphysical phenomenon!" he barked.
"Bah! Attempt to obfuscate *me*, will you?" He stopped
more or less in the middle of the Evil Horizon—which
was more in the way of a rapidly-receding tunnel,
now—and began making peculiar gestures with his one
hand while fingering various grotesque carvings on the
staff with the other.

"The principle is well established!" he proclaimed.
"I refer you to Chandrasekhar Sfondrati-Piccolomini's
magisterial pandects, in which the limit of irredeemable
moral collapse is set precisely at 1.4 times the mass of
preexisting wickedness from which, however—take note,
ethereal ignoramus!—must be subtracted the degree of
coercion involved in attempting to force said collapse,

the which—attend, spectral wretch!—must in turn be calculated—and calculated *only*—by use of—"

Hrundig and Benny and I raced into the opening at the center of the Evil Horizon, passing Zulkeh in a flash.

"—not forgetting, of course, to factor out all manner of sins which are not germane—"

And emerged back in the outer cavern just in time to see the fallen angel and the fallen saints rise shakily from the state of scholarly stupor in which Zulkeh must have sent them before he started his pedant's charge into the Horizon.

I almost felt sorry for them. Not quite.

Zulkeh came out himself a moment later. Behind him, what was left of the Evil Horizon seemed to tighten into a ball. Like a whipped cur.

The mage glowered down at the angel and the saints. "Shocking!" he pronounced. "To see such incompetence in official authorities!"

"We were just following the rules," whined one of the fallen saints. "Decreed by the Old Geister Himself!"

Zulkeh sniffed. "A sad state of affairs, when God Almighty fails to stay abreast of the literature." Then, sighing: "But—'tis well said. Mathematics is properly the province of the youthful scholar. I fear me the Lord is past His Prime."

The fallen saints glowered and the fallen angel seemed about to make some kind of protest, but Zulkeh's glare cowed them into silence.

"Bah!" He turned to the rest of us. "Come, my fellow adventurers—let us be off. For even as I correct divine error, time wanes!"

Zulkeh began striding toward the door leading back into the Infernal Regions. "We may still make good our escape before the equinox of galactic oscillation!"

∽   ∽   ∽

And—we did.

Just by the skin of our teeth, mind you, and we probably wouldn't have made it at all if Zulkeh hadn't decided to gamble with the Osirian Detour. Which was no fun at all, what with having to fend off a giant serpent in pitch darkness riding the most primitive damned boat you ever saw with only a ragpatch doll of a so-called deity to steer the blasted thing. But at least we were able to circumvent all the Joe relics and the Nun and the Beast From Below and the deadly Worm of the Deep—the *other* Worm of the Deep, the really nasty one; not Apep, who's just a glorified snake—and the Slathering Sanguine Skulker and the Creeper from the Crevasse and the Undulant Umbellant from Under and the It and the Thing and the Them and the They.

We did have a moment's unpleasantness with the Torrid Terror. And the Flaying Crutchman. But the Minions of the Minotaur were pretty small potatoes and the Minotaur himself never made a showing. And now that I've had a bit of a set-to with troglodytes I can assure you that their reputation is grossly exaggerated.

The Mesozoic ones might have been a bit of a handful, true. But with Greyboar along that encounter was pretty much a picnic. Actually, it *was* a picnic. The troglodytes mistook Greyboar for a distant cousin and insisted we stay for lunch. Don't ask me what we ate. The less said about Mesozoic troglodyte cuisine the better.

But at least we didn't run into any poetry, except for when Hrundig got tipsy at the picnic—on what? don't ask—and he started matching lays with the Mesozoic troglodytes and got adopted into the clan himself.

In fact, when we finally got back into our house we

discovered that only thirty-six hours had elapsed. At least, according to the grandfather clock which Jenny and Angela had bought at an auction and installed into what they called our "foyer."

Zulkeh was ecstatic. "Proof positive!" he exclaimed. "For this alone, the expedition was worth it! Irrefutable evidence that time passes in the netherworld at a rate precisely"—a bunch of incomprehensible twaddle here—"and that Greenwich Laebmauntsforscynneweëld is every bit the dunce that I have named him in treatises too numerous to detail. To which," he added, stalking toward the library, "I shall now add yet another."

So he was happy. Marvelous.

So was Shelyid, needless to say, because while the wizard spent the next several days in nonstop scribbling at the writing desk in the library, the dwarf could lounge around without any of the onerous duties which Zulkeh usually saddled him with. Dust the mage off, once or twice, and that was it. Spent the rest of his time with Hrundig and Greyboar and the Cat getting plastered down at The Trough. Marvelous.

Magrit must have been happy too, judging from the way she decamped in the middle of the first night back. I caught a glimpse of her by candlelight passing through the front door, cackling something about Finally Getting Even with somebody or other. Wittgenstein mooned me on the way out.

Marvelous.

Gwendolyn and Benvenuti? Oh, they were downright ecstatic—in that ridiculous star-crossed-lovers' achy-breaky way of theirs. Because of the "rigors," as they say, of our trek out of the netherworld, they hadn't been able to talk much until we got back. Then they spent a few hours holding hands on the couch in the salon, having what people call a "heart-to-heart." Much as I tried, I couldn't help overhearing some of it. The gist of which was that As He Was Still Committed To Art—and had apparently picked up some kind of silly Foul Wrong To Be Righted In The Blood Of The Evildoer along the way—and She Was As Always Bound Body And Soul To The Cause and, furthermore, Disapproved Of Personal Vengeance, their love was every bit As Hopeless As Ever and therefore They Must Part Again.

Which, once settled, didn't stop the two of them from spending the next several days not moving once out of their bedroom on the third floor. Well. "Not moving" in the sense of leaving the bed. I began to fear for the structural integrity of the building. Marvelous.

On the morning of the fourth day after our return from the netherworld, Benny stopped into the library to bid me farewell. Hrundig was with him, waiting in the doorway.

"Adieu, good Ignace!" he exclaimed, in his perfect baritone. "I must be off! There is a wrong to be avenged! In the blood of the perpetrator!"

I'd been wondering why he was garbed all in black. He even drew his rapier out of its scabbard and inspected the razor-sharp blade with great satisfaction. Which was a bit unusual. Despite appearances, Benvenuti really wasn't much given to dramatic excess.

"Off, I say! Godferret Superior #3 is a doomed man!"

I hadn't realized Benny had a grudge against the guy as much as Hrundig did. Normally, I would have asked about it, but I was too mired in my own misery to care much about the travails of others.

I did manage to summon up enough civility to inquire as to his plans After The Wrongdoer Met His

Just Desserts. Given that Benvenuti had pretty much scuttled his prospects as an artist anywhere in Sfinctria. Benny shrugged and said that he was thinking of perhaps trying his fortune in Kankria.

"Kankr?" I choked. *"Kankr?* They haven't got a pot to piss in!"

"All the greater the challenge, then!" he replied. His perfect teeth gleamed under the perfect mustache. Then, with a flourish of his cape, he was gone and Hrundig with him.

A few hours later, after nightfall, Gwendolyn made her own departure. She took the route through the Underground Railroad, of course. Even at night, Gwendolyn wasn't going to risk being seen on the streets of New Sfinctr. Not with Queen Belladonna having just issued a new writ for her arrest.

She kissed me on the cheek before she left, and we hugged for maybe ten minutes and I'll admit that warmed me up a bit. Well, okay, a lot. Even though I blamed her almost as much as Greyboar for the disastrous state of affairs we found ourselves in, I was still glad that the old feud was over. The truth is, I had a soft spot in my heart for that woman. Squishy soft, to be honest.

Then Greyboar wandered in and gathered us both up in his own embrace. It was the three of us again, like it hadn't been in a lot of years. An awful lot of years. Even if it was only for a moment, before Gwendolyn went off to her crazy revolution and Greyboar and I went off on even crazier feats of derring-do.

The arms around me got tighter. Then tighter. Gwendolyn's even more than Greyboar's. I'd forgotten how strong the woman was. But I hadn't forgotten her, it seemed. And so there was a little strange part of me—that maniac that resides somewhere in everybody—that was happy as a lark.

Stupid bastard. All these years I'd spent, trying to pound some sense into him. And here he was, back again, just as crazy as ever.

Gwendolyn left then, after giving me a last kiss. Greyboar escorted her out of the room. I stayed behind, simultaneously basking in the warmth of the present and shivering at the bleak bitter cold of the future.

Reconciliation. A marvelous thing, indeed. Marvelous. Still—

A disastrous state of affairs is a disastrous state of affairs, no matter how you slice it.

And what was I doing all this time, you're wondering?

Ha!

Working like a dog, what else? It's the old story. The proles can play when the shift is over. But responsible management stays on, working weak and weary into the night.

Chapter 32.
Saved by the Rules

Sure, sure. Everybody else could lounge around, basking in the splendor of our glorious deed and our even-more-glorious newfound moral stature.

Professional Heroes, Excelsior! Marvelous!

Well . . . To be precise, *Greyboar* was a Professional Hero, Excelsior. I wasn't. I wasn't even a Professional Hero's manager and agent, to my chagrin. The first thing I discovered upon our return—we'll get to it; hold your horses—is that a Professional Hero *can't* have a manager and agent. Matter of professional ethics, don't you know? Seems that by the nature of the trade, a Hero must always act out of High Principles, and a manager/agent would tend to bring that principle under what they call a "cloud of disrepute."

Which meant . . .

That I was now officially a Professional Hero, Auxiliary, Sidekick. With the wondrous prospect of eventually advancing—should the sidekick Prove His Mettle

In Deeds Of Renown—to the august status of Professional Hero, Auxiliary, Companion.

Marvelous.

All this was explained to me the day after our return from the netherworld. At the crack of dawn, there came a furious pounding on our door. Bleary-eyed, I opened the entrance and beheld three stooped and withered old men, clad in rags, each clutching a bundle of tomes.

They charged into the foyer without so much as a by-your-leave. "Where's the dining room?" demanded one. "We'll need the largest table in the house," quavered another.

The third one didn't say anything. Jenny and Angela had appeared in the foyer, rubbing sleep from their eyes, and the oldster was ogling them. Not that they weren't worth ogling, mind you, dressed as they were in those gauzy nightgowns which they favor (and I normally do except when lechers are in the vicinity). But I still thought it was grotesque. The way the geezer was wheezing, I was half-sure he was about to expire on the spot. Which I wouldn't have minded in the least, except I'd have to deal with the body. From the looks of them, if his two companions tried to carry him out they'd drop dead themselves.

"It's that way," yawned Jenny. She pointed the way to the dining room and started back up the stairs. Angela followed. "Call us if you need anything, Ignace," she mumbled.

All three of the *vieillards* ogled them until they passed out of sight. Then, they nodded in unison.

"Excellent! Excellent!" exclaimed one. "Flagrant libertinism," proclaimed another. "The Second of the Sure Signs," he added gleefully, cackling and rubbing his hands.

I had no idea what they were talking about. I was just coming awake enough to order them out of the house when they charged down the hallway toward the dining room. By the time I got there, they had all the tomes spread out and open, covering the entire surface.

I was about to toss them out bodily when they spoke the horrid words.

"Ahem. Sirrah Ignace. We are the Rules Committee of the Professional Heroes Guild. Here to welcome you into our ranks and instruct you as to your new responsibilities. I am Pathos. This is Bathos, and the other goes by the name of Cannabis."

"We also double as the Ethics Committee," added Bathos. Apologetically: "I'm afraid we're required to do so by our small numbers and meager purse. We are not, as you are perhaps aware, one of the more populous and prosperous guilds."

The two of them turned to Cannabis, as if waiting for him to speak. But he was just ogling the walls, apparently oblivious. Perhaps he was hoping that more nubile damsels might spring forth from the woodwork. I got the feeling his mind wasn't entirely there.

Pathos cleared his throat. "Well. He's had a bit of a rough time of it for the past few decades. Ever since that unfortunate episode with the dryads."

He heaved a small sigh. "To be honest, Sirrah Ignace, we're the smallest and the poorest of the professional guilds. In fact, the three of us are pretty much it, in the Excelsior class. Except for Hamhead Jones, if he recovers from his injuries. And the Apprentices Rafael and Ethelrede the Younger." Again, he cleared his throat. "Assuming that Rafael comes out of his coma. And Ethelrede the Younger escapes from the rock to which he's currently chained in the netherworld, after carving himself a new wooden leg."

"Oh, no," I croaked.

"So pleased to welcome you into the Guild!" exclaimed Bathos. "I think I speak for all of us when I say we were delighted—"

"Ecstatic!" qualified Pathos. Cannabis flopped his head around, drooling a bit. Agreement, perhaps, but I suspected he was lost in unfortunate memory.

"—to hear the news that Greyboar the Great has eschewed his wicked ways in favor of a Hero's Life."

"*Oh, no!*" I wailed.

It was all downhill from there. By the end of the day, when they finally left, the Guild All-Committees-In-One had made clear our new professional ethics and standards.

Starvation loomed, assuming we survived that long.

Just to drive home the point, our first job showed up on our doorstep that same afternoon.

"We're the village elders from the small province of Rockandahardplace," pronounced the gap-toothed swineherd at the front. "Terrible it's been, the way the Dragon devours our maidens. Which puir lasses we moost chain up outside the Creature's lair 'pon every full moon."

"Terrible! Terrible!" intoned the other dozen or so peasants. "Been the ruination of all moral standards! 'Tis nary a maiden to be found past the age of twelve! The foul slatterns!"

The swineherd cleared his throat. "Fortunate, as it is, th'Dragon's no really so fussy."

They beamed at me. Then, two of them hauled up a small cart filled with potatoes. A none-too-plump piglet was tied to the cart, looking none too pleased.

"O' course," announced the doughty fellow in charge, "we has brought th'customary Gift To The Hero. As stip'lated in the Rules."

Words failed me.

Alas, they didn't fail Angela and Jenny.

"It'll be great!" squealed Jenny. "We can be the maidens of the month! Tantalizing bait for the Dragon, while you and Greyboar get ready to pounce!"

"You're not maidens," I protested.

Angela stuck her tongue out at me.

"And since when have you complained about *that?*" demanded Jenny.

"Doesn't matter anyway!" proclaimed Angela. "You heard what the Doughty Villager said. The Dragon's not fussy. No more than you are."

A moment later they were charging about their sewing room, hauling out material for The Costumes. By the next day they were well into the project.

Why they were spending so much time on it was a mystery to me. Given that Jenny and Angela's design for their "sacrificial maiden" costumes seemed to consist mostly of Revealing Rents in the Rags.

I couldn't even find solace in The Trough. By the time I got there, Greyboar and the Cat and Hrundig and Shelyid had already spread the news. My entry was greeted by a thunderous round of applause.

"The Hero's Sidekick!"

"Behold! He comes!"

This ruffian ribaldry was followed by fifteen minutes of lowlife derision, followed by the Unkindest Cut of All. Leuwen plopped a pot of ale in front of me, where I sat glumly hunched over at Eddie Black's.

"On the house, Ignace," he announced. "Just this

once, seeing as how you've entered the land of pover-
tee." Guffaw, guffaw, guffaw. It was *so* tiresome.

"But don't despair," he added, his double chin
quivering. "Kenny the Beggar says he'll buy you half
a pint of bitters if you survive the Dragon."

Guffaw, guffaw, guffaw. It was *so* tiresome.

Not knowing what else to do, I spent the next few
days sharing the library with Zulkeh. At my insistence,
the Committee had left all their tomes behind so I
could undertake a study of our new professional rules,
regulations, guidelines, and code of ethics.

Hour by hour, I slogged my way through the books.
It was just as bad as I feared.

Fatality rate: expected to be astronomical.

Casualty rate: all-encompassing, universal; a given.

Recompense: nil, save the voluntary "gift."

Selection of clients: nil, save that preference goes
to the poorest, least privileged, and most downtrodden.
Those with only a pot to piss in must be serviced first.
Do not accept the pot as a "gift."

And so on and so forth.

"We're going to starve," I groaned. "If we live that
long."

But then—

But then—

I started noticing something. Didn't think much of
it, at first. Until, in book after book, a pattern began
to emerge.

I started studying more intently. Then, earnestly.
Then, feverishly. By the end of the second day, I had
gone through each and every tome.

And found no exceptions! None! The principle was
established! The rule as clear as day!

I was quivering with excitement. But I forced myself

to think it over carefully, before I made the Fateful Decision.

Oh, for maybe ten seconds.

Screw it. Even if I'd lost everything else on account of Greyboar's philosophical obsessions, I'd gained the one thing that mattered the most to me.

So it was with a light heart and a lift to my steps that I charged into Jenny and Angela's sewing room. They left off their cheerful chattering and their sewing (well—mostly rending what had already been sewn) and looked up at me from their chairs.

Smiling like liquid sunshine.

"Well, and will you look at this?" chuckled Jenny.

"He actually doesn't look like a barrel of pickles," chortled Angela.

"Marry me," I choked.

The smiles vanished from their faces. Jenny and Angela stared at me. Then at each other. Then, back at me.

Tears started to form in Jenny's eyes. "Which one?" whispered Angela. "We thought you loved us both."

I was probably hopping up and down with glee, by then. I don't remember clearly.

"That's it! That's it! *Both of you!*"

I managed to bring myself under a semblance of control. "Well, not exactly that, since that would be polygamy or something and given the way you two are—well, you know, it's like a three-way thing—so what happens is that I marry Jenny and you marry Angela and she marries me, and maybe we can do it back around again the other way just to make sure everything's on the up and up."

They were back to staring at me. Blank-faced.

Then Angela croaked: "That'd be illegal, Ignace."

"Can't be done," added Jenny, very sadly.

By then I'm *sure* I was hopping up and down.

"Bullshit! Doesn't apply to us! Me and Greyboar are official Heroes! On this stuff—*there's no rules! We set our own!*"

Jenny and Angela still didn't believe me, so I more or less hauled them by the scruff of the neck into the library, jolted Zulkeh out of his scholarly trance, and put the matter before him.

"Well, *of course!*" he expostulated, stroking his beard fiercely. " 'Tis as plain as the nose in front of your face. All Heroes, by the nature of the trade, are profligates when it comes to matters of the heart. Cannot be held accountable to society's rules. Nay—fie on it! What sort of wretched Hero would settle for such a timid boundary to his Vaulting Spirit?"

He gave Jenny and Angela a stern look. "As for the other—this trifle concerning sexual orientation—the matter is plainer still. My dear girls! The principle was established by the very founder of the Hero's Trade himself. I refer, of course, to Gilgamesh Sfondrati-Piccolomini and his grotesque liaison with the man-beast Enkidu, in which homoerotica was intermingled with the most perverse aspects of sadomasochism and bondage. And whatever doubts might still have remained were *surely* dispelled by the great Achilles Laebmauntsforscynneweëld, in his unseemly hither-thither between the captive slave girl and comely Patroclus, in which—"

Chapter and verse, chapter and verse. The one and only time in my life I blessed pedantry!

Zulkeh even offered to speak on our behalf should the Rules and Ethics Committee prove obstreperous. But, in the event, his intercession was quite unnecessary. When I consulted with them, the Committee was every bit as emphatic as the mage.

"Of course!" stated Pathos.

"Practically a necessity, under the code of professional ethics," intoned Bathos.

Cannabis didn't say anything coherent. He just drooled at Angela and Jenny, muttering something about shinnying up a tree. I think.

So that was that. Jenny and Angela and I got married that same evening. Before a standing-room-only crowd at The Trough. I insisted on the venue, and since there Are No Rules For Heroes when it comes to this kind of stuff, who could object?

I even insisted that the Oldsters at the Old Bar preside over the ceremony. Which they did, or tried to, until their argument over precedents and hallowed traditions got so snarled up that Greyboar got disgusted and went ahead and finished the ceremony himself.

Then there was a gigantic celebration, in which Leuwen broke every tradition and footed the entire bill. Almost broke my heart, that, because I wasn't able to participate in more than a round or two before Jenny and Angela hauled me back to the house and upstairs to the Connubial Bed, as it was now renamed.

But my incipient heartbreak was gone before we even got home and after that I didn't give it the least thought. Truth is, I didn't give much of anything what you could properly call thought for quite a few hours.

I woke up early the next morning, before sunup. Our bedroom was still dark. Somehow or other, I'd wound up in the middle, and I could hear Angela murmuring something in her sleep to my left and felt Jenny move in her sleep to my right.

I can always tell them apart, even in the dark. Even though I couldn't have begun to tell you whose leg was which, in that tangle we were in.

So I knew it was Jenny's hand which made that

funny little caressing stroke on my ribs that tells you
the sleeping person who made it wants you there. And
I knew it was Angela's hair I was kissing. And I remembered the way her face had looked when it had been
floating somewhere over me earlier and the way Jenny
had laughed and she and Angela had each put a hand
on my chest and squeezed me really tight and Angela
had laughed too and said, "See, Ignace? You don't miss
that hole in your heart at all, now that it's gone."

And the funny thing is, I really don't. Even though
we're all going to starve to death if we live that long.

Screw it. Bring on that sorry dragon!

Comes down to it, I'll bet Hrundig knows a recipe
for cooking the mangy beasts.

I guess I was talking out loud, and woke the girls
up. Jenny chuckled, stroked me again, and whispered:
"He does. We got it from him before he left."

Angela nuzzled me. "So don't whine about the
money we're going to spend on onions and mushrooms," she murmured. "We'll need it for the stuffing."

Amazons 'r Us

The Chicks Series, edited by Esther Friesner

When it comes to the best
in science fiction and fantasy,
Baen Books has something for *everyone!*

IF YOU LIKE . . .
YOU SHOULD ALSO TRY. . .

Marion Zimmer Bradley .... Mercedes Lackey,
Holly Lisle

Anne McCaffrey .... Elizabeth Moon,
Mercedes Lackey

Mercedes Lackey .... Holly Lisle, Josepha Sherman,
Ellen Guon, Mark Shepherd

Andre Norton .... Mary Brown,
James H. Schmitz

David Drake .... David Weber, John Ringo,
Eric Flint

Larry Niven .... James P. Hogan,
Charles Sheffield

Robert A. Heinlein .... Jerry Pournelle,
Lois McMaster Bujold

Heinlein's "Juveniles" .... Eric Flint & Dave Freer,
Rats, Bats & Vats

Horatio Hornblower .... David Weber's
"Honor Harrington" series,
David Drake's, "RCN" series

The Lord of the Rings .... Elizabeth Moon,
The Deed of Paksenarrion

IF YOU LIKE ...
YOU SHOULD ALSO TRY...

Lackey's "SERRAted Edge" series .... Rick Cook, *Mall Purchase Night*

Dungeons & Dragons™ .... "Bard's Tale"™ Novels

Star Trek .... James Doohan & S.M. Stirling, "Flight Engineer" series

Star Wars .... Larry Niven, David Weber

Jurassic Park .... Brett Davis, *Bone Wars* and *Two Tiny Claws*

Casablanca .... Larry Niven, *Man-Kzin Wars II*

Elves .... Ball, Lackey, Sherman, Moon, Cook, Guon

Puns .... Rick Cook, Spider Robinson Harry Turtledove, *The Case of the Toxic Spell Dump*

Alternate History .... Gingrich and Forstchen, *1945* James P. Hogan, *The Proteus Operation* Harry Turtledove (ed.), *Alternate Generals* S.M. Stirling, Draka series Eric Flint & David Drake, Belisarius series Eric Flint, *1632*

SF Conventions .... Niven, Pournelle & Flynn, *Fallen Angels* Margaret Ball, *Mathemagics* Jerry & Sharon Ahern, *The Golden Shield of IBF*

Quests .... Mary Brown, Elizabeth Moon, Piers Anthony

Greek Mythology .... Roberta Gellis, *Bull God* and *Thrice Bound* Eric Flint & Dave Freer, *Pyramid Scheme*

IF YOU LIKE . . .
YOU SHOULD ALSO TRY . . .

Norse Mythology ...... David Drake, *Northworld Trilogy*
Lars Walker

Arthurian Legend .... Steve White's Legacy series
David Drake, *The Dragon Lord*

Computers .... Rick Cook's "Wiz" series
Spider Robinson, *User Friendly*
Tom Cool, *Infectress*
Chris Atack, *Project Maldon*
James P. Hogan, *Realtime Interrupt*
and *Two Faces of Tomorrow*

Science Fact .... Robert L. Forward,
Indistinguishable From Magic
James P. Hogan, *Rockets, Redheads, and Revolution*
and *Minds, Machines, and Evolution*
Charles Sheffield, *Borderlands of Science*

Cats .... Larry Niven's Man-Kzin Wars series

Horses .... Elizabeth Moon's Heris Serrano series
Doranna Durgin

Vampires .... Cox & Weisskopf (eds.), *Tomorrow Sucks*
Wm. Mark Simmons, *One Foot in the Grave*
Nigel Bennett & P.N. Elrod, *Keeper of the King*
and *HIs Father's Son*
P.N. Elrod, *Quincey Morris, Vampire*

Werewolves . Cox & Weisskopf (eds.), *Tomorrow Bites*
Wm. Mark Simmons, *One Foot in the Grave*
Brett Davis, *Hair of the Dog*